Wherever Grace Is Needed

Center Point
Large Print

Wherever Grace Is Needed

ELIZABETH BASS

Center Point Publishing
Thorndike, Maine

This Center Point Large Print edition
is published in the year 2011 by arrangement with
Kensington Publishing Corp.

The text of this Large Print edition is unabridged.
In other aspects, this book may vary
from the original edition.
Printed in the United States of America
on permanent paper.
Set in 16-point Times New Roman type.

ISBN: 978-1-61173-099-9

Library of Congress Cataloging-in-Publication Data

Bass, Elizabeth, 1965–
Wherever Grace is needed / Elizabeth Bass. — Center point large print ed.
p. cm.
ISBN 978-1-61173-099-9 (library binding : alk. paper)
1. Single women—Fiction. 2. Sisters—Fiction. 3. Families—Fiction.
4. Domestic fiction. 5. Large type fiction. I. Title.
PS3602.A84723W44 2011
813′.6—dc22

2011012681

Prologue
Memorizing the Sky

June 1988

In the living room, she went through the same ritual she'd performed everywhere else, joining the tips of the corresponding fingers of her two hands to look through, like a viewfinder, and then slowly walking around the room, examining every little thing. She needed to commit it all to memory. This might be her last chance to see this old house, with its odd-shaped cabinets and closets perfect for hiding, and the fireplace framed by faded multicolored tiles.

She noticed everything through her viewfinder hands, even the single cobwebby strand suspended between a knight's horse head and a pointy black bishop's hat on the fancy marble chess set. Her oldest brother, Steven, had given the game to their dad this past Christmas, and it hadn't been touched since that day. The old chess set, on the other hand, kept its spot on the spindle-legged table between two armchairs, its shiny wooden blond and black pieces poised for battle.

The wall of shelves behind the armchair contained the stereo she wasn't supposed to touch and the records she could touch so long as she was very very careful. She knew those album covers, of landscapes and brass instruments and swans, as well as she knew the pictures in her old fairy-tale book. She'd hardly ever get to see them now.

She turned slowly, inspecting the room frame by frame until she came to the old globe standing in the corner. She had to stop and find Austin, and then trace her finger all the way over to Oregon. People kept telling her Oregon wasn't really far, but here was proof they were lying. Oregon was practically in the Pacific Ocean. On the globe, several strings of bumpy mountains stood between here and there, like a series of fences.

When she gave the globe a spin, watching the smooth seas and bumpy mountains whirling by caused her stomach to cramp a little. And then she heard jangling keys from upstairs, a sure sign that her father was getting ready to take her back to her mom's. A wave of panic gripped her. She wasn't ready! There was so much she hadn't gone over yet. And what about the yard? She had forgotten to say good-bye to Desdemona!

She turned and ran out the front door and around the side of the house. Desdemona, a dachshund, pressed her sausage belly against the chain-link fence until Grace joined her on the other side.

"Des!" Grace flopped onto the grass and let herself be attacked by frantic snuffles and licks.

After Des had calmed down a little, Grace stretched out on her back on the grass and made a viewfinder of her hands again, this time pointed straight up at the sky overhead. Thin clouds streaked across the blue, not the puffy clouds Grace liked better. She couldn't make pictures of the wispy shapes, except maybe a trail of toilet paper or an earthworm. It disappointed her. This might be her last time to stare up at the sky in Texas. Everybody kept telling her that she would come back, but how did they know? And how could she be sure the sky would look the same all the way over in Oregon?

But what was the point of memorizing a sky that wasn't actually like the sky you wanted to remember?

Grace wouldn't let herself cry. She could cry all the time at her mom's house, but here when she cried, her brothers made fun of her. They *never* cried. She had seen tears in her father's eyes once, back when she was really little. He'd been reading a book and explained to her that he was crying because what he was reading was moving. The idea had startled her, so she'd asked to see this book. It had taken her a second or two to work up the courage to look, only to discover that all the usual lines of squiggles were just sitting there on the page in the normal way, perfectly still. When she assured her dad there was nothing to be afraid of, he had stared at her in confusion for a moment and then burst out laughing.

Of course he'd told everyone. Even now when

her brothers saw her crying, they always asked her if she'd seen something moving.

While she was still looking through her makeshift viewfinder, a shadow fell over her. She feared it was her dad . . . but it was only Sam. He was seven years older than her—twice her age—but he was the younger of her two half brothers.

"What are you *doing?*" From the alarm in his voice, you would have thought she was about to stick her finger into a light plug.

"I'm trying to memorize everything."

"Like what—the sky? That's *really* pointless!" He twisted to check if there was something up in the sky he'd missed. "There's nothing up there!"

"Usually there's more."

Sam wouldn't understand. Steven wouldn't either; anyway, he was off at some kind of science camp.

Sam sat down next to Grace, and Desdemona raced around to wedge her body between them, nudging Sam's hand with her moist snout until he gave in and scratched her ears. "Dad said to tell you he's ready to go."

She felt a sharp stab of jealousy. Why did *she* have to go? Sam didn't even like it here all that much—he was always arguing with their father now. It all started when Sam had become, to put it in his own words, political. To Grace, this phase had come on so quickly it seemed as if someone had just flipped a switch in his head. The change dated from the week the Johnson family had moved into the rental house on the corner. The family had two kids, Seeger and Rainbow, and Sam had started hanging out with them.

Now Sam was always predicting that one day he would hit the road and never come back. But Grace had never wanted to hit a road. Ever. Why couldn't *Sam* go to Oregon?

"It's not fair," she blurted out. "It's all because of my stupid mother, and stupid Jeff! If she had to go and get married again, why couldn't she have found someone from here?"

Sam was silent for a moment, but then apparently he remembered he was supposed to be making an effort to cheer her up. "Oregon's going to be great. It's . . ." He frowned for a moment, obviously reaching. "It's really green there."

"Austin is green. How is Oregon green any different?"

"It just is, because it rains more there. I've seen pictures. They have a huge mountain, and a volcano."

Okay, maybe Austin didn't have a huge mountain. Certainly not a volcano. But she'd never missed having mountains—not like she was going to miss this house, and Des, and her brothers . . . even though they mostly ignored her anyway. And Peggy. And her dad . . .

Tears stood in her eyes. She was determined not to let a single one drop, but the effort of holding them back caused her entire body to quiver. The gate squeaked open and a renewed sense of doom filled her.

"What's going on?" her father asked as he approached them. "I've been scouring the house for you."

Sam squinted up at him. "She doesn't want to go, Dad. I don't blame her. Whatever happened to free will?"

A troubled look flashed across their father's face. For a split second, Grace wondered if he was going to let her stay, but then in the next instant he drew back his shoulders like he always did when he was irritated with someone. That someone was usually Sam, but today, her last day, it was her. "How can you not want to go with your mother?"

"Because I like it *here.* This is my home, not Oregon."

" 'Go where he will, a wise man is at home,' " her father said.

Sam tapped her foot with his sneaker. "See? Whenever you feel homesick, just think of Dad quoting at you."

To her surprise—and probably Sam's too—their father sank down to the grass next to them. It was weird, because he wasn't a sit-on-the-grass kind of dad. Most of her classmates' fathers were younger. She could imagine *them* sitting on the grass, or playing touch football with their kids and not worrying about grass stains. But her father was more of a chair person.

She and Sam and Desdemona scooted over a bit, as if they were all scrunched on a sofa, not sprawled in an empty yard.

"None of us have ever been to Oregon," her dad said. "You'll be striking out into new territory. The Christopher Columbus of the Oliver family."

"Except you won't be giving out diseased blankets to slaughter the natives, hopefully," Sam interjected.

Their father leveled a withering stare at him. *"One hopes."*

"I don't want to be an explorer," Grace declared. "I just want to stay here."

"That's a shortsighted way to think. Where would the world be if Christopher Columbus had been a mousy little homebody?"

Sam cleared his throat. "Well, for one thing, a lot of native Americans would probably still be alive. . . ."

Their father glared at him. "Would you forget the Indians for just one moment?"

"Sure," Sam grumbled. "Why not? Everyone else has."

Their father turned his attention back to Grace. "The thing to remember is that Columbus didn't stay in the New World forever. He kept returning home. And it was a whole lot harder for him to return to Europe than it will be for you to come back to Austin. He had a grueling months-long sea journey. You'll just have a four-hour airplane flight."

"I don't think this is going to make her feel any better, Dad," Sam said. "Seven-year-old girls don't dream of becoming explorers. Mattel hasn't come out with Conquistador Barbie yet."

Grace rounded on her brother and with the palm of her hand gave his shoulder a shove that nearly knocked him over. Sam wasn't very big. She never could have knocked over Steven. "Shut up! You don't know anything!"

Normally, she would have gotten in trouble for yelling at someone to shut up, even Sam. Her father would have called her a little barbarian. Today, though, he looked almost proud of her. "Grace isn't just any seven-year-old girl." His admiring tone clapped her shoulders back and lifted her up.

She darted a triumphant glare at Sam, who had weebled back into an upright position. Why shouldn't she be like Christopher Columbus? Grace Oliver—the famous adventure person. She could almost imagine it.

Almost.

"But now, if we don't hurry," her father announced, starting to unfold himself awkwardly, "the adventuress won't have time to stop at that port of call I intended to make on the way back to her mother's."

"Is the port of call Amy's Ice Cream?" Grace asked.

Her father stood up and dusted his hands together. "It might be."

She sprang to her feet.

"Wow!" Sam exclaimed in disgust. "Someone offers you a little ice cream and suddenly everything's hunky-dory. Ice cream is the opiate of enslaved children."

She scowled at him. "I'm just glad he's not taking me back right away."

She followed her father out of the yard. Sam trailed after them. "Sure, that's how you justify the way you can be bought off. . . ."

Her father waited at the gate, and when Grace passed through, he shut it.

Both Sam and Des pressed up against the chain-link fence, looking abandoned.

"Hey!" Sam called after them. "Can't I come, too?"

At the busy ice cream store on Guadalupe, she and Sam stood in line while her father went to run an errand. When he returned, they were perched on a bench outside the shop, eating cones. Lou approached them carrying a gift bag, which he deposited in Grace's lap.

Careful not to drip her Mexican vanilla with crushed Butterfingers on her present, she reached into the silver bag with a white bow and pulled out a book. It was a blank book with a red cloth cover. On a card tucked into the first page, her father had written something in his spidery script.

"Oh, wow," Sam said, deadpan. "A blank book." He craned his head around her shoulder to read the inscription aloud in a flat, unenthusiastic voice.

" 'Where we love is home.
Home that our feet may leave, but not our hearts.
Oliver Wendell Holmes' "

Grace snapped the book closed to keep it away from any other unappreciative eyes, and held it to her chest. She liked her book. It wasn't a girly gift. It was serious. "Thanks, Daddy," she said, throwing caution to the wind and putting her arms around him. For once he didn't seem wary of getting chocolate down his white shirtfront. Despite how hard she'd tried not to cry, tears splashed her cheeks. "I'll miss you so much!"

"I'm going to miss you too, Gracie."

When she looked up, Sam was staring at his ice cream. For a moment, he looked depressed. Then he snapped to. His mouth tugged up at the corners as Grace settled back on the bench again, her ice cream braced in one hand and her book clasped in the other. She was shaking her head to clear her eyes of tears.

"What's the matter, Grace?" Sam asked, although his voice lacked its usual taunting gusto. "Did you see something moving?"

1

Exile with a K-tel Soundtrack

June 2010

For the very first time in her entire life, Jordan West hated summer. Summer usually meant freedom—from school, at least. She wasn't the school type. Her mom had always told her that these were supposed to be the happiest years of her life, which was so not comforting. In Jordan's opinion, school was an extralong basic training for life as a brainless office hemorrhoid.

But summers had always been great. In summer, the only classes she'd had to worry about were the ones that her mom had always arranged for her, and they were fun. Last year she'd gone to an arts camp, which had been a little like boot camp, too—but boot camp for art freaks and weirdos. Her people.

In summers past, she'd only had piddling little responsibilities to tend to—like taking Dominic and Lily to the pool or movies, or baby-sitting them when the 'rents weren't around. Actually, Nina had been the one who usually did the baby-sitting while Jordan hid in their room, drawing, or occasionally sneaked out to a friend's house. But

Jordan always got equal credit for babysitting because Nina never narced on her. They'd been a perfect team, she and Nina. Jordan could be bad, knowing Nina would drag her back from the dark side when necessary, and in return, just enough Jordan had rubbed off on Nina to keep her from being a nauseating Little Miss Perfect.

But now there was no Mom, no Nina, and summer stretched before her like a long, hot prison sentence. She'd thought getting out of Austin would bring some relief. She had begged her father to let her stay with her grandparents this summer. But bad as her life in Austin had become, with memories and guilt assaulting her everywhere she looked, it was beginning to seem like heaven compared to living with her grandparents in Little Salty.

What had she been thinking?

She hadn't been thinking. That was the problem. No one was thinking anymore—just reacting, and she was the worst of them all. For the first time in her life she slept fitfully in rooms all by herself, going to bed crying, waking up headachy and dazed. Life was something she never could have imagined a year ago, or even a few months ago. Even her grandparents' house and the little town they lived in, which when she was a kid had seemed fun to visit, now felt suffocating, almost unbearable.

The first thing each morning, her grandmother

checked the newspaper for coupons. Coupons ruled their world. A coupon could mean a trip to Midland, even if it was just to buy canned green beans, two for ninety-nine cents. Granny Kate refused to let Jordan stay in the house alone—as if Jordan was nine years old again—and so they both had to pile into the Ford Focus and drive thirty miles of dreary country road listening to *The Best of Bread* and Barry Manilow, because Granny Kate's musical taste, which apparently had never been cutting edge, had fossilized sometime around 1978.

Jordan knew there was good music from way back then because Jed Levenger, her really cool art teacher at camp last year, had played the Rolling Stones in the studio all the time. But no way you'd hear Mick Jagger coming out of Granny Kate's car speakers, any more than you'd hear Cannibal Corpse or Rancid. The Ford Focus was an easy-listening bubble of pain.

During these drives, Jordan sometimes wondered if Jed was still teaching at arts camp. It wasn't that she had a crush on him or anything—Jed was as old as her father and sort of sloppy and grizzled looking. But he was the first—and only—real artist to say that she was talented. Although maybe a guy teaching at a rinky-dink arts camp couldn't be considered a real artist. Still, he wasn't a hemorrhoid. He wasn't a normal adult who was all food-work-food-sleep.

Once they arrived in Midland, she and her grandmother would hit the grocery stores. "Stocking up," Granny Kate called it, though it was hard to figure out what calamity they were preparing for. After shopping, they would splurge on lunch at Applebee's. Big treat. Granny Kate was usually unnaturally chipper as the waitress seated them. She'd hum "Copacabana" as she inspected every single item listed on the menu, even though they both knew she was going to order the pecan crusted chicken salad. She always ordered the pecan crusted chicken salad.

The worst part came after the ordering was over, when the two of them would sit across the table from each other, straining for something to say. Once, right in the middle of the noontime crowd, Granny Kate had stared into Jordan's face and burst into tears. It had been awful, and so embarrassing. People had actually turned in their chairs and gaped at their table. And then Granny Kate had wailed out an apology to the room and honked her nose into her napkin like some kind of crazy woman.

And Midland days were the good days.

When they didn't go to Midland, they stayed in Little Salty. Jordan would crawl out of bed, usually sometime during *The View*, and Granny Kate would jump up and pop a couple of Family Dollar frozen waffles into the toaster, all the while fussing about what a late sleeper Jordan was. Then the day's schedule would be laid out—usually involving some grisly combination of bridge club, errands, church, and Jazzercise.

As far as art was concerned, the best Jordan could hope for was that Granny Kate would be taking her afternoon nap during the Bob Ross reruns on PBS. The show would lull Jordan into a trancelike state as she sat on the couch and ate bowls of ice cream. Bob Ross was the best company available in Little Salty, and he was certainly more effective than that stupid counselor she'd been sent to back in Austin, after the accident. All the shrink had ever done was stare at her in a condescending way that absolutely convinced her that everything was all her fault.

Bob Ross was better. That soothing voice. Snowy white mountaintops and happy little trees. Happy little world where nothing bad happened.

At six-fifteen every night, her grandfather would come home. Pop Pop was a pharmacist who had been on the cusp of retirement as long as Jordan could remember. She suspected his reluctance to hang up his white smock had something to do with the coupon-and-Jazzercisey alternative. It seemed unlikely that he would ever quit now that his home had become funereal as well as tedious.

When Jordan had first arrived in Little Salty, after that first wince of greeting, Pop Pop had tried to put a happy spin on things. "I'm sure you'll liven us up!" he'd said, giving her a big bear hug. It was the first time anyone had touched Jordan in three months.

But she hadn't livened things up. In fact, she had a hunch that her arrival had actually bumped up the gloom quotient. The grandfolks tried to hide it, but she could tell her presence made them uncomfortable. And sad. She occasionally felt their eyes on her, searching for someone who wasn't there. When she met their gazes, they would snap to and guiltily turn away.

Jordan despaired. Was this how it was going to be from now on, forever? Were people always going to look at her and remember someone else?

One night she finally lost it. The eruption occurred during a typically silent dinner. Nothing but cutlery against china and the loud ticking of her grandmother's kitchen clock could be heard. No one talked here during meals. There was nothing to say. Jordan started to feel stir-crazy and punchy. The tension of it all caused her to giggle.

Granny Kate, who had been lost in thought, glared at her. The glare seemed horrible because there were tears standing in her grandmother's eyes. It wasn't hard to guess what—who—she'd been thinking about.

Jordan sprang suddenly from her chair. *"I'm sorry!"* she yelled, tossing down her napkin.

"What for?" Pop Pop asked, mystified, like a

man who'd just been shaken out of a dream. "What's going on?"

"I'm sorry that I laughed!" she raged. "I'm sorry that I'm me! I'm sorry that I'm here!"

Even as she shouted the words, Jordan couldn't believe this was her. But she couldn't help herself. Anger and sadness had been corked up inside her for months and spewed out in a Krakatoa of fury.

"We *wanted* you here," Pop Pop argued.

Granny Kate remained noticeably purse-lipped and mute.

"But now you're sick of the sight of me," Jordan said. "Don't you think I am, too? Do you know what it's like to not be able to look at myself without thinking about my dead twin sister? I wish I could break every mirror in the world!"

She ran to her room and slammed the door, but immediately felt sorry. And so dumb. This wasn't her. This was some screwed-up teenager throwing a melodramatic fit, like in one of those hokey old after-school specials. She needed to strangle her inner Kristy McNichol and get herself under control.

This was when she needed Nina. Nina had always been able to shake her out of these emotional explosions. If Nina were here, she would have sat on the edge of the bed, cross-legged and calm, while Jordan stomped around the room punching pillows and howling about how screwed up everybody was. Then, after

Jordan had tired herself out a little, she would have ventured a thought or two.

What are Granny Kate and Pop Pop supposed to do, Jordan? It would be really weird if they didn't look at you at all—that *would piss you off even more. They can't help it.*

Jordan snorted, as if Nina had actually spoken to her. "They probably can't help blaming me, either."

She lifted her head, tilting it to hear some reply. But Nina's voice was gone.

Of course it was gone. She would never know what Nina felt. Nina was dead. Their mother was dead. And it was all her fault.

She flopped on the bed and cried herself to sleep, and she slept right into the next day. When she finally staggered out to the kitchen again, Barbara Walters was on the television talking about Lasik surgery, and her grandmother was just dropping two Family Dollar waffles into the toaster and singing "Can't Smile without You."

Nothing had changed. Nothing was ever going to change. It was so depressing that she sank down in front of her plate and almost started crying again. If only there was someone to help her. If only Nina were there.

If only she could stop thinking about Nina.

Then she remembered. In junior high they'd had to write a paper on a historical figure they admired. Jordan had picked John Adams from a list of suggestions, scribbled a few boring paragraphs about him during lunch before class, and had received a D. Nina had picked Gandhi, and she hadn't just typed a five-page paper including pictures and an index of links to Web sites, she'd also spent weeks talking about him, and watching that boring movie, and plastering the room they shared with inspirational quotes. For a month "Be the change that you want to see in the world" was taped to their closet door.

At the time, Jordan had rolled her eyes, because the only change she'd wanted to see was a world where she didn't have to do dumb papers. But apparently the quote had penetrated her thick skull, because it came back to her now.

If she wanted her life to be different, she was going to have to make the changes herself.

As she gnawed on waffle number two, she started to devise a plan for the next trip to Midland.

"Any good coupons in the paper today?" she asked her grandmother.

2

Grace, Interrupted

At first, no one could hear the phone ringing. Small wonder. The decibel level in the duplex was just short of what it would have taken to have the cops called on them, but loud enough to have traumatized Grace's two elderly and mostly deaf cats. In addition to the saxophone quartet playing "Powerhouse" in the small back room, the kitchen was crammed with people talk-shouting over the noise—friends, friends of friends, and a few strays with way too much beer in them. In the smoke-filled living room, where four card tables were wedged between all the other furniture, the long-awaited Tournament of Stupid Games was in full swing. Grace didn't recall Mousetrap being such a noisy enterprise, although heretofore she'd only seen it played by the under-ten set, and sober.

It was Amber who finally heard the ringing, perhaps because her current Twister position cocked her ear in the right direction. "*Grace!* Your phone!"

Grace realized she would never be able to carry on a conversation down here and made a dash for the stairs, just missing the card table where the Operation round of the game battle was raging. A few inches to the right might have upset the outcome of hours of ferocious competition.

By the time she reached her upstairs bedroom, she was out of breath. She toed the door shut to block out the noise from below and picked up the phone. "Zoo! How can we help you?"

"Grace?"

Every trace of high spirits was flushed out of Grace's body in a rush of worry. "Steven? What's wrong?"

Her oldest brother wouldn't call her unless there was an emergency. Frankly, she was a little surprised that he had called her for any reason. She usually communicated with him now through his wife, Denise, who was also a partner in his medical practice.

"The thing is . . ." He faltered, and she held her breath in dread. "Dad's had an accident."

"Oh, God." She collapsed forward. She'd been braced for bad, but now that the bad had arrived, she still felt like Jell-O inside. "What happened? Is he okay?"

"It was a car accident. That is, a Chevy Tahoe hit him as he was walking across Guadalupe near campus."

"On the drag? But is he—?"

"His leg's broken."

"Oh, no." Even as she said it, though, she felt relief. It could have been so much worse.

On the other hand, a broken bone was no picnic at any age. And it had to be especially trying for a seventy-six-year-old man. Especially a peppery seventy-six-year-old man who was used to being independent.

"Poor Dad!" she exclaimed.

"No kidding," Steven muttered. "Felled by a Chevy! I can't imagine what he was doing on the drag. It's not like he has a reason to be anywhere near campus anymore."

Pondering why the victim of an auto accident

had positioned himself in front of a car and gotten himself run over was typical of Steven. It wasn't a case of blaming the victim so much as assuming the victim had indecipherable motives for wanting to be maimed.

"When did the accident happen?" she asked.

"Yesterday."

"Yesterday?"

The reproach was duly noted. "He was okay, Grace. He's just been in the hospital."

Just been in the hospital! Spoken like a surgeon. A hospital was a second office to Steven—a humdrum bone repair shop.

So for a day her father had been laid up in a hospital bed with serious injuries. During that same day she had been blithely absorbed in planning for this party, a housewarming of sorts. Ben had just moved in to her duplex on Friday.

"I'll call Dad right away," she told Steven.

"Good . . ." He hitched his throat.

A throat hitch from Steven meant that he wasn't quite finished. Grace waited for it.

"Actually, I was wondering . . ." The hitch again. "The thing is, I'm worried about when Dad gets discharged. He's not going to be a hundred percent. He'll need home care. I was thinking about hiring someone . . ."

Hired home help. Lou Oliver would never go for that.

"It would be a different matter if things were

normal here," Steven continued. "But I've got this blasted conference in St. Louis coming up this week, and Denise . . ." He paused a moment and began again. "Denise . . ."

Grace leaned forward. "Steven? What's happened?"

He coughed. "The thing is, Denise . . ."

During their recent phone conversations, her father had been muttering about Steven and Denise having problems. The bust-up must have come, which would explain the reason Steven's brain was short-circuiting every time he said her name. Highly charged emotional situations often affected him that way.

"Oh, Steven. Have you two split up?"

"Yes."

"When did it happen?"

"Friday."

And Denise seemed so perfect for him. In fact, she was exactly like his first wife, Sara. The two women both had bulldozer personalities, which seemed to be what Steven gravitated toward.

Poor Steven. "I'm so sorry."

"It's fine," Steven said. "I'll have to leave Orthopedic Partners and start my own practice, though. I don't know what I'll call it. Orthopedic Loner or something."

"Why should you have to leave?" she asked.

"Because Denise and Jack—Dr. Gunther, the other partner . . . He and Denise . . ."

Oh, God.

He coughed again. "Anyway, I'm speaking at a conference this week. And since there's no question of Sam helping out . . ."

Sam, a journalist, was stationed in Beirut.

"I know it's a lot to ask, Grace. . . ."

"I'll come down right away."

Now that she had agreed, Steven seemed doubtful. "But you've got your thing there. Your CD thing . . ."

Her "CD thing" was her life. Music stores were a sputtering business model, but so far Rigoletto's was still clawing at the ledge of profitability by its fingertips. It helped that she had specialized. The store had practically no other brick and mortar competition in town for the dollars of classical music obsessives. It also didn't hurt that she'd cleared a room in back where she brewed good coffee and had live music on weekends.

"Ben can baby-sit Rigoletto's for a while," she said.

"Ben? Really?" He sounded surprised.

"Really," she assured him. "I can leave tomorrow."

"No, I meant, you're really still with *that guy?*"

The one time Ben had met her Austin family, he hadn't exactly made a big hit.

That was another reason it had taken them so long to move in together—although not the biggest. Mild family opposition had added to

Grace's hunch that they weren't fated to be. A fate deficit was a goofy reason to put off doing the couple thing—she knew that—but she couldn't help it. Beneath the realist face she showed the world, there lurked a mushy center of romanticism. She blamed this on an early addiction to the Brontës, which gave her the unrealistic expectation that there was a man wandering the world who would become attached to her with a fervent, though preferably not doomed, devotion. All her life she'd kept an eye out for her Heathcliff, her Rochester, a man who would be able to hear her heart's desire if she opened the window and called his name on a stormy night.

Instead, she'd been sent Ben, who a lot of the time didn't hear her when she said something from across the living room. But they had been together for two years. Maybe it wasn't devotion, but even dogged inertia had to count for something. In five months she would be thirty. Most of her friends were married, with kids. She didn't want to look back at fifty and realize she'd wasted her life waiting for Brontë man.

"I'm still with him," she told her brother. "And thanks to *that guy,* I can swing a short trip without having to shutter the doors."

"Well, that's useful, I guess," Steven said. "This is a load off my mind, Grace. The family owes you one for this. Big time."

She shouldn't have felt pleased by the pat on the head, but she did. Most of her life she'd been an Oliver in name only, a sort of satellite Oliver in her own orbit ever since her mother had hauled her halfway across the country, married again, and started a second, happier marriage. And a second family that Grace had never felt completely a part of, either. Her Oregon half siblings were a decade younger and looked on her almost as a different generation. And while she loved her mother and stepfather, they had a habit of chalking up anything she did that they didn't approve of to the Oliver in her, as if her blood were tainted.

Grace's too-brief visits to her dad had been the highlights of her adolescence. She loved hanging out in the old house in her dad's neighborhood, which was so different than the various suburbs her mother had dragged her to. And she loved her dad, with his starched shirts, sharp tongue, and brittle exterior, all of which would melt away as he discussed a book he loved. They filled their holidays together with chess games, which she always lost, and rambles across central Texas in a never-ending quest to find the ultimate barbecue joint. All to a soundtrack of their mutual favorites: Telemann, Mozart, and Chopin.

But those visits had been few and far between, and usually too brief to make her feel that she actually belonged there. She always clicked with her brother Sam, but he had moved away early, and the difference in her and Steven's ages meant she really hadn't had a chance to get to know him all that well. When the time had come to decide where to settle, she had decided to stay in Oregon, which over the years had become her natural habitat. But she'd always felt a tug toward her native city, too, and the old house of her earliest memories. And her dad.

"I'll be there tomorrow," she promised.

"To Austin?" Ben stood amid the party debris, flabbergasted. "When did this happen?"

She briefed him on Steven's call and her travel arrangements as she surveyed the kitchen, which looked as if all its cabinets and drawers had been turned guts' side out, like something from a horror movie. It would take all night to get the place in order.

Her flight was at ten. Eight hours from now.

"Why?" Ben asked, bewildered even after she had explained it to him. "Just because the guy has a broken leg?"

"He's not *the guy,* he's my dad. And he's seventy-six."

He immediately looked contrite. "Duh—of course. Sorry." He focused on a point on the counter, thinking. "What about the store?"

"Could you handle it for a couple of weeks?" Ben had been working at Rigoletto's for two and a half years. It was how they had met.

"*Me?* But there are orders to deal with, and bands, and employee problems."

"What employee problems?" she asked.

"Well . . . for one thing, Amber's leaving."

Now it was Grace's turn to be shocked. "What? Who told you that?"

"She did. Just recently. She's going to grad school in Washington."

"When?"

"In the fall."

"Why didn't she say anything? To me, I mean."

He looked uncomfortable. "Well . . . you're the boss. I'm not."

"I know, but . . ." She swallowed, trying not to feel hurt. It was ridiculous. They were friends; she was happy for Amber. Who could blame her for not wanting to spend the rest of her life as a clerk in a CD shop?

Still . . . People didn't get accepted into grad schools overnight. This had to have been in the works for a while. Months and months.

"And what about the cats?" Ben asked, continuing to take stock of his own troubles.

"What about them? You just feed them, and change the water."

"They're old and vomity," he said, "and they have to eat that special food, and Heathcliff has his medication, and I really don't think the little one likes me. She's always giving me that glassy stare."

As if they could help being old. And surely Ben knew the name of her cats by now?

"Her name is Earnshaw, and she stares at everyone that way," she ground out between clenched teeth. "She has cataracts." She took a deep breath before she went all angry mother bear on him. *Air in, air out.*

Ben had a point, after all. She was accustomed to her geriatric cats, but they were a handful. "I'll lay up lots of food tomorrow morning," she promised, "and write out a schedule for taking care of them, including all the vet info."

"This is so nuts." He reached for her hand. "We've been planning my moving in for years—and now here I am for less than two days, and you decide to pick up and go."

"The timing's awful," she agreed. Although, to be honest, they hadn't actually *planned* this for two years. They had *put it off* for two years and finally caved in to the inevitable. "But we have years ahead of us, and my dad needs me now. It'll just be a week. Maybe two." For good measure, she added, "Three, tops."

Ben nodded. "Well . . . just don't be surprised if you come home to find a new jazz section in your precious store."

"No jazz."

It wasn't that she didn't like jazz, or lots of other types of music. But as far as Rigoletto's was concerned, a Miles Davis CD was just a gateway drug. Allow that in and next thing you knew there would be rock and country and—she shuddered—top forty. Then she would be just another music store. Just another music store going out of business.

"Promise me—no jazz, no indie rock, no Top 40," she said.

"Promise me you won't leave me stranded here in a cat nursing home and catering to your lunatic customers forever."

Out of the blue, Grace felt a sharp sudden pang about leaving that had nothing to with Ben or even with her decrepit old cats. This was a thunderclap of concern for Rigoletto's. For years her store had felt like her home, the home she'd finally managed to make for herself when the real things didn't pan out. While her contemporaries had been setting out on career paths or spending years in graduate school, she had thrown the best years of her life into Rigoletto's. She'd regularly worked eighteen-hour days and scrimped pennies to pay off her bank loan and become an amateur plumber and carpenter to keep from hiring expensive labor. She'd survived a recession and the encroaching gentrification of the store's once dirt cheap neighborhood.

Now she worried that if she didn't watch over her flock of repeat customers, these nuts she had spent years ministering to—the students, the Volvo drivers, the misfits—they would scatter into the retail wind.

"Of course I won't leave forever," she assured him, feeling torn between two geographical points. Between Texas and Oregon. Between family and family substitute. "I'll be back as soon as I can. I just need to make sure Dad can look after himself."

"No worries, Grace. I'll hold down the fort." Ben smiled. "Just leave it all in the hands of the Life champion."

"Champion? Really?" She'd forgotten all about the tournament.

Ben shrugged. "Well . . . just at Life. After that I got Tiddly-Winked down to fifth place and knocked out of the competition by a disastrous showing in Operation. I guess there's a reason surgeons shouldn't drink three beers before they cut somebody open."

She laughed. Still . . . to be Life champion. Even if it was only temporary, Grace would have settled for that.

3

Iago Is Missing

No one was there to meet Grace at the airport, which was no big deal. She could get to the hospital on the bus. The only downside was that she wouldn't really be able to clean herself up before she saw her dad. Coming off the plane she felt unwashed, wrinkly, and droopy. Also, she was dressed in comfy jean shorts and jogging sneakers because she'd read somewhere that you should wear loose-fitting clothing and athletic shoes on planes, in case of a crash. Easier to vault over your fellow passengers and hurl yourself toward the exits, she presumed.

Her father would say she looked like a slob. He was always bemoaning the *Tobacco Road* fashion standards of the day. He could hold forth on the sloppiness of the general public almost as long as he could decry the poor reading habits of the average undergrad. During her last visit, she'd begun to tense up every time they were in public and she heard the slap of backless sandals; a flip-flop sighting could trigger an hour-long lament.

Even now that he no longer went to work, her dad was a jacket-and-tie man. Shirts were always starched, pants creased. In the old days he'd played tennis, always in proper attire bleached to an eye-straining white. Ever since his sore knees had forced him to give up that sport, his exercise routine was to get up early, dress in a polo shirt tucked into khakis and his Mr. Rogers boating sneakers, and walk his dog around the neighborhood.

As she settled herself on the bus, Grace juggled bag, purse, and a container of barbecue she'd bought at the Salt Lick stand at the airport and marveled over the dips and twists of life. How had her father ever thought he could be happy with her mother? Cindy Oliver Wainwright probably didn't own an article of clothing that wasn't cotton knit, and the suggestion of ironing anything would elicit gales of laughter. Grace hadn't seen her mother read a book in decades that wasn't written by some incarnation of Nora Roberts, while Lou was suspicious of anything post–Edith Wharton. As far as Grace could tell, love between her parents had withered shortly after "I do," but the marriage had sputtered on for five more years. It was the biggest mistake either of them had ever made.

And she was the result.

By the time Grace arrived at the hospital, it was already past three. Her dad was sitting up in bed, his plaster-encased leg jutting out in front of him, his eyes trained absently on the opposite wall. She'd rarely seen him when he wasn't absorbed in a book or some other task. He looked slightly different, although it took her a second to figure out the problem. His hair was longer. His cheeks were covered with a grayish shadow.

When he caught sight of her, his face remained a blank, then it morphed into a puzzled frown.

"Let me guess . . ." She tilted her head. "Steven didn't tell you I was coming?"

In the next moment, he snapped back to his old self. "Of course he did," he responded in his usual clipped voice. "But he didn't tell me that you intended to move into the hospital with me."

She laughed and dropped her bag and purse on the ground so that she could give him a quick air hug, which in the Oliver family translated into a lavish display of affection. As she leaned over him, he relieved her of the greasy white sack she was carrying.

"Salt Lick," she explained.

"Isn't fifteen hundred miles a long way to go to smuggle lunch to an old man in the hospital?" He peeked into the sack.

Grace twisted to scope out the room. "Is there an old man here?"

"Old enough to not be able to scoot out of the way of an oncoming vehicle. I never should have given up tennis," he grumbled as he extracted the takeout container. "Although that behemoth was barreling down on me so fast, I would have had to be Usain Bolt to outrun it." He shifted uncomfortably. "The police insist the accident happened because I was jaywalking."

"Jaywalking on the drag? Why?"

"I don't know why!" he replied, almost yelling. "Your brothers keep asking me that. First Steven, then Sam on the phone. How should I know?"

He seemed truly agitated, so she let it drop. She sat down on the bed and gave his leg a tap. "Good thing I did come all this way. You obviously haven't had many visitors. No one's signed your cast."

"Truman offered to. I told him to keep his mitts off my leg."

Truman was her dad's older brother. "How is Uncle Truman?"

"He hasn't been run over by any Mac trucks lately, so he's a damn sight better off than I am."

"Listen to the self-pity! It was an SUV."

"It was a behemoth." He took his first bite of barbecue and his face melted into a mask of bliss.

"Better than hospital food?" she asked.

"Much. Thank you."

"So when can I spring you from this place?"

"Soon, I hope. I think they would have pushed me out two hours after I got here, except for Steven. Seems to think I can't cope on my own."

"You will be a bit mobility challenged. That's why I'm here—to help out for a while."

A dark eyebrow darted up. "Don't you have a store to run?"

"Ben's looking after things."

He made a face. "Scruffy Ben?" Her father's nose wrinkled in distaste. "I don't trust a grown man who tells me he skateboards to work. You don't worry he's going to dip into the till?"

"I'm more worried that he'll try to update the inventory."

Her father, who had cosigned the original loan for Rigoletto's, seemed more horrified by the idea than she was. "You need to get back up there.

There's not going to be anything for you to do here anyway."

"Not so sure about that." She nodded at the crutches in the corner. "Do you intend to hobble back and forth to the grocery store on those?"

"If I have to. It will be good exercise."

"How will you carry anything?"

"I do have friends, you know." He leveled his paternal glare on her, which he had never managed to make very menacing. "I'm not entirely alone in the world."

"I know you're not. And now that I'm here, you're even less alone."

He looked up at her and, almost grudgingly, his face broke into a smile. "It's good to see you, Grace."

"Even in sneakers?"

He eyed her feet. "Well . . . they're better than those awful flip-flop things. Do you know people wear them even here? Visitors! Can you believe it? I can hear them coming from two hallways over. *Fwap, fwap, fwap!* It's as if the whole world had turned into the shower room at the YMCA. . . ."

She smiled and settled in for a lengthy diatribe on the world's deteriorating standards in footwear. *Welcome home.*

Dr. Allen, Lou's doctor, wanted him to stay another night. Evidently, there were problems neither Steven nor Lou himself had seen fit to mention to her. His blood pressure had been spiking; they were trying to get his medication adjusted. The doctor told her they had also feared a head injury when he came in, because he'd been disoriented. But now the doctor was also attributing that to the blood pressure problem.

So in the afternoon, when her father slipped into an impromptu siesta, Grace grabbed his keys and made her way to his house.

By the time she stepped off the bus in the old neighborhood, she realized that she was ready for a nap herself. The afternoon was warm; every time she visited, she had to readapt to the heavy humid heat of Texas. As she lugged her stuff up the front porch steps of the old Craftsman house, her lack of sleep announced itself in every muscle of her body and the scratchy feeling behind her eyes. First she would take a long shower, and then she would collapse onto the old chenille coverlet of the spare bedroom. *Her* bedroom—though it hadn't been officially hers for twenty-two years now.

She let herself in, welcoming the fifteen-degree drop in temperature even as something in the air made her wary. Her nose wrinkled. A malodorous trail led her into the kitchen. The culprit sat right in the middle of the old chrome dinette table in the kitchen: a half-eaten bowl of cereal and a milk carton, spout gaping.

She picked up the milk carton with her fingertips and upended it into the kitchen sink.

Then she brought the bowl over and dumped its contents in, too, before flipping a switch and sending the whole mess gurgling down the garbage disposal. Why would her father have left his breakfast out and set off for campus?

She was scrubbing the sink with cleanser when she heard a knock at the door. Drying her hands on a paper towel, she hurried to answer it. When she opened it she found herself looking down into the face of a boy, probably eleven or so, judging by the awkward, half-formed look of him. His mop of brownish blond hair, chubby cheeks, and round brown eyes brought to mind little animals in old animated movies. The kid was born to be a Disney chipmunk.

"Is Professor Oliver back?" he asked.

"No, he—"

"Is he dead?"

She straightened, taken aback by the blunt question. "No! Why?"

"I heard he got run over."

"And you're . . . ?"

"I'm Dominic," he said, as if she should have known this. "I live next door."

Ah! Now she remembered. Her father's neighbors, a couple that had moved in about ten years earlier, had a flock of kids. It was sweet that her dad had befriended one of them.

"I'll be seeing Dad tonight," she said. "Would you like me to take him a message?"

His face scrunched up. “Why?”

“Well . . . maybe to tell him to get well? Or that you look forward to seeing him soon?”

The kid gaped at her as if she were insane. “He barely knows me!”

“Oh.” Grace lapsed into silent confusion.

“I was just worried he might be dead,” Dominic told her.

The matter-of-fact way he kept repeating that unnerved her. “He broke his leg, but they’ve set it and he’s able to hobble around. He’ll probably be back tomorrow.”

“Tomorrow!” Dominic exclaimed, as if this news would upset some important life plan of his.

“Or maybe the next day.”

He tilted his head, puffed his cheeks, and blew out a long breath. “Well, okay. Thanks.”

He turned and clomped down the stairs.

Odd.

Maybe Dominic just saw it as his duty to make sure everyone in the neighborhood was present and accounted for. It was summer vacation. Kids had to do something.

She turned and went back inside. She was feeling a little headachy now, and she realized she hadn’t had any caffeine since the Styrofoam cup of so-called coffee on the first leg of her plane trip. Which now seemed half a lifetime ago. She usually slurped down a few espressos per day—a perk of owning her own business-slash-café.

She opened the kitchen cabinet where the coffee had always been kept and found six boxes of Grape Nuts, a long shiny box of aluminum foil, and a tangerine. In her current state of fatigue, the incongruous still life was too taxing on her brain. She shut the cabinet.

In the drawer where the coffee filters usually were, she discovered a stack of printed paper. She reached in, grabbed the sheet on top, and saw that it was a mundane but very detailed to-do list.

Monday, the 22nd:

Let Iago out. Coffee. Iago in. Dog food. H/W pill. Breakfast. Vitamins. B/P pill.

Shower, shave, dress.

Walk, read, lunch.

PM: Pharmacy. (This item was written in her father's hand in blue ink.)

Dinner. Iago's dinner. Walk.

Everything off.

Doors.

Each item had been ticked off when completed. She leafed through the pages underneath, which had been carefully typed and printed, double-sided. On some days, there were extras scrawled in, such as *"Dr. Franklin,"* or *"Dinner at M's 7:30."* These activities would be scored through when finished, just as the others were.

She scanned the list again, but this time her gaze

arrested on one word. *Iago.* Iago was her father's dog. She'd completely forgotten.

Frowning, she glanced down at the two stainless-steel bowls resting on an old newspaper on the floor. One was empty, and the other one had about two inches of water and an overturned dead cockroach floating in it. Iago's bowls. But where was Iago?

Her father hadn't mentioned the dog to her; in the back of her mind, she'd just assumed he would be here. Had she overlooked a sixty-pound basset hound? She made a quick sweep through the house, although it seemed unnecessary. Iago usually trotted up as soon as someone came in. He wasn't in the house, and a quick glimpse around the yard revealed no dog out there, either. All the gates were closed, so it didn't look as if he had escaped.

Steven must have found someone to take care of Iago. Or boarded him somewhere. She picked up her phone and dialed her brother's cell number.

He picked up immediately, although his voice sounded harried. "Oh, Grace. I've got a cervical column seminar starting in five minutes."

Typical Steven. No nonsense like *How was your trip?* "Sorry, just a quick question. Where's Iago?"

"Iago?" he repeated.

"Dad's dog. Big, black-and-white slobber machine. What did you do with him?"

The line went so still for a moment that she feared she had lost the connection. "Steven?"

"I didn't do anything with him," he said.

"Well, didn't you have to make arrangements for him when Dad went into the hospital?"

"To be perfectly honest, I forgot all about him."

Great. "Dad didn't give you any instructions about him?"

"No—none. He never mentioned Iago."

She frowned. Stranger and stranger. "I guess I should call him."

"Shouldn't you look around first?" he asked. "I mean, you wouldn't want to upset him if he's just temporarily lost."

"It's not temporary—he's already been gone two days. Besides, Dad might know where Iago is. What if he left him at the groomer?"

"Then the groomer will have left a million messages on Dad's phone. Does he have any messages? His phone will beep when you pick it up if he does."

She picked up her dad's land line. "The dial tone sounds normal. This is bad."

Steven cleared his throat. "Sorry, Grace—I'm one minute to magic time here. Can you handle this? You might start by calling around to shelters."

He hung up. She went to the shelf where her father kept his Yellow Pages and was about to start looking up shelter numbers when there was another knock at the door.

This time, she knew the visitor at a glance. "Peggy!" She opened the screen door and threw her arms around a small roundish woman with snow-white hair.

Peggy, a retired teacher, lived across the street and down a few houses, and had been Lou's first wife's best friend. She'd been Grace's best friend, too. Her very first. As soon as Grace had been old enough to get on her tricycle, she had headed for Peggy's house every summer morning to pester her while she worked in the yard. "Helping Peggy," is what Grace had called it. Afterward, if she was lucky, she got invited in for M&Ms and a game of Old Maid. When her parents had divorced, Grace had missed Peggy almost as bitterly as she had missed her dad.

Peggy and Lou had stayed friends through all the ups and downs in their lives, and the closet romantic in Grace always waited for the call telling her that they had finally decided to tie the knot. Their ornery insistence on not getting married had frustrated her for years.

"I couldn't believe it was you!" Peggy said, pulling back to inspect Grace's travel-bedraggled person. "I saw you walking up the sidewalk and asked myself, *'Is that Grace?'* I thought I was imagining things. It's so good to see you." Peggy's smile collapsed. "I've been so worried about Lou."

"Have you been to the hospital?"

Peggy shook her head and said the word *no* on an inhale, so that it caught in her throat.

"He's doing fine," Grace assured her. "He was eating smuggled barbecue and complaining about everyone's footwear."

"Truman told me he'd broken his leg."

Uncle Truman had told her? Peggy hadn't even spoken to Lou on the phone?

"His leg's in a cast. He's supposed to be coming home tomorrow."

"That's good." Peggy tilted her head in curiosity. "And you're here for . . . ?"

"Just a week or two, till Dad's on the mend and he can take care of himself."

"Oh." The older woman's face pinched a little as she drifted off in thought.

Something felt peculiar. In the old days, visiting a sick friend in the hospital—especially if that sick friend was Lou—was something Peggy would have been all over.

"Is everything all right?" Grace asked.

Peggy snapped back to attention. "What?"

"I guess I was hoping you could fill me in on what Dad's been up to. Whenever I call him, all he talks about are books and music."

"I don't know if I'm the right person to ask."

Grace frowned. Who else *would* she ask, if not Peggy? "You and Dad haven't gotten into an argument, have you?"

Peggy hesitated. "Well . . . in a way." Her face

registered a brief, agonizing mental tug-of-war. "I didn't want to say anything. You know how I feel about your father—about all of you. And Lou and I have never had any conflict."

"Until now?" Grace guessed.

"Well . . . he's seemed moody. Maybe I've been getting on his nerves. One evening we went to a Mexican restaurant and I guess I fussed at him a little too much, and he blew up."

"Dad?" Her dad enjoyed needling people, jokingly, but he didn't *blow up.* Especially not in public. Especially not at Peggy. Blowing up at Peggy was akin to blowing up at the Easter Bunny.

But Peggy's tale was still half-finished. "He left me there, actually. Just got into his car and drove off. And the restaurant was all the way over on South Congress."

Grace lifted her hand to her forehead, where that ache was starting to get a little stronger. "What happened afterward?"

Peggy shrugged. "I finished my enchiladas and called a cab."

"I mean *afterward* afterward. Did you talk to him about it? Did he apologize?"

"No. We haven't spoken. Not for three months."

Three months! Grace had never been at her dad's house three days in a row without Peggy popping by once or twice. "I'm so sorry," Grace said. "I hadn't heard anything about this."

Peggy nodded, and in that instant, something of her old breeziness returned. "Well! These little bumps in the road happen in all friendships, don't they?"

Complete ruptures after fifty years? That seemed more than a *bump* to Grace.

"I hope you'll come over and visit me while you're here," Peggy continued. "I don't keep M&Ms anymore, but I can usually rustle up some Chex Mix."

"I'll be over," Grace assured her. "You'll be sick of the sight of me before too long."

"I doubt that!" Peggy gave her arm a quick, strong squeeze. "Unfortunately, I need to run, and you probably have a million things to do, too. I just wanted to dash over and say hi."

"I'm glad you did. But wait—you haven't seen Iago, have you?"

Already halfway down the steps, Peggy turned. "No. Is he missing?"

Grace felt a sinking feeling in her stomach. "I was hoping that he'd left him with you."

"No, not with me. Your uncle Truman hasn't said anything about the dog, either."

She bit her lip. Not with Peggy, not with Uncle Truman. "Can you think of anyone else around here he would have left Iago with?"

"Your father wouldn't trust anyone with that dog," Peggy said.

"I know . . . but why wouldn't he have said

something to Steven about taking care of Iago? Or me?"

Peggy frowned down at the floor. "Have you called shelters? Vets?"

"I was just about to start. I'm still hoping he's not really lost. Dad might have just taken him to the groomer's. . . ." She was back to clinging to that unlikely scenario.

"I'll keep an eye out," Peggy promised.

After Peggy left, Grace felt more uneasy. Not just about Iago. And not because Peggy and her dad had had a fight. It was that everything seemed the same, and yet not the same. She skipped the nap she so desperately wanted and spent the afternoon calling around to shelters and vet clinics instead. Later, when she returned to the hospital, she had to tell Lou that Iago was missing.

At the news, the creases in his face went slack with shock. "How can he be missing?"

"That's what I was wondering. There's the doggy door in the back, so he might have gotten outside, but the gate was firmly closed. And he couldn't have dug out, or there would be a hole the size of a crater next to the fence."

"He's not a digger."

As far as Grace could remember, Iago wasn't an anything-er, except perhaps a sit-arounder. She returned to her original suspicion. "Did you take him somewhere Saturday? The groomer, maybe?"

Her dad looked almost offended. "I can still get

out a water hose and wash my own dog, thank you very much."

"I wasn't saying . . ." She sighed. "He must have gotten out. Maybe the gate was open, and then someone came by and closed it later."

"He's never run away before."

"He might have gotten panicked when you didn't come home."

Lou didn't look convinced. "Someone must have taken him."

"Dognapped him, you mean?"

She stopped just short of laughing. Iago, a lumbering black-and-white mass of tongue and ears and floppy skin, didn't strike her as a canine theft object. He wasn't even a purebred—at the animal shelter her father had adopted Iago from they described him as a basset hound-poodle cross, which just meant that he was a slightly taller basset with peculiar tufts of wiry fur on his eyebrows, his chest, and in a line along his back. He resembled a canine life form that had been haphazardly sprinkled with Miracle-Gro.

But of course her father would consider his companion of these past five years to be a highly desirable dognapping target. "The house on the corner turned into a rental and now it's crawling with students," he said. "They might be up to some kind of shenanigans."

"I'll make a tour around the neighborhood and check the animal shelters again," she promised.

"I'll also make some flyers tonight on the computer."

"There's a good picture of him on my desk, in the office," he suggested.

She gingerly segued onto another topic. "I asked Peggy if she had seen him, but she said she hadn't."

Lou's jaw clamped shut.

"What's going on, Dad? I can't believe you've been fighting with Peggy."

"Is that what she says?"

"She says you abandoned her at a restaurant."

"I never did! Why would I do such a thing?"

"I don't know. . . ." She lifted and dropped her shoulders. "But it sounds as though you two are avoiding each other now."

"She's always nagging at me. Of course I've been avoiding her."

What was going on here? Peggy wouldn't make up a story about being abandoned at a restaurant out of whole cloth. What would be the point? Yet Grace had a hard time believing her father would lie, either.

"It's a shame, Dad. You were always such good friends."

"A history of friendship is not an excuse to be irritating."

Grace decided to let it drop for the moment, but in the back of her mind she set a rapprochement between Lou and Peggy as her goal for her stay.

"I should probably go now before the nurses kick me out. I'll be back tomorrow." She gave him a quick kiss on the crown of his head, which he endured with a wince. "Take it easy tonight, Dad."

She was almost out the door when he stopped her.

"When you get home, Grace, could you make sure to give Iago a treat for me? Poor guy's probably wondering where I've been."

4

Paint It, Black

Jordan had lain in wait for the perfect moment, and Sunday that moment arrived. After oversleeping church and then eating the requisite two waffles when her grandparents returned, she crawled back into bed with the cheap MP3 player she'd bought at Wal-Mart. Later—how much later it was impossible to say, because she was in a Mick Jagger-induced trance—she felt a hand on her shoulder and found herself staring up into Granny Kate's face. Her grandmother's lips were moving, but Jordan had no idea what she was saying until Granny Kate reached down and yanked a bud out from one of her ears.

"We've got to get to Bonny's." Her grandmother's voice was tight. She'd been on edge ever since their last trip to Midland.

"What for?"

"Bridge club. Why else do you think I made lemon squares?" She gave Jordan an exasperated nudge. "You're not even dressed yet!"

"I have a headache," Jordan lied.

"It's from listening to your music too loud. Those little ear thingamabobs aren't good for you. You'll go deaf."

"What?" Jordan asked.

"I said—" Belatedly, Granny Kate caught on to the joke. Instead of laughing, she heaved a sigh. "You can't be too careful when it comes to your ears. You might not care now, but you will when you're being fitted for your hearing aid, believe you me."

"It's just I've got this throb in my temple," Jordan explained. "If I went with you to that bridge club thing, I'd be *seriously* cranky."

"But honey, I can't just abandon you. Your Pop Pop is playing golf and won't be back all afternoon."

"I'll be fine. Swear to God."

Granny Kate hadn't really trusted leaving her alone since she learned that Jordan had seen a psychologist back in Austin. In Granny Kate and Pop Pop's world, *seeing a psychologist* equaled dangerously unbalanced. But over the past week, ever since Jordan had escaped in Midland and made tracks for the nearest hair salon, Granny Kate had seemed more open to the idea of not carting her around everywhere. In fact, the few times they had been out together in Little Salty since Jordan had shown up with Deep Cerulean #68 hair, her grandmother had walked around with a permanent wince on her face.

"Well . . ." Her grandmother's gaze slipped in the direction of Jordan's scalp.

The tide was turning in her favor, Jordan could tell. *Deep Cerulean #68 saves the day again!!*

Granny Kate relented. "I'll just be over at Bonny's. You know where that is."

"Bonny's," Jordan repeated. "Gotcha."

"The phone number is on the list taped to the refrigerator. So's your Pop Pop's cell phone number."

"On the refrigerator. Check."

"There's chicken salad in the fridge for your lunch. Don't just eat ice cream."

"Ice cream. Lunch. Check."

"I said *don't* eat just ice cream."

Jordan laughed. "I know. I was just messing with your mind."

"Well, don't! My mind's been in enough of a mess since the menopause."

When Jordan finally heard the front door shut, signaling her grandmother's departure, she bounded out of bed and practically did a jeté across the room. A whole afternoon to herself. This was too good to be true!

First thing after throwing some clothes on, she

padded over to the room they called Pop Pop's office, which actually was just a large closet with an antique computer and a lot of old fishing magazines in it. She perched on the computer chair. Usually when Jordan was on-line, her grandmother would find a million reasons to breeze through, checking on her. Granny Kate had read an article about on-line predators and teenage girls uploading naked photos of themselves, so naturally she couldn't imagine that Jordan would be doing anything on the Internet but making herself a target for pervs.

First she looked up the hours for the local hardware store. It was open Sunday afternoons. Excellent. She took a quick visit to her e-mail inbox.

Today there was a message waiting from Dominic. Nothing from her dad. Nothing from Lily. *Seventeen* magazine wanted her to subscribe, and Amazon.com thought she might be interested in something called *I Wasn't Ready to Say Goodbye* because she'd bought *Healing after Loss*, but Amazon.com had its head up its butt. She'd only bought that stupid book because her therapist had told her to. Did a company really think people wanted to sit around consuming grief books one after another, like bonbons?

She ticked off the two messages she didn't want and pressed the delete button, then turned to Dominic's message. In his e-mails, her brother tended to spit out his ideas in little disjointed bursts. He was like a painter Jed had shown her once, that French guy who painted with dots. Seurat. If you gathered Dominic's correspondence from about three months together and read it all at once, you might actually get a coherent narrative out of them. But reading just one random e-mail was like looking at a couple of dots from that painting *A Sunday Afternoon on the Island of La Grande Jatte* and trying to decide if they belonged to an umbrella or a monkey.

Today's e-mail was a case in point.

hi. how r u? i'm okay i guess but its boring here! lily took me to see a movie but i fell asleep in it and she said it was a waist of dads money and her time to take me to movies that she doesnt want to see in the first place if i'm just gonna conk out.

oh. i went next door and the guy's not dead after all. the lady told me his legs just broken. now I have to give lefty back or figure out a way to keep him but i wonder how that would work.

when are you gonna come home? egbert fell off the wall the other day for no reason. it was so weird!!!

bye, dominic

What was Dominic talking about? Who was *the guy?* Who was *the lady?* Who or what was *Lefty?*

She typed a quick reply, then grabbed her purse and headed out the door. It was a blazing sunny day, so hot she could feel the heat of the road burning through the soles of her sandals.

What was the deal with Egbert? Last year at arts camp, Jordan had painted a melted smiley face in oils. It was meant as a joke for Nina, who was always complaining that, because of the configuration of their beds, she ended up looking at Jordan's dismal midnight blue side of their room, while Jordan woke up with a view of light yellow painted walls, posters of pro tennis hotties, and picture frames with hand-painted daisies and smiley faces all over them. At arts camp, Jordan had decided to make a warped smiley face to hang on her side of the room for Nina to look at. It was sort of a goth smiley that looked as if it were melting.

Nina had laughed when she saw the painting. She'd named it Egbert.

Dominic didn't say whether Egbert had suffered any damage. Jordan felt a sharp stab at the idea of anything happening to that painting. Then she told herself that was completely stupid. It wasn't a Van Gogh or anything. It was just a dumb picture she'd made. A joke.

Her errand at the hardware store took practically no time at all because she'd plotted it all out in advance. She whizzed through the aisles grabbing Styrofoam paint pads and a plastic tray. She'd halfway expected the guys in the store to look at her funny when she asked for the black paint, but the stares they gave her weren't different from the ones she'd received from everybody else in the week since she'd dyed her hair blue. Their eyes followed her while they continued their conversation about how the guy at the register had had a fight with his girlfriend and ended up at a bar watching the Rangers game and drinking *way* too much Jack Daniel's.

When the guy behind the register finished bagging the pads and the tray, he handed them to Jordan with the barest of smiles. "That's the bluest blue I've ever seen."

Taking her stuff, she pinned a puzzled gaze on him. "Blue?"

"Your hair."

"I don't know what you're talking about," Jordan said. "I've been a blonde all my life."

"Girl, I'm telling you, your hair's blue."

She grinned. "You really did drink too much Jack Daniel's last night, didn't you?"

His coworkers laughed and Jordan could hear them ribbing the counter guy as she strolled out of the store.

She smiled halfway back to Granny Kate's, until she realized that the exchange with the hardware store clerk seemed like the first real human interaction she'd had in months. At least interaction that wasn't all bogged down by tension and guilt and other emotional dreck.

It didn't matter. Anyway, she didn't have time to think about stuff like that now.

She had been thinking about her painting project for days, imagining it, wondering how she could pull it off. Now it turned out to be not so difficult after all. True, the last time she'd painted a room—her room at home—she'd had more time and Nina had done all sorts of prep. But she doubted taping and laying down plastic made all that much difference anyway. As long as the walls got painted, who cared?

Two hours later, she realized she maybe should have cared. Though she was pleased with the room, even she had to admit she'd been a little sloppy. Dribbled black dots speckled the robin's egg blue carpet, and in a couple of places trickles of paint streaked black teardrops down the wall. Still, as she stood back, she surveyed the result with satisfaction.

Three walls of her bedroom were glossy black, and in the center, over her bed, she'd used leftover white paint she'd found in the garage to create her ode to Bob Ross. It looked like one of his signature snowy cedar trees, only in negative. The effect was heightened by the fact that the black paint hadn't thoroughly dried when she'd done the tree, so its branches were a smudgy gray in some parts. In an arc over the tree, she'd written HAPPY LITTLE TREE! in thick, blobby letters.

She smiled. It felt like eons since the world

around her had actually lifted her spirits. *Thank you, Nina. Thank you, Gandhi.*

She did anticipate a little dismay from the grandfolks. Black was a major change from the pastel walls they were accustomed to. Also, the black didn't really go with the curtains, which were yellow with little bouquets of violets embroidered on them. (Now they had little black polka dots, as well.) Maybe her grandmother would let her make new ones.

When the front door opened, she braced herself, especially when she heard voices and realized Granny Kate had brought a bridge club crony back with her for coffee. Evelyn Webb—a woman with a long face that pinched up in disapproval whenever she was around Jordan.

"I smell fumes!" Granny Kate's voice sounded alarmed.

"Smells like paint!" Evelyn exclaimed, knocking herself out with her Nancy Drewiness.

Seconds later, the two ladies appeared at the doorway. Both women's faces slackened in shock as they stood at the threshold, slowly scanning the room. Their gazes froze when they reached HAPPY LITTLE TREE!

"Oh . . . my . . . word," Evelyn breathed.

Granny Kate rotated her head, as if reading the letters at another angle would make the whole thing clearer to her. Her expression was hurt, almost offended. It was as if Jordan had scrawled profanity all over the walls, or drawn a huge swastika.

"You told me to make myself at home," Jordan said, waving them into the room. (One good thing: they both were too wigged out to notice the carpet splatters.) She attempted to talk them through it, assuming the tone of the guide at the art museum Jed had taken their class to last summer. *In this work, Claude Monet was attempting to express . . .*

"I wanted to make my room a little more me," she continued. "I mean, I'm not really beige walls and violet sprigs, am I? So I tried to inject a little of my Little Salty experience into the décor. It's like, what do you get when you cross Bob Ross with Mick Jagger?"

Something caught in her grandmother's throat. Jordan looked at her and saw there were actually tears standing in her eyes.

Evelyn Webb saw it, too. Concern for her friend emboldened her to march right up into Jordan's face. When she spoke, her voice had the fake urgency of adult concern. "Are you taking drugs?"

Jordan looked into the woman's weasel eyes and then burst out laughing.

After that, the situation deteriorated rapidly. And when Pop Pop walked in a few moments later, things only got worse. Jordan had hoped he might defuse the situation, but instead, as he stood in his green golf pants and gawped at the black walls and HAPPY LITTLE TREE!, his face went crimson, as if he was going to burst a blood vessel. She'd hardly ever seen her grandfather angry, except maybe at baseball umpires on television, or at Congress. Certainly never at her. But now he was practically quaking. Evelyn Webb fled before he could explode; Jordan wished she could scuttle out, too.

"What the Sam Hill were you thinking!" her grandfather shouted at her.

Good question. She supposed she'd been thinking that it was only a room. She tried once more to explain her motives, finishing with, "Anyway, it's just paint. It can be painted over."

Pop Pop went ballistic. "Painted over? Do you know how much painters cost?"

"*I* can do it," she said.

The wrong thing to say, apparently.

"You're not getting anywhere near a paintbrush in this house again!" he raged. "Even leaving aside the black walls, you splloopled paint all over the carpet! I don't know who this person you said you've been watching on television is . . ."

"Bob Ross," she said.

"And the Rolling Stones!" her grandmother interjected. Now that she'd found her voice again, she seemed most disturbed that after decades of her vigilant efforts, Mick Jagger had finally managed to penetrate her Barry Manilow world. "She's been listening to them on the sly, evidently."

"I just downloaded a few songs." As evidence, Jordan showed them the little MP3 player.

"You see?" Granny Kate snatched the device from Jordan and pivoted toward her husband. "She's been *downloading!*" As if downloading songs was just the kind of nefarious Internet activity they'd been worrying about all along. "And Evelyn thinks she's on drugs."

Jordan rolled her eyes. "Evelyn's a hemorrhoid."

"Don't you dare call our friends hemorrhoids!" her grandfather bellowed.

Jordan shrank back. "I was only expressing an opinion."

Her grandmother swooped down on her. "Your mother always said you were difficult to love, but we took you in for her sake. Now I realize our Jennifer had the patience of a saint! Well, I'm not a saint, and I'm fed up with your sulking and snippiness and blue hair. *Fed up!*"

Granny Kate fled the room in tears.

Jordan's face burned. *Difficult to love?* Her mom had said that about her?

She heard a weird noise and looked down. It was the muffled sound of her own foot tapping against carpet. She tried to still the movement but couldn't. Something was trembling so deep inside her that her brain couldn't send out waves strong enough to make it stop.

Granny Kate must really hate me, she thought. Why else would she have mentioned that about her mother, except to stick a knife in her gut and twist it? And Pop Pop wasn't saying anything. He probably felt the same way. *Difficult to love.*

Well, here was proof. They were the most mild-mannered people in the world, and she'd still managed to cheese them off.

She barely had the nerve to look into Pop Pop's face. "I just wanted things to be different," she said. "At least to *look* different. Wouldn't you, if you were me?"

He didn't say anything.

"Pop Pop?" she asked, her voice small.

A muscle in his jaw twitched. "Your grandma's upset. This has been a difficult year, and you . . ."

And you're not just the reason why, you're also a walking reminder.

He didn't have to say it. She knew.

"I think you'd better start packing your things," he said.

5

The People in Your Neighborhood

The next day, Grace decided to canvas the neighborhood for news of Iago. There was a black SUV in the driveway of the rental house next door, so she assumed that the person who lived there wasn't at work. For some reason—perhaps because of the bungalow's perky yellow paint job—she didn't expect a tall, blue-eyed Dirk Squarejaw type to open the door.

When he saw her, he leaned against the doorframe and grinned as if Grace had materialized for his amusement.

"I'm your neighbor from . . ." She tilted her head in the direction of her dad's house.

"Really? I thought the old guy lived alone."

"The *old guy* is my dad," she informed him. "He's in the hospital."

"Oh. Sorry to hear that." He shook his head, but that boyish smile remained firmly in place. "I'm always the last to know anything that's going on around here. Too busy buzzing around the skies to keep up, I suppose."

"Hallucinogens?" she guessed.

He chuckled. "Airline pilot. My name's Wyatt Carter. I fly for SunWest Airlines. They're based in Dallas, but so's my ex-wife. So I've based myself here."

He paused like a lame stand-up waiting for laughter, but the most she could manage was a cough of sympathy for the ex-wife. She tried to steer the conversation back to the point. "The thing is, Wyatt, my father's dog is missing. You haven't seen him, have you?"

"You mean that black-and-white dog, looks sort of like a mutant basset hound?"

Hope leapt inside her. "Yes! Exactly!" She picked a newly-minted flyer off the stack in her hands and thrust it at him.

He gave it a cursory glance. "Nope. I've seen him when your dad's walked him, but I haven't noticed him loose. I hope there's nothing wrong with him."

"He's lost," Grace said.

"I meant, nothing wrong with your dad."

"He was hit by a car."

"Oh." Wyatt squinted. "Wait . . . The dog?"

"No, my dad," she said. "His leg's broken."

"That's awful. Poor old guy."

"He'll be fine, they say. But he's very upset about Iago."

"Who?"

"His dog—the missing dog?" *The reason I'm here.* "So if you do see him . . ."

"Let you know? Roger Wilco." He grinned. "What did you say your name was?"

"Actually, I didn't."

He laughed. "So, ActuallyIDidn't, are we permanent neighbors now?"

Until that moment she had never realized how much she could look forward to a casual conversation being over. "I'm just visiting for a couple of weeks."

"We should get together sometime."

Unbelievable. "I'll be pretty busy."

"Well, if you're ever not busy, you know where to find me."

And I know how to avoid you. She attempted a smile and made her escape. The door didn't close behind her, and she could almost feel that laser gaze on her butt as she walked away.

Next to Wyatt Carter's bungalow stood another one-story house, although this one sprawled across the entire corner lot. In the old days, Sam's good friend Seeger and his sister, Rainbow, had lived there. Now it was a student rental. Several beat-up cars with orange UT stickers on them sat in the drive.

Two guys lounged shirtless on an old couch on the front porch, nursing beer bottles. They noted her approach with easy smiles and sleepy, half-hooded eyes. Students. No wonder her father despaired.

"Hey," they said in unison.

"Hi," she said. "I'm visiting my dad, two houses down. He's in the hospital."

"No shit! The old professor? Wha happened?"

"An SUV ran him down on the drag."

"No way!"

"That's cold."

"He'll be okay, but he broke his leg." This information was met with more exclamations of disbelief. They seemed genuine. In fact, she couldn't buy her father's suspicions that these guys had been up to any shenanigans. They didn't look as if they had the initiative for dognapping, or anything beyond keggers and Frisbee tossing.

"The thing is, his dog is missing. You guys haven't seen him, have you?"

She handed over two copies of the flyer, which the guys gaped at for a moment.

"Oh, no! That cool sawed-off-looking thing? Great dog."

"Seriously great dog."

"Well, if you happen to see him, could you let me know?" Grace prompted.

"Will do."

The other guy sent her a mock salute with his beer bottle and drawled, "Rest assured, ma'am, we will definitely be on the eyeball for said dog."

"Thanks." As she walked away from this Bill and Ted's Excellent Dogwatching porch, for the first time she began to lose hope that she would actually find Iago.

Her phone rang. It was Ben. She picked up, eager to hear news from home.

"Am I glad—"

Ben's panicky voice interrupted her. "Where's the key to the storage cabinet?"

This was not a just-wanted-to-hear-your-voice call, evidently. She squinted down at the sidewalk, trying to switch mental gears. "What storage cabinet?"

His voice was tight with impatience. "The one with the credit card machine paper in it! I'm going nuts here, Grace!"

"It's on the shelf under the register."

"What would a key be doing there?"

"Not the key, the little rolls of paper for the credit card machine. The storage room key is on the key-shaped brass holder hanging on the door of the employee coat closet. It has a red plastic key ring with the words *storage closet* written on it."

"Well, how was I to know?" he asked in a testy voice.

"I didn't mean—"

"I have to go," he said, cutting her off.

"Wait! How are—"

He stopped her before she could finish. "Vomiting. Vomiting all the time."

She frowned. She'd been on the verge of asking him about himself, but she presumed he was talking about the cats. "Oh God. I'm sorry, are—"

"I *really* have to go, Grace. I've got a customer waiting for some purchasing action here."

"Of course. I'll call you—"

The line went dead. As she stood in the middle of the sidewalk with her phone still unfolded in her hand, she felt so dislocated it almost made her queasy. It was hard to believe that just about thirty-six hours ago her most pressing concerns had been running out of chips at the party and who would win the Tournament of Stupid Games.

Impulsively, she dialed the number for her mom's house in Portland. Her mother had once owned an escape artist Pomeranian; she might have some tips for hunting a lost dog. Plus, she just felt like calling someone who would really talk to her.

Her half sister, Natalie, picked up the phone and let out a breath when she realized who was calling. "Oh, Grace." A yawn traveled over the line. "I'm *so* tired. I was at work until one in the morning."

Grace frowned at the sidewalk. "Pools are open until one?"

"What?" Natalie asked, confused.

"I thought you were a lifeguard."

Natalie sputtered. "*Hello?* Lifeguarding was last summer. This year I'm working at the Crab Shack. I'm making more money, but I smell like a fish stick."

"Oh." Her mother hadn't told her what Natalie's summer plans were, or her little brother Jake's, either. And when Grace went by the house now, sometimes she felt as if her younger siblings looked at her like the old baby-sitter who'd dropped by for a visit. "Is Mom at home?"

"No—work. She's doing morning shifts these days."

When Jake and Natalie were both in elementary school, their mom had gone back to school and become an LVN.

"I can tell her to call you when she gets home," Natalie said, obviously eager to crawl back into bed.

"No—I'll call her. I'm in Austin."

"Why?"

"Visiting my dad."

"Oh! Right!" She yawned again. "Mom mentioned that, I think. She's worried about you leaving the store with what's-his-name."

"Ben."

"Right. I thought it was weird. The only other times she mentions the store is when she's complaining about how you're a slave to it. Now when you finally do get away . . ."

"It's because I'm home. In Austin, I mean. She and my dad—they've never been on the best of terms."

Natalie snorted. "No kidding! I can't imagine Mom marrying an old man. She must have been really desperate or something."

"He wasn't so old back then. Just forty-five."

"Like I said—an old man."

Grace bit her lip. "I'd better go. I'll call Mom back later."

" 'Kay. Good night."

Grace said good-bye and hung up, feeling even more disconnected than before.

"Can I help you?"

At the sound of a woman's voice just behind her, Grace spun on her heel. She had spotted this woman earlier working in her yard. The blonde, who appeared to be in her mid-thirties, lived two houses down on the other side of her dad's property, next to the white two-story house where the weird kid named Dominic lived. She wore a sunny yellow linen tank top, white shorts, and espadrilles. Not exactly the clothes Grace would have chosen for working in the yard.

"My name's Muriel Blainey." She extended her head forward and tilted it slightly like a curious bird. "I've seen you going door to door. Is there some sort of problem?"

The neighborhood watch, Grace presumed. She introduced herself and explained, "My father's dog has disappeared."

"Iago? I am *so* sorry! Was this before or after the accident?"

"I think it must have been just after," Grace said.

"Well, the poor doggie hasn't been around my house," Muriel informed her, making a sympathetic pouty face. "Have you tried the animal shelters yet?"

"I called them." The creases in Muriel's forehead alerted her to the fact that this was the wrong answer. "But I guess I'll go in person this afternoon. Of course."

"I assume you've called every vet in the phone book by now."

"Well, not *every* one."

Not good enough, Muriel's expression said. "And you have flyers?"

Grace handed one over.

"Every pole should have one," Muriel instructed her. "And all the local businesses. If you need to borrow a staple gun, my husband has one. He's away on business in California, so it's not as if he'll be needing it this afternoon. I'll get it for you right now and we can have all your flyers out in a jiffy."

Grace felt the negligible weight of the small packet of thumbtacks in her pocket. Totally inadequate. Everything about this woman made her feel unprepared. "I think Dad might have one somewhere," she said, edging away. She couldn't shake the alarming suspicion that if she actually accepted Muriel's aid, she wasn't going to get away from her until the very last flyer was stapled to the very last phone pole.

"I'll knock on your door if I need it," Grace promised her. "Thanks."

She hurried to the house and shut the door. Staple gun! A normal person would have kept his toolbox in the garage, but this house had no garage and her father was definitely not normal. She searched the closets, the little mudroom to the side of the kitchen, and even the window seat in the dining room, which had been used as a junk repository for decades. Nothing. Finally she remembered the upstairs storage closet.

Growing up, she'd always loved the closet because it resembled a little room. It even had its own tiny window. She'd always imagined setting up a sort of clubhouse in it. Not that she, a lone kid visiting from halfway across the country, had any friends to invite to join this club. . . .

Forgetting the staple gun, she picked her way over storage boxes and old vacuum cleaners and made her way to the window. It was just a tiny vertical rectangle, but it had the same woodwork and double panes of glass that the windows downstairs had. Beneath a heavy layer of dust, the paint was pinkish beige. A color from long ago, she supposed. Now the trim inside was off white. Her dad had just had the whole place repainted a few years ago, inside and out. The exterior was a deep red color with rich brown trim that made the old craftsman design look sharp, especially against the gray stonework around the porch. It was one of the oldest houses in the neighborhood, and her father's pride.

Something captured her attention through the accumulated grime on the window glass. At first it was hard to credit what she was seeing, because it seemed to be just a black-and-white smudge in the distance. Impulsively, she used the tail of her T-shirt to wipe a semi-clear spot on the glass and pressed her face close. Unbelievable!

Iago lay in the neighbor's yard, surrounded by a privacy fence, in the shade of an old pecan tree. The furry truant hadn't just landed there recently, either, by the looks of things. He'd dug himself a cool trough to relax in.

So that was why Dominic had looked so anxious. Nervy little dognapper.

In less than a minute, Grace was standing at the front door of the neighbor's house. The first doorbell wasn't answered, although she caught the rustle of a curtain out of the corner of her eye. She buzzed again, leaning on it this time.

She was braced to give the dog thief a dressing-down. But when the door finally opened, instead of Dominic, she found herself looking down at a girl. Her face was a teenager's, but she was still at that awkward late-bloomer stage where the head seemed unnaturally big for the body, like a Pez dispenser. Her dark hair was pulled back from her face in a severe ponytail, and her Harry Potter glasses made her brown eyes appear larger than they were.

"I had nothing to do with it," the girl declared. "I told Dominic it was dumb, unethical, and maybe even illegal. Are you going to call the police?"

The matter-of-fact way she asked that last question made it sound as if troopers coming to haul away her little brother would not be an entirely unwelcome development.

Grace crossed her arms. "Before we get the authorities involved, can I just see Iago?"

The girl hesitated a moment before cautiously stepping aside and letting Grace in. She ushered her through a short entrance hall that led on one side to a dining room. The table piled with books and mail indicated the room hadn't actually been used for eating in a while. On the other side of the hall was a living room with a grand piano and music stand.

"What a pretty piano," Grace said. "Do you play?"

The girl tossed the instrument a somber look. "I play clarinet. My mother played piano, but she died."

"Oh, I'm sorry," Grace mumbled.

Double doors led out from the living room to a deck and the backyard beyond. When he saw Grace cross through the doors, Iago heaved his belly up from the dirt and waddled toward her, his heavy tail flopping from side to side in greeting. She bent over and scratched the soft droopy ears, which he loved. Wriggling, he sank down on his rear and let out a yodel of pleasure.

Dominic appeared, his face crinkled with worry. He wasted no time justifying his theft. "The thing was, I could hear the dog on the other side of the fence. He was whimpering. I thought the old man had died. I couldn't just leave him there."

She darted a skeptical glance at him. "And when I saw you yesterday . . . it slipped your mind?"

"You didn't even mention the dog!"

True. She hadn't noticed Iago was missing at the time. Still . . . "I assumed a neighbor would inform me if my dog was sitting in his yard."

"He's not your dog, technically. You're just loosely related."

"And you're just a dog snatcher."

He rubbed his hand over his hair, unable to deny the charge. "I took really good care of him. I even spent all my allowance this weekend buying a bag of dog food."

His face was so white with panic, and she felt so relieved to have found Iago, she couldn't keep up the pretense of anger. "Don't worry—I can tell you were a good dog-sitter. Dad'll be glad that Iago was taken care of while he was gone."

The boy deflated in relief. "I call him Lefty, on account of his left paw is black. But I'll understand if your father wants to change his name back."

Chutzpah. She laughed. "You can talk it over with Dad. He'll be back home tomorrow."

The boy's eyes widened. "You mean go over there?"

"Iago might not understand if you don't pay him a visit or two," she pointed out.

He registered her lack of anger and smiled. "Okay."

Grace turned to lead Iago out via the backyard gate, but Dominic's sister blocked her way. She looked stunned, even a little outraged. *"That's it?"*

"What's it?" Grace asked.

"He *stole a dog!* The only consequence is you're going to invite him over for a visit?"

"Iago's fine. I can tell Dominic wasn't being malicious."

"He was *hiding* him," the girl pointed out.

Whose side was she on?

Dominic seemed to wonder the same thing. "Please don't tell anybody else," he begged Grace. "Especially not my dad. Please?"

"Where did your father think the dog came from?" she asked.

"He still doesn't know about the dog," the girl said.

Grace felt her jaw go slack. The father didn't know? Iago had been there for two days. How could a man cohabitate with a basset hound for two days and not know it?

"Dad hasn't seen him yet," Dominic affirmed.

"Hasn't seen what?" a deep voice asked.

At the sound of the deep voice, they all jumped and turned. Standing on the deck was a tall man with hair and brown eyes like Dominic's. But that was where any father-son resemblance ended. Dominic had a doughy quality to him, while the man was tall and lean. And his expression was as reserved as Dominic's was open and readable.

"Dad!" Dominic said, clearly alarmed. His Adam's apple bobbed visibly.

The man took Grace in warily through his wire-framed glasses. "Hello."

She smiled. "I'm Grace Oliver. I'm staying with

my father for a while after he gets home from the hospital."

"I was sorry to hear about Lou's accident," he said.

"And you're . . . ?"

"He's my dad," Dominic explained unnecessarily.

"Ray West."

"I'm Lily," the girl interjected before shooting her father a curious look. "Why are you home so soon?"

"Is something wrong?" Dominic asked.

Grace sensed that this was her moment to slip away.

"Actually, there is," Ray said. "At the office, I got a call from your grandfather."

In a flash, the atmosphere changed. Grace stopped. The kids' bodies went rigid, and Dominic's face was suddenly as pale as his sister's.

"They're sending Jordan back," Ray announced.

"Back!" Lily exclaimed. "Back *here?* Why?"

Her father shook his head. "I don't understand it myself. She was so certain she'd be happier there, and now . . ."

"What happened?"

Ray let out a breath. "I don't know. I couldn't get much out of your Pop Pop. I'll have to call back tonight when the dust has settled. Jordan's on a flight from Midland right now. I've got to go meet the plane."

"Yes!" Dominic gave a hop and then spun toward Grace. "Jordan's one of my—I mean, she's my other big sister."

He seemed so thrilled that it was impossible not to smile back at him. Yet it was also impossible not to notice that they were the only ones smiling.

Lily's face was a thundercloud of unhappiness. "Oh, great!" She stomped into the house.

The father said nothing more, but trailed after his daughter, head lowered mournfully. He seemed to have forgotten Grace was there.

And he never did notice the dog.

6

Going, Going, Gone

Whatever pleasure Lily could have received from Jordan's getting kicked out of Granny Kate and Pop Pop's house—what *on earth* could she have done?—was completely overshadowed by the fact that she was back now. Apparently for good.

Lily was rinsing off the breakfast dishes when she heard a rumbling upstairs from Nina and Jordan's bedroom. (She refused to call the room *just* Jordan's.) What was she doing up there? Jordan had been home for two days . . . two days fraught with tension. She had been relatively quiet until now, and careful to stay out of their dad's way, but it didn't matter because bad feelings and conflict just seemed to ooze out of Jordan anyway.

The only positive Lily could take from Jordan's being back for good was that *for good* might not be all that long. In two years Jordan would be eighteen, and there was no way she'd want to live at home after high school. So two years was all they had to endure.

Two years of being known as the sister of the freak with blue hair. The geeky little sister.

The ugly duckling. She always tried to get that horrible expression out of her head, but it stayed there anyway, dancing around in her consciousness, mocking her.

In her opinion, Hans Christian Andersen had a lot to answer for. People told that dumb story as if it was supposed to be a source of hope to less attractive kids. As if every ugly person ended up being a swan! A true fairy tale. As far as Lily was concerned, the incredible aspect of the whole tale was that it took so long for the swan—to say nothing of its mother—to figure out that he was an entirely different species. The story should have been called *The Stupid Swan*, because that poor bird could have saved himself a lot of trouble and heartache if he'd just looked at his reflection and realized that he was in the wrong family to begin with.

Unfortunately, there was no doubting Lily was in the right family. Everyone said she resembled

Granny Kate's older sister, Jeannie, when Jeannie was a kid. Family photos confirmed this, and it was *not* comforting. Even as a teen, Aunt Jeannie looked like an undernourished refugee from the land of bad fashion decisions. Her plain, ill-fitting shirts always emphasized her pancake-flat chest, and the tweedy skirts she wore bunched awkwardly around her thick waist. The girl could have had a flashing neon sign over her head: FUTURE SCHOOL LIBRARIAN AND AFRICAN VIOLET ENTHUSIAST.

Lily shuddered whenever she looked at those photos, because apparently that's how other people saw her. But that's not how she saw herself. It wasn't how her mother or Nina had seen her, either.

One of her best memories was of Nina, eight going on nine, parading her through the halls of their elementary school to Lily's first grade classroom on her first day of real school. Other kids had looked at her like she was special, because her big sister—a third grader who already had the poise of a sixth grader—had escorted her right up to the teacher's desk and announced, "Miss Collins, this is my little sister, Lily. She should probably be in second grade, because she already knows how to read and add and everything."

(If only Miss Collins had listened—it would have saved Lily two very boring years until her third grade teacher had gotten a clue and bumped her up to fourth.)

Nina had waited for her outside the classroom after school at the end of the day, too, and had taken her to the girls' rest room to help her unstick the two braids that Tommy Dewes had glued together during storytime. "The first day is the hardest," Nina told her. "Tomorrow afternoon will be better."

She'd looked blurry through Lily's hot tears. "How do you know?"

"Because tomorrow at lunch, Jordan will punch Tommy Dewes in the nose." And then, before they left the bathroom, she'd given Lily a fierce, bracing hug. "You don't even belong in first grade anyway."

Nina had always known what to say to her. She'd been her cheerleader, and confidante, and practically her best friend. Her only friend, sometimes. When they got older, Jordan started treating Lily like a pest, but even when Nina was with her school friends she sometimes invited Lily along to movies or whatever. Nina would play tennis with her, too, though Lily stank at tennis. Nina would laugh when Lily worried about not being good enough. "Who cares? It's just to have fun together, right?"

Lily's throat tightened. She really shouldn't think about Nina, not unless she was sure she was alone. She didn't want to get all upset and set

Dominic off. It had been horrible those first weeks to hear him crying in his room. Almost four months later, they were all just now getting back to normal. The new normal. That was what made Jordan's return so especially awful. She was one of those people who seemed to rampage through life like a demented rhinoceros—as if she were the only person in the world and the rest of them were just little rodents who had to scatter or get squished.

Something crashed upstairs, shaking the ceiling hard enough to set the light fixture over the dining room table swinging. What the heck was Jordan doing?

Dominic ran into the kitchen, skidding the last few feet across the linoleum in his socks. "Did you hear *that?!*"

"What's going on?"

Her brother's entire torso lifted in a shrug. "I've knocked at the door, but she won't let me in."

Lily bit her lip. She wondered if Jordan was doing drugs. That would explain why Granny Kate and Pop Pop had been in such a hurry to get rid of her. She'd asked her dad for details, but he wouldn't explain anything.

She dumped baking soda down the drain and flipped the garbage disposal switch. During the ten seconds the disposal was making its god-awful noise, Lily reconsidered her suspicions. Not that she knew anything about it, but she doubted taking drugs involved anything that sounded like dropping a large boulder on the hardwood floors. After she flipped the switch off and quiet descended on the kitchen again, she announced, "I'm going to find out."

Her brother barred her path. "You know how she is when she doesn't want to be disturbed."

"So? Who does she think she is? The queen?"

At that moment, Jordan herself slouched into the room. "I prefer empress, if you don't mind. Or tsarina. Sounds more . . . well, like a bossy person."

Lily smirked. "I think the word your tiny brain is reaching for is *dictatorial.*"

"Yeah, whatever," Jordan said. "Could you guys get the door if the bell rings? Some people are coming by."

"What people?" Lily hadn't seen any of Jordan's friends at the house in months and months. Did she still have any? "Who?"

"Never mind," Jordan said. "Just answer the door and show them up to my room."

Nina's room. Lily fumed.

"I'm not your maid," Lily told her.

"I'll do it," Dominic said quickly, before a fight could erupt.

"Thanks, Dominickel."

When she was gone, Dominic turned back to Lily, who tried not to convey what a traitor she thought he was.

Apparently her effort failed. “I’m just trying to help,” he said defensively.

Lily was determined not to waste any more of her time thinking about whatever it was that Jordan was up to. She had more important things to do, like read *Hamlet.* Her original goal for the summer had been to read the complete works of Jane Austen, but that had taken her less than a month. After *Pride and Prejudice* she hadn’t been able to stop herself. It was like eating M&Ms. She’d just popped one down after another.

It would take her more than a month to get through all of Shakespeare, she was pretty sure. Just this one play was probably going to take her more than a month. Every other line she had to stop and figure out what the heck was going on. She hadn’t even reached the part with Hamlet in it. There were just a lot of guys running around exclaiming, *Tush!* and *Peace!* and *Stand, ho!*

Her task was made a little more difficult because she couldn’t stop tensing up every time she heard a noise outside. She kept thinking it would be those mysterious people Jordan was expecting. But the first time she heard a car door shut and stood up to peek through the curtains, it was just that lady from next door, bringing Professor Oliver back. He had cut off the leg of one of his pairs of khakis at midthigh, just past where his cast began.

When the doorbell rang, Lily jumped up,

forgetting she wasn't going to answer the door. She reached it the same time as Dominic, who was running full tilt from the dining room. The two came inches away from colliding like cops in an old silent movie. As Lily opened the door, she expected to find a teenager on the other side of the threshold, but instead there was a scruffy guy who had to be at least sixty. He had on baggy jeans and wore his scraggly gray hair in a ponytail. Behind him stood a younger guy—younger, as in forty-five or so.

"I'm here about the dresser," the scraggly one announced.

"The *what?*" Dominic exclaimed.

Maybe *dresser* was code for "I'm here to sell drugs." She debated calling her dad. Or the police.

Then she heard Jordan call out from the staircase, "Hey! The stuff's up here." She gestured with a roll of her shoulder and headed back up, with the scruffy men trailing.

As Lily and Dominic exchanged confused glances, a paneled van pulled into their drive. Another middle-aged guy popped out and came loping up the stairs. "This is the sale, right?" he asked as he shouldered past them.

"Sale?" Lily repeated.

Dominic ran upstairs and came racing down again a few minutes later as more people trickled in. This time there were women too. An invasion had begun.

"She's selling everything!" Dominic announced excitedly.

"What do you mean, everything?"

"I mean *everything.* All the furniture, and clothes, and books and CDs. She told me she put an ad on Craigslist."

"Is she selling Nina's stuff?"

Dominic nodded.

"She can't do that!"

Lily ran to the staircase but couldn't get up it because the first two guys were now carrying down Nina and Jordan's old dresser. Quivering with impatience, she flattened herself against the wall. When they were finally out of her way, she took the stairs two at a time, nearly knocking over someone on his way down with a boxful of loot.

She stopped short at Nina and Jordan's door. The room was filled with people dragging open drawers and holding up articles for inspection. Stuff was strewn everywhere—all of Nina's clothes and books and purses. Everything. The vultures were picking through it. They were looking at Jordan's things too, but Lily didn't care about that.

"You're selling everything!" she yelled at Jordan.

Jordan tossed her an annoyed look. "Brilliant detective work there, Lils."

"But you can't!"

"But I am."

A lady picked up Nina's tennis racket, and Lily felt a pain shoot through her heart. She turned on her heel and raced back downstairs to the phone. When her father answered on the second ring, she didn't waste time with niceties.

"Dad, you have to come home. *Now.*"

Tension crackled over the line—that palpable fear disaster had struck again. "What's wrong?"

"Jordan's selling everything in her and Nina's room!"

There was a slight pause before her dad answered, but when he did, it was with exasperation. Aimed at *her.* "For Pete's sake, Lily. You scared me half to death."

"They're taking away all the furniture, and Nina's tennis racket!" she said, trying to convey the extreme urgency of the situation.

"Well, just see they don't start hauling away things from the rest of the house."

"But—"

"I need you to keep your eyes open, Lily. Make sure all the other doors are shut and watch to make sure no one makes off with the family silver. Can you do that?"

"But *Dad*—"

"I have to go now," he said, cutting her off. "I'm supposed to be in a meeting."

She hung up, feeling more and more panicky. And outraged. This was really going to happen! All that was left of Nina was just going to be carted away like so much garbage. Thank goodness she had already pilfered a few of her sister's books.

Dominic trooped through the hallway with the neighbor lady. Grace. He was tugging her up the staircase and telling her to "come see." As if this were a carnival going on instead of a tragedy.

The terrible thing was, Lily couldn't think of a way to stop it. She wanted to run up and screech at everyone to get out, but what words would make a dent in the determination of these estate sale buzzards? She wished she were a soldier with a sword and could charge in yelling, *Stand, ho!* She wished there was another person left in the world who would understand her anguish at seeing a stranger carrying a stuffed toy rabbit and a tennis racket out the front door.

7

Back Home

When Grace came back from next door, her father was installed in his favorite wing chair in the living room next to the old chess board, his injured leg jutting out onto the area rug. He glanced at her newfound objet d'art and recoiled like a vampire exposed to sunlight. "What is *that?*"

"It's Egbert," she announced.

He didn't even ask for a translation. "It's awful."

She flipped the painting around and inspected it again—a yellow smiley face melting into a black backdrop. Something about it made her smile. According to Dominic, his blue-haired sister had painted it herself, though you couldn't have told it from the girl's reaction when Grace had forked over her five dollars. Jordan had barely spared the picture a glance.

"It'll look good in the kitchen," Grace said.

"Here?" Lou said, horror-struck.

She laughed. "In Portland. Ben will get a kick out of it." She thumped her dad's cast playfully. "*Ben* has a sense of humor."

She crossed the room to lean the picture against the closet door, out of the way. She was almost afraid to turn around again. Her father was planted next to that chess board like a threat. She didn't mind chess, but when she played her dad she needed to be in a losing frame of mind.

"How about a game?" A casual onlooker might not have caught the subtle yet sinister gleam in his eye.

She relented. After all, he was an invalid. "Okay, just let me put some coffee on first." She remembered that he couldn't drink regular coffee now, and they were out of decaf. "You want some juice or something?"

"No, no—but Iago would probably like a . . ."

"A what?"

"One of those little things he eats all the time."

Actually, what Iago wanted was rarely in doubt. The dog waddled after her to the kitchen, where Grace took out his box of biscuits and handed him one. He snapped it out of her hand and trotted away with it to savor in paranoid solitude under the dining room table. Five years on, he still hadn't grasped the idea that no one was going to snatch his bisky back.

When she returned to the living room, Lou was practically rubbing his hands together in anticipation. To give him credit, he never seemed to realize the game would be a massacre. In fact, as they began, so did his usual gasps of shock whenever Grace made a bone-headed move. As the carnage piled up and her downfall became eminent, he started adding interjections, trying to stop her before she could take her hand off her piece.

"You do realize that's your queen, don't you?" he asked in a doleful tone.

She was just trying to figure out what calamity would befall her queen when the doorbell rang. Lou reached for his crutches.

"I'll get it, Dad. By the time you critch over to the door, our visitor might have given up hope and gone away."

"Depending on the visitor, that might be the best outcome."

As if to prove his point, when Grace opened the door, Uncle Truman brushed past, removing his summer straw hat and fanning himself with it as he eyed his brother. "You look pitiful!" he exclaimed.

Lou chuckled.

"Do you intend to walk around for six weeks with half a fraying trouser leg?" Truman asked.

"He just got home from the hospital," Grace protested.

But Uncle Truman's bluntness never fazed her father. "I was going to have Grace take a few pairs to a tailor to have them altered."

Truman sank down in the chair Grace had vacated. "Grace can't do it herself?"

"No, she can't," Grace said.

Her uncle shook his head. "Women today are pitiful! That's what I was just telling Peggy."

"I'm sure she was tickled to hear it," Lou said dryly.

"I didn't mean *her,*" Truman said.

"You meant me." Grace and her father exchanged smiles.

If Truman entertained a suspicion that he was the object of their mutual mirth, he didn't show it. "Peggy's making peach preserves today. You should see it! I took her out to Fredericksburg yesterday and we bought a few bushels, and now she's going at it like a house afire. Mason jars everywhere, kitchen all steamed up. And I know for a fact she can make clothes, and garden, and crotchet—and I don't know what-all."

"All hail Peggy," Grace said without enthusiasm.

One talent the woman evidently lacked was visiting her old friend to welcome him home from the hospital. “Right now I’m taxing my meager housekeeping skills making a pot of coffee. Would you care for some, Uncle Truman?”

His face collapsed in a frown. “Oh . . . I don’t know. Is it decaf?”

“No, it’s caf.”

“I’m only supposed to drink decaf.” He tilted his head. “But I don’t guess a cup’ll kill me.”

Grace didn’t guess anything would kill Uncle Truman, except maybe a strict regimen of enforced tact.

Since when did he drive women out to peach orchards? she wondered as she marched into the kitchen. And why Peggy?

She loaded up coffee cups and carried them into the living room on a tray, waitress style, along with a glass of orange juice for her dad.

“How about a game, Tru?” her father asked his brother.

Truman almost spilled the cup Grace was handing to him. “Do you think I’m a fool? You might be an invalid now, but you’re probably still a cheat.”

Lou raised his hand to swear. “I never cheated in my life.”

“Then how is it you always win?” Truman argued.

“Because I’m a better player than you. Always have been.”

"Winning all the time," Truman grumbled in disgust. "Where's the sport in that?"

"It beats losing all the time," Grace said, settling onto the sofa by the front window.

Lou changed the subject. "Grace had to hunt down Iago while I was in the hospital. The neighbor's boy was taking care of him. Thought he had been abandoned."

Truman shook his head more mournfully than a temporary dognapping seemed to call for. "That accident was a bad business."

At first Grace assumed he was referring to Lou getting run over. But there was a decided shift in the air in the room—a gloomy silence that couldn't be attributed to a broken leg.

"What accident?" she asked.

Her father looked as if he regretted bringing up the subject of the neighbors. "The family next door was on vacation earlier this year," he explained. "While the mother was driving somewhere with one of the girls, the two of them were in a head-on collision. Both were killed."

Grace remembered Lily mentioning her mom. The pianist. She'd had no idea the loss was so recent. "How awful! The daughter who was killed, was she the oldest?"

Lou nodded. "She was a twin, and the better half by a long shot. That sister of hers hasn't been around lately, though."

"She's back." Grace understood now. They were

talking about the teenager selling all her things. The sister whose return had made Lily so upset, and Dominic so happy.

She couldn't imagine the devastation of an accident like that. It explained some things, though. Such as why an eleven-year-old boy would seem preoccupied with whether his old neighbor, a man he didn't really know, was dead. And whether his dog had been left abandoned. It also explained Ray West's shell-shocked expression.

"I invited Dominic to visit Iago," she said. "He stopped by today to tell me about the sale, but he didn't want to come in. I think he still expects to be arrested."

Truman grunted. "Serve him right!"

"He's welcome," Lou said. "Maybe I can convince him to wear his cap the right way around. Strike a blow for civilization."

Truman stood up. "I can't laze around here all day," he announced irritably, as if they had been holding him there against his will.

"Glad you dropped in," Lou told him.

"I'll be back." Truman glanced at the cast and then sent his brother a sly look. "I'll let you know if I hear about any marathons you can enter."

He exited laughing.

After closing the door behind him, Grace paced across the room to stand in front of the dormant fireplace. "Spreading sunshine wherever he goes.

What's he doing squiring Peggy around to peach farms all of a sudden? I never even knew they liked each other all that much."

"You think people can't change just because they've got AARP cards? Not everybody's opinions and feelings harden right alongside their arteries."

"I know that."

"Peggy and Truman's business is their business."

"All right," she said, sorry now that she had said anything.

"You know what I think?" He studied her with one of those sharp, penetrating gazes of his. "I think you're gossiping as a way to avoid getting the pants whupped off you in chess."

"Ha! You're so sure of yourself." She crossed over to the chair adjacent to his, which from her perspective might just as well have been dubbed the chair of perpetual sorrow, seeing how it was usually ground zero for soul-crushing defeat. Hope sprang eternal, however. "Where were we?"

"You had just done something very foolish," he said, whisking a bishop over to gobble up her queen.

She blinked. "Where did *he* come from?"

Her father chortled.

She concentrated on the board, as always hoping that if she stared fiercely enough at all the pieces, a survival strategy would suddenly occur to her.

"Have you ever considered the possibility that I've just been letting you win all these years so that you'll let your guard down, laying yourself bare for the ultimate chess smackdown?"

"You mean it's all been a big set-up?" He laughed.

"Just you wait," she said, sliding her castle to take one of his pawns.

He twinkled a smile at her and then nodded toward the board. "Checkmate."

8

You Again

The next day, Steven came back from St. Louis. Of all her siblings—in Texas and in Oregon—Steven was the tallest and best looking, with wavy dark hair and intense blue eyes. He usually kept his feelings hidden, at least around her, but today he walked with a tired stoop, and the sadness in those eyes gave Grace's heart a sharp wrench. He looked as though he needed a hug, but they'd never been close, so he appeared caught by surprise when she leaned in and gave him a quick, awkward clutch.

"Where's Dad?" he asked after he'd pulled away from her.

"In the kitchen, eating lunch."

"Has there been trouble?"

"Not *trouble,* exactly." She debated whether to say more. Many of the things Lou had said over the past few days, and some of the things he'd forgotten, had made her nervous. Perhaps she was overreacting, though. "Talk to him, and then you tell me."

She led him back to the kitchen, where their father was leaning over a bowl of tomato soup. Lou took a look at Steven and let out half a chuckle. "You again."

Steven stopped just feet in front of the entrance to the kitchen. He pivoted toward Grace for an explanation of that remark, but she was as clueless as he was.

"You were just here yesterday," Lou said.

Steven laughed uncomfortably. "Uh . . . I just got back from St. Louis, Dad. Maybe I have a double?"

"And maybe somebody's been doubling up on the painkillers." Grace sent Steven a raised brow before turning back to Lou. "You sure you're not thinking of Truman, Dad? You probably just *wished* it had been Steven."

Steven looked alarmed. "I look like an eighty-one-year-old?"

Grace handed him a cup of coffee. "How was the trip? Are you feeling all right?"

He shrugged and sank into a chair with a sigh. "I'm fine. A lot of work to do, of course."

She sent him a look to convey the fact that she

hadn't said a word to their father about his marital and professional situation.

Steven shook his head. "Dad knows, Grace. I told him Saturday."

"Told me what?" Lou asked.

"About Denise," Steven said.

She'd been living with her dad for days and he'd never dropped the slightest hint that he knew what Stephen was going through. Never uttered a peep. Times like these, she longed for Sam. Sam liked to hash things out from every angle.

"Oh, yes," Lou said. " 'An arrant traitor as any!' "

Steven sank down a little farther in his chair.

"I'm so sorry, Steven," Grace said. He looked so sad, she wanted to give him another hug. But she refrained.

"It's okay. We've been working out how to divide up the practice. I'll have to hire a new office nurse and tech, but Emily, our office administrator, is coming with me. I guess I need to get busy finding us a new home. It will take a while to set up."

"What about you—won't you need a home, too?" Grace asked.

"Denise moved out. I'll stay." He pulled a roll of Tums out of his pocket and crunched on one for a moment before taking a sip of coffee. "I think my ulcer's coming back."

For a moment they all sat staring into their coffee cups.

"Won't you be selling your house?" Grace asked. "I mean, it's community property."

"No one's said anything about a divorce yet."

Lou looked at him in disbelief. "You don't mean you're still hoping for a reconciliation?"

"Well, no—maybe. Naturally, the practice is broken up, and that's terrible . . ." His shaking hand pushed another Tums out of the roll, and it went shooting across the table. He lunged for it. "This job is so stressful! It drives us all crazy sometimes."

Grace tried to hold back criticism, but she couldn't help herself. "Stress makes people drink too much, or throw temper tantrums, or eat too many Oreos."

"But everyone's different, aren't they?" Steven asked.

Out of the corner of her eye, Grace caught sight of a face peering at them through the window of the side mudroom door. She jumped, startled—but then she recognized Dominic. She got up to let him in.

Lou seemed amused by the arrival of their new visitor. "Creeping around the side, are you? Planning another heist?"

Dominic's face went red. "No—my sister Lily she said y'all were in here, so I came to maybe see Iago?"

"How did Lily know we were here?" Grace asked.

"Lily knows everything." Dominic regarded Steven with a shy, curious smile.

“This is my brother,” Grace explained, making the introductions. “Steven, Dominic.”

Steven extended his hand. “Hi, Dominic.”

Dominic shook it briefly before stepping back again. “I only meant, Lily knows where everybody is practically all the time because she keeps up with things like that. Plus her bedroom is on this side of the house, and she has our mom’s bird-watching binoculars now.”

“I suddenly feel like a specimen under a microscope,” Grace said.

“Oh, don’t worry,” Dominic assured her. “Lily doesn’t usually tell anybody anything. Especially not anything interesting.”

“Thank heavens for that, at least.”

“She writes it all down instead. In her diary.”

“The Samuel Pepys of Hyde Park,” Lou mused.

Dominic looked confused. “Is Iago here? Or maybe you’re so mad I stole him you wish I’d go away?”

Lou chuckled. “To err is human, Master Dominic. We don’t want you to go away. Iago is having his afternoon nap in the backyard.” Lou grabbed his crutches and thumped one against the linoleum in the determined way that Grace was beginning to understand signaled his intention to get up and move.

Dominic seemed alarmed by the effort Lou had to expend on his behalf. “I can go by myself.”

Lou laughed. “I need to keep my eye on you.

How can I be sure your dognapping days are behind you?"

Dominic started to protest, but Lou rummaged through the biscuit box, brought out two bone-shaped biscuits, and handed them to him. "I have a hard time carrying things—and managing doors. I could use your help."

"Oh, sure," Dominic said.

After the two went out, Steven took a sip of coffee. "Dad seems about the same as always."

"He confused you with Uncle Truman!" she reminded him. "You've got to admit, that was weird."

"He's always been absentminded."

"Since when?"

Steven frowned. "Well, since he retired. I guess in the last year I've noticed it more."

Grace hadn't. But she hadn't been around to notice.

"The other night in the hospital he forgot Iago was missing five minutes after we had just talked about it," she said.

"That could have been the painkillers."

Grace wondered if Steven's patients had to battle his skepticism to make him believe their symptoms. "Also, I've been finding odd stuff around the house."

"Like what?"

"Like a cabinet holding nothing but six boxes of Grape Nuts."

"Maybe they were having a sale somewhere. He was stocking up."

She crossed to the kitchen drawer in the corner. "While he was in the hospital, I ran across these." She pulled out the printed lists notated in their father's spidery script and handed it to her brother.

Steven read the top one and flipped through a few others. "Lots of people make lists."

"These aren't just to-do lists," she argued. "These are blueprints. He's making sure he doesn't forget."

"Correct me if I'm wrong, but isn't *not forgetting* what a list is for?"

"Yeah, but he's been making sure he doesn't forget to take a shower. To eat. Who forgets to eat?"

For a moment, Steven searched for a response. He folded his arms, frowning. "What do you think we should do?"

"I was going to ask you."

"I'm not a neurologist, Grace. If a rotator cuff needs fixing, I'm your man. But memory loss . . . I haven't thought about this since I was an intern. I do know that medications can cause memory problems."

"But now his blood pressure dosage has been readjusted."

"Or it could be a thyroid issue."

Her phone rang, and as she fished it out of her

purse, Steven stared quizzically at the mark on the old chrome dinette where Sam had once left a red Magic Marker uncapped.

The number was Ben's. Grace's chipper greeting was met by a moan of despair.

"There's water everywhere! What am I supposed to do?"

That quickly, she was plunged into a remote catastrophe. "Back up a step, Ben. Where are you, and why is there water everywhere?"

"The hot water heater!" he shouted. "It must have busted overnight. How can I open the store while this is going on?"

"Wait. It's the water heater at the store?" That one had been replaced recently.

"No—I'm at the house. I came back to feed the cats and noticed . . ."

She frowned. It was just before ten o'clock, Portland time. If he was just coming back to the house, where had he spent the night?

He heard the unspoken question and sputtered, "I crashed at Danny's, okay? He got a new Wii. The thing is, what am I gonna do about all this water? I have stuff stored down here. My box of H.P. Lovecrafts is all soggy."

"Call the landlord."

"I don't even know who that is."

"Never mind, *I'll* call the landlord. Go tend to Rigoletto's and I'll get the water heater situation straightened out from here. I'll call you back to let you know if and when you'll have to return to the house to let the plumber in."

"Do you think your renter's insurance will pay for my books? Some of them are really valuable."

"Mmm . . . doubtful." Before he could whine, she added, "But I'll check. Is everything else all right?"

"Huh?"

"Heathcliff and Earnshaw?"

"They're fine, Grace. Well, still alive. The one only comes out from under the couch to eat or upchuck." He sighed raggedly. "*I'm* not fine, in case you're wondering."

"I can hear that," she said. "I'm sorry. I'll tend to this, Ben."

When she hung up, Steven was still sitting with arms folded. "You obviously need to learn how to be in two places at once."

"I practically am, thanks to this doohickey." She searched through her phone's list and called the landlord, who told her to call the plumber herself, which she did. Then she sat down to text the meet-up time to Ben.

Steven sighed and slid down in his chair, stretching his legs out under the table. "Wherever Grace is needed."

She shot him a look as she punched the tiny keys.

He smiled. "Like when Sam was on his first foreign assignment and came down with meningitis. How long did it take you to get on a plane? Two hours?"

"Of course. Sam reimbursed me, so it was a free vacation."

"To Belarus?"

"Not many people get to see Belarus." She added, muttering, "Or get the opportunity to navigate its healthcare system."

The Belarus jaunt was always spoken of in joking terms in her family, on both sides. Her mother had thought she was mad for going. But in truth, Grace had jumped at the chance, because Sam's turning to her during that crisis had made her feel like an essential Oliver family member. Not the odd man out, which is how she usually thought of herself.

The look in Steven's eyes told Grace that he had been using the time she was on the phone with Ben to chew over their dad's situation. "Last month, I was driving Dad to Llano to eat barbecue, and halfway there he asked me where I was taking him."

Grace thought about this for a moment. "The trouble is, we can probably come up with lots of anecdotes about his forgetting things, but what we need is to get him to agree to see a doctor. You need to broach the subject with him."

"Me?"

"You're a doctor. He respects you."

The back door shut and Iago jogged into the

kitchen, followed by the sound of Lou's crutch-thump gait. Grace's gaze met her brother's, and by the time their father reached the kitchen, they were both mutely staring into their coffee cups as if not a word had passed between them since he had left.

"The dognapper scooted back over to his house. You know what he wanted? To apologize for stealing my dog and then to hit me up for a job! He wants to walk Iago twice a day."

"Not a bad idea," Steven said, studying Iago's flesh jiggling as he perched before his water bowl. The kitchen echoed with the sound of dog tongue slapping water.

"You can't take Iago out on walkies now," Grace pointed out.

"He wants me to pay him," Lou continued. "Two dollars per walk!"

"That's just twenty-eight dollars a week," Steven said. "A service would charge you nearly that much *per day.*"

"But a service wouldn't be coming from right next door. It's not as if he's paying for insurance, or transportation. He's not bonded. He's not paying into Social Security."

"Dad," Steven said in exasperation. "You're going to have to accept a little help sometime. Grace can't stay forever."

"Who said I wanted her to?" he asked, his tone growing spiky. "She can leave whenever she wants. I've been taking care of myself quite well without anyone's help!"

"You got run over by a car," Steven pointed out.

"An accident! Haven't you ever had an accident?"

"Dad—"

"What have the two of you been doing in here—conspiring?" Lou laughed, not even noticing their guilty expressions. "Meanwhile, I was wheeler-dealering. And managing just fine, I might add. I told that boy I'd pay him thirty-five dollars per week and not a penny more."

He jutted his chin and continued to glower at them for a moment. Then, he turned and thumped back out to the living room.

Grace and Steven slumped in their chairs, frowning in confusion. So while grumbling about Dominic's demands, Lou had actually offered Dominic more than the kid had asked for.

Maybe his math skills were just faltering.

Grace wondered if there was really a situation at all, or if she was just blowing things out of proportion. "Lots of people make lists," she said, trying to reconsider.

"And forget things," Steven agreed.

"It's probably all . . ." She searched for the right words.

"Much ado about nothing," he finished for her.

"Exactly."

They both sat in silence for a moment.

"I'll talk to him," he said, getting up. "And I'll call Dr. Allen and see if we can get him in for a checkup ASAP."

She stood and smiled at him gratefully. "Thank you!" He endured another of her hugs. "I'm sorry about everything, Steven. About you and Denise, I mean."

"Don't be." He sniffed, and then squared his shoulders. "It's losing my practice that's the blow." But his effort to keep a stiff upper lip was defeated by a sad sigh. "I really loved our imaging equipment."

9

If I Had Anywhere Else to Go, I'd Be There Already

After a morning of sitting in her bare room, Jordan was so bored she resorted to going downstairs. She went to the kitchen, foraged until she found the only thing to eat with sugar in it, then breezed into the living room. Unfortunately, Lily was in the comfy chair with the ottoman, reading some book that was thick enough to be an encyclopedia.

On closer inspection, it *was* an encyclopedia, from their dad's old set.

Jordan let out a sigh and flopped into the chair

opposite, sitting in it sideways so that her knees crooked around the armrest.

Lily glanced up briefly, scrunched her lips, and went back to reading.

"Good book?" Jordan asked her.

Except for a nearly imperceptible shrug, Lily ignored her.

"I know *M* was always *my* favorite," Jordan said. "So much more absorbing than *F-G,* or" she snorted—"*C!* That one is *such* a bore."

"Ha. Ha."

Jordan exhaled on a long slow breath. "You know, you could probably look up anything in there on your computer. Then you wouldn't have to lug a ginormous book around."

"I *like* lugging books around." Lily peered at her through her glasses. "Are you eating cake icing?" She squinted at the tub in Jordan's hands. Her face pinched in disgust. "You are!"

"It was the only thing I could find with chocolate in it." As Lily's face froze in a scrunch, Jordan said, "I've seen you eat cake icing."

"On *cakes*. Not spooning it out like it was ice cream! That's revolting."

Jordan scooped up an extra large dollop and stuffed it in her mouth. It *was* sort of revolting. "I'd go to the store to get a Kit-Kat or something, but I'm broke."

"What about all the money you made selling everything?"

"It's . . . in a place where I can't touch it."

Her sister looked at her mistrustfully. Jordan foresaw a significant portion of Lily's life today being spent trying to figure out where all the money had gone.

Lily went back to reading. Or seemed to. A few seconds later, she asked, "Didn't Dad send you money while you were at Granny Kate and Pop Pop's? I thought he said he gave you enough for the whole summer."

Lily was a repository for details like that. She could tell you how much people got for their allowance at what age, and what Aunt Jeannie had sent you for your eighth birthday, and what grade you'd gotten in Social Studies when you were eleven, even if you hadn't shown her your report card, which of course you would never do in a million years. Lily knew. She was a ferret in Keds.

"I spent that money," Jordan confessed.

Her sister's jaw dropped. "How could you spend a summer's worth of money in one month?"

"I got my hair done. And I bought some stuff."

"What kind of stuff?"

"None of your business."

Lily's eyes narrowed and she turned back to her encyclopedia, but Jordan could tell she wasn't really reading by the way her right foot was jangling. "I bet it had something to do with why Granny Kate and Pop Pop kicked you out," Lily said.

"You don't know anything, so shut up."

The front door opened and slammed shut and Dominic came in. His face registered surprise to see the two of them sitting together in the same room.

"Where were you?" Jordan asked him.

"Next door," Lily and Dominic answered, in unison.

"With the woman who bought my picture?" Jordan asked him.

"Egbert wasn't *your* picture," Lily said, as if she were actually supposed to be part of this conversation, which she wasn't. "You gave the picture to Nina, remember?"

"Yeah, I *do* remember that."

Lily glared at her. "Sometimes I wonder. She doesn't exist here anymore, thanks to you."

Jordan froze. "What do you mean by that?"

"You *sold all* her stuff!"

Jordan leapt up. "That's not what you meant by *thanks to me,* though, was it?"

Lily stared back up at her, her lips turned down at the corners in that really irritating way she had. The girl was a natural-born hemorrhoid. Jordan considered wringing her skinny little neck, but the last thing she needed now was to get into more trouble.

She spun around and practically dove onto the couch. "I never should have come back here," she moaned, only slightly comforted when Dominic sat down next to her.

"As if you had any choice," Lily scoffed. "The only reason you're here is because Granny Kate and Pop Pop wouldn't have you. Now *we're* stuck with you."

"Believe me, if I had anywhere else to go, I'd be there by now."

"What did you do?" Lily asked.

"I'm not going to tell you, so quit asking."

"I know," Dominic piped up. "You painted a room."

Jordan lifted her head. "Who told you that?"

Dominic shrugged. "Dad." He squinted at her. "It's true, isn't it?"

She nodded.

Lily's eyes were like two full moons. "*What?* They sent you back here for painting a room? That's insane!"

"Tell me about it," Jordan muttered.

"There *had* to be more to it than that," Lily insisted.

"She painted the spare bedroom at Granny Kate and Pop Pop's without permission. And she wrote *'happy little tree'* on a wall." Dominic looked to Jordan for confirmation. "That was it, wasn't it?"

Jordan nodded again.

" 'Happy little tree?' " Lily repeated. "What does that mean?"

"You wouldn't understand."

"Would I?" Dominic asked.

Jordan smiled and nudged him with her knee. "Maybe."

Lily looked like she was about to explode. "There *had* to be something else. Granny Kate wouldn't kick you out of her house just for writing *'happy little tree'* on a wall."

"Sorry to burst your Granny bubble, Lils, but that's the way it went down."

"You're a liar."

Dominic shook his head. "Dad said. He told me Granny Kate said she had painted the room black and painted *'happy little tree'* on a wall."

"Black!" The word brought Lily out of her chair. Her forehead wrinkled. "Why black?"

"Granny Kate told Dad it was on account of she had been listening to satanic music," Dominic said.

Jordan squinted at him. "Dad didn't tell you *that.*"

He ducked his head. "Well . . . I kinda sorta listened in on the phone when Dad was talking to Pop Pop. The night you came home."

"That's eavesdropping!" Lily exclaimed.

Dominic answered, "I've seen you do it."

Lily didn't deny it.

"Anyway," Jordan said, "the music was not satanic. It was the Rolling Stones. They have a song called 'Paint It, Black.' "

Lily stood in the middle of the room, mouth agape. "You painted a room black because a song told you to?" She tossed her head back and let out a sharp laugh. "Only an idiot would hear a song and then do what it said! It was probably like a metaphor or something!"

Dominic frowned at Jordan. "What's a metaphor?"

"What are you asking *her* for?" Lily asked. "She made a C-minus in sophomore English."

"It doesn't matter," Jordan told him. "Nobody cares about stuff like that except people like Lily. And people like Lily think they're way too good for you and me."

"You don't know anything about me," Lily said. "You don't know anything about anybody, because all you care about is yourself!"

"Whatever," Jordan grumbled, knowing that if there was anything that drove Lily insane, it was being dismissed with a *whatever.*

Sure enough, she was practically quivering.

Jordan smirked at her. "You might want to go get a glass of water or something, Lils. Your face is all splotchy red. It looks like your zits are having a rave."

Dominic laughed.

Lily glared at him now, too. "I can't believe you would take her side."

"What did I do?" he asked.

"Dominickel always takes my side." Jordan pulled Dominic to her, tickling him so that he laughed even harder. After another moment of stewing, Lily stomped out of the room and Jordan released Dominic. "Well, that got rid of her."

Dominic leaned back on the couch, frowning. She was afraid he was going to ask more pesky questions about what had happened in Little Salty, but instead he asked, "Can I have some icing?"

"I only have one spoon," she said, handing it over.

"That's okay, I'll use my finger." He dipped a stubby forefinger in and scooped it out. Then he leaned back and sucked on his finger.

"So, to get back to what we were talking about before Little Miss Mensa interrupted us . . ." Jordan arched a brow. "Where were you?"

He pulled a slimy finger out of his mouth. "I already said. Next door. I got a job."

"No way! Doing what?"

"Walking Professor Oliver's dog."

She gave him a congratulatory shove. "You enterprising little bastard! How much are they going to pay you?"

"Thirty-five dollars a week!"

"Oh." That didn't seem like much. But then, walking a dog wasn't exactly strenuous work. "Wow."

"I know," Dominic said excitedly, "I was kinda shocked by how much he offered me."

As long as he felt good about it, she supposed that was what mattered most. Anyway, it was more than she was bringing in. She should have stayed home this summer and gotten a job. Now summer was halfway over and it seemed too late. "You'll be rich and you'll be able to loan me money."

"You've got money—you sold all that stuff."

"The money's already gone."

"How could you have spent it all? You haven't been out of the house!"

"Yes, I have." The day before she'd walked to the post office, bought a money order, and sent it off to Granny Kate and Pop Pop. The idea of letting all that money out of her grasp still stung, but it was done now. They couldn't fault her for leaving them in the lurch financially, at least.

"Lily said you made over four hundred dollars," Dominic said. "How could you have spent it all so fast?"

"I owed someone."

"Four hundred dollars?" he squeaked.

She sighed. "Probably more than that."

Dominic shook his head and dipped his slobbery-looking finger into the icing again.

Jordan's stomach flipped. "Take the rest," she offered. "I'm definitely not going to eat any more of that stuff. It's nauseating."

At least, it was now.

"It'd be better if there were some saltines," Dominic said, digging in. "I did that with the other tub we had, but it was strawberry. This is better. Where did you find it?"

"It was crammed behind some old canned asparagus."

"No wonder I didn't see it."

Asparagus was Dominic repellent.

"Why isn't there any food in the house?" she asked. "Any decent food, I mean. Where's the Cap'n Crunch? Whatever happened to Chips Ahoy?"

"Dad does the shopping once a week, and he hardly ever gets stuff like that. Most of the time we just have sandwiches and soup, or frozen pizzas and salad, or if he's late we just go to Taco Cabana. And the only cereal he buys is Shredded Wheat or bran flakes. I have to spend all my allowance money just on candy bars. Otherwise I'd die of malnutrition."

She nudged his thigh with her foot. "Now that you're the big breadwinner among us, you'll be able to keep us all in candy bars."

Dominic ducked his head modestly and scooped another blob of icing into his mouth. "I'm really psyched about my job. And Professor Oliver said he'd teach me to play chess, too."

"Why?"

"For fun."

"Sitting around with an old geezer doesn't sound like fun to me, but whatever."

"I just worry that he'll think I'm stupid. Maybe he'll fire me."

"Not likely! You're just walking his dog—you're not trying to teach it calculus."

His forehead was still pillowed with wrinkles.

She nudged him again. “Stop worrying so much, Nickel. Everything’s going to be great for you.”

He sent her a tentative smile that was just a shadow of the one he would have given her six months ago. It was so full of doubt, so lacking in joy. That little smile would have broken her heart, if her heart hadn’t been shattered into a thousand pieces already.

10

What You Need to Know

Lou knew where he was, what day it was, and who was in the White House. Dr. Allen, his GP, chuckled through most of the interview, especially when Lou grumbled that his children had forced him to come.

“Kids ganging up on you, Lou?” The doctor winked at Grace, who was perched uncomfortably in a chair in the corner. She hadn’t wanted to come into the examination room, but her father had insisted, as if to prove to her how wrong she and Steven were.

Dr. Allen elbowed his patient. “Well, you should know—‘How sharper than a serpent’s tooth it is. . . .’ ”

Her father kept his eyes trained on the doctor’s face. “I’m sorry?”

Grace dug her nails into her palms to keep from blurting out the rest. *Was he kidding?* Her dad knew *King Lear* like she knew *Seinfeld.*

Dr. Allen's brow furrowed a moment before he chuckled again and asked Lou to count backward from one hundred by sevens. "I have a colleague you should meet," he said, already reaching for a pad to start scribbling the name as Lou faltered at eighty-six. "A neurologist—big brain like you, Lou. Jacob Franks wrote the textbook they teach at Johns Hopkins. I'm just a horse doctor next to this guy."

Grace jumped to her feet, eager to get out of there. Dr. Allen wasn't joking about being a horse doctor—he obviously didn't know what he was talking about. Even though she had made the appointment to see him and practically dragged her father here, she felt like giving the quack a piece of her mind. A lot of people couldn't do math in their head, and forgetting one little quote wasn't proof positive of anything, either. Her father was always reading and learning new things. He played chess, for Pete's sake.

Besides, he was seventy-six. Didn't everybody start to lose a few gray cells at that age?

Why had she instigated all this?

As they walked out to the car, Lou was still clutching the piece of paper in his fist. "Can I borrow your cell phone? I want to call this number."

Two days later, at the neurologist's, Lou hobbled after the nurse by himself, while Grace stayed in the waiting room. The lighting was soft and Audubon prints of wild turkeys and woodpeckers decorated the deep forest-green walls. Several ficus plants stood in corners and served as screens between clusters of armchairs. Grace took a seat near the glassed-in receptionist area. Magazines fanned across an oak table next to her, and a pamphlet display hung on the wall above it.

Each pamphlet title she read seemed grimmer than the last: *What Is a Migraine? . . . Living with Epilepsy . . . After You've Had a Stroke . . . When the Diagnosis is Alzheimer's . . .*

Her gaze rested on the last. *Alzheimer's.* That word had been skittering around her mind for days, unacknowledged and unspoken.

She reached over to grab the pamphlet but recoiled before her hand actually touched it. What was the point in looking? The diagnosis *wasn't* Alzheimer's. There wasn't any diagnosis yet. And she wasn't a doctor. Steven had suggested the changes in Lou might be chalked up to a malfunctioning thyroid. Dr. Allen had run a blood test and they had yet to hear back on the results. No sense panicking prematurely.

Still, the furrow in Dr. Allen's brow when Lou had failed to finish the quote from *King Lear* would not be banished from her mind.

She snatched the Alzheimer's pamphlet out of its slot and inspected it. The cover was a collage of old people of all races and both sexes, usually hugging another old person or a child, or being hugged by someone else. It appalled her that her father—dignified, sharp-witted, sardonic—should be associated with anything this insipid. She flipped it open in irritation. *Alzheimer's disease is a disease of the brain that impairs thinking and memory. It may also change behavior. It is not part of the normal process of aging.*

Who on the planet didn't know that already?

She slapped the pamphlet shut again and tapped it against her palm. The trouble with these things was that they were written for idiots. They were pointless.

She wondered if there was a section about symptoms and opened it again, just to check.

Memory loss.

Well, duh.

The second on the list was *Difficulty performing simple tasks.* But her father managed very well on his own. Except for the accident.

People with Alzheimer's disease are apt to forget common words.

That wasn't Lou, either.

She frowned. *Dog biscuit.* That was a word he had forgotten the other day. She hadn't thought anything of it at the time.

But that was just the trouble. Why would she?

All of these symptoms were problems everyone had. By these criteria, *she* suffered from Alzheimer's. If it wasn't for the words *thingamajig* and *whatsit,* there would be days when she couldn't communicate with anyone.

She put the pamphlet in her purse and decided to check messages on her phone. Her inbox contained the usual mix of spam and messages from family and friends in Oregon. Her mom wanted to know whether she would be staying in Austin until August, in which case she would miss Jake's birthday party. (The last birthday party of Jake's that Grace had been to was his eighth.) She said she didn't envy Grace having to live through the heat, or with the Olivers. Grace wondered if the thought of her in Austin was causing her mom to have flashbacks. Something seemed to be ginning up the long-distance maternal concern.

There was no message from Ben; Grace hadn't heard from him since he'd called to let her know the water heater had been changed. One message came from Sam. Sick of chess yet? the subject line read. What followed was a typical communiqué from her brother, giving her his news and speculating about how things were going at home. The tone reminded her that she hadn't bothered to update him about their father's health concerns.

She started to text a reply, but then stopped. There was really nothing to tell him at this point that wouldn't fall into the category of alarming him prematurely—perhaps unnecessarily—or leaving him in the dark.

The door to the inner office opened and her father came hobbling back out with a folded piece of pink paper protruding from his breast pocket.

"What did he say?" Grace asked as she held the building's door for him on the way out.

"I'm going to have an MRI."

"When?"

"They'll call me with the appointment. The doctor said there's a chance that I might have had a small stroke. Or maybe some kind of head trauma."

She slowed as they reached the car. "But if you'd hit your head, wouldn't you remember?"

"Not if hitting it caused me not to remember."

She frowned, trying to decide if that made sense or not.

On the drive home, she asked, "What did he do?"

"Who?"

"The doctor."

Within the confines of his shoulder belt, her father shrugged. "Tests."

"What kind of tests?"

"Just tests, Grace. Reflexes. Questions."

"What kind of questions?"

"What does it matter? It was me in there, not you," he said sharply. "I don't give you the third degree every time you come out of a doctor's office, do I?"

At the change in his tone, heat leapt to her cheeks. "No, of course not. I'm sorry."

The drive through the next blocks was so tense Grace fiddled with the air conditioner just to block out the rigid emptiness. A blizzard of cold air streamed from the vents.

"When this is all over," Lou said, "I want you to go home."

Grace glanced over at him sitting straight and still in his seat, his hand resting on his cane. "When what's all over?" she asked.

"The tests. Whatever happens, I don't want you staying here any longer than necessary. I'm not helpless."

"You'll still need me, Dad. You've got a broken leg. You can't drive."

"You've got a life in Portland, and the store to tend to."

"Ben's handling it for now."

"That's why I'm concerned," he said.

"I worry about you, Dad. Sam's thousands of miles away and Steven's life is crumbling and . . ." She almost mentioned something about Peggy evidently not being someone he could count on—she still hadn't been over to the house once—but she stopped herself. "Who can you depend on?"

"I'll manage," he said. "Life's not a children's game, Grace. I don't get to count to ten before the action starts. Ready or not, here it comes. I'll figure out a way. I'll adjust."

"But—"

She was about to argue, but when she opened her mouth, she realized she had no words. And as she pulled into the driveway, she noticed Dominic sitting on the steps of Lou's front porch, next to Iago. Both of them got up when she'd parked, and Dominic crossed to open Lou's door.

"Where've y'all been?" he asked.

"Out and about," Lou said as he began the process of extracting himself from the front seat.

"I walked Iago," Dominic said, "but you said you were going to teach me chess."

"I did, didn't I?" Lou laughed. "Well, there's no time like the present."

Without a look back, he and Dominic made their way to the house, slightly impeded by Iago, who, with the whole yard to walk in, still managed to be underfoot.

11

Smoke Signals

Have you bought your plane ticket?" her father asked her, for about the tenth time in two days.

The frequency of the question had been increasing over the past week, to the point that

Grace was ready to scream if he asked it one more time. Convincing her to leave was becoming an obsession with her father.

"You should see if you can get a last-minute deal on-line," he said.

She grunted as she wiped after-breakfast crumbs from the kitchen counter. "I'm not sure I should leave."

"There's no need for you to stay here. There are people in town who can help me, if I need it. But I won't really need help for a long time. You heard what the doctor said. It's a gradual thing."

She'd also heard the doctor say that it was impossible to say how quickly his condition might worsen. She spent nights now reading Alzheimer's case histories on the Internet, trying to figure out what *worsen* might actually entail. She felt almost nauseous with anxiety. If she left him alone now, it would be like snapping herself in two.

"Dad, who are the people in town you can rely on?" she asked. "Steven, and who else?"

"Truman pops by all the time."

"I wouldn't leave a pet hamster with Uncle Truman."

Her father looked offended—as if she had just compared him to a hamster.

"Not that I . . . well, you know what I mean."

He straightened to his full height. "I enjoy having you here, Grace. You know that. But for you to stay here permanently would be throwing yourself on a pyre."

"Dad, *please.* That's crazy talk!"

Their eyes met, and she regretted saying it. She regretted saying anything.

He tapped his cast. "Don't worry if you have to take a flight in the next day or so if it would save you money."

"You're really that eager to get rid of me?"

His face remained a blank. "You can use my computer."

"For what?"

"To make your reservations."

On her last nerve, Grace thumped the sponge she was using into the sink. "All right. I'll go upstairs now and get myself on the next affordable plane out. I'll even take the red-eye tonight if that makes you happy."

"Don't be angry, Grace. Of course I'll be sorry to see you go."

"Of course," she grumbled. "So sorry I wouldn't be surprised to feel your crutch nudging me into a taxi."

She tromped upstairs and logged on the Internet. Why was she even arguing with him? Even if he was sick, she didn't belong here. Most of the time she wondered if the Olivers really considered her part of their family. Sure, they'd always been welcoming to her when she'd showed up for her summer visits, or on the rare holiday. Yet she had never felt that she'd progressed beyond honored guest. In terms of family, she could claim only second-class status at best. Which, of course, was also what she had at her mom's house. But at least in Oregon there was Ben, and Rigoletto's.

Within fifteen minutes, she'd bought a ticket for a flight at ten the next night. At least they wouldn't have to discuss it anymore. She was tired of repeating the same argument they'd been having for the past two weeks. It was surrender time. This ticket was her white flag.

She marched downstairs, where Lou had already installed himself in his chair. "I bought a ticket for tomorrow night," she informed him.

"Good."

"Maybe we could go out tonight. You know, a sort of farewell dinner. Something that's actually edible for a change."

"Your food is *edible,*" he said. Faint praise, even for him.

"I just thought it would be a little more special if we went out. I've been here for weeks and we haven't gone on a barbecue run."

"I don't see the need to go out," he said. "I'd just as soon stay home."

Unaccountably, tears stung her eyes. Was he doing it on purpose? Nothing she said was right.

She worried if she stayed in the house on her last night there, she'd spend the whole time weeping, and that would drive her father crazy. "Would you mind if *I* went out?"

"I think that would be a good thing," he said.

"Fine."

She went out the front door and let it slam behind her. It was childish, but she didn't care. She pulled out her cell phone to call Steven, but when she got his voice mail she remembered that he was out of town again. Maybe she would be able to catch up with him tomorrow.

She looked one way down the street, then the other. The black SUV was parked in the drive next door. Impulsively, she hopped off the porch, marched across the yard, and knocked at the pilot's door. A few seconds later, when he swung it open, his eyes bugged.

"Am I bothering you?" she asked.

He smiled. "My door's always open to a pretty lady."

Evidently it was a revolving door. In the past several weeks, she'd seen a steady stream of women, many in flight attendant uniforms, going through the yellow bungalow.

"I need someone to have dinner with tonight," she announced.

"Where?"

"I don't know."

His face screwed up in confusion.

"I don't have a destination in mind," she explained. "I just thought we could go out."

"Oh—you mean like on a date?"

She sighed. A fine time for the playboy of the western world to turn all bashful and fluttery on her. "I'm leaving tomorrow," she assured him. "It would just be a one-night thing."

Those magic words, *one night,* made the sale. "Sounds fun," he said, grinning. "Where do you want to go?"

"You can choose. I don't really want to think."

"My dream woman!"

Over the next eight hours, she regretted her decision to go out with Wyatt several times. She'd been hasty. Her dad had only been terse with her because he hadn't seemed to want to go anywhere since his diagnosis—even to the grocery store. He probably dreaded running into people he knew and having to pretend that everything was okay.

But as evening approached and a gloom descended on the house, she wondered if it wasn't actually good that she was going. Otherwise she and her dad would both sit at home moping. Already she was dreading the long next day leading up to her flight out. What would they do?

"I'll leave some soup out for you," she told her dad, just before she decided it was time to go up and get dressed. When she put the can of Progresso chicken noodle on the counter, she felt a stab of guilt. This is probably how he would feed himself when she was gone. Cans of soup.

Though, come to think of it, most of the time a can of soup was all she fixed for them herself.

She hoped Wyatt Carter didn't want to go anywhere fancy. It was a strain for her makeshift visitor's wardrobe to handle even dress casual. She put on a clean pair of shorts, a tank and a gauzy overshirt, slipped into a pair of sandals and decided he would just have to deal.

She was relieved when he knocked on the door wearing jean shorts himself. They were already in his car before he announced, "I thought we could go to the Salt Lick."

Her hand faltered on the seat belt. That was her dad's favorite place to go around Austin. For a moment she felt almost guilty.

"Is something wrong?" he asked.

She shook her head. "No, that's great. I like it."

He fired up the engine.

The restaurant was about twenty minutes away from town. Luckily, on a Tuesday it wasn't as jam-packed as it usually was when she'd been there before, during weekends. The host pointed them to one of the rustic wood tables, and Wyatt pulled two Shiner Bocks out of a bag he'd brought with him. Grace had forgotten the place was BYOB.

"You look like you could use one of these,"

Wyatt said, twisting the cap off a beer and handing it to her.

"You have no idea," she said, taking a long first swig.

He brightened and waved at a nearby table. "Hey, look who's here!" He nodded to his right. "It's like old home week."

One table over, Peggy sat in a bright yellow shirt-and-shorts set. Across from her was Uncle Truman. A pain pierced Grace's heart. In all these weeks, Peggy had never made the time to visit Lou. And now . . . here she sat at a barbecue joint with Truman. *Traitor!*

She faced forward, turning away before they'd spotted her. Of course, she herself was a traitor, too, leaving her dad and coming here tonight.

Wyatt looked confused. "Don't you want to go over and say hello?"

She shook her head and fanned herself with the laminated menu. The air was warm and muggy—the building was baked from the hot summer air outside and the huge round open barbecue pit inside. She wished she'd sat closer to one of the fans.

"Who's that old guy with Peggy?"

"My uncle Truman."

"Your uncle?" He looked surprised. "Then maybe you really would like to—"

"No. It would probably make his evening *not* to have to talk to me," she said, trying not to look at them. She wondered if they had spotted her yet. Probably not. They seemed completely wrapped up in each other.

Wyatt looked at Grace oddly and then stared down at his own menu. "You're different than I thought you would be."

"How?"

"Well—I imagined you as more of a Miss Congeniality type."

Unable to help herself, she glanced over as Uncle Truman took hold of Peggy's hand. Grace felt herself levitate a few inches. Part of her wanted to jump up and separate those two, to tell them to think about the spectacle they were making of themselves.

"Grace?"

"Huh?" She swung her attention back to Wyatt. "I don't know where you would get the idea that I would be Miss Congeniality." It seemed especially funny now that her fist was clenched and aching to clobber a little seventy-five-year-old lady.

Wyatt frowned. "I don't, either." He taxed his brain for a few moments and shrugged. "I guess I sort of thought you reminded me of my son."

She narrowed her eyes. "Your *son?*"

"Only personality-wise, you understand."

"I didn't know you had a son."

"That's because he's in Dallas."

"How old is he?"

"Fifteen."

"Fifteen!" She laughed.

He leaned forward. "Do you think that makes me seem old?"

"I was laughing because you seem to have a fifteen-year-old mentality yourself."

He preened. "I try to stay young."

"I didn't mean it as a compliment." She took a sip of beer. "What's your son's name?"

"Crawford. He's nothing like me, really. He's into band, and computers, and . . ." He shrugged. "The one thing we really agree on is that we both detest my ex-wife's new husband. Mel. He really blew his stack a month ago when Crawford hacked into his e-mail account and discovered he was having an affair with his secretary. Now the whole family's in counseling." He seemed especially peeved by that. "Sharon never suggested counseling when *we* were married. Maybe forgiveness is something women learn as they age."

"Don't bet on it," Grace said.

A waitress came by and took their orders. While Wyatt was engaged in flirtatious banter with the poor trapped server, Grace couldn't help glancing over at her uncle and Peggy. Uncle Truman was pouring out champagne. Grace crossed her arms over her chest. *Champagne,* at the Salt Lick?

"Anyway," Wyatt continued, once the waitress

had left, "when I say you remind me of Crawford, I guess I'm saying you remind me of Sharon, because he takes after her. Young Sharon. Before all the problems started."

"When was that?"

"Right after we drove away from the church."

She laughed. "People who've been married make it sound fantastic."

"Yeah, I've learned my lesson. I know it's probably a blow to all the prospective Mrs. Wyatts out there—"

"I don't believe it!" Grace exclaimed. Her gaze had strayed back over to Peggy and Truman's table just in time to see Truman pop open a small square jewelry box. Grace did a double-take and glared back at Wyatt. "He's giving her a ring! An engagement ring!"

Wyatt's jaw dropped. "That old horndog."

"This is not right." Truman was actually proposing to the woman whom Lou had been in love with for decades? She jumped up. "This is not happening."

Wyatt tried to grab her arm. "Whoa. Grace. It's not your business."

"That's where you're wrong."

She marched over to Truman and Peggy's table and stopped, planting her arms on her hips just as Peggy was trying the ring on for size.

"Very nice!" Grace exclaimed sarcastically.

The two of them looked up at her in surprise.

"Grace!" Peggy said. "Truman just—"

"Your mother had Alzheimer's, didn't she, Peggy?" Grace demanded.

Peggy's face screwed up in confusion. "What?"

"Or dementia. Right?" Grace remembered that now. "You probably knew what was going on back at that Mexican restaurant."

"I'm not sure what—"

"And when I couldn't find the dog," Grace said, cutting her off, "you probably realized then why Dad hadn't mentioned Iago. Am I right?"

Truman huffed at her. "Have you finally flipped your lid, Grace?"

"Were you just waiting for confirmation that Dad wasn't ever going to get better?" she asked Peggy. "That you really needed to latch on to someone new before you got stuck?"

"What is she talking about?" Truman asked Peggy.

"And you!" Grace yelled at him. "Stealing your own brother's girl—kicking him when he's down. You even brought her to his favorite restaurant to do it!"

"Simmer down!" Truman said, starting to stand. "You always were the type to find something to bust your bloomers over."

"I'm perfectly calm!" Grace said.

To prove it, she picked up a champagne glass and tossed its contents into her uncle's face.

• • •

"Lovely evening," Wyatt growled. "Thanks so much."

They were the first words he had spoken in twenty miles. They were just pulling off Guadalupe into the Hyde Park neighborhood, so he was probably hoping to get his licks in before dumping her off.

"I told you I was sorry," she said.

"Don't be," he drawled sarcastically. "It was entertaining. First time I've seen anyone unhinged enough to take a slug at an eighty-year-old."

"I didn't hit him. I just spilled a little champagne on him."

He smirked. "You're the only person I know who spills upward, with perfect aim." He shook his head. "At your own uncle!"

She shuddered. Her behavior had been abominable. But she hadn't seemed to be able to help herself—it had been as if she were another person entirely. Jerry Springer girl. "You wouldn't understand."

"No, I wouldn't. Frankly, I think you must be nuts."

"Well, you won't have to worry about dealing with me anymore. I'm leaving tomorrow night."

"Good," he said. "Although if tonight was anything to go by, I don't think we'd be having too many more nights on the town in any case."

"Don't go breaking my heart," she said. "Anyway, you didn't see me at my best."

"What worries me is that I might not have seen you at your worst," he replied as he turned the car onto their block.

It was dark, but the street was lit up with colored flashing lights, and the inhabitants of practically all the houses had spilled into the street to look at the fire trucks, police cruisers, and the ambulance—all parked right in front of Grace's dad's house.

"Stop!" she yelled, at the same time Wyatt said, "What the hell?"

"Oh God!" Grace moaned, clawing at the passenger side door to get out. Wyatt parked the car as close in as they could get and she jumped out and flew toward the house. A policeman held out his arm but she broke right past, only to be snagged by another cop.

"My dad's in there! Professor Oliver!"

"No, he's not," the policeman said. "He's with the doctor, by the ambulance. He's okay."

A breath of relief gushed out of her lungs. "Thank God! What happened?"

"It was a kitchen fire," the policeman said. "Appears to have been caused by a pot of soup left on the stove."

"And Dad called the police?" she asked.

"No, ma'am. The kid next door did."

Dominic! "A little boy?" she asked.

“No, ma’am, it was a girl. Lily West. Said she spotted the fire as she was looking through a pair of binoculars.”

“But you said you were going to be coming in tonight.”

Grace gripped her phone more tightly. “That was yesterday, Ben. Today I’m telling you that it’s going to be a couple more weeks.”

“Weeks?” he asked in that petulantly forlorn voice that was beginning to grate on her nerves.

“The house caught fire,” she said. “I can’t just walk out now.”

“But isn’t your brother there?”

“As it happens, he’s not. I called him this morning—he should be coming back around noon. But there’s nothing he can do.”

“Then how is there anything you can do?”

“Because I’m living here. I don’t have anything else to think about, while Steven’s whole life is falling apart.”

Ben sputtered.

“What?” she asked.

“You abandoned your life,” he said. “Doesn’t that count as falling apart, too?”

She mulled that over for a moment and felt anger rising in her chest. What was he trying to do to her? Couldn’t he see that she was under stress here? “Are you trying to tell me that you can’t handle the store?”

"No, I'm handling it fine. Getting the knack of it, actually."

"Is the house a problem?"

"Not really."

"Then is it the cats? What?"

He sighed. "It's *you,* Grace. You're not here, and you're supposed to be. I miss you, and I worry that your brothers are taking advantage of you."

As quickly as her heart melted at his telling her he missed her, she got riled up all over again. "They are not. Steven's just going through a really rough patch—he's not the best caretaker in the world at the best of times—and Sam has no idea what's going on. I was going to try to e-mail him today."

"And I'm sure he'll catch the first plane out of wherever," he said, his voice dripping sarcasm.

"Beirut. I don't want him to catch a plane out. I'm here. I can handle this. I just need a little more time."

There was a silence, and then he let out a ragged breath. "Is there anything I can do to help?"

"Yes—be patient. Just for a little while longer."

"Of course," he said. "Don't worry about things here, Grace. I'm sorry if I upset you. Your call just took me by surprise. I was all ready to break out the champagne."

Aw. "Everything's okay there?"

"Boompsa-daisy."

She smiled at the sound of him sipping his morning coffee, and she braced herself against the sudden longing to be there with him, in her own kitchen, with Heathcliff draped over her shoulder, the cool morning air lightly riffling the miniblinds. She closed her eyes.

"Grace?" Ben asked. "You there?"

No, I'm there—with you.

"You're sure everything's fine?" she asked, suddenly feeling as if one tiny problem would send her rushing back to Portland.

"Everything's cool. There was a panic there when Amber left, but then Jerry said he wanted to start working more hours anyway, so that was, like, providence or something."

"That's right—Amber's gone now." Grace made a mental note to e-mail her old friend and see how she was settling into her new life in Seattle.

"She had to store a few boxes in our basement—they didn't all fit in her Honda. Hope that's okay. She said she'd come back sometime in the next month or so and pick them up."

"Perfectly fine. Or maybe when I come back we can load them up and drive them up to her ourselves. Treat ourselves to a road trip."

"That sounds awesome. I'll hold on to that thought."

"Me too," Grace said.

And then, coming from the direction of the living room, she heard the sound of something glass falling. She begged off the phone and ran downstairs to clean up the teacup her father had dropped on the floor.

12

The Boy in the Binoculars

Lily kneeled at the window behind her bed with a copy of *Peterson Field Guide to Birds of North America* draped across the pillow, frustrated to not catch sight of the object of her search. Over the past few days, the only birds she had managed to identify were a couple of cardinals and a few greasy grackles hanging out on the telephone wires. None of the birds seemed particularly binocular-worthy. But earlier in the week she had spied something that was.

It was a boy. His brown hair was curly but cropped short, giving him a Roman god appearance, and he had light-colored—maybe green?—eyes. He seemed to be about fifteen or sixteen. She'd first spotted him coming out of Wyatt Carter's house two days ago. She hadn't known that Mr. Carter was married or had a kid, but she had told Dominic, and Dominic had mentioned the newcomer to Grace, and Grace said that Wyatt was divorced and had a son named Crawford.

Lily liked Grace. Grace had baked her an entire batch of oatmeal cookies after Lily had spotted the fire at the Oliver house and called 911 before anyone else. The cookies had disappeared within a day—Dominic and Jordan gobbled down most of them—but Grace had also called Lily a hero, and that was something that didn't go away. Weeks later, that word still made her sit up a little straighter.

Dominic had said that Grace was going to leave at the beginning of August. But she never had left, and Lily was glad. Even though Lily didn't go over to the Oliver house like Dominic did, Grace was always friendly to her when she saw her in the driveway, and would call hello to her if she happened to be sitting on the porch when Lily walked by.

School was about to start up. Lily wondered if Crawford would go to her school, and if so, if he would be in her class. Yesterday she'd heard the sound of a trumpet coming from the Carter house, so he was bound to be in the band. They'd have something in common.

Just when she was beginning to despair of ever getting a sighting of him that day, Crawford appeared around the side of his house pushing a lawn mower. Lily leapt into high gear. She changed into her jean shorts and her newest summery shirt—a halter shirt her mother had bought her last August, when things were on sale. The yellow sleeveless top tied in the back and wasn't too tight, so it didn't really emphasize the fact that she had nothing going on chest-wise. The halter showed more skin than she was used to, but it was nothing close to the skimpy stuff Jordan wore sometimes.

If her mother had been there, she would have counseled that the important thing was to feel good in her own skin. Lily had heard her say that sometimes to Nina. Maybe to Jordan, too. Lily could see the sense in it, but at the same time, she didn't feel comfortable. Her body failed her daily—with hair that went nuts if she didn't tie it back, and skin that either broke out or looked blotchy, and feet that she sometimes imagined she could actually see growing. Her bra size may have flatlined at AAA, but the way things were going she was destined to be the only sophomore girl wearing a size ten shoe.

Nevertheless, she summoned her mother's voice in her head and, shoulders back, casually strolled down the sidewalk while Crawford Carter mowed his yard. She and Dominic had hardly ever gone to the pool this summer, so the skin on her shoulders looked bluey-white, like the underbelly of a fish. She should have worn a T-shirt, but it was too late now. Crawford had reached the front porch of his house and was turning the mower just as she passed directly in front of him. He glanced up but quickly looked back down at the ground directly in front of him without acknowledging her.

Lily trudged on, disappointed. She really didn't have anywhere to go, so she walked to the convenience store a few blocks away.

When she got there she grabbed a six-pack of Cokes out of the refrigerator cabinet and took it to the cash register. The clerk, the same teenage clerk who'd been selling her soft drinks and ice cream bars all summer, rang her up without glancing at her. Not that she cared what a convenience store clerk thought, but the one time she'd come in with Jordan the slumpy bored teenager had suddenly become alert as a bird dog. As they'd paid, he was all curiosity about what "you girls" were up to that afternoon, even though he was only looking at Jordan.

Now this same clerk shoved her six-pack of Cokes into a plastic bag and handed them to her as if she were invisible.

"Thank you," she made a point of saying, refusing to sink to his inarticulate level.

He grunted and went back to reading *Sports Illustrated.*

During the walk back, Lily practiced things she would say to Crawford Carter. She considered introducing herself formally, but she decided that would be uncool. Best to make it seem spur-of-the-moment, as though she hadn't ever noticed him before, but now that she had, *of course* she would say hello. No big deal.

She arrived at her street, turned at the student rental house on the corner, and got smacked in the chest with a Frisbee. Which actually hurt.

"Oh, hey, sorry about that!" one of the three guys standing in the yard called out.

Hopping back awkwardly, she picked up the green Frisbee and flicked it back to him, an easy distance. Unfortunately, the disc went wild and landed on the overhang of the front porch.

The guys watched their Frisbee disappear and then unleashed a series of groans and exclamations.

"Damn!"

"Nice one, kid!"

A hot flush leapt into her cheeks. "I'm so sorry . . . I didn't mean to . . ."

The three guys ignored her now. They were casing the front porch, pacing back and forth like cats, trying to figure out the best way to get up there to retrieve the Frisbee.

She scurried away as quickly as possible. Worse luck still, at the pilot's house Crawford was nowhere in sight. The newly trimmed grass displayed the striped pattern of the lawn mower's tracks, but the buzz of the lawn mower had stopped.

As she stood frozen in disappointment, Crawford came around the corner with a push broom. He flicked a nervous glance at her—no doubt wondering why a girl was standing there staring at his grass—and began sweeping the clippings off the sidewalk.

Taking a deep breath, she walked up to him, stopped, and pulled a red can out of her sack. "Would you like a drink?"

Those eyes—yes, they were very green—registered confusion at first, but then his face relaxed and he reached out and took the Coke from her. "Thanks." He snapped the can open and chugged down several swallows, his Adam's apple bounding in his throat. He had dust clinging to the fine hair on his arms, and some of his curly hair was sweaty and sticking to his temples.

He was even cuter right up close than he was in the binoculars. The view through the spyglass had made her curious, but now it felt as though the earth had shifted beneath her feet. Was this how Marianne Dashwood felt when Mr. Willoughby scooped her up on that hillside in *Sense and Sensibility*?

Not that Crawford looked like he was about to scoop her up, or even touch her. Still. It was hard to make her mouth form words.

"I live in the house two doors down," she finally blurted out, inclining her head in that direction. "My name's Lily."

He shrugged to wipe his mouth with the arm of his T-shirt. "I've seen you over there."

He'd noticed her? *Her?* "Really?"

He laughed. "Really. My name's Crawford."

It was all she could do to keep herself from saying, "I know." Trouble was, she hadn't planned what else she was going to say to him. Just walking up to him and introducing herself had been as far as her imagination had stretched.

"D-do you live here now?" she stammered.

"Yeah, I used to live with my mom in Dallas, but I don't get along so well with her new husband."

"Oh." She wondered if she should say *that's too bad,* or something like that, even though it wasn't bad at all from her perspective. "So you're going to go to school here?"

He nodded.

"Are you going to—"

"Hey, dude!" One of the college boys jogged toward them. "You wouldn't have a ladder, would you?"

Crawford turned. "Yeah."

"Our Frisbee's stuck on the roof. Some idiot girl—"

Seeing Lily, his words broke off.

Lily looked away, heat creeping into her cheeks again.

"Oh, sure," Crawford said. "Just a sec." He started to trot off, but then he turned back to Lily. "See you around, Lily."

Just hearing his voice say her name made her forget her embarrassment, her disappointment at their having been interrupted, and her smarting left breast.

13

When the Bough Breaks

Grace moved quietly around the kitchen making coffee, almost as if she were performing a pantomime. A noisy summer storm had blown in just past midnight. Then, after it had died down, late into the night the sounds of Horowitz playing Beethoven sonatas had drifted down the hallway from her father's bedroom to hers. She would be surprised if her father had managed to get to sleep at all before dawn.

Lou had always been an early bird, but now later mornings were becoming a pattern for him. What did he think about at night as he played his CDs, or even just listened to the wind in the trees outside his window?

Following the initial diagnosis, her father had spoken of doing things just the same as always. That had been back when Lou was pestering her to return to Portland. Everything had changed with the fire. The fire had given the diagnosis teeth.

She'd spent the following week arranging to get the Sheetrock above the stove replaced. After that, the kitchen had needed repainting, which she had done herself. A new stove was going to be delivered the next day—an electric stove, so they could hook up an automatic shut-off device that Steven had found on the Internet.

She had been busy, but not so busy that she hadn't noticed the change in her father. He'd stopped griping at her to leave and didn't fuss at her for doing things. He never spoke of his worries, but she sensed them nevertheless.

After all her efforts to be so quiet this morning, the knock at the front door struck her nerves like a gong. She glanced at the old kitchen clock as Iago exploded in a series of yodeling barks that lifted his front paws off the ground. It was still just after seven, a little before the time Dominic usually made it over. But Dominic rarely came to the front door. He was at home enough now to traipse around the side yard and bang on the kitchen door. If no one answered, he knew the hiding place for the spare key.

Iago finally worked up enough steam to launch himself into a lumbering run. Grace was then forced to wrestle past him to wedge the front door open.

Ray, Dominic's dad, was waiting, his expression impatient. The step down the porch put him just slightly above eye level to her.

"What are we going to do?" he asked.

Alarm gripped her. "Has something happened to Dominic?"

He looked as if the name jarred a distant memory. "Dominic?"

"Your son."

"I know, but . . ." He stopped, confused. "Haven't you seen your tree?" He angled to one side, making way for her to join him on the porch.

At once the problem became clear. The storm had taken out a massive branch from the elm tree, which now bisected Lou's front yard and half of Ray's, too. By some miracle, Ray's car hadn't been demolished; the limb had missed his vehicle by inches. Unfortunately, his Prius was now trapped between the branch and the garage.

No wonder he was perturbed.

"We've got to move it," he said.

We? The branch was big, it was heavy, and it was still attached to the tree by a sinew of bark. She could no more move it than she could have picked up his Toyota and carried it to the street.

"I need to get to work," Ray said. "I have meetings."

"I'll have to call a tree company," Grace said. "I'll try to get someone out as soon as possible, but after a storm like this . . ."

Ray gave the branch the evil eye, as if hoping to move it through sheer willpower.

Didn't his office accept acts of God as an excuse for absenteeism? She'd never seen someone seem so mournful at the idea of missing business meetings, but she shouldn't have been surprised. From what she could gather, he certainly wasn't throwing himself into his home life. Dominic made it sound as if Ray spent most of his evenings at home hibernating in his den.

At a loss for what else to say or do, she and Ray ambled over to the tree, stopping where the fallen branch seemed its thickest and most immovable. The elm had been there as long as Grace could remember. Would they have to chop it down now? She hoped not. But it was frightening that something so solid looking could just come crashing down without warning.

"I'm glad no one got hurt," she said.

Ray toed the branch a couple of times, testing it, and glanced back at her. "Hurt?"

"It could have fallen on someone."

"It was the middle of the night."

"I know, but if it had happened during the daytime . . ."

"Oh, I see," he said, apparently not interested in following her train of thought.

Maybe he'd had enough of real tragedy to know better than to go looking for the hypothetical kind.

The screen door to Wyatt Carter's house banged opened, and Wyatt's teenaged son came out and jogged around to their garage. He yanked open the manual garage door, rooted around for a bit, and finally emerged with a pair of protective goggles around his neck and a chain saw in his hand.

"I can clear it out for you," he said. "A hundred dollars. And the firewood."

Grace frowned.

"That's not too much, is it?" the boy asked.

"No, but . . ." She shook her head. She barely knew this kid. "It's Crawford, isn't it?"

He nodded.

"I'm sure a hundred dollars is a lot less than what a tree guy would ask," she said. *A damn sight less.* "But I'm not so sure you should be out here wielding a chain saw. Is that your dad's?"

"Dad won't care."

"*I* would care if something happened to you. You're fifteen, right?"

"Practically sixteen," he said.

She tossed a questioning glance at Ray. "What do you think? Is practically-sixteen chain-sawing age?"

"I wouldn't let my sixteen-year-old anywhere near a chain saw," Ray said, arguing against his own interests. "For the safety of the community."

Crawford shifted back to Grace. "You can ask my dad, if you want. I've done this kind of work a lot. My granddad has a Christmas tree farm. I'm very responsible."

"Okay, I'll ask him." Grace looked at her watch. "But I'm not sure he'll be up at this hour." On his days off, Wyatt usually stumbled out in his robe to retrieve the *Statesman* sometime around ten.

"Oh, he's up," Crawford assured her, beckoning her toward his house.

Just as they reached the porch, the door crashed

open and a blonde in a maroon uniform jacket and skirt hurtled out the door. *"Bastard!"*

The woman nearly plowed into Ray, who jumped back, embarrassed and confused.

"Not *you,*" she assured him in an irritated voice, thumping her compact wheelie suitcase down the porch steps. She stopped, eyed them all, and gulped in a breath. "Do any of y'all know where there's a bus stop?"

All together, they pointed mutely toward the corner. The blonde rolled her eyes and let out a huff. "How often does it come by?"

"About every twenty minutes?" Grace guessed.

At that moment, a bus could be heard trundling down the street.

"Crap on a stick!" The woman took off running.

Wyatt appeared at the door in a red robe, a cup of coffee crooked in one hand. "Enjoy Albuquerque, Susan!"

"Go to hell!" she hollered without a backward glance.

They all turned back to Wyatt, who was smiling appreciatively after her. "You should see her on an airplane. Woman wields a drink cart like a weapon."

"Lucky for you she didn't have a weapon handy this morning," Grace observed.

He shrugged. "My day off, and she expects me to drive her all the way out to the airport. Go figure."

Crawford cleared his throat. "Dad, will you tell them it's okay for me to use the chain saw so I can get the branch out of the driveway?"

Puzzled, Wyatt glanced left, finally noticing the world beyond his own front porch. "Holy Moses!"

"They're afraid I'm going to saw my leg off or something."

"He won't saw his leg off," Wyatt said, stepping gingerly by them in his bare feet to take a closer look at the damage. "Damn!" He took a slurp of coffee. "What were you trying to do, Grace? Get yourself a chip for the other shoulder?"

Ignoring the father, Grace turned to the son. "One hundred dollars and firewood. And please be careful. If you could start by clearing the West driveway, that would be best. Ray has to get to work."

"Sure!" Crawford said, eager beavery.

She turned to Ray. "Okay?"

He nodded and then pushed his glasses up to the bridge of his nose, studying her. "Were you over at my house one day?"

She laughed. "Evidently I made a big impression."

"I had forgotten," he explained.

Wyatt chortled. "Way to turn a woman's head, West!"

Ray looked at him, confused, and then, as realization dawned he turned back to Grace with a mortified expression. But she could tell it wasn't just mortified on her behalf. He seemed equally stunned by the idea that someone would think that turning a woman's head was anywhere on his agenda.

"Don't worry," she reassured him. "I have that effect on people. Remarkably unmemorable."

Whatever Ray intended to say was swallowed by the earsplitting whine of the chain saw.

Since the incident at the Salt Lick, Uncle Truman had been avoiding the house almost as assiduously as Peggy had been. But a fallen branch was too much for him. He knocked on the door and barged in past Grace.

She was as relieved to see him as she was irked. It would have been bad if her losing her temper had cost her father the companionship of his brother, geriatric old coot though he was.

"You have a branch down," Truman announced.

The town crier of the blatantly obvious.

"I know." Her father had barely managed to make it out to the living room assisted by his cane. His cast was gone, but he still treated the leg with distrust.

"I don't know why it decided to fall like that," Truman wondered. "Storm wasn't that bad. Are you going to chop down the elm? It's a big'un."

"Not as big as it was last night," Grace muttered. The absence of the one branch had exposed one patch of yard to the sun for the first time in decades.

Lou sat down in his chair. "I hope we don't have to chop it down."

"Are you feeling all right today?" Truman asked, his brow crinkling. Grace could read his thoughts. *My brother's going downhill fast. And he's five years younger.*

"Of course I am."

Truman sat down next to him. "That boy out in your yard looks like he's doing an okay job. I watched him for a good long while."

"Grace hired him," Lou said. "A neighbor boy."

Truman darted a nervous glance at her.

"Do you want something to drink, Uncle Truman?" Grace asked.

"No, thank you."

"Well, what do you want?" Lou asked.

Truman pivoted. "Pardon?"

"What are you doing here? You surely didn't come by just to tell me that the elm tree had lost a branch. I had that all figured out on my own."

"I just happened to see it, was all," Truman explained.

"How did you happen to see it this early in the morning?" Lou tightened his grip on the foam handle of his cane. "Coming by to see if I'd fallen apart yet?"

Truman looked shell-shocked.

Grace stepped forward. "Are you sure you don't want something to drink, Uncle Truman?"

"I'm not going to suddenly go catatonic, you

know," Lou continued. "That's not the way it happens. I do have some time. Not that we've seen too much of you since I was diagnosed."

Her uncle looked so stricken, even Grace felt sorry for him. And guilty. It was probably her fault he hadn't wanted to come over. "I don't think that's why Uncle Truman was in the neighborhood, Dad."

"Well then, why?"

"I was over at Peggy's."

"What were you doing over there at this hour?" Lou asked.

Truman darted an uncertain glance over at Grace.

"Also, I think there's still some banana bread left," she said, "if anyone would care for a piece. I'll go check."

She fled to the kitchen just as Dominic, Iago, and Crawford were filing in for a break through the side door. Iago trotted toward the living room, while the boys beelined it for the fridge.

It hadn't taken Crawford long to figure out the routine, Grace thought.

"Are you out of root beer?" Dominic asked, put out.

"Uh . . . yes. There's ginger ale, though. And orange juice."

Both boys reached for cans of ginger ale and flopped into chairs at the table.

"How did it go?" Grace asked.

Crawford looked exhausted, and perhaps Dominic had exhausted himself through osmosis because he let out a sigh and said, "There's a lot of wood out there now! It'll make a huuuge pile. What're you going to do with it all?"

"That's up to Crawford. It's his."

"I'm gonna sell it." Crawford looked up at Grace. "You should take some first, though. Y'all have a fireplace, right?"

Her first instinct was to say that they really didn't need to be setting fires on purpose. But then she realized how crazy that was. Life couldn't stop. Her dad had always loved having fires in the winter, especially during the holidays. "Yeah, we do. That would be great."

"I hate the thought of winter," Dominic said. "I don't want to even think about having to go back to school in a few days, and starting sixth grade."

"Sixth grade!" Crawford laughed. "Come *on.* Sixth grade is, like, no pressure."

"I hate my school," Dominic said. "I wish I could go to public school, but my parents went to this school, and so all of us are supposed to go there until high school. We have to wear uniforms, and all mine are gonna be too small."

"There's a solution to that problem," Grace said. "It's called new uniforms."

"Yeah, but then I have to ask someone to take me to buy them."

"Wouldn't your dad take you? Or Jordan?"

Dominic's eyes were huge. "My sister? Are you joking? I don't want my sister buying my clothes!"

"Just to drive you there," Grace explained. "She wouldn't have to follow you into the dressing room."

"Jordan doesn't drive," Dominic said.

"Your sister, the girl with the blue hair?" Crawford asked. "How old is she?"

"Sixteen," Dominic said.

Crawford slammed his ginger ale down on the table so hard that a little fountain of pop spurted out. "She's sixteen and she doesn't know how to drive? Why didn't she take driver's ed?"

"She did. But she never drives."

"As soon as I can," Crawford said, "I'm going to get a license, then a car, then a job, then an apartment." He ducked his head. "I mean, after I graduate, I'll get an apartment. Then I won't have to ask anyone's permission for anything, or be shuttled from house to house."

"I hear that," Grace said.

Crawford looked surprised. "Were your parents divorced?"

She nodded. "When I was really little. And then my mom moved to Oregon and I had to go with her, even though I wanted to stay here with my brothers."

"See?" Crawford said. "That sucks yangers."

Dominic nearly spat out his ginger ale. "You shouldn't say yangers in front of Grace!"

"Sorry," Crawford said.

"No, you were right," she said. "It sucked. Yangers."

The front door shut, and Grace left the boys for a moment. In the living room, she found her dad alone, intently scratching Iago's ears.

"What happened to Uncle Truman?" she asked him.

"He left. He told me he and Peggy plan to get married."

She flopped into her usual chair. "They're nuts."

"So you knew." He frowned. "Did you tell me about their engagement already?"

"No, I didn't. I don't know why. I guess I didn't want to upset you."

His head snapped up and his eyes suddenly focused on her like laser beams. "Why? Why shouldn't they? They're not getting any younger."

"Why *should* they? What's the matter with the way things are?"

"They're lonely."

"Okay, but do they have to suddenly become simpering lovebirds? Cooing at each other in restaurants and exchanging rings?"

"What are you talking about?"

Oops. She had just assumed that Truman had spilled all the beans about that incident. "When I was with Wyatt at the Salt Lick, I saw Uncle Truman give Peggy a ring."

"Did you congratulate them?"

She shrugged. "After a fashion."

"You should have told me," he said.

She should have, she saw that now. But that had been the night of the fire. The ring incident hadn't seemed too important after that.

For a moment she thought her father was going to go upstairs to be alone. He was putting on a brave face, but she knew that deep down he really had to care about what he'd just heard. Instead of leaving, however, he lifted his head and called out, "Who's up for a game of chess?"

Lickety-split, Dominic appeared and settled himself in the martyr's chair. "Today I'm going to win," he said.

Lou chuckled. "Just keep telling yourself that, son."

Crawford drifted in and pulled up a stray dining room chair to observe the game for a bit. Grace put on a record, and after that the only sounds were Mozart and Dominic's anguished groans until a light knock sounded at the door.

"I wanted to bring your plate back," Lily said when Grace opened the door. "From when you gave me the cookies."

Grace reached out and took the flimsy plastic platter she'd bought at the dollar store, which hadn't even cost a dollar. "Thanks. You didn't have to trouble yourself."

"I know."

Lily stayed rooted to the welcome mat, her arms

held tightly at her sides. There was something different about her. Finally, Grace pinpointed what it was: lip gloss. And instead of a ponytail, her hair was brushed straight and ornamented with a red headband. She peered around Grace's side to check out the scene inside and then gazed pointedly at Grace.

"Would you like to come in?" Grace asked.

"Well . . . okay," Lily replied, as if Grace had talked her into it.

14

Adult Education

The thought of school starting made Jordan sick to her stomach. Junior year. In ten years of school, even leaving out kindergarten, she'd never had to face that first day by herself.

She'd always sneered at Nina and her methodic annual back-to-school preparations. Every August Nina wanted—and got—new outfits for school, which would hang in a place of honor on her side of the closet for weeks like a new fall collection awaiting its big unveiling. And no one took school supplies more seriously than Nina. Ever since first grade, the annual pilgrimage to Target had stretched out five times longer than necessary because Nina angsted forever over which box of crayons she wanted, and debated three-subject versus five-subject notebooks, and took forever deciding whether it was really worth splurging for the protractor with all the circles and curlies.

Then there were the lists. God, the lists! Sometimes Nina had even written them up on poster board, decorated with stars and ribbons: *Seventh grade goals . . . Ten mistakes I made as a freshman that I will not repeat sophomore year . . . Resolutions for an awesome sixth grade!!!*

If Nina hadn't been funny and popular, she would have been the biggest dweeb on the planet. (She would have been Lily.) But somehow Nina had made compulsive geekiness seem like an endearing mental illness. It used to drive Jordan crazy, but now she would have given anything to be draped over her twin bed, watching Nina sitting on the floor designing one of her stupid posters.

As long as Nina had been there, Magic Markering her way toward academic and social success, Jordan had felt as if she had a toehold on the success ladder, too. She could be snide and slack off, knowing that Nina would intervene if she were about to lose her way completely. It was hard to claim a place in a family as big as theirs. Nina was the mature one, Lily was the brain, Dominic was the baby, the cute one. Jordan had coasted along, sloshing around in the middle until she'd discovered she could be the edgy one, the troublemaker, because Nina would always be there to anchor her from going too far wrong. In the past two years alone, Nina had prevented her from: failing Algebra I, wearing a yellow kimono to Spring dance, failing geometry, and losing her virginity to Wayne Loscalzo.

Now she just felt adrift. She had no one to talk to . . . no one she wanted to listen to, anyway. No one to save her. All her friends were morons. Not one of them had called her this summer—which was probably because most of them thought she was in Little Salty. Also, she *had* sort of chased them away. Before school had ended in May, her friend Abbie had made this big point of telling Jordan that because she was being *so totally* melodramatic, everybody was really tired of her moods. So Jordan had told her and all of her other so-called friends where they could go.

She didn't want to see any of those people anyway. Nobody knew what she was going through, and even if they did know, what would it matter? No one could help her. Nothing anyone could say would make her forgive herself. She could only hope that somehow, someday, she would forget.

At the vegetarian restaurant near her house, she ordered a carob-soy smoothie to go. While the woman behind the counter was making it, Jordan sat down on the bench by the door. On the windowsill behind her, there was a little pile of fall course schedules for Austin Community

College. She picked up one and flipped through it. God, she wished she were in college! Why couldn't she be one of those really smart kids who could test out of the last few years of high school? It was the one thing she envied Lily for—Lily had skipped third grade, so she would graduate when she was seventeen.

Jordan pored over the art class listings. The school offered a lot of bogus stuff, including two levels of tie-dyeing and lots of beading. But there was wood carving—that sounded cool. She had never really done any carving or sculpting except a cat made out of modeling clay at school. Her school's piddly little art class was so lame. Every year it was the same thing. Collages, still-life drawing, watercolors. Lame.

Her gaze traveled down the page and then stopped. *Oil Painting—Levenger.*

Jed Levenger was teaching at ACC?

She read the course description and felt her chest squeeze painfully at the unfairness of it all. She *would* be stuck doing poster board collages while the rest of the world got to do really interesting stuff. Unless . . .

She was flipping through the catalog to see what the requirements were for taking a class when the waitress brought her the smoothie.

On the walk home, she read the beginning of the booklet, where it talked about registration. It said high school students could take classes, they just wouldn't get credit. The real hiccup was, you had to get parental permission.

Oh, and there was a small matter of $105 to register, plus another $30 for materials. She shouldn't have sent all that money to her grandparents. Now she'd have to go begging.

She began plotting the best time to talk to her dad about giving her the money and permission. He was usually in his best mood when he was walking out the door in the morning—escaping. The downside of mornings was, while he might be in a reasonable mood, this was also the time when he was most likely to forget whatever you said to him.

When she opened the front door to her house and stepped inside, her breath caught. The house was filled with piano music—it sounded as though her mom was back, sitting at the piano. But in the next moment, she realized the music was coming from their dad's study. It had to be a recording.

She crept to his office door and opened it slowly. Her father was at his desk, leaning back in his chair with his eyes closed.

That music! It was a piece her mom had played sometimes, a simple but mournful song, not like the intricate classical pieces she usually favored. Jordan's throat tightened and she had to suck in hard to take a breath. It actually sounded like her mom.

Her dad's eyes popped open. Seeing her, he

tipped forward and lunged for his mouse. A click of his forefinger and all sound ceased. "I didn't hear you come in," he said.

"That was Mom playing. It had to be."

His nod was barely perceptible. "I recorded her once."

How could he stand to listen to that recording? Or maybe a better question was, how could he keep himself from listening all the time?

"Was that Chopin?" Her mother had tried to teach her piano, but Jordan didn't have any talent or interest in that kind of music. Although now she wished she'd at least tried a little harder to absorb some of what her mother had been trying to teach her.

"Erik Satie," her father told her. " 'Gnossienne.' Where have you been?"

She felt a pang. He so obviously didn't want to talk about her mom. At least not with her. Which was understandable, she guessed.

"I was at Mother's Café, getting a smoothie. Why?"

"I don't know . . . I came home at five-thirty and no one was here."

"You're usually not home till six-thirty," she reminded him.

"Do you know where Dominic and Lily are?"

"Do I look like Nanny McPhee?" she fired back.

He blew out a breath, and with that sigh she could feel any hope of taking Jed's painting course evaporating. *Way to go, Jordan.* "Tranquilize, Dad. They're probably with Grace."

He blinked in that absentminded way he had. "The woman who lives with Professor Oliver? What would Dominic and Lily be doing over there? I thought he just went over to walk the dog."

It took an effort not to shake her head. "Well, yeah, but Dominic also likes to hang out there, along with some kid named Crawford."

"The teenager with the chain saw?"

Jordan made a face. "I don't know anything about a chain saw. He's just a boring-looking normal nobody kind of a guy. Completely beige."

"So what's Lily doing over there?"

"You'd have to ask her," Jordan said. "I don't know why Lily does anything."

His expression was thoughtful. Maybe this wouldn't be the worst time to ask him for a favor.

"Hey, there's this art class at ACC I want to take on Saturday mornings."

His brows rose. "*You* want to get up early on Saturdays?"

She hated it when adults were sarcastic. As if nothing was more important to a teenager than sleeping late. And as if she was just an average teenager. "The teacher's a guy who taught at my camp last summer. I'd really like to go."

He mulled it over for a few seconds. "Sounds like a possibility."

She might as well get the big obstacle out of the

way. “It’ll cost around a hundred and fifty dollars,” she warned him.

“We’re not paupers, Jordan. If it’s important, the money’s not a problem. We’ll see.”

He looked back at the screen of his computer. Back to work. Music off, Mom forgotten, daughter . . .

Dismissed.

She hesitated a moment, wondering if she should salute and leave, but decided to dig in her heels. “Who’s we?”

He glanced up again. “What?”

“I asked, who’s *we?*” She gestured around the room. “There’s me, and my mind’s made up, so that leaves you. Did you mean ‘*I’ll* see’? Or were you just trying to make me feel bad?”

His eyes widened. “Why would that make you feel bad?”

“Because that’s what you used to say when you meant you and Mom would have to confer. *We’ll see.* But now Mom’s not here anymore and whose fault is that?”

“Jordan, would you—” He stopped whatever he was going to say and lowered his voice. “It was just something I said, okay? Without thinking. *I’ll* see what I can do for you.”

“What you could do for me is let me take this stupid class so I’ll have something to do with myself besides wishing I’d never been born. Ever since the accident—”

Her father wheeled his chair back and lurched to his feet, cutting her off. He yanked his wallet out of his back pocket. "A hundred and fifty?" He pulled out a handful of twenties and tossed them across the table at her. "Here."

"Oh, thanks. Very kind of you to offer," she sassed back, knowing she was pressing her luck. She couldn't help it. He'd practically thrown the money at her to get her to shut up.

"I'm giving you what you asked for," he said. "What more do you want?"

I want someone to tell me it wasn't my fault. To forgive me.

Did he really not know?

Her adrenaline was pumping and there were tears in her eyes, but she forced herself to remain calm. She stepped forward and then took the money. "I need special permission from you. You might even have to go register with me."

"Just tell me when."

"I'll call them tomorrow and find out," she said.

"Fine."

They both stood frozen, facing each other as if they were each waiting for the other to say something conciliatory. After a few seconds, he fell back into his desk chair and returned his focus to the screen.

She made a dash for the door.

"Jordan?" he asked.

She stopped, her heart in her throat, praying he

would say something to her that would make her hate herself a little less.

When she turned, though, his face was screwed up in puzzlement. "Do *you* ever hang out next door with Grace?"

She drew back, then let out a laughing breath. "I'm bored, but I'm not *that* bored."

15

Unforgettable

On the first day of school, Grace cradled a mug of coffee in her hands as she sat by the front window, watching the melancholy exodus. Crawford left first, followed by Lily, carrying a brown clarinet case, her small frame weighed down by a backpack large enough to take to tackle Kilimanjaro. After her, Dominic burst out of his house, appearing slightly frantic and already hot in a maroon jacket, black pants, and black shoes that made him look like he was attending a school for doormen. The uniform was a little tight, and Grace kicked herself for forgetting to say something to Ray.

But honestly, shouldn't Ray have been able to tell when his son's clothes didn't fit?

Jordan, the straggler, came out five minutes later. For her back-to-school outfit she had chosen a black tank top, a lime-green miniskirt over brown-and-white striped leggings, and platform boots worthy of a seventies stadium rock star. Instead of a backpack, she was lugging an old carpetbag that made it hard to tell if she was headed for school or running away from home.

Despite the fact that none of them looked thrilled to be embarking on a new school year, Grace felt a ridiculous stab of nostalgia. For a crazy moment, she wanted a do-over—a blank slate. Not that she missed school, or God forbid, being a teenager. She just wanted the world back the way it had been when she was sixteen.

Or maybe she just wanted the world back the way it was when her father was well.

Around noon, she went to check the mail and nearly walked right into Ray, who was standing on the front porch. She drew back, startled. She hadn't spoken to him since the tree episode, weeks ago.

He looked worried. "You wouldn't happen to have seen one or two of my kids around here, would you?"

Unbelievable! The man didn't know that this was the first day of school? Where had he been?

"You won't find Jordan here ever, and you won't find Dominic or Lily here today," she said, annoyed for the kids' sakes. "They're in school, Ray. It's the first day of school."

He absorbed this information and then blew out a breath. "That's right. Of course."

"Please tell me you knew that." Otherwise she would have to think those kids really were alone over there.

"I knew that," he confirmed. "I forgot."

"Pardon me for asking, but how could you forget? This was a big day for the kids, Ray. Well—I don't know about Jordan, but I know it was important for Lily and Dominic. They could use a little attention from you, Ray."

"You think I'm not interested in my own kids?"

She backpedaled. "It's not what you feel, it's what you show. Even the basics—like seeing that Dominic needs new uniforms."

She'd expected him to take offense. Instead, he nodded. "You're right. I only noticed his uniform this morning."

"I probably should have said something," she admitted. "He mentioned it earlier . . ."

As she spoke, Ray zoned out before her eyes. He sat down on one of the two Adirondack chairs on the porch, his face pinched in a strange, distracted expression. "I know that music," he said.

Grace listened. "Probably." She assumed everybody knew it. "It's 'Moonlight Sonata.' "

"Is that what it is?" he asked. "Jen used to play it—my wife, Jennifer."

Jennifer. Dominic and Lily's mother. The woman who'd died in the crash with Nina, the other twin. Grace had never known what their mother's name was. Dominic and Lily never talked about her in detail.

He shook his head. "I know you're right about the kids, Grace. And I did talk to them this morning, but then . . . I don't know, I just spaced out or something. Odd, isn't it? I forgot it was the first day of school *because* it was the first day of school."

She didn't say anything—because she really didn't have anything to say that wasn't along the lines of *wow, you're crazy.*

"I started out this morning thinking about the first day of school," he explained. "I came downstairs as Dominic was leaving, and I saw him in his uniform. Seeing him flung me back in time. All morning I couldn't concentrate at work. Finally, I told my boss I was going to work from home today."

"You went to the same school Dominic goes to?"

"Yeah." He shook his head. "Stupid, isn't it? And then I was actually surprised to find the house empty, because the thing that was preoccupying me had been triggered by seeing my son in his school uniform. I started thinking about the first day I saw her, at St. Xavier's."

Grace stood still for a moment, as if any sudden movement might scare Ray away before he could tell her more about this woman. "You met her at school?"

"Actually, we'd met before, but I didn't remember." He smiled. "I didn't go to St. Xavier's till I was in seventh grade. The first day I got there I felt a little lost. I had to wear a uniform, and everything seemed so regimented. When I arrived at that first homeroom, the teacher sent me to the back of the room because my name started with W. As I was walking past her, Jen—her name was Webber—said, 'Hey Ray!' Which was really startling, because I had no idea who she was.

"It happened again in Chapel. Then in another class. I'd see Jen and she'd beam a smile at me and say, 'Hey Ray!' like we were best friends. Finally, at lunch, I was sitting by myself at the end of a long table and she came and plopped her plastic tray across from mine and said, 'You don't remember me, do you?'

" 'Not really,' I admitted. Although a more truthful answer would have been *not at all.*"

"How did she know you?" Grace asked.

"Turns out, we'd been in peewee soccer together. I mean, it had been years and years before—back when I was five or six. I'd forgotten all about it—all about her. Probably I blanked it out because I was the worst kid on the team. I *hated* soccer."

"But she remembered you," Grace said wistfully. "That's so cool—so sweet." So Cathy and Heathcliff . . . if Heathcliff had been a math geek.

"That's what I thought. I spent the rest of the day on a sort of high because this cute girl remembered me. Walking down the halls during the following weeks I felt like I was a couple of inches taller. I looked forward to the classes with her, and all those tedious lineups they made us go through, just so I could see her smile and hear her voice saying 'Hey, Ray.'" He shook his head. "'Hey Ray.'"

Grace could almost hear it herself.

"Did you two go together in school?" she asked.

"God, no." He laughed and explained, "That high I was talking about? It didn't take me long to figure out that Jen smiled that way at the whole world. Whenever I tried to really talk to her between classes, I could hardly get a sentence out because she greeted *everybody. 'Hey, Jake!' 'Hey, Carla!' 'Hey, Sara!'* It was so irritating." He shot a sharp look at Grace. "Do you know that when I looked at Jen's Facebook page after she died, she had over 1,300 friends? I have forty-two. And most of those are from work."

Grace smiled. "So when did you and Jennifer start going out?"

"Well, the first time we got together—sort of—was right before high school ended. We'd been friends for years, but only from being in classes together, and clubs. But Jen was really popular. She wasn't a cheerleader type, just a girl everybody liked. In school she dated the captain of the junior varsity basketball team, then the debate club president, then Kevin Early, then a guy named Eddie Carter, who was her date to the senior prom."

"Who did you go with?"

"Sonia Krohn, my chemistry lab partner."

"What happened with her?"

"She gave me a concussion. Then I think she went to MIT."

Grace sputtered. "Wait—back up. A *concussion?*"

"In Sonia's defense, I behaved badly. After we arrived at the prom, I went to get her a sparkling apple juice, and then on the way I walked by Jen. I almost didn't recognize her because she was standing all alone. I mean, I hadn't even seen her standing by herself *in six years,* and then suddenly, there we were at the prom, not another person around. Turns out, her date, Eddie, had had a Sea-Doo accident on Lake Austin that day and was in the hospital, so Jen had come to the dance with a couple of friends. And then Sinead O'Connor started singing that 'Nothing Compares 2 U' song, and I asked her to dance, and she said yes, and before I knew what was what, two dances had gone by, and Sonia was glaring at me next to a Styrofoam rock."

Absorbed in the story, Grace eased herself into the other chair. "Styrofoam rock?"

"The Seniors' theme was 'Blaze of Glory,' because of the Bon Jovi song, so they'd decorated the hall like the Grand Canyon, like in the video. Anyway, long story short, Sonia shoved me into the Styrofoam, which made the Grand Canyon wall start to wobble, and then it was just me holding it up, and several people gasped and ran over for fear that the whole thing was about to come down. A football player named Bryan Bennett pushed me out of the way, and somehow I lost my balance and ended up clunking my head against the corner of the refreshment table. So, technically, I guess Sonia didn't give me the concussion. She just gave me the shove that started it all."

It was amazing to hear all this. Grace got the impression that Ray had barely communicated with anyone for months, but here he was, opening up to her. It was like the moment when a wild animal inched up toward you to take a piece of food.

"Jen and I left the dance together and ended up driving out to Mount Bonnell and sneaking up the stone steps after curfew to look at the view. It took a quarter hour of city gazing and passionate hand holding for me to work up the nerve to kiss her. When I finally bent down and touched my lips to hers, it was nearly overwhelming—really. At first I thought I was just seeing stars because of how great the kiss was. Then I realized that I was about to black out from a headache.

"Jen drove me to the hospital and visited Eddie

while I waited in the ER. I felt like an idiot. My parents came and my dad drove Jen home before he took me back to our house. He kept calling Jen Sonia—I'm not sure I ever made him understand what had happened."

"So you and Jennifer didn't actually go out in high school?"

"No, we didn't really get together until college, and that was sort of by accident, too."

"Where—"

"Hello, you two!" someone yodeled at them from the street. It was Muriel Blainey. She turned up the walkway and stopped just at the porch steps. She wore a lime-green shirt and lemon-yellow pedal pushers. "You two sure look comfy cozy, porch-sitting together."

Ray shot to his feet. "Hello, Muriel."

"Don't get up on my account. Y'all looked like you were deep in conversation about something or other."

Then why did you butt in? Grace wondered, annoyed.

Ray was already edging away, taking the stairs backward so that he looked as if his feet could easily miss a step. Grace worried she would never be able to look at him without imagining the Grand Canyon about to crash down on his head.

"I need to get back to work," he said.

He fled back to his house, and then Muriel

rounded on Grace. "You sure are playing your cards right. Maybe befriending the children *is* the way to a widower's heart."

Grace was so surprised she almost laughed. "We were just talking."

Muriel sent her a knowing smile. "And how many people in the neighborhood do you think Ray's actually talked to since the accident? I'll give you a hint—goose egg."

"Maybe it's easier to talk to me because I'm an outsider. I never knew Jennifer or Nina."

"That's probably to your advantage," Muriel said.

Advantage? "I'm not trying to—" Grace choked on the words. It was stupid even to be having this conversation. In fact, she was beginning to feel angry.

"How's that boyfriend of yours?" Muriel asked. "The one you talk about but we never see."

"He's good. How's your husband?" Grace asked. Two could play at this game.

"Fine," Muriel said, adding, "in California, at the moment."

"It must be hard, having him away so much."

Muriel's lips twisted at the corners. "Yes, it is."

After Muriel left, Grace went inside but glanced once or twice out at the two empty chairs on the porch, almost as if she could imagine herself and Ray sitting in them. A sharp desire to know what happened when he and Jennifer met again plagued her the rest of the afternoon. It was as if she'd been left with a series cliffhanger and now had to wait till the new television season. But what were the chances Ray would ever open up to her again?

16

Good Morning

For the first painting class, Jordan started out early. The studio was located in one of the farther-flung ACC campuses and she had to catch two buses to get there.

It would have been so much simpler if she could drive. Well, she *could* drive—that is, she knew how—but she didn't have a license. The thought of driving made her ill now. Nina had always been wild to get behind the wheel, which is probably why she'd volunteered to drive their mom last spring, the day of the accident.

The whole thing had played out in Jordan's head so many times. It was like a short film she'd pieced together from scraps of her own memory, what Lily had told her, and a police report. Some details she'd filled in herself, from her imagination, just from knowing her mom and Nina.

On a Friday afternoon in March, while all the family except their dad were on a spring break vacation in the country, Jordan had been forced to call home just before dinner. Their mom had been making a pizza, aided by Lily, who had answered the phone first.

"What's going on?" Lily had asked, sensing something odd in Jordan's voice.

"Just put Mom on," Jordan had told her in a clipped voice.

Lily had done as asked, and then had come the confession, spoken by Jordan in a wobbly but defensively pissed-off voice. "Mom, I'm at the police station."

She'd given a brief, humiliating explanation right there in the middle of a bunch of cops and other people standing around, who were all staring at her as the dumb story came out. Knowing that she had an audience, Jordan had responded with growing exasperation to her mom's sputtered questions.

"Look, I'm sorry, okay? Can you just come get me? Please?" she'd asked her mom in her most irritable voice.

The last words she'd ever spoken to her mother.

After hanging up, her mom had instructed Lily to carry on with the pizza preparation but to hold off actually putting it in the oven for another thirty minutes or so. Lily had probably been delighted to be left in charge. Her mom had then taken the keys off the hook by the door and was just about to step out when Nina came racing in, volunteering to drive her mom wherever she was going. Lily had reported that their mom hadn't given anyone any details about Jordan's call, but after a moment's thought she'd looked glad to have Nina along.

After that, Jordan could only imagine. Nina would have gone around to the driver's side of the Jeep and driven very carefully on the rural roads. On the way to town, she would have asked their mom what was going on, which their mom would have told her because Nina was mature and responsible—the only one their parents ever really confided in. Maybe she would have asked Nina for advice on how to get Jordan under control. And Nina would have been sympathetic to their mom's frustration yet taken Jordan's side, too, and tried to smooth things over. Nina had always been the peacemaker.

They would have been deep in conversation when they rounded the curve and found the truck coming straight at them. The truck had been passing another vehicle illegally. DO NOT CROSS DOUBLE YELLOW LINES IN YOUR LANE TO PASS, the signs read, and the truck was in the wrong lane. According to the police, both vehicles had been going approximately sixty miles per hour.

And now came the part Jordan replayed most often in her mind, over and over, a constant loop of torment: The instant of surprise and fear in Nina's eyes as a truck barreled toward her, then a sickening impact of crushing metal and shattering glass, then intense pain, then semiconsciousness during the eternal wait for an ambulance, their mom already dead in the seat next to her, the paramedics arriving just as Nina's world turned to dark.

When Jordan told people she didn't want to drive now, most who knew her would nod in sympathy. They remembered the collision, and probably thought she was afraid to get behind a wheel. Afraid.

It wasn't fear that made her not want to drive. It was shame. *Nina* should be the one who was alive—Nina, the best of all the Wests. And their mother should still be with them, too, taking care of Dominic and Lily and playing piano and feeding birds and being the only woman their dad had ever loved.

If she lived to be a hundred, she would have to endure this pain of having lost everything—her mom, her sister and best friend, the love of what family she had left. Everything. And it was all her fault.

She'd left the house way too early. But that was okay. She'd be able to talk to Jed while he was setting up. She imagined he'd have the music cranked and he would be slurping some coffee from a battered mug. Jed was a natural-born teacher. He might put on a cranky curmudgeon act, but he was always full of energy in class, as if being around students gave him some kind of performance buzz.

She was so early that she had time to swing by a coffee shop and buy a to-go cup and a couple of stale doughnuts. Jed would like that. He was one of those bearish-looking guys who didn't mind that he had a gut.

She walked into the community college building, loving all the smells of paints and glues and turpentine that made art seem a little like alchemy. She got to her classroom, dropped all her stuff at a place close to the door, and was a little surprised by the quiet. She peered around the forest of empty easels until she spotted a lone seated figure with blond cornrowed hair slumped over a table at the front of the class. It was a woman, and she was zonked.

What should she do? Wake the person up? Call security and inform them that a strange lady had crashed in Jed's classroom?

Where was Jed?

The woman snorted, shaking herself out of sleep, and then raised her head and examined Jordan through red puffy eyelids. She wasn't wearing any make-up, and her blotchy skin still bore the traces of sheet line. Her pale eyebrows blended in with her skin, and together with her blue eyes gave her a forlorn look.

"Is it time for class?" she asked Jordan.

"It's . . ." Jordan didn't know what to say.

"Where's Jed? He's teaching the painting class, isn't he?"

"What gave you that idea?"

"Because his name was on the schedule? Levenger?"

The woman sat back in her chair with a sigh and combed a finger through her cascade of snaky braids. "*I'm* Levenger," she said. "Heather Levenger . . . much as I wish I weren't."

"Oh." Jordan's disappointment was so sharp she couldn't have hid it if she'd wanted to. She'd been looking forward to being in Jed's class. That was the whole point.

The woman smirked. "Don't tell me . . . one of Jed's groupies?"

Jordan shook her head. "No—I had him in a class once. I just liked him."

"Yeah, so did I. Once." Heather narrowed her puffy eyes on the cup Jordan held. "Where did you get that coffee?"

"I bought it down the street."

"Oh." The woman sagged. "I thought maybe it was free."

Maybe because she worried that she would have to spend the next three hours with a near-comatose instructor if she didn't, Jordan offered the cup to Heather.

She raised a barely-visible brow. "Are you sure?"

"Yeah. I've had a cup already."

Heather reached out her hands to take the cup,

looking almost moved to tears by the gesture. "Thank you so much."

Jordan looked in her bag. "I got a couple of doughnuts, too. One cakey one with chocolate, and a cruller."

A childlike gleam appeared in her teacher's eyes. "Oh . . . cakey chocolate?"

Jordan handed it over and Heather took a bite and washed it down. She started to look less like the undead. Watching her, Jordan had an odd feeling in her chest—the same feeling she'd had when she and Nina had dropped off gifts for a giving tree for the underprivileged at Christmas. That little glow of maybe having made someone's day slightly better.

She offered her the other doughnut, too, but Heather shook her head. "No—thank you. My ass is already as big as a barn."

Jordan doubted this was true. Although the crinkly skirt she was wearing probably didn't help matters.

Heather tilted her head and eased her hand toward the bag. "I might just take the other one for later. Would that be all right?"

Jordan didn't want to say no. She was still trying to think when she'd ever heard an adult talking about her ass in front of her, and actually using that word. Maybe never.

She took it as a sign of respect. At least Heather didn't see her as just a high school dweeb.

"So Jed never mentioned me?" she asked. "Jordan West?"

Heather sent her a blank stare. "You were at that camp thing he did?"

"Yeah."

The woman shrugged. "No, but to tell you the truth, last summer is when we were hitting rock bottom, relationship-wise. We separated in September. Almost a year ago, exactly . . ."

"Oh, well . . . it's no big deal or anything. I was just hoping . . ."

"I know—you were hoping for Jed." Heather sighed. "Well, you got me. I'm guessing that sucks. Which reminds me, I'd better get going here. Got a class to teach. Would you mind sweeping up a little? It looks like they had a shop class in here or something. All this dust is a disaster with oils."

Usually having someone boss her around like that was a huge turnoff. But something about this woman—exhausted, abandoned, with crazy hair—made Jordan reach for the broom. Heather was an artist living a real life. A kindred spirit.

Heather was all alone too. Maybe the oddballs of the world, like herself and Heather, just would never fit in, not even with their own families. Maybe they had to find families of their own, through friendship.

Jordan started sweeping.

17

Eight O'clock in the Morning

It was hard to get the timing exactly right. If she left too soon, she ran the risk of being in the awkward position of walking in front of Crawford all the way to school, because there were only so many ways you could dawdle so that someone would catch up with you, and she'd tried most of them already. If she pretended her shoe had come untied one more time, Crawford would probably think she didn't know how to dress herself.

On the other hand, if she left too late, he would have too big a head start and she'd be forced either to run and catch up—and she really wasn't good at running without her breathing turning wheezy—or call out to him, which would seem really dorky.

So she waited at the doorway until she could just see a movement at his front door. Then she hurried out, managing to cross in front of the Carter house just as he'd reached the end of his walkway.

"Oh, hi," he said, surprised.

"Hey," she said.

The door to his house banged open again and a beautiful red-headed woman wearing a flight attendant uniform hurried out. She stopped at an unfamiliar economy car parked in the Carter driveway and glanced up at Crawford. "Would you like a ride, sweetie?"

Lily's heart stopped. Not because the woman had called him sweetie—you could tell by the way streaks of red appeared in Crawford's cheeks that he was embarrassed to have some woman calling him that. No, her heart stopped because she worried Crawford actually would take the ride, and where would that leave her? Hurrying to school all on her own.

To her relief, Crawford shook his head. "No, thanks. I don't mind walking."

The redhead flashed a big toothy smile at him. "Suit yourself, sweet stuff."

Crawford hurried on. Lily had to do a little skip step to keep up with him.

"Who was she?"

"My dad's girlfriend," he grumbled. "One of them. I think that one was Bev."

"Your dad has lots of girlfriends."

"Tell me about it! According to my mom, he *always* did."

Her parents had always been so boring. They never even fought. Oh sure, there were moments when she'd been able to tell that her mom was exasperated with her dad—because he was forgetful, or something like that—but she'd never had to worry that her family would break up because her dad was a philanderer. “I can’t imagine,” she said.

“You’re lucky!” As soon as he’d blurted out the words, Crawford faltered a step. “God—sorry.”

“Why?”

“I didn’t mean . . . well, you know. I know you’re not lucky. I should just shut up.”

The accident embarrassed people sometimes, like this. Nobody knew how to act around so much loss.

“No, I see what you mean,” she said. “I guess when it comes to families, there’s no perfect situation.”

He slanted a thoughtful look down at her, and she had to turn away. Crawford’s green eyes always caused her to feel feverish when he looked at her. She was just waiting for the moment when he would murmur to her in a low voice, *“You really are amazing, Lily West.”*

For a moment, it looked as if that moment had come.

Then she heard shouting from behind them. “Hey! Heeeeeeey! Crawford, wait up!”

Dominic.

Lily rolled her eyes and just barely bit back a huff of exasperation. She couldn’t say anything about her pesky little brother because Crawford liked him, which might have been endearing if it weren’t getting in the way of moments with romantic potential. Although, honestly, she had to admit that there probably wasn't much chance of a romantic moment out on the sidewalk on the way to school.

Dominic came galumphing after them, breathing heavily. When he caught up, he had sweat trickling down his temples, but that probably had more to do with the jacket he was wearing in the eighty-degree weather than with the half a block he'd just run.

"Why are you wearing your jacket in this heat?" she asked him.

He swiped the maroon sleeve of the jacket over his brow. "We get a demerit if we show up in chapel without a jacket. If I don't wear it every morning I might forget."

Lily bit her lip, determined not to tell him in front of Crawford how dumb that was. But she couldn't help saying, "You could get to your school faster if you walked up Forty-fifth."

Dominic shrugged. "I'd rather walk with you guys, even if it takes a little longer."

"Aw, dude," Crawford said, in a way that managed to be both sarcastic and nice. "I'm touched."

Her brother laughed. "What were y'all talking about? It looked serious."

"Nothing," Crawford said casually.

Disappointment pierced Lily. It hadn't felt like nothing to her.

Dominic chattered all the way to the intersection

where he absolutely had to peel off in the direction of his own school. Then, as Lily and Crawford were about to cross the street, Crawford darted a glance over his shoulder.

"I think your sister's behind us. Should we wait?"

Jordan was moseying along at a snail's pace, glowering at the ground as she went.

"Wait for Miss Technicolor Dream Hair?" Lily asked. "No, thanks."

He laughed. "Great name!"

Lily couldn't actually take credit for the name—she'd overheard two mean girls calling her sister by that name in the girl's rest room the week before—but she let him think it was a product of her own wit. "You know how you were saying I was lucky?" She jabbed her thumb over her shoulder. "Well *that's* the reason you were wrong. I have to deal with the punk prima donna every day of my life. Believe me, it's not easy."

He looked behind them again. How could he help it? If the word *weirdo* had needed a mascot, Jordan could have been it.

"She's never even said hello to me," he said.

"Yeah, well, she wouldn't, would she? She probably doesn't consider you cool enough." She looked over at him as they were crossing another street and saw that his brows were knit together.

"I guess she likes weird dudes," he said.

"Omigod, you have no idea. Her last boyfriend

was Alex Plummer, who looks like the undead, only with a Mohawk and lots of piercings. And whenever Jordan's walking around the neighborhood, she always stops and talks to the strangest guys. I even saw her once on Guadalupe, sharing a Twix bar with a homeless guy who was missing half his nose."

"That was sort of nice of her," he said.

Lily frowned. Maybe it was, but he was missing her point. "The Twix part was, but sitting down and talking to him for forty-five minutes? That seemed excessive and weird."

"Were you spying on her?" Crawford asked.

"No! Why would I do that?"

He shrugged.

"I can't help it if my sister and I have to walk around the same neighborhood. Believe me, I try to avoid her whenever possible."

He laughed. "One big happy family!"

"Yeah."

Not so big as it used to be, she couldn't help thinking. And as the thought crossed her mind, she had to try extra-hard not to toss another angry glance back at her sister.

18

Setting the Date

Grace put a deadline of mid-September as the time she was supposed to go home. But then her father fell sick—they worried it was pneumonia—and she stayed.

The first week of October, one of Lou's teeth had an abscess, and Grace stayed with him for a week while that was taken care of.

Everyone had started to pester her about the amount of time she was spending in Texas. Ben, of course. And her mother had phoned her several times, worried that Grace was being sucked away from her real life.

"This is real life, too," Grace reminded her.

"But you've never stayed so long before."

"Dad's never needed me before. And it's not forever. Just a few more weeks."

Even Steven expressed worry over her lingering in Austin.

"Why should *you* be dragging Dad to the dentist and things like that?" he asked her one afternoon as they sat in a coffee shop. They had just dropped Lou off next door to get a haircut, with instructions for him to join them when he was done.

As she looked across the table at Steven, it

occurred to her that she had probably socialized with her brother more in the past months than she had in her whole life. When they were kids, the nearly ten-year gap in their ages had seemed an unbridgeable gulf. And after she'd finished school, Steven was always married to some disagreeable woman or another. But now, alone, sharing their troubles and their concerns about their dad, he seemed more human.

"For that matter, why should you be here at all?" he continued.

"Because he's my dad."

"He's my dad too. Why should we both be here? Now that my personal life has exploded, I can move back into the house so you can go home."

She shook her head. That would never work. "You've got office appointments or surgery every day. You're busy, and unreachable most of the time. Emily practically demands a secret password before she'll let me through to you."

Emily, the office gatekeeper.

He smiled. "Emily's deciding to come to the new office seems like the one thing that's gone right in my life lately."

God, how grim. Grace liked Emily, as much as anyone could like a woman who seemed to thrive on scheduling appointments and filing insurance claims. One time when Grace was visiting the office she had asked Emily if she was seeing anyone. Emily had smiled politely, if a little impatiently, and informed her that she was much too busy these days for socializing.

"What are you busy with?" Grace asked her.

Emily had frowned at her, as if it should be obvious. "With the new office! There's tons to do!"

Grace could remember being that involved in Rigoletto's at one time. But that was her own store. She had a sink-or-swim stake in its success.

After much prying—interrogation, really—she learned Emily had no family. None. She had spent her very young years in foster care and her teen years in a group home. "My job is my life," she confessed to Grace, almost bragging.

But even with Emily the office assistant extraordinaire devoting herself 24/7 to overseeing his professional life, Steven still didn't have enough time to take care of Lou.

"We could hire someone during the day," he suggested when she pointed out this problem. "And then at night I'll be there. It doesn't matter to me where I live anyway. Denise . . ." He swallowed. "Well, we'll have to sell our house at some point."

Poor Steven. Denise had left him squished like romance roadkill, and he was still carrying a torch for her. Grace imagined her brother up in his old room, dejected and alone with his bug collection and his Top Gun poster.

He took a deep breath. "The point is, you've got

your own life to take care of. You can't martyr yourself to Dad's illness."

She resented that idea, for her dad's sake. "I love being around Dad. We have fun. We've sort of fallen into a strange *Odd Couple* existence. Most of the time I forget he's sick at all."

Steven nodded. "Most of the time he seems so normal that I wonder if he hasn't been misdiagnosed."

Unfortunately, at this moment the barber from next door streaked back and forth down the sidewalk. Grace and Steven craned their heads toward the window and followed him in time to see their father, with his barbershop poncho billowing around him in the afternoon breeze, stepping out into the middle of Duval Road.

"What's Ben like?"

It was that lull between the end of school and dinner, and Lily was sitting backward in a chair, elbows propped on the backrest, watching Grace make granola, which at the moment was just a sludge of oil and molasses at the bottom of a mixing bowl. Most of Grace's mind was focused on how she was going to whisk that gluey syrup together with oil. She didn't give Lily's question much thought.

"I guess the first thing I'd say about him is that he's funny." She added, "In a cranky guy sort of way."

"Funny's good," Lily said. "Although it seems to me that lots of guys think they're funny when they're not, and girls giggle and laugh at them anyway."

"I'm not a big giggler," Grace replied, frowning at the recipe, which said to add water. Water in granola? Who knew?

Lily persisted with her inquisition. "Is he cute?"

"He's not the Old Spice guy, but I think he's cute in a shaggy kind of way."

Lily's brows knit together. "So he's cranky, arguably funny, and not all that good-looking."

Grace laughed. "Well, love is blind, maybe."

"Love!" Lily exclaimed. "You don't seem like you're in love to me."

Grace wasn't aware that the look of love really existed outside of Burt Bacharach songs. "Why not?"

"Well, for one thing, you're here and he's in Oregon. And you never talk about him."

"Not everybody wears her heart on her sleeve. Ben and I call each other all the time."

"Every day?" Lily asked.

"Well . . . twice a week. Usually." She frowned. Come to think of it, it had been a week and a half now since they'd spoken.

"So you really do miss him, then," Lily said, and Grace couldn't help noticing that she sounded disappointed. "I thought maybe it was all off with you guys, and maybe you'd move here. It's better with you here."

"That's sweet of you to say."

"If you weren't here, it would just be the professor and the guys, and I'd feel weird about coming over so often. But with you here, I feel better about just hanging out."

Grace laughed. She'd never quite met anyone who could be so sly and guileless at the same time.

"But if you actually miss him . . ." Lily shrugged.

Grace started whisking, and then hopped back to evade the splatters she'd kicked up. "I do miss him. He seems so far away. They all do."

"Who is all?"

"Ben . . . my friends . . . Heathcliff and Earnshaw."

"You have friends named Heathcliff and Earnshaw?"

"Heathcliff is a big orange cat, fifteen years old, a furry lummox, and Earnshaw is a seventeen-year-old tabby female."

"Wow," Lily said. "That's really weird."

"What?"

"You just volunteered a lot more about your cats than you ever did about Ben."

"Well . . ." Grace busied herself mixing oats into her mixing bowl. Now that she studied it more closely, the recipe called for a lot of oats. Almost the whole box. No wonder she'd had to make so much goop to coat them in.

"It's also weird that you'd name a female Earnshaw," Lily said. "We read that book last year in school, and the woman in the book was Cathy. Earnshaw was her last name."

"I know, but I worried that if I called her Cathy it would sound like I'd named my cats after two defunct cartoons."

"Did you actually like that book?" Lily asked. "When I read it, I thought Heathcliff was a lunatic."

Grace stopped stirring for a moment. "Oh, no—he was just wounded, and hopelessly devoted to Cathy."

Lily laughed. "*Hopelessly devoted* reminds me of that stupid song the girl in the movie *Grease* sings."

"Olivia Newton-John?" It had been years since Grace had seen that movie, but she'd loved it when she was a teenager.

"But when you think about it," Lily said, "they're sort of similar."

"Who?"

"Heathcliff and Olivia Newton-John. Heathcliff is hopelessly devoted to Cathy, who is faithless and flighty—even though I personally think she made the absolute right choice to go live in the nice house with the civilized people—and Sandy is hopelessly devoted to John Travolta, who is, you know, greasy. Yuck."

"Heathcliff was always my idea of a romantic hero," Grace said. Until now. "Now I'll always think of him as a lunatic, or as Olivia Newton-John man."

Lily stood and came closer to inspect Grace's granola-making progress. "You can buy granola in the store, you know. They sell it in bulk at Central Market."

"I can put my own stuff in it this way. Like pumpkin seeds. They're good brain food."

Lily angled a serious glance up at her. "It's for Professor Oliver, isn't it? There's something wrong with him—it wasn't just that he broke his leg, was it?"

"He's . . ." Grace swallowed. The kids would find out soon enough. Really, she was surprised they hadn't guessed before now. "He's got Alzheimer's."

Lily frowned. "That's really bad, isn't it?"

Grace nodded. "But it's gradual." Although she couldn't get her mind to erase the vision of her father walking across the road in that poncho. It was a miracle he didn't get run over again.

Someone knocked at the front door. Dominic and Crawford were outside somewhere with Iago, so Lily twirled around. "I'll get it!"

Grace followed her, and when she saw the strange man on the other side of the screen door, she was glad she did. The guy was about thirty-five years old, wearing a torn T-shirt and old jeans, and he apparently hadn't shaved in days. He kept his gaze focused down on the welcome mat, not on their faces.

"Grace Oliver live here?" he asked.

Lily turned to Grace, her brows darting up like question marks.

"I'm Grace."

The man finally looked at her. "I'm from Portland."

Grace tilted her head. "Do I know you?"

"No, see, I answered a classified. Someone was looking for someone driving to Austin from Portland? Guy named Ben?"

Grace gasped. Ben was here? She scooted past Lily and shot out onto the porch, looking around.

"Ben asked me to bring you something," the stranger explained.

He pointed down to two beige plastic cat carriers sitting in the front yard.

In shock, Grace launched herself off the porch and fell to her knees in front of the metal grill of the cages. "Oh my God—Heathcliff! Earnshaw!" She looked up at the man. "You drove them here?"

He nodded.

"But—"

"Your friend paid me two hundred dollars. It sounded like a lot of money four days ago, but now . . . I'm not so sure if I'm ever gonna get that smell out of the upholstery."

Grace couldn't work up too much sympathy for

the man, although she was grateful he actually got them to Austin safe and sound. But her surprise and happiness at seeing Heathcliff and Earnshaw were quickly being displaced by a rising tide of anger. How could Ben have handed her cats over to a total stranger? From a classified ad! Anything could have happened to them!

"Well, I can't say that guy Ben didn't warn me. 'Course he didn't warn me about the sound of one cat yowling for twelve hours straight, days on end, right in the back of your head as you're trying to drive."

"Thank you for bringing them to me safely." The man seemed hesitant to leave, like those bellboys you see in movies lingering in the room hoping for a tip, but he finally took off when he saw her and Lily picking up the cat carriers and taking them into the house.

"This is so weird," Lily said. "You were just telling me about them, and now here they are. It's like it was fate."

Fate, shmate. Grace's blood pressure was soaring. The boys came in from the back, along with Iago, who started barking up a storm, which in turn caused Heathcliff to bristle, growl, and hiss. In the other cage, a series of esophageal gulps had commenced, the prelude to a hairball.

"I guess I'll take Iago back out," Dominic said, just as Lou, roused from his afternoon nap by the commotion, came down the stairs.

“What’s going on?” he asked. “What’s that smell?”

Grace clenched her hands in fists and ran upstairs, closed the door to her room, and got on the cell phone. She speed-dialed Ben, pacing as she waited for him to pick up. When he did, she lit into him. It was early afternoon in Portland and he was probably at Rigoletto’s, but she didn’t even care.

“How could you do this?” she asked. “How could you be such a thoughtless jerk?”

“Wait a second!” he replied. “What did I do that was thoughtless? I sent the cats down to you. Aren’t you glad to see them?”

“Of course I am!” she yelled. “That’s not the point. That guy who drove them down could have decided that it wasn’t worth the trouble and dumped them on the side of the road in Wyoming! Or he could have been some crazy who sells cats to labs for medical experiments.”

“Wouldn’t labs be interested in healthy cats?” Ben asked.

“It doesn’t matter—the point is, you didn’t know this guy from Adam. Why didn’t you at least tell me what you were doing?”

“Because I wanted to surprise you.”

She cursed under her breath.

“And I knew you’d have a cow,” he added, “which you are. For no reason. The cats obviously got there safe and sound.”

"Why did you feel the need to send them at all? The last time we spoke, I was talking about coming home this week. For all you knew, by the time the cats arrived, I wouldn't even be here."

"But you *are* there," he pointed out. "Sometimes I wonder if you're ever coming back."

She sighed in frustration. "So, this was a passive-aggressive move to get me to go back to Portland?"

"Maybe so." Uneasy silence crackled over the line until Ben spoke again. "Everything's fine here, Grace. You could even say your leaving has been good for me. I manned up to the challenge. The store's eking out a profit, the duplex is spic-and-span, and I feel good about that. But you know what? It wasn't supposed to be this way. We had finally decided to be together, remember? Instead, I've never felt more alone in my life. I miss you. I know you feel your dad needs you, but the fact is I need you, too."

As he spoke, the anger seeped out of her. She sat on her bed and then sank back on the mattress.

"What can I do?" she asked.

"Come home. It's crazy, you staying there so long."

"I know. I should just set a date . . ." Another one.

"But you should make it a do-or-die date, and make it realistic," he said. "Don't tell me you're coming the day after tomorrow and then freak out again because your dad stubs his toe or something."

"It's been a little more serious than that," she said.

"I know, I know," he said apologetically. "But I'm serious. By what date do you think you can get things arranged there and get yourself ready to come back?"

She bit her lip. "Thanksgiving?"

"That's a month away."

"I know. But I've promised Dad I'll be here for Thanksgiving anyway, because he wants everybody here. Even Sam's flying in. And that will give me time to get together with Steven and arrange things. He's even mentioned moving into the house here, so if we could find some day help . . ."

"Great!"

"And—oh!—you should come for Thanksgiving, too."

"I'm not sure about that."

"Why not?"

"It's a long way to go just to eat turkey," Ben said. "And what about Rigoletto's? Put on your capitalist thinking cap, Grace—Thanksgiving weekend? Black Friday? Do you really want to give that up?"

She took a deep breath. She had imagined him flying in and the two of them driving back together. He had sounded so eager to have her there.

A silence fell over the line . . . though it wasn't quite as silent as she would have liked. She could make out a rhythmic pulsing beat in the background . . . a tambourine . . . and was that a banjo? "What are you playing?"

"Just music," Ben answered in a staccato voice.

"But it's—"

"It's the Freelance Whales, okay? I put in an indie section. Just a small one. It's very popular."

"Oh."

And to think a few months ago she'd been worried he might play a Miles Davis record. Her line in the sand hadn't just been crossed, it had been obliterated and washed out to sea with the tide. Yet she couldn't bring herself to say a word of reproach. He was there and doing his best.

"I guess I could find someone to sub for me," Ben said, relenting. "Or maybe we will have to close the store for the weekend. But if it's important to you, Grace, I'll be there."

19

The End of the Story

After three months, Steven's new office still had an unfinished feel to it. The waiting room still bore the sharp smell of fresh paint and carpeting, and the walls were bare except for a single framed print of a dancer in an impossibly bendy position. Hard to tell whether this was meant to soothe, inspire, or taunt his patients.

"Would you like to speak to your brother?" Emily asked her.

"We're supposed to have lunch today."

"Dr. Oliver didn't tell me that. We're rather busy." When Grace glanced around the deserted waiting room, Emily looked at her with long-practiced patience. "He's in with his last morning patient now. Naturally I've blocked out the schedule for his lunch, but he only has thirty minutes."

"I'll try not to keep him late."

"Dr. Oliver's next appointment is at one."

"Do you always call him Dr. Oliver?" Grace asked her.

"Of course," Emily said.

"Never Steven?"

"No." Two red stains appeared in Emily's cheeks, but Grace couldn't tell if she was embarrassed or offended.

"Emily, how would you like to come to my father's house for Thanksgiving?"

Emily flinched a little. "I couldn't intrude."

"An invited guest isn't an intrusion." Grace laughed. "Unless your name is Uncle Truman."

Emily's blank stare sobered her, however, and Grace remembered Lou saying that he wanted the holiday just to be close friends and family. So maybe he would consider Emily an intruder. Then again, with her history littered with unhappy foster homes and group houses, if Emily didn't intrude on someone sometime, she would never get anywhere. Besides, she'd worked with Steven forever. That had to qualify her as a close . . . something.

"I appreciate the offer. . . ."

"It's more than an offer. I want you to be there."

Emily smiled so politely, it was maddening. The woman was a tough nut to crack. "If you'll just take a seat, I'll let Dr. Oliver know you're here the moment he is free."

It was twelve-thirty by the time that moment occurred. Grace was surprised Emily didn't drag the poor patient out bodily for this incursion on her carefully planned schedule. Steven came out, looking a bit harried himself. "We can grab a sandwich next door," he told Grace.

"I invited Emily over for Thanksgiving," she told him as they were in line to place their orders.

Steven frowned. "Why?"

She gave him a quick whack on the arm. "To be polite."

"What did she say?"

"She said no, but I want you to work on her. Make her change her mind."

"If she doesn't want to go . . ."

"She will, if you second the invitation."

"You mean if she's coerced?" He extracted a little bottle of orange juice from a hill of chipped ice.

"I've worked with Emily for years, Grace. She's the best admin worker I've ever come across—I'd be at sea without her. I don't want to upset her by forcing her into awkward social situations."

"Trust me, she's not going to quit over a meal at our house. Our family isn't that bad, is it?"

He darted a quick look at her and then placed his order.

When they were settled at a table, she decided she might as well plunge in with the plans she was making. Emily's clock was ticking away. "I'm leaving after Thanksgiving," she told him. "Back to Portland."

"That's good."

"So I was looking at your room the other day. We could get it painted and fixed up a little. Also, I should start looking for someone who could come in during the day."

His smile collapsed. "To tell the truth, I've decided against that."

"The home help? What else can we—"

"No, I mean I've decided against moving back home. I don't think that would work. It might sound selfish, after you've been here all these months, but I'm not sure that I would want to be pushing forty and living with my dad. It's not as if I'm looking to get married again—obviously, I'm not even divorced—but I don't quite want to give up the idea of any kind of social life in the future. And a man living with his father . . ."

Grace nodded. What he said made sense. It would be a little *Sanford and Son*ish. “We should be looking for a full-time person, then. Live-in, too.”

Something rumbled inside her just to think the words, much less say them. Their father would never go for this, even if they could find someone. But she couldn’t force Steven to move home against his will.

“I’ll ask around,” he said. “I’m sure some of the doctors I know have had to recommend home help for patients. There’s probably an agency that deals in this.”

“I wouldn’t want it to be someone different all the time. I think Dad would feel better with someone regular, who he could trust.”

“I know what you mean,” Steven said. “Just leave it to me.”

After ten more minutes, Steven had to get back to his patients, and she needed to get home in case her dad arrived home early. Truman and Peggy had driven him out to Llano to eat barbecue.

“Don’t forget to ask Emily,” she said as they parted.

“I won’t,” Steven promised. “But don’t expect her to come, Grace. She’d probably feel like the odd man out at our family gathering.”

Grace knew something about feeling like she didn’t quite belong at a family shindig. She also understood the longing to be there anyway. “Just ask her.”

• • •

That evening, as she stood on the back porch, wondering how she would ever work up the nerve to broach the subject of live-in home help with her dad, she caught sight of Ray dashing around his backyard. He was so tall that she could see the top of his head from her vantage point on the porch. Ray was hauling the ladder toward the pecan tree in the center of the backyard. Closer up, he looked a little demented.

"Are you going to pick pecans?" she asked. A lot of them were still wearing their green husks.

He halted in midmovement and darted glances all around, trying to pinpoint where the voice had come from. He spotted her and exhaled in relief. Maybe he'd thought he was hearing voices.

"I've been neglecting the bird feeders!" he said. "I haven't even thought about them."

She noticed there was one hanging from a large branch on the pecan tree. It was fairly high up.

"You'd better let me spot you on that ladder," she said.

"I'll be all right."

"Famous last words." She hopped down and came around the side of his yard and let herself in. On the other side of the fence, Iago was showing his discontent at being left behind by attempting to claw through the wood.

"I never once thought about the bird feeders till this morning," Ray said. "Can you believe that?

All these months—who knows what the birds have been living on."

"Well, it was summer. Now is the time when you *should* be tending to them, I think."

"Really?" He looked somewhat relieved as he crawled up the rungs and unhooked the house-shaped glass-and-wood structure. He climbed back down holding the bird feeder away from him with his fingertips.

"I assume birds survive okay in the warm weather just eating worms and whatnot," she said.

"I hope so," he answered, scoping out where the other feeders were. Now that Grace had an eye out, she spotted several. Ray headed for a hummingbird feeder hanging off the back porch. "Jen would have been able to say for sure. There wasn't a bird that came into this yard without her noticing it. She knew them all, and what they ate, and where they wintered."

"She was a bird-watcher?"

"A bird freak," he corrected. "She set up this backyard as a sort of private, open aviary." His gaze snagged on a birdbath full of leaves, pecan shells, and what looked like the petrified remains of an old baseball. He shook his head. "But now look at it. I wonder how long it took the birds to realize they needed to decamp."

"They'll come back," she said.

He furrowed his brow at her. "Do you know anything about birds?"

She laughed. “Zilch, actually.” Then she nodded at a bird feeder hanging off a linden tree by a window. “You missed one.”

He obediently moved the ladder. “I wonder how often I should be checking these things.”

“You could put Lily on it,” she said.

He swung his head around. “Lily?”

She nodded. “She lives to observe. She’s over at our house right now.”

“I know.” She squinted at him and he explained, “They leave me notes. I don’t know how to thank you for being so patient, letting them invade your home all the time.”

“No thanks necessary. Dad loves having them over. I do too.” She felt a pang about Ray, though, abandoned by his loved ones, rattling around the house all by himself, angsting about bird feeders. “I think they’re about to start watching *The Lord of the Rings*. Have you seen it?”

He laughed. “Asking a software engineer if he’s seen *The Lord of the Rings* is like asking him if he reads Dilbert or has ever tried Indian food. Jen and I had seen it twice by the end of opening weekend.”

She watched him unhook the feeder that looked like a little red barn. “Jennifer was an engineer?” She hadn’t known that. “Is that how you two finally got together? Work?”

He climbed down. “It was earlier, actually—in college.”

"You went to the same college?"

"We weren't supposed to. I went to Stanford, but then in my second year, my dad had a stroke and had to stop working, so I transferred to UT and lived at home to save money."

"That couldn't have been easy."

"No, it wasn't. Most of my friends from high school had left, and I was living at home, so I didn't really feel part of college life at first. Then one day as I was walking to my electromagnetics class, there was Jen in the hallway. I nearly walked right by her, until I heard her say my name. She was on her way to chemistry. We were taking some of the same courses, but in different sections. Later on we met in the student union and caught up. Her parents had moved to Little Salty, so I had lost contact with her for a while. She asked me if I was dating anyone—I thought this was my big chance—and then she told me she wanted to set me up with her roommate. Cheryl. So I went out with her roommate for a while."

Grace felt as if someone had slapped her. He had gone out with *someone else?* "Why?"

"Because Jen already had a boyfriend."

But Jennifer was your true love, she wanted to say. He was supposed to be a hopelessly devoted, tortured Olivia Newton-John man. Why would he have settled for Cheryl?

"It was sort of devious," he admitted. "I didn't like the guy Jen was going out with—he was a really slick business school guy. I thought if I kept an eye on him, I'd find out he was cheating on her. Sure enough, he was. After a while, it was really obvious. He was being incredibly edgy around the apartment, and sometimes he even looked guilty. And one time on campus I saw him making out with a girl—I couldn't see her, but I suspected it was not Jen.

"Afterward, I invited Jen out for a pizza—at Milto's—and she seemed distracted and upset. It was clear she knew. I was about to tell her what I knew, just to confirm her suspicions, when she suddenly blurted out, 'That bitch!' Really loud—right in the middle of the restaurant. Then she apologized for ever having introduced me to her."

"Who?" I asked.

"Cheryl," Ray explained. "It was Cheryl who Jen's boyfriend was cheating with. *Cheryl!* I couldn't believe it. He wanted Cheryl when he already had Jennifer. And at the same time, Jen said something like, 'I can't believe she'd rather go out with him than you!'

"Well, that stopped both of us. We sort of gaped at each other for what seemed like a minute or so, and then I said, 'But you preferred him, too.' And she said no, she didn't, and I said she obviously had because she had been going out with him and not me for five months, and she said that was because I had never asked her. And I explained that I hadn't asked her because I assumed she'd turn me down flat, and she said that was the stupidest thing she'd ever heard of, and I argued that it was actually perfectly logical since we'd known each other forever and had never dated. Then she repeated that if I had asked her that might not have been the case, and I replied that we'd never know now because it was all in the past, and she said it wouldn't be all in the past if I would just finally for once ask her out on a damn date. And then it struck me—she *really did want me to ask.* So I did."

Grace felt like a kid listening to a fairy tale. Never mind that she knew the ending, her attention was rapt. She just needed to hear the words. "And what did she say?"

"She looked at me like I was the biggest jerk in the world and practically yelled, 'What the hell took you so long!' " He grinned. "And that's how we finally got together."

And they all lived happily ever after.

For a while.

The sadness of his loss hit her full force.

"You two must have gotten married pretty soon after college," she said.

"The month after we graduated. Jen didn't want to wait to have a family. She was an only child and had always dreamed of having a big family, but at the same time, she wanted them all out of her hair by the time she was forty-five, when she would still be young enough to try skydiving or take trips to the Amazon without worrying about anything happening . . .”

As his words hung in the air, Grace’s smile faded, and she looked down.

Ray busied himself with birdseed. “Thanks for helping me,” he said. “I can manage on my own now.”

She didn’t want to go—though he clearly expected her to. Without thinking, she blurted out, “Would you like to come to Thanksgiving dinner with us?” At his look of surprise, she continued, “Dad wants to have all his friends and family over, and I’m sure he’s going to want to invite Dominic and Lily.”

“Thanks, but my in-laws mentioned coming down.”

“Oh. Well that’ll be even better, for the kids. And probably for you, too.” His expression seemed so serious, she worried she had embarrassed him. Or maybe he thought that she was being pushy, or God forbid, coming on to him. “I just thought I’d make sure you weren’t alone for the holiday. We’ll have lots of people coming over. My boyfriend is coming from Portland.”

“Your boyfriend?” He seemed startled, as if he didn’t expect that she would have one.

She nodded. “His name’s Ben. We live together.” He laughed, and she felt her cheeks burn. “Is that so hard to believe?”

“Well, it’s hard to believe you’re actually living

together when you're here and he's two thousand miles away."

"True, but it's only temporary. In fact, I'm probably going back with Ben after Thanksgiving. My being here was never supposed to be permanent."

"I couldn't imagine being away for so long from someone I love." He turned back to his tree. "Not voluntarily."

The implied criticism in his words hit her with a glancing sting. She felt like defending herself, but that was foolish. She didn't have to explain herself to this neighbor who didn't know the first thing about her.

Not knowing what else to say, she settled on "Well, I'm sure the birds will be back soon."

"What?" His head snapped up as if he had already forgotten she was there. "Oh, sure. Thank you for your help."

She wandered back to her side of the fence and was greeted by an ecstatic Iago. For the rest of the evening, and for much of the next few days, she felt a bitter regret for not clearing up the idea that she was somehow a bad person because she had abandoned Ben. Because she hadn't abandoned him, really. She had just extended her stay. And why should she feel compelled to justify her actions to Ray? She didn't care what he thought.

Besides, it wasn't as if he was the king of interpersonal relationships himself.

20

Heather's World

When Jordan got to her art class there was a notice on the board informing the students their teacher was sick and that this week's class was canceled.

As Jordan read the scrawled message, she was surprised by how disappointed she felt.

Heather wasn't the most inspiring art instructor in the world. Most Saturday mornings, she barely looked awake. Jordan always tried to arrive early with coffee; she liked to listen to Heather rattle on about all the stuff she'd been doing on Friday night. There was always someone's "show" she'd gone to, or else she'd been out hearing a band until the small hours. From the sound of things, going to bed before three was almost unheard of in Heather's world.

Heather's life was perfect. She just did what she wanted and didn't worry about what anyone thought of her. And she didn't pigeonhole people into little categories like most adults Jordan knew. Jordan had helped her haul a really heavy statue back to her apartment complex once, and the whole way there Heather never asked her boring questions about school, or her plans for college, or any of that crap. She'd just asked if she had a boyfriend, and when Jordan had answered no, Heather had said they'd have to work on that. *They'd* have to work on that. As if they were really friends.

She didn't have Heather's phone number, but luckily, she knew where she lived.

She took the bus as close as she could get to Heather's apartment and walked the rest of the way, stopping at a convenience store to buy a fresh coffee for Heather.

When she knocked, it took a minute to get an answer. Heather finally poked her head through the door, and Jordan let out a yip of surprise. Bloodshot eyes stared out at her from a pale, greenish face. Heather's wild hair was looking wilder than usual; several braids seemed to be stuck together.

"Oh, hey." Heather blinked her eyes like a rodent peeking out from its burrow. She brightened slightly at the sight of the cup. "Coffee—you're *so* welcome to come in with that." She stepped back, leaving the door open for Jordan to follow her.

Jordan hesitantly stepped across the threshold, wincing at a stench in the air.

Heather flopped on the couch, which was loaded with a pile of laundry. Clean, Jordan hoped. "Shut the door," Heather told her. "Buns could get out."

Buns was Heather's brown lop-eared rabbit, which had apparently been a bone of contention—

one of many—between Heather and Jed while they were married. Now Jordan could see why. There were round bunny poop pellets all over the place.

Heather took a slurp of coffee and then leaned back against her laundry, her elbow hooked over her eyes to shut out what little light managed to penetrate the blue plastic miniblinds.

"Class was canceled today," Jordan said. "I was worried."

"Were you? That's so sweet."

"Have you been to the doctor?"

"Christ, no. For a hangover?"

"Oh." Jordan relaxed a little. "I didn't know what was wrong. I thought you might be really sick or something."

"I might not be diseased, but I can swear that two hours ago I was truly sick."

Jordan's stomach turned. That's what the stink was. Vomit. And rabbit. And overflowing ashtrays.

Heather lifted her head. "You didn't happen to bring anything salty to eat, did you?"

"Uh, no."

Her head plopped back again. "Oh, well. Maybe we can send out for a pizza later." She sighed. "It's so nice you came to take care of me. I guess I really could use some help here."

Jordan hadn't realized she'd volunteered for "taking care" duty, or what that would entail. But

Heather did look bad. "I think you should open a window."

"Go to it, girl," she said, lying back. "I just need to rest my eyes a minute longer."

A minute later, snores rose from the couch.

Jordan didn't know what to do. It would be rude just to walk out. And Heather did feel bad, even if her illness was self-inflicted. She decided to tidy up.

Thirty minutes later, she was starting to feel as if she was making some headway. Finding an ancient pair of rubber gloves under the kitchen sink had emboldened her. She'd torn through the dirty dishes in the sink, hit the bathroom with a can of scrubbing bubbles, and done a poop pellet patrol through the apartment with the dustpan. Making as little noise as possible, she stacked papers and pushed clutter into already-overflowing drawers and closets. It was a superficial fix, but it looked better. Finally, she decided she needed to fire up the vacuum, but she hesitated to, fearing the noise would wake Heather or set off Buns's bowels, or both.

Heather, hearing the vacuum being rolled out of the bedroom closet, sat up and stretched. "Wow! Look at this place—you are a miracle worker."

Jordan glanced around. The discouraging thing was, it still looked like a dump.

"You know what I feel like?" Not waiting for Jordan to answer, Heather continued, "Chinese food. Tell you what—while you run the vacuum, I'll hop in the shower and then we can go to this great buffet I know. All you can eat for four ninety-nine. It'll be my treat."

An hour later, Jordan was slumped in a booth at Ho House, staring at a plate of sweet and sour chicken with sauce so orange it glowed.

"Is that all you're getting?" Heather asked, flopping down opposite her. Her plate was loaded down with food—fried rice and gloppy, greasy entrees as well as a pyramid of egg rolls. Jordan didn't see how someone could possibly expect to eat that much, especially with a hangover.

Eyes furtively scanning the restaurant, Heather produced a large Ziploc baggie. With hand movements as fast and direct as a frog's tongue, she transferred all the egg rolls to the baggie and then hid it in her purse.

"I don't think you're supposed to do that," Jordan warned.

Heather rolled her eyes. "These places always have tons of leftover food anyway."

"Yeah, but—"

"Hey, I'm not a millionaire. I gotta take what I can get."

Jordan frowned. She'd never been so poor that she needed to steal food.

When Jordan didn't answer her, Heather chuckled. "You're cute, you know that?"

"Cute?"

Heather gasped under the power of a brainstorm. "You should come to my place for Thanksgiving! You could be my Little Sister—for my parents. They're coming down from Denver."

Jordan tried but failed to understand. "Won't your parents remember that you don't have a little sister?"

"I don't mean a *real* little sister, I mean, a *Little Sister* little sister. You know—the program that pairs an older person with a kid? See, it's important because . . . well, long story short, I've had to borrow a little money off my folks and they *never* would have given it to me if I'd just asked for myself. They'd have just gone all tough love on my ass. So what I did was, I made up an underprivileged Little Sister to tell my parents about so they'd lend me money to help *her.* So now maybe if they saw this underprivileged Little Sister, preferably looking kind of scrungy, they'd feel like they should help some more."

"Wait a sec," Jordan said. "You'll tell your parents that you've been spending money on *me?*"

"Well, not *you,* actually, but the person you'll be representing, yeah. Mostly to help pay for your ear operation."

"What?"

Heather's eyes lit up. "Yes! That's it—it would be so cool if you could just pretend to be a little bit hard of hearing."

"I don't know . . ."

Heather leaned forward. "You're not offended, are you? I mean, it's not like you really are a poor deaf kid. That would be exploitive."

"But this is a big lie," Jordan pointed out.

Her new friend let out a sharp cackle. "Right, but it's lying for a good cause—me!"

Jordan couldn't help smiling.

"Please say you'll come—it will be miserable if you don't," Heather said. "My parents are both CPAs. If you're not there, the whole afternoon's going to feel like The Attack of the Phil Collins People."

Jordan laughed. "What are you going to have? For Thanksgiving, I mean. Are you going to make a turkey and all that?"

Heather laughed. "If you'd pitch in here, we might just have a great big platter of frozen egg rolls."

As Heather was driving Jordan home, her ancient Geo Metro started belching smoke from the hood, but Heather didn't seem to notice. She didn't seem to notice her windshield had a sunlike crack that made her have to lift herself up and crane her neck to see over it, either.

"Is that normal?" Jordan asked.

"Is what normal?"

"The smoke."

Heather lifted her shoulders in a careless shrug. "It goes away sometimes."

"Sometimes?"

Heather glanced at her sidewise. "I guess I should get it fixed, huh? The trouble is, once you start fixing things, it never ends."

Jordan knew something was faulty in that logic, but she couldn't pinpoint what exactly. She tried not to be judgmental, but she wasn't in the best of moods.

Heather glanced at her warily. "Hey, I'm *really* sorry about the buffet thing, Jordan. I swear—I've been going there for years and I've never gotten caught. It was just bad luck. And I had no idea that restaurant owner was so insane. The way he treated you!"

Jordan shuddered in humiliation as she remembered the angry Chinese owner threatening to call the police and making Heather upend her huge purse. When all those egg rolls had spilled out, Jordan would gladly have sunk through the floor, but Heather just shook her head and acted amazed that the egg rolls had managed to find their way into her bag.

They'd offered to pay the owner—Mr. Ho, evidently—an extra five dollars to keep him from calling the police. He took the five dollars, but then had insisted on calling Jordan's parents. Jordan had experienced an awful flashback to last March; she just couldn't bear the idea of someone calling her father and telling him she'd screwed up again. So she'd resorted to a desperate measure—the first thing that had popped into her head.

A few weeks earlier, she'd been trying to reach Dominic and had run him down by telephone at the professor's house next door. She had programmed the number on her phone.

So, with Mr. Ho hovering over her, she'd whipped her phone out and speed-dialed the number. Thank heavens Grace picked up, though she sounded confused when Jordan blurted out, "Hi, *Mother,* it's me, *Jordan.*"

"What?" Grace asked.

Jordan's voice had trembled. "I'm in trouble again. I'm so sorry—but could you please please please talk to this restaurant owner, Mr. Ho, and tell him that I'm not a thief?"

"What? *What?* What's happened?" Grace sputtered.

"He wants to know that I'll be disciplined at home so he won't *call the police.*"

"Oh my God . . ."

"Please, Mother?"

Taking a deep breath, she handed the phone over to the Chinese dude.

Jordan had worried that Grace would blow it, but it turned out she barely had a chance to. Mr. Ho started shouting down the phone, declaring that if he ever saw Jordan in his restaurant again he would call the police and have her hauled off to jail. Then, in his anger, he'd hung up before handing the phone back to Jordan. She hadn't had a chance to talk to Grace again, which was probably just as well.

"So have you thought any more about Thanksgiving?" Heather asked her, as they pulled onto Jordan's street.

"You really want me to come?"

"Would your folks mind—I mean, your dad?"

Jordan had told her that her mom and her sister had died in an accident, but she hadn't given her all the details.

"Probably. But I don't care."

Heather stopped where Jordan told her to, across the street from the house. She started to get out of the car, but the door was stuck, compelling Heather to go around and open it from the outside. When Jordan stepped out, Heather gave her a big hug. "Remember, we've got a date. Hasta luego!"

Heather got back behind the wheel, but when she turned the key, the car wouldn't start. She tried again several times, but the engine would just let out a few mechanical growls and then fall silent. Jordan looked over and saw that woman Grace heading toward them.

Great.

Finally, the engine made a reluctant whirring sound and picked up. With a grinding of gears and a wave, Heather rattled off down the street, streaming smoke like an old locomotive.

"What is going on?" Grace asked. "What was that man on the phone saying? I could barely make out a word."

"Nothing—it was so stupid. The guy caught Heather stuffing an egg roll in her purse and had a cow."

Grace stared after the smoke-belching car. "Was that your partner in crime?"

"Yeah. She's my painting teacher at ACC."

"Your painting teacher takes you out to steal food? Geez, Jordan."

Jordan rolled her eyes. "Yeah, *geez,* someone who doesn't treat me like a pariah. Must be something wrong with her!"

"She could have gotten you arrested!" Grace said. "As it is, this whole situation's put me in an awkward position."

"I should have guessed," Jordan huffed. "You're going to run squealing to my dad. That will be great. Really cheer him up!"

"*You* might have thought of that earlier," Grace said.

"I didn't do anything! I told you, the owner was just being a dick. Is that a good reason to cause a family crisis? You think my dad doesn't have enough to worry about? That his year hasn't been bad enough already?"

Grace frowned, and Jordan could tell she was getting through to her. Finally. "Okay, I won't say anything to him," she said. "But please don't do this to me again. And you really should be careful about who you're friends with."

"Heather's okay—she's just going through a rough patch," Jordan said.

"She's sort of old to be running around with, isn't she?"

Jordan felt her spine stiffen. "What would you know about it?"

They watched the Metro make a squealing left-hand turn at the intersection. It exhaled another cloud of black before disappearing from sight.

"She should have that car worked on," Grace said. "It's an environmental disaster."

"Thank you, Madame Earth Muffin!"

Grace shook her head. "You make it seriously hard for people to like you, don't you?"

Jordan's cheeks felt hot. *Your mother always said you were a difficult child to love. . . .*

"I just don't care whether they like me or not," she declared.

"That's not a very pleasant attitude," Grace said.

Jordan snickered. "It's not pleasant to be a hemorrhoid, either, yet here you are."

While the shock was still fresh on Grace's face, Jordan stalked away. Just because the woman had done her a piddling little favor, that didn't give her the right to tell her how to live her life.

21

T-DAY MINUS ONE

When Sam appeared at the mouth of the airport concourse, he clasped Grace to his muscular, wiry frame for a marathon hug and then presented her with a ridiculously large bouquet of flowers that he swore he'd held in his lap the entire flight. "I bought them as I was running to catch my connection in Newark," he explained, "but I think they began life in Columbia."

"They're better traveled than me," she said.

He arched a dark brow. "What, better traveled than the Christopher Columbus of the Oliver family?"

She whacked him playfully with a tip of a carnation.

She'd always had a soft spot for Sam. Maybe it was because he was the closest in age to her—albeit the farthest in geography. She sometimes felt that if she dropped off the face of the earth, none of her other brothers or Natalie would notice. But Sam would. Even though he hadn't always been there during the few holidays she'd spent in Austin, or during the summer visits to her dad's, Sam had always kept up with her life, and he was known to nag her about working too much or not having enough of a social life . . . the very things that his own life suffered from. But e-mails and telephone calls couldn't compare to the fun of seeing him in person. It always felt like running into a long-lost friend.

Having him here, she started to feel excitement about the holiday. A real Oliver holiday—she hadn't been here for one of those in years. Only now that she'd had a hand in organizing Thanksgiving, she felt at the center of it all instead of just being a drop-in guest.

On the drive back, she listened as Sam caught her up on all his news. His paper was squeezing out the foreign offices all the time, so he was worried about losing his assignment. "I might end up in L.A. churning out copy about Lady Gaga."

"Good—I'd probably read you more often. Although we both know that you'll never come back to this side of the world as long as Seeger's in . . . where is he now?"

He slumped a little. "Malawi."

Poor Sam. When it came to Seeger Johnson, Sam had a little Olivia Newton-John man in him. He had been lucky enough to find a kindred spirit as an adolescent; unfortunately, he and Seeger had spent their entire lives not quite managing to live in the same place. Or even on the same continent.

"I heard from him a few weeks ago," he said. "He still hopes to get the tree planting project funded by the Malawi government. Now he'll never leave that place." Seeger, who actually listed environmentalist as his profession on his tax return, had been working for years on a project called Trees Across Africa. "The man's a disgusting idealist with a Johnny Appleseed complex."

"You've got a little bit of that in you too, don't you?"

He turned, drawing back. "Me? I observe. I analyze."

"Okay, but you *aren't* in L.A. writing about celebrities. You're where the trouble is."

"The difference is, I prefer to keep a safe distance, especially if there's the slightest chance of cholera."

She shook her head.

"Oh God, let's not talk about my problems anymore." He shot her a wry look. "Let's talk about Steven's. Is he going to be moping the whole holiday?"

"I doubt it. I think he's mostly over Denise, but you know Steven. He's not exactly Mr. Emotive. He reminds me a little of Ray, but of course I think Steven has blocked Denise from his mind, while Ray—"

Sam stopped her. "Wait, wait—back up a moment. Who is Ray?"

"Our neighbor. I mean, Dad's neighbor."

His brows lifted. "And?"

"And it's not what you're thinking," she said. "He's a widower, he's still grieving, he's got three kids. I e-mailed you about them—Dominic and Lily."

"That's *two* kids."

"Oh, there's this other girl, but we've never hit it off. In fact, last time I saw her she called me a hemorrhoid."

"What does *that* mean?"

She'd been wondering that herself. "I haven't the foggiest idea. But it can't be good, can it?"

He laughed, but in the ensuing silence, it became clear that they'd been tap dancing around the person who was really on their minds. "How is he?" Sam asked.

She didn't have to ask who *he* was. They'd talked about everyone else. "Dad's fine." In spite of her words, Sam looked anxious. "You might not even notice anything wrong at first," she told him. "Or at all, if it's a good weekend. Keep your fingers crossed."

"But you guys still think he needs live-in help?"

At the mention of this topic, her grip on the steering wheel tightened. "We've finally found someone." Here, it was harder for her to sound upbeat. "She seems very nice."

"Who is she? What's her name?"

"Her name's Darla Swinton."

Sam's mouth set in a grim line. "What's she like?"

"She's very nice."

"And?"

"Well—you know. She's had some nursing

experience, then she lost her husband and she wanted a change."

"But what's she like? Does she have a sense of humor?"

"She's a home-care nurse, Sam. She's not a comedian."

"But does Dad like her?"

"During their one meeting, Dad barely said a word," Grace answered truthfully. "He's still resistant to the whole idea. But once I'm gone . . ."

She hated saying the words *he'll get used to it.* It felt as if he were a person who'd lost all independence, and that they were condemning him to a life he'd hate. "I don't want to leave him."

Sam sent an alarmed look over at her. "But you are. Scruffy Ben's coming down to take you back with him, isn't he?"

"Yeah. Once I drop you off at the house, I have to turn around and go right back to the airport and pick him up."

"Do I detect a lack of enthusiasm in your tone?"

"It's not because of Ben," she assured him. "It's because I'll be going back with him. To Portland. I always hated leaving Austin. You know that."

He smiled faintly as he squinted into the windshield. "Dad always tried diversion tactics to get you back on the plane to Oregon—as if a quick jaunt to the ice cream shop or a bookstore would make you forget you were going to the airport."

"It worked when I was little. Then one time

when I was around twelve we ended up at Holiday House with me wailing into a milkshake for an hour. That was the end of the bait-and-switch."

"But you're okay with going back this time, right? You've made your decision."

She had—or thought she had—but when the reality of leaving hit her she felt less resolute. "I hate it." She reached down to her purse for a tissue and shot Sam a warning look. "No cracks."

Sam darted his left hand toward the steering wheel. "I won't make fun of you for being weepy if you promise to stay in your lane."

She laughed.

"You're doing the right thing," he told her. "You've got a great life in Portland. Your cool store, family number two, friends, and let's not forget scruffy Ben . . ."

"But when I think of Dad, none of that seems to matter."

"Believe me, it matters," Sam said. "You're lucky you've found someone who wants to live with you. You don't know what it feels like to wake up and have no one . . ." Sam muttered a curse and reached for a Kleenex.

"But that's just the problem," Grace told him. "I keep thinking about Dad waking up feeling that way. He'll be so alone. Some days he probably won't see anyone but this Darla Swinton person. Or maybe he'll have a visit from Uncle Truman to look forward to."

Sam sank against the passenger door. "God, that's gruesome."

Because Sam's plane had been a little late, Grace barely had time to drop him off at the house before she needed to turn around to retrieve Ben. Foreboding took hold of her, though, as she drove up to the house and found Muriel Blainey practically blocking her way into the drive.

"Hello, Grace!" Starched and pressed in autumn hues, Muriel darted a glance at Sam and walked right up to the car before Grace even had a chance to get out. "Hello, Sam. You probably don't remember me."

He smiled, but the split-second gap between his mouth opening and his words said it all. "Who could forget?"

She came nose-to-nose with Grace as Grace was trying to help unload Sam's stuff. "I was just wondering what you were having tomorrow."

Grace straightened. "Turkey."

"Well, yes, I assumed . . . but do you need me to bring anything?"

Grace gaped at the woman, trying to compute what she was saying. "Food, you mean?"

"When I bumped into Lou, he didn't mention what I should bring."

Her father had invited Muriel to the family dinner? *Muriel?* To the dinner that he had insisted should be only family?

"What about John?" Grace asked, referring to

the rarely-sighted Mr. Muriel. "Is he coming, too?"

"Unfortunately, he had to stay in California." In the next second, Muriel was back to food. "I'd be happy to make my mother's Jell-O salad recipe. It's old school, but it's always a big hit, especially when I make it in my special holiday turkey mold."

"Yum!" Sam exclaimed, almost managing to cover his sarcasm.

Grace shot him an exasperated glance. She was still trying to come to terms with Muriel getting invited. When had her dad invited her? How had they bumped into each other?

Something about that struck her as odd. "Where exactly did you bump into Dad?"

"He was out walking—over past Koenig Lane."

Grace froze in panic. That was almost a mile away. "Did he have Iago with him?"

"Oh, yes."

"Okay." Grace looked over the roof of the car at Sam. "Let's go dump this stuff."

Muriel glanced from one to the other. "Is something wrong?"

"No—not really," Grace said. Apart from Lily, she hadn't told anyone in the neighborhood about her father's illness. She hadn't felt it was her place to blab to her father's friends and neighbors about his diagnosis, and she certainly didn't want to go into it with Muriel now. "I just worry about him walking that far on his bum leg."

"Oh! I didn't think about that," Muriel said. "I should have offered him a ride, I guess. Though I don't usually like having dogs in the car."

"It's okay," Grace said.

She prayed it *was* okay as she nodded to Sam to start heading toward the house.

"What about the Jell-O salad?" Muriel asked.

"Fantastic," Grace told her. She couldn't have cared less about food right now.

"What time tomorrow?"

"Noon."

"Though you'll probably want me to come a little early, right?"

"No, not really," Grace said, too distracted to candy-coat things.

Inside the house, she dropped Sam's suitcase and gave her hysteria free rein. "We've got to find Dad," she said. "Now."

"Grace, you need to get back to the airport."

She stopped in her tracks. The airport. Ben. She'd forgotten.

She shouldn't have left her dad alone so long! He'd insisted he didn't want to go out, though, and that he'd be fine. How could she have been so stupid?

And to think she was worried that Darla Swinton wouldn't take good care of him!

"You go to the airport," Sam said. "I'll go look for Dad. He probably just wanted to stretch his legs."

"You'll need the car." There was only one car. She looked at her watch. "I have time."

As they prowled the streets, worry and frustration ate at her. Her father had said he was going to lie down before Sam showed up. Why had he suddenly decided to take off?

"What if he gets hit by a car again?" she asked, hugging the steering wheel and peering out the side window.

"He might be hit by you if you don't keep your eye on the road," Sam said. "Just drive. I'll look."

At that moment, Grace mashed on the brake. Peggy and Truman were walking down the sidewalk, hand in hand. They looked over, startled by her squealing of tires, and practically jumped apart when they saw who it was hanging out the opened window.

"Dad's missing!" she blurted out.

Sam got out and poked his head over the roof. "He wandered off on a walk."

"So?" Truman asked.

Peggy elbowed him. "It's good to see you, Sam." Then she assured Grace, "Don't worry about your father. We'll get the car and look for him, too. I've got your cell phone number."

Grace felt like weeping in gratitude. "Thank you!" She accelerated, forgetting about Sam being half in and half out until she heard his cry of alarm. He was about to duck back into the car when she told him to shout after them that Lou had last been seen at Koenig Lane. He did this and then sank back into the passenger seat, blowing out a breath.

They zigzagged around the neighborhood, peering around each street and yard and asking anyone they saw if they'd seen an old man walking a fuzzy basset hound. No one had.

"We're on the wrong track," Grace said after ten minutes of this.

"Maybe I should go home and wait while you drive out to the airport," Sam suggested.

She shook her head. "You take the car, and I'll take the bus to the airport."

"But—"

Grace wasn't willing to argue the point. "And keep looping by the house regularly to see if he's shown up there."

They switched sides and Sam dropped her off at a bus stop just as a bus was pulling up.

"We'll find him, Grace," he assured her.

"I'll be back as soon as I can," she said.

She boarded the bus and rode it to the capitol building, where she had to get on the airport shuttle. Luck was with her. It was waiting right there.

She bit back the urge to tell the driver to step on it and flopped on a seat near the front of the empty bus, which started its journey just as her phone rang. It was Peggy.

"Grace, we found him. He's with us."

Grace nearly collapsed in relief. In that moment, the animosity she'd felt toward Peggy all these months disappeared. At least she'd come through in the pinch. "Thank you so much!"

"We're driving back to the house now."

As she was hanging up, Grace saw a message on her phone she hadn't noticed. It was a text from Ben that had come a few hours before. She had accidentally left her phone on vibrate until she'd turned on the ringer, hoping for news about her dad. Ben had probably texted to let her know his plane was delayed.

She decided to call Sam first and tell him the good news.

"Thank God," he said. "I'm going to go home and root through the liquor cabinet now."

"Leave a little for me," she said.

After she'd hung up, she looked at her phone again. As she scrolled down Ben's text, her forehead furrowed in confusion.

Not on plane. I'm so sorry.

She pressed speed dial. On the other end, the phone rang and rang. She hung up, stewed for ten seconds, then dialed again. When there was no answer, she sank back in frustration and watched suburban Austin whiz by through the window for a block. The third time she called, Ben picked up.

"Okay, Grace," he said, as if they were already midargument, "I'm sorry. Okay?"

"What happened?"

"I have to go to Seattle. In fact, I'm halfway there now."

Halfway to *Seattle?* "What's in Seattle?"

"Amber. She's all alone up there during the holiday, and swamped with school stuff besides."

Grace would have laughed if she hadn't been so irritated. "Are you going there to help her study?"

"She needs me, Grace."

"Why?"

His long sigh crackled over the line. "Nobody knows this yet but me. Amber's pregnant."

The response threw Grace. And, frankly, she couldn't help feeling a little hurt. She and Amber used to be good friends, but they'd barely communicated at all since Grace left Portland. She hadn't even e-mailed her the big news. "Why would she tell you this?"

"Because." When he realized *because* wasn't enough, Ben confessed, "Because I'm the father."

"What?"

"I knew you were going to react this way."

"What way?"

"Mad."

But she hadn't been mad. She'd just been shocked. Flabbergasted.

Now she got mad. "For God's sake!"

"You left, Grace. You've been gone forever."

"For *five months.*" She sputtered wordlessly before asking, "What happened? Only a month ago you were begging me to go back to Portland.

Thanksgiving was going to be our big reunion."

"I know." He sighed. "The truth is, the thing with Amber happened before."

"Before you asked me to come back?" she said, her voice finally reaching toward hysteria. "Before we made plans for today?"

"The thing with Amber was nothing," he said.

"Obviously not!"

"She'd just come down one weekend to get those boxes in our basement," he explained. "And I was feeling lonely, and so was she, so—"

Grace cut him off. "I get the picture."

"I thought that was the end of it. Obviously. But now, with the kid . . ." He sighed. "I asked you to come home all summer, Grace."

"But I didn't know you meant that if I didn't come home you would get our mutual friend pregnant!"

The bus driver, a woman, glanced up at her through the rearview mirror.

"You'd been gone so long, Grace," Ben said. "How was I to know what was going through your mind?"

"By asking me!"

"I did—and you always set dates for returning and then broke them. How could I be sure that *you* weren't seeing someone down there, like that Ray guy."

"That's absurd! How do you even know about him?"

"Because you talk about him and those stupid kids *all the time.* Every time we talked, you mentioned them."

For some reason, hearing Ben refer to Dominic and Lily as *those stupid kids* made her madder than anything else. "You are crazy and wrong, but it doesn't matter anymore. I don't even want to talk to you right now."

"Fine. You don't have to talk to me ever, if you don't want to," he announced. "I'm moving to Seattle."

Grace felt as if her heart should have been breaking at the announcement, but her first thought was, *Who's going to take care of Rigoletto's?*

When she finally hung up the phone, the bus was pulling into the airport. "Do I get a price break for taking a round trip without getting off?" she said to the driver.

Eyeing her through the mirror, the driver pursed her lips. "Sounds like if the city of Austin doesn't give you a break today, nobody will."

22

The Pleasure of Her Company

Maybe she just hadn't been paying attention, but when she came home from school Wednesday afternoon and saw the Ford Focus in the driveway, Jordan was stunned. She scooted in the front door, heard voices in the kitchen, and flew up the stairs before anyone could see her.

She darted into her room, shut the door behind her, and dove onto the futon lying on the bare floor. *Why didn't anyone warn me they were coming?* Granny Kate and Pop Pop hadn't acknowledged her existence since kicking her out of their house. God, this was going to be so awful.

Plus, she'd promised to go to Heather's for Thanksgiving, which was going to be awkward to explain to her grandparents after they'd driven all this way to visit.

Her door opened and she held her breath until she saw that it was just Dominic. "Why didn't anyone tell me that Granny Kate and Pop Pop were coming for Thanksgiving?" she asked him. "I just assumed we'd skip it."

"Skip Thanksgiving?" Dominic's eyes bugged.

"Are you crazy? Why would we do that? Granny Kate brought a little turkey and two pies."

"I made plans to go to a friend's house. How am I going to explain? Everybody'll be so pissed off."

"Couldn't you cancel?" Dominic asked. He sank down next to her. "It'll be awful if you're not here."

Those big eyes under that brown mop of his made her reach over and muss his hair. "Aw, Nickel—you're probably the only person in this whole world who would say that."

"I'm serious," he said, ducking away from her hand. "I'll be really bummed if it's just me and Lily."

She sank down onto her elbows, giving him a playful shove with her foot. "You'll forget about me the second you see a pecan pie."

"I will not."

She laughed.

"This really bites!" he said. "It's our first Thanksgiving without Mom and Nina. And we don't get to go over to Grace's house. And now you're not even going to be here."

"Why would you want to go to Grace's for Thanksgiving?"

"Grace and the professor are really nice. And Iago's there."

"Okay—spending a holiday with the dog, I can see. But wanting to go to an interminable family dinner with that 'rhoid and her pompous daddy? No, thanks."

“You don’t even know them,” Dominic argued.

“Thank God.”

To her surprise, he jumped up, angry. “Fine! Go wherever you want to go. You’re going to get in trouble for it, though.”

She watched him stomping away, and laughed. “What did I say to get you in a huff?”

He slammed her door.

“Dominic, don’t be mad!” she called after him.

A second later, *his* door slammed.

She lay back again and weighed her options. She could cancel on Heather, but that would really suck, because she’d probably actually have fun there . . . at least more fun than she was going to have with her own family. But if she didn’t cancel her plans with Heather, she was going to be everybody’s anger sponge here at home. But then if she did cancel and stay home, she would probably be in a pissed-off mood all day and end up cheesing everybody off anyway.

As usual, she couldn’t win.

Lily poked her head in.

“No, don’t bother to knock,” Jordan told her. “It’s just my room.”

“What did you say to make Dominic so angry?” Lily asked.

“*Nothing.* He’s just being a little emotion monkey today.”

“You must have said *something.*”

“Do you think I’d tell you anyway? You’d just

run to your lame little diary and scribble it all down."

"I only write down thought-provoking things," Lily said.

God, it was so hard to believe that they sprang from the same loins. There had to have been a mistake—a hospital switch or something. Maybe somewhere in the world Mr. and Mrs. Bug-Up-Their-Butts were wondering how they had lucked into such a cool daughter instead of the four-eyed little priss pants who rightfully should have been theirs.

"So, are you going to tell me or not?" Lily persisted. "What's going on?"

"*Nothing.* Dominic's bent out of joint because I told a friend that I'd go to her house tomorrow for Thanksgiving dinner."

"But Granny Kate and Pop Pop are here!"

Jordan rolled her eyes. "Yeah, thanks, figured that out."

"Dad's going to be really mad."

"Why should *he* get upset? He sees me every day. Not that he wants to, of course."

"That has nothing to do with it," Lily argued. "It's about decorum. He'll be mad that you've offended Granny Kate and Pop Pop. Especially after last summer."

Jordan rose to her feet. "Okay, yes, I suck. So before you feel the need to go playing town crier with that bulletin, let me just go tell them myself."

"There's no reason to get persnickety," Lily said.

Could she be any more annoying? "If you keep talking like that your tongue is going to get stuck in permanent geek mode. Repeat after me: *There's no reason to be pissy.*"

"I don't like pissy," Lily said. "It's vulgar. I like persnickety."

"Fine. Doom yourself to freakdom. I've done my best."

"I'm not a freak!"

Jordan laughed. Lily's face turned red and she did an about-face and stomped to her room. Another door slammed.

Sighing, Jordan picked up her phone and called Heather. She was still wavering over what to do when her friend picked up.

"Oh, good!" Heather said as soon as she heard her voice. "I've been meaning to call you. We're going to need food. Do you have anything?"

"Um, I guess I could scrounge something." She felt pulled in the other direction now. "So you're still expecting me?"

"Of course! You're going to be the life of the party. Maybe the only life." When Jordan didn't even chuckle, Heather asked, "There's no problem, is there?"

"Not really. It's just that my grandparents showed up."

"Good, they'll be company for your gloomy dad."

"They'll add to his gloom, more like."

Heather sighed. "Well, don't angst. This year will suck, but by next Thanksgiving your dad will have found somebody else."

Jordan froze. "What do you mean, 'somebody else'? Who?"

"Just anybody. Believe me, it won't be long."

Jordan tried to laugh. "You don't know my dad. He and my mom were together forever. Since elementary school! I don't think he was ever with anybody else. He was devoted to her—still is."

"God, that's sad." Heather let out a long breath. "Still—happens all the time. Think of Paul McCartney. His fantastic vegetarian wife who he was completely devoted to for years and years died, and then lickety-split he married that one-legged model. *Huge* mistake. But the guy couldn't help himself. Men don't do lonely."

For some reason, the whole idea made her furious. "You can't compare my dad to Paul McCartney! The one good thing about Dad is that he *really* loved my mom."

Heather backed off. "Chill, okay? Maybe your old man *is* different," she conceded. "I'm just sayin', life might be grim now, but just wait till the stepmom shows up."

Jordan bristled. The idea that some strange woman would sashay into their mom's house made her physically sick. How could her dad be that fickle?

Suddenly, she laughed. “God! The woman doesn’t exist yet, and already I hate her.”

“Oh, she exists—she just might not have materialized yet. Or maybe she has and you don’t know it.”

Jordan frowned.

“So . . . you think you could bring eats tomorrow?” Heather asked.

“Sure,” Jordan said, absently twisting a strand of hair around a finger. “I’ll find something.”

“Great! And don’t forget—dress scrungy.”

After she hung up, Jordan squared her shoulders and marched down the stairs before she could chicken out. Granny Kate, Pop Pop, and her dad were all sitting around the kitchen table, drinking some of the diet soft drinks that Granny Kate always brought with her. The three of them looked up in surprise when she came in.

“Hi, folks.”

“Well, hello there,” Pop Pop said, amiably enough.

Granny Kate didn’t really greet her, except to ask, “What was all that door slamming upstairs about?”

“Me, of course,” Jordan confessed. “I’ve screwed up again. I promised a friend I’d go over to her house tomorrow and eat lunch with her family, and Dominic and Lily think you’ll feel insulted that I’m abandoning you.”

There was a split second of silence—a catch in

the air—and then Granny Kate said, "Of course we won't be insulted."

Pop Pop smiled at Jordan. "If you've made a promise, you've made a promise."

Her father's expression remained neutral for a moment as he studied Pop Pop and Granny Kate, then he looked back at Jordan, his lips tweaking into a little smile.

And that's when she knew. They weren't angry, or disappointed.

They were *glad.* Relieved.

Relieved that she wouldn't be there.

"We just want you to have a good holiday," Granny Kate said.

Her grandparents both beamed dopey grins at her. It was the happiest she'd seen them since the accident.

23

Four Kinds of Pie

The mattress sank and squeaked, waking Grace with a start. Her eyes popped open; she was so tired it felt as if her eyelids were being dragged across sand.

She lifted onto her elbows and discovered Sam poised on the edge of her bed like Rodin's *Thinker.*

"What is it?" she asked.

He glanced at her with red eyes. "Why didn't you tell me?"

"Tell you about what?"

He drew back. "About Dad! He's *really* not doing well at all."

She shot up to sit. "Has anything happened?"

"Grace, he got lost!"

She dropped back against the pillows. *Yesterday.* "I was worried that something was going on now."

"I didn't realize it was this bad," Sam said.

His words made her want to pull her hair out. Hadn't he been reading her e-mails? Or listening during phone calls?

He sat up straighter. "I've made my decision, Grace. I'm coming home. For good."

She tilted a skeptical glance at him.

"What?" he asked. "Why shouldn't I?"

"Because you'd go crazy here, for one thing. And you and Dad don't even get along all that well when you're together. It's not like you would be a soothing presence."

"I'm bound to be better than this Darla What's-Her-Name."

"No, you won't. Because she at least has training dealing with old people. She won't start weeping when Dad forgets the word for broccoli."

He looked offended. "That just took me by surprise."

"All along, I've told you what's been happening."

"I know, but I didn't expect him to have deteriorated so quickly. He even looks rumply. When was the last time he got his hair cut?"

"A few weeks ago. I don't like to badger him. He really hates being nagged."

"Tough. It's for his own good."

His imperious tone irked her. "He's not a different person, Sam. He still has a will of his own."

"If he's the same person, I doubt he would want to look as if he slept in his clothes." He shook his head. "Anyway, there's no reason I can't take care of him as well as anyone else. He'll hate a home-care person, and you . . . well, you've already had your life screwed up completely by this."

At that moment, Grace would have liked to whip the covers over her head and pretend to be invisible. She'd barely slept last night for chewing over what Ben had done. Now she had to deal with Sam envisioning himself as Florence Nightingale. And Thanksgiving. Why had she even woken up?

Sam glanced over at her, eyes narrowed and forehead scrunched. "Grace, you're crumpling again."

She sat up straighter. Poor Sam. She'd cried on Sam's shoulder most of yesterday. "I just don't know what I'm going to do now."

"What do you mean? It's decided. You're going to go home and get back to your store and your friends and that other family in Oregon. I'm going to stay here."

"You can't, Sam. You have a fabulous job, a dream job. You would be wasted here. What would you do for work?"

He shrugged, but she could see the dread that lay behind his stoicism. "I'll find something. I imagine I can land some local gig and write about city planning commissions and the school lunch menus."

She shook her head. "There's no point. We've got Darla. And even if you moved here and found a job, we'd still need her." But in her mind, she was thinking, *On the other hand,* I *could stay.* "Anyway, you and Dad together are a train wreck."

"That was before." Her expression must have been doubtful, because he lifted his chin. "Look, I'll prove it. You've got enough to do today. Let me take care of Dad."

"Sam, Dad was looking forward to your visit so he could hang out with you. Not so you could harass him about his hair."

"I know how to be tactful," he said, growing as prickly as their father would have under the circumstances. "Besides, you've got enough to worry about with dinner."

"That's practically all done."

He sent her an incredulous look. "You've mastered the art of cooking in your sleep?"

"I didn't sleep. I got up in the middle of the night last night and loaded up the turkey. It's already baking. In fact, it should be done soon."

"A little early, isn't it?"

"Better too soon than too late." At least, that's what she had been thinking at four in the morning. She went through the checklist in her head. "I made the cranberry sauce yesterday, and the stuffing is in with the turkey. The potatoes are peeled and sitting in water in the fridge, waiting to be boiled and mashed. Even the table is set."

She needed to keep focused on today, minute by minute. If she ran out of tasks, she would just have to redo things she had already done. Mash potatoes into oblivion and reset the table until she fell into bed tonight in a stupor. Most of all, she needed to not think about Ben, or the fact that she was alone again and two years older than the last time she had had to date, and that she didn't feel like dating at all because her life was unraveling at the seams. She didn't even know the answers to the basics anymore—like where she belonged.

"I need to get up," she said.

Sam was eyeing Egbert with horror. "What is *that?*"

Glancing at the silly melting smiley face immediately had the opposite effect on Grace. She grinned. "Egbert. He cheers me up."

Sam's gaze then fell on Heathcliff, who was crouched on one side of her in his brooding chicken pose. The flaps of fat at the bottom of his belly seeped away from him like a furry puddle. "Too bad the painting can't do something for your cat. He does not look good. Do they make kitty amphetamines?"

"He's just old."

"Pathetically old. You should get him a friend or something."

"He has a friend. She's under the bed. She's old, too."

"Having an old friend under the bed probably doesn't do him much good."

"Those kitties are devoted to each other. The shelter I adopted them from said they couldn't be separated. Heathcliff is probably just glad to know his old friend's there." She gave him a gentle nudge with a sheet-draped knee. "Kind of like having an old brother in Beirut."

After Sam left her in peace so that she could get up and get dressed, she fought the urge to burrow under the covers and go back to sleep. She craved oblivion. But there was too much to do today to waste time wallowing in self pity. She sprang out of bed in the hope that brisk movement would bring on a more zippity-doo-dah outlook. The strategy worked—at least until the view of her closet stopped her cold. All her boring clothes.

No wonder Ben had dumped her.

After that, every routine seemed to contain a mental sand trap. In the bathroom mirror she noted blemishes that hadn't been there before, and she began to wonder about teeth bleaching. Amber had perfect teeth.

Downstairs, Sam and Lou were already in a fracas over his record collection.

"They don't need rearranging," Lou was saying, his voice tense.

"But I could alphabetize them."

"I don't want them alphabetized! I want them where I can find them."

She swerved away from the argument, but of course the idea of music made her start chewing over the possibilities for Rigoletto's. If she did decide to stay in Austin permanently, what would become of the store, and its customers?

The trouble was, the thought of Rigoletto's didn't pain her like it had before. She didn't feel the pull toward Portland that she had during the summer. Yet for so long, Rigoletto's had been her baby, her life. Could she give that up for good?

In the kitchen she was surprised to find Dominic sitting alone at the table, staring intently at the salt and pepper shakers. Iago, obviously walked and fed, was under the table, his backside propped on one of Dominic's sneakers. The dog looked up at Grace when she entered the room and smacked his jaws in greeting.

"Hey." Dominic's tone was somber.

"What's going on?" she asked him. "Didn't I see another car in front of your house?"

"My grandparents are here," he said in a monotone.

"That's great. Must be good to see them."

"It's awful," he said. "I don't think they even wanted to come—they just thought they had to. And now they're acting as if everything is normal. Lily's all dressed up and keeps trying to impress everybody, but nobody cares, and Jordan went to a friend's house. Nobody mentions my mom's name, or Nina's. It's like they're trying to pretend they never existed. Sometimes I even wonder myself, except they had to have existed or I wouldn't feel this way, would I?"

"What way?"

"Like someone hit my chest with a rock." He started fiddling with the salt and pepper shakers.

And she thought she had problems. She sank down in a chair. "Did . . . your mom always do a lot for the holidays?" She'd almost referred to her as Jennifer, as if they'd been acquainted. After hearing Ray talk about her, Grace did feel like she knew her. A little.

"From Halloween on, Mom was always busy," he said. "Before Thanksgiving she made food for days. I'd help her sometimes. We ate leftovers for a week afterward. Last year was really great. Nina and I made three kinds of pie, and then Granny Kate brought a pineapple chess pie, so we had four. Just the pies took up a whole counter. It was crazy. This year Granny Kate brought two, but Jordan stole one."

"That's awful!"

"And now when I'm in the kitchen and I look at the one sorry pie, I keep thinking about last year. I can't help it. Last year was so much better—we had everything."

She nodded. Poor Dominic. To lose so much, so young. She couldn't imagine how he felt.

He sighed and stood up. "I have to go back."

"Come over later, if you have time. Dad will probably be glad for a rest from Sam and Steven and me."

After he'd left, she got up to check the oven. There was shouting in the next room.

A moment later, Sam skittered in as if he'd been ejected from the living room by a boot to the rear. "Some people just refuse to be helped!" he snapped.

"Not me," she assured him. "You can help me by hauling this turkey out of the oven."

He did as he was told, donning oven mitts and then wincing under the weight of the bird as he pulled the rack out. "What's this stuffed with? Gravel?"

She laughed. "I hope not. But I'm never thinking my clearest at four A.M."

A car door slammed outside and Iago let out several sharp barks.

"That might be Emily," Grace said. "I should go see."

"Who's Emily?"

She was already on the way out of the kitchen, although she nearly bumped into her dad on the way through. "I think someone's here."

"I know, Dad. I'm heading for the door."

"What's going on in here?" Lou asked, gaping at the opened oven. "Why is Sam taking the turkey out already?"

"Because it's done, Dad," Sam said.

"We're not about to eat, are we?"

"It doesn't matter. You can't let it sit in an oven forever or it will have the consistency of shoe leather."

She left Sam to sort out the turkey situation with their father and ran to the front door.

The new arrival was only Steven. He smiled, holding up a foil-covered platter.

"Where's Emily?" Grace asked.

"She couldn't make it. She sent along something for us, though."

As the arguing from the kitchen ramped up into shouting, Grace peeled back the foil on the plate Steven was holding, revealing a festive ring of three-colored, wriggling Jell-O. "This is really weird. Did I miss the memo on the retro Jell-O revival?"

Steven frowned. "What are they yelling about in there?"

Grace waved her free hand as she took the plate from him. "Don't mind them. They've been spatting all mor—"

A clattering crash from the kitchen cut her words short, and was followed by Sam's voice, yelling, *"Oh, great! Just great!"*

Steven and Grace hurried toward the kitchen.

Shoulders and heads bowed, Sam and Lou were standing in the middle of the kitchen in a puddle of turkey juice, which Iago was frantically lapping up as fast as he could. The turkey itself was sprawled on its side on the floor, looking like a crime victim with its stuffing guts spilling out over the linoleum.

"*This* could be a problem," Sam observed.

24

Paul McCartney All Over Again

Between Emily's gift and the Jell-O turkey that Muriel brought over, Grace felt she had consumed more gelatine-based food in one meal than she had in all the years since preschool. The real turkey had been a lost cause, though Truman had questioned whether some part that hadn't touched the floor might still be perfectly good. But Sam was a witness to the fact that the bird had rolled once it hit the floor, and neither he nor Lou could vouch that Iago hadn't slobbered on it before being shooed away.

But even if the balance of the food had been Jell-O, Grace wasn't off the hook in terms of dishes. She did them all, washing the good china by hand to preserve the gold pattern. She was glad for the time alone, and even gladder to hear her father laughing with everyone in the next room. When Peggy came in to ask if she needed help, Grace sent her back to the others. She felt much more generous toward her neighbor since the rescue of the day before.

"Dad is so happy to have you all here," Grace said. "You should stay with him."

Peggy held her gaze for a moment. "Promise we'll have a chance to talk again before you go back."

That word, *back,* stabbed at her heart. "We'll have a chance," she assured her.

As she was finishing up, the back door opened and Dominic came in, followed by Lily. "Are people still here?" Lily asked.

"Some people," Grace answered. "Muriel, and my brothers. You should go in and meet Sam."

"Okay," Lily said, passing on through.

Dominic saw the huge piles of dishes and went closer to inspect. "Did you do all those by hand?"

"Yes."

"We were lucky. Granny Kate did all the dishes before she and Pop Pop decided to leave." He grabbed a leftover roll from a basket on the counter and took a bite.

"I thought your grandparents were supposed to stay the weekend."

"They were, but I think they got tired of us. They left right after we ate, so we came over here."

"What about your dad?"

Dominic shrugged. "He's having one of his zombie days. He was probably hoping we'd all leave so he could sit in his office and listen to Mom's piano music."

Grace pictured Ray over there, holed up in his office lair, and a little of her self-pity melted away.

When Dominic joined the others, the sounds in the next room spiked up again. Crawford appeared, and a Monopoly game was suggested.

Grace went upstairs to fetch her brothers' old game that she'd seen in the storage closet, but instead of staying to play, she slipped on a cotton cardigan and went out onto the back porch. Iago, who had been put outside because all the food was putting him on snuffle overdrive, waddled over and nuzzled her. She buried her face in the soft roll at the nape of his neck and breathed in his comforting doggy smell. Part of her couldn't wait till everyone went home and she could be alone again.

Although, come to think of it, she was all alone now.

Or so she thought. Someone nearby cleared his throat.

She jerked her head up. It was Ray.

"I didn't expect to see you all alone today," he said.

She laughed. "I didn't expect to be all alone."

"Can I join you?"

He sat down next to her. "Am I right in thinking all my kids are over here?"

She smiled. *Not* sitting in a funk and listening to piano music, then. That was an improvement. "And probably will be for a while yet. They just started a Monopoly game."

His brown eyes studied her face. "You're sad. Or worried about something. What's wrong?"

She lifted her shoulders. "Oh, it could be a lot of things. The past twenty-four hours haven't been the greatest. First my father got lost, and then today he and my brother wrestled with a twenty-pound stuffed turkey and dropped it on the floor, and I got next to no sleep last night. Oh, and yesterday Ben broke up with me over the phone as I was on the bus on the way to the airport to pick him up."

Ray looked gratifyingly horrified. "Why didn't he tell you before?"

"Just a coward, I guess. See, he had a very good reason for breaking up with me. He'd gotten a mutual friend of ours pregnant."

"Oh God."

She drew in a ragged breath.

"How long had you and Ben lived together?" he asked gently.

"Two days."

Ray gaped at her, obviously thinking she'd misspoken.

She couldn't help smiling at his reaction. "He had just moved in when Dad had his accident. We had planned for Thanksgiving to be our big reunion. But instead, he left me."

"Hmm."

She glanced over at him. "What do you mean, 'hmm'?"

He hesitated. "Well, some people might say that you were the one who did the leaving, Grace."

"But I had to—to take care of Dad."

"*Had* to?"

"Wanted to." She sighed. "Chose to. And you're right—it was mostly my fault. Not the pregnancy, of course, but leaving Ben, and then stringing him along and telling him I'd be back, and then not coming back. I didn't intend to string him along, but I guess that's how it seemed to him. I should have thought more about how he was feeling, but I was so wrapped up in what was going on here."

"It's natural that you would be."

"I know, but you said it yourself. If I'd really loved Ben, I wouldn't have left him at all."

"I said that?"

"Well . . . you implied it." She sighed. "The problem is, I wanted an Olivia Newton-John man, but I wasn't willing to be hopelessly devoted myself."

Ray shook his head. "You've lost me."

She smiled. "Ask Lily sometime. She'll explain it."

He took a moment to think. "So it sounds to me that you're not completely broken up by losing Ben?"

"No, not entirely. But now I'm uncertain about what to do. Everyone tells me I should leave, that I would be giving up too much if I stayed with Dad. The word *martyr* comes up a lot. But it doesn't feel that way to me. I keep thinking that I wouldn't be able to forgive myself if I did leave."

"You'd be missed."

His words gave her heart a gentle lift, even though she knew she was being a dope. *He's not talking about himself.* He meant Lily and Dominic. Or he was just being polite.

The trouble was, she had almost developed an addiction to these quiet conversations with Ray. She'd almost . . .

No. She would not go there. She was still less than twenty-four hours away from having been dumped by one guy, and wasn't going to tell herself fairy tales about falling in love with anyone else. There was no basis for it. Yes, they had talked—but usually about Jennifer, and their extended courtship. Was it possible to fall in love with someone for the way he had fallen in love with someone else?

Possible, perhaps, but certainly not wise.

She cleared her throat, wanting to veer the conversation away from her problems and back to his. “I heard the in-laws left early.”

“It wasn’t much of a visit for them. Now I can’t imagine why they wanted to come in the first place.” He looked down at his feet. “It was tense. Jordan was the smartest—she just went to a friend’s house. The rest of us sat around pretending we were all glad to be there. Pretending to be thankful. The holiday felt like a sham to me. I can’t help thinking about how it was before, thinking of . . .”

His words broke off, so she finished for him. “Four kinds of pie.”

He looked baffled “What?”

“Dominic told me your family had four kinds of pie last year. Riches.”

His brows scrunched together over his glasses. “Dominic said that?”

She nodded.

“I hadn’t remembered that. But yeah, I guess this holiday must have seemed pretty awful to the kids.” He shook his head. “There are so many hurdles to get over before any of us can settle into some kind of normal. I can’t even think about Christmas, or . . .”

“Or what?” Grace asked.

He turned to her. “The twins’ birthday is coming up.”

Jordan’s birthday. Nina’s birthday.

"December sixteenth. I'd like to just forget it," he said.

"But you can't. It wouldn't be fair to her."

His jaw remained clenched.

"It wouldn't," she said. "Look, I can see how Jordan might be . . . a handful. I don't know exactly what's happened, but I do remember that sixteen can feel awful even when everything's going right. You make mistakes that five minutes later cause you to cringe and want to be invisible. Knowing there are people around who will forgive you is essential to survival."

She waited for him to say something, but for a moment it looked as if she might have shut down conversation between them for good.

When his gaze focused on her, his dark eyes were bright. "You remember from experience?"

She held back for a moment, but caved in to impulse. What the heck. She stripped off her cardigan sweater, then yanked her V-neck T-shirt down off her left shoulder. Ray's eyes bugged in surprise.

"Look," she said, twisting toward him.

"I don't see anything," he said.

She wiggled her shoulder a little. "You don't see a scar?"

"Uh, no."

Her bra strap was probably in the way. She flicked it off her shoulder and then told him to look again. "See? There should be a faded scar."

It was the remnant of a tattoo she'd gotten at age eighteen—a tattoo of her first serious boyfriend's initials. Trouble was, she and Mike Mulcahey had broken up three weeks later. She'd attempted to have the letters removed, but now the spot on her skin just looked like a giant botched vaccination scar.

Ray leaned so close she could feel his breath on her skin. She closed her eyes. "So what do you see?" she asked.

"MM . . ." he said, sounding the letters out so that it sounded like a murmur.

A door slapped shut behind them, and they both whipped around to see Jordan towering over them with a glare. "This is just great! I leave my friend's house early to be with my family, and not only do I have to hunt everybody down next door, I find my father pawing the neighbor!"

Several more faces peered around her as a pileup occurred at the side door. Crawford, Dominic. Truman and Peggy. Her dad.

"Did you guys sneak back here to make out?" Jordan's voice was charged with outrage.

Ray flipped Grace's bra strap back into place and surged to his feet. "Grace was just showing me her scar."

Grace couldn't help smiling to herself as she stood up.

"Look at her—smirking!" Jordan turned to make sure everyone else took note. "See?"

"Grace and I were just talking," Ray explained.

Jordan sneered. "Really? 'Cause it looked to me like you were trying to get her bra off."

"Don't be ridiculous," Ray said. "It's just Grace."

Grace did a double take. *Just* Grace?

"We were just—"

"I can't believe you're already forgetting about Mom!" Jordan railed. "And with *her,* of all people!"

"I'm not—especially not with Grace," Ray said.

"Wait," Grace said. Where did all this *especially not, of all people, just Grace* language come from? What was the matter with her?

Jordan crossed the porch to get right up into Grace's face. "Just because my little brother befriended your dad doesn't give you the right to try to take over our whole family!"

"Jordan," Ray said in a warning voice. "Apologize to Grace. And go home."

The girl rounded on him. "I can't believe how you're acting!" she yelled. "Heather was right. You're Paul McCartney all over again!"

Everyone stood in puzzled silence until Sam laughed.

His laughter just riled Jordan up further. "I can't believe I'm the only one who even seems to care about Mom anymore!" She turned on her heel and ran toward her house.

Ray raked a hand through his thick hair and

released a ragged sigh. "I'd better go." He turned, and caught the glances of Dominic and Lily, who were blinking at him in confusion and, it had to be said, mistrust. Maybe they didn't believe that he had been tearing Grace's clothes off, but they didn't seem to believe his story in its entirety, either. "Why don't y'all come home with me?"

"We haven't finished our game," Lily said.

"Yeah," Dominic echoed.

"Oh." Ray turned back to Grace, lifting his arms in an exasperated, helpless gesture. "I'm sorry, Grace. I just can't . . ." His words petered out, and all the warmth seemed to drain from his features. "Have a good trip home."

Something between them—a tentative connection—had ruptured.

"Thank you," she said, sadly.

After Ray had gone, the rest of their audience filtered away. Except for Muriel. She hovered at Grace's side. "You sure are moving in fast."

Grace closed her eyes and took a deep breath. "Nothing happened. It was just like he said—I was showing him my old tattoo."

"Wow. There's a tactic I never tried."

"It wasn't a tactic!" With a growl of frustration, Grace said, "I'm going for a walk."

"Good idea. Try to get him out of your system."

As Grace turned to shut the gate to the side yard behind her, she saw that Crawford was gaining on her.

"I thought I'd go next door and check on Jordan," he said, a flush creeping up his neck. "She seemed sort of upset."

"That's nice of you."

She attempted to sound neutral, although the idea of Crawford chasing after Jordan gave her a chill. Like watching a bunny chasing a fox.

He shrugged and peeled off to the left, to the West house. A few seconds later, she heard someone calling Crawford's name. It was Lily, standing on Lou's porch, facing the Carter house. She obviously didn't know where he'd gone.

Or who he'd gone after.

Grace took in a deep breath and then breathed it out slowly. This was life. It went on. There were always more tattoo scars in the making.

25

Grace, Readjusting

This is going to take a while."

Crawford's straight-up, matter-of-fact observation was obviously not intended to have the demoralizing effect on Grace that it did.

Not that it took Crawford to tell her that she was going to be tied up in this current project for . . . well, maybe forever. All she had to do was look around her. The bedroom that had once been Steven's now served as command central for

Rigoletto's on-line. Grace's computer sat on Steven's old student desk, next to a three-drawer file cabinet containing the store's paper records going back to 2006, which she still needed to sort through.

In Portland, over Christmas, she had been too distraught to do much more than toss everything in boxes and load it onto the U-Haul. Now she was paying for her disorganization. New and used CDs lay everywhere, piling up on tabletops and windowsills. And these were just from the boxes she had opened. The unopened ones were stacked in the closet alongside Steven's abandoned early eighties wardrobe items. Milk crates dotted the floor, filled with LPs and even some 78s that in moments of madness she had accepted as trades.

Also scattered about the room was her push puppet collection. She'd opened that box by mistake and then had been unable to resist taking them all out and showing Crawford, who'd seemed underwhelmed. Dominic had been more impressed by the old-fashioned toys. Grace owned about forty of them, most given to her by her dad when she was little, or more recently sent to her by Sam on his travels.

She absently fiddled with one now—a milkmaid her father had sent her when she was a girl, from a trip to Switzerland. Push the plunger under the pedestal that the little segmented figure stood on and she collapsed in a heap. Release it, she popped back up again. The action seemed to soothe her, like those Chinese worry balls some people used. There was so much work ahead. She wished she could make herself rebound as quickly as a push puppet.

Transferring the inventory of Rigoletto's to its new on-line home was taking longer than she'd thought it would. And that was even with many of the used CDs going into batches for immediate eBay auction. Crawford was tackling that task now—sorting through several hundred used CDs and making sure the batches of twenty-five to be auctioned didn't have duplicates. Meanwhile Grace cataloged, photographed, and priced the better selections.

"I should have done this years ago," she said, putting the milkmaid aside.

"Why didn't you?" Crawford asked.

"Because I had my store. It kept me busy enough."

"Why don't you open a store here?"

She shook her head. She didn't have time now for a brick-and-mortar store. She could take care of her on-line business from home and keep an eye on her dad at the same time.

So maybe everything had all turned out for the best.

Sure. Time to write Ben a thank-you note.

"Grace?"

She turned abruptly.

"You know how you told me to tell you if you started to space out?" Crawford asked.

"Yeah."

"You're spacing out."

She laughed. "Thanks."

Lou came down the hall and poked his head in. "You're not putting any of my records on the Internet, are you?"

This was a running concern with him. He eyed the records with suspicion.

"No, Dad. This is all Rigoletto's stock."

He shook his head. "You shouldn't have done it."

"What?"

"Gotten rid of your store."

"I haven't, Dad. I'll still have it—it's just in cyberspace now."

"It's not the same, though, is it?"

"It's better," she said. "I don't have to pay rent on a building."

She kept her voice cheerful, but it was a lie. Even if sometimes she had felt like a slave to it, she had loved going to the store every day. When she went back to Portland in December, staying at her Mom's while she cleared out the duplex, closed up shop, and packed all her inventory away, it had been hard sometimes to get work done at the store for all the knocking on the door. Old customers came by to lament the closing, and several of her musician friends who had played at

Rigoletto's talked her into having one last big New Year's bash. When Sasha, her friend who was a cellist with the Oregon Symphony, had started playing "Auld Lang Syne," she'd feared she just might lose it.

What am I doing? she'd wondered. Suddenly it had all felt like a mistake, as if she'd fishtailed on the highway and discovered herself going in the wrong direction. And her doubts were compounded by the subtle yet constant echo of doom her mother kept up as she was staying at her house.

"I hope you're not making a mistake," she'd kept repeating, with the underlying meaning that there was very little doubt that Grace *was* making a grave error. "It's selfish of Lou and the boys to pressure you to move down there."

"The *boys* are both in their thirties, and no one's pressured me to do anything."

"Well of course they wouldn't come right out and say it . . . But look what you've already given up—your store, and Ben."

"I didn't give up Ben. He left."

"But if you had been here . . ."

The very idea had made Grace huff in frustration. "You didn't even like Ben!" she reminded her mom. "But now when he's gone, you act like losing him is the tragedy of my life."

"I just don't want you to end up alone."

"I won't." She smiled. "I'll have Dad."

Her mother had looked on her pityingly and shook her head.

Her stepfather had no opinion about her moving, and Natalie and Jake reacted to the news as if it wasn't that big a deal anyway. And it probably wasn't, to them. They were both so wrapped up in their teenage lives, her problems could only seem dull and remote. Strange, Grace thought, that she missed Dominic and Lily over Christmas more than she'd ever missed her own stepbrother and stepsister in Oregon.

Someone was at the front door. When Lou left the room to get it, Crawford asked, "It's on account of him that you came back, isn't it?"

She opened her mouth to deny it but admitted, "Mostly."

"I wouldn't move across the country to take care of my dad," he grumbled.

"Maybe in twenty or thirty years things will look different."

"Or maybe Dad'll still be married and I won't have to worry about it."

"*Still* married?" Had Wyatt gotten married while no one was looking?

"Dad's engaged," Crawford said. "To Pippa."

"Who?"

"Pippa—his girlfriend." He scowled and added, "One of his girlfriends. He said he thought we needed stability. I think he just means he wants somebody in the house to stay with me while he's away. But I'm sixteen."

"I'm amazed."

"Amazed by what?" Lily asked from the doorway. She leaned against the frame, hugging her book to her chest. Grace recognized it as her journal—the Lily West equivalent of Linus's blue blanket.

Grace didn't feel at liberty to discuss Wyatt's impending marriage with the neighbors, since she'd just heard about it herself, so there was a short, awkward pause before Crawford told Lily the news. "Dad's engaged to Pippa."

"I thought he liked the other one better," Lily said.

"I think he did, but turned out she had a husband."

So it was Pippa by default, evidently.

"Wow." Lily sat in the folding chair next to the desk and looked at Grace. "Can I borrow a pen?"

Grace obligingly slid a ballpoint across the desktop. "You're going to have that book filled up before long."

"I know." Lily lamented, nibbling her lip as she started making notes.

"I'm surprised you don't blog," Grace said, "or use Twitter."

Lily gaped at her for a moment. "I'm not an exhibitionist! I'm writing *private* thoughts. That way, if I ever decide to become a writer, I'll have lots of material. I mean, it'll all be here, right?"

"That might depend on what kind of book you'll want to write."

"Coming-of-age books are *perennially* popular," Lily said. "And I'm coming of age right now, so it's important to get it all down, and experience everything." She paused to write for a moment before adding casually, "Like the spring dance, for instance."

Crawford didn't pick up on her cue, so she continued, "Last year I didn't want to go, but I really need to go to the spring dance this year to see what it's like. Maybe I should be helping you all out so I could splurge on a new dress."

At last she'd caught Crawford's attention. "A dress!" he exclaimed in disgust. "Why would you waste your money on that? Money should be saved for important things."

Lily sat up straighter. Grace, too. It wasn't often Crawford got riled up.

"Important things like cars?" Lily guessed, a hint of disdain creeping into her voice despite what was probably a mighty effort to keep it out.

"Well . . . yeah," he said. "Anyhow, you could get a dress for next to nothing at Goodwill."

Lily tapped the pen on the desk, evidently visualizing herself at the big dance in a thrift store prom dress. "That sounds a little Jordany."

There was a pause before Crawford ventured to

ask, “I guess Jordan always has plenty of dates to the dance?”

“She hates dances!” Lily said. “Who’d want to take her anyway?”

Grace was torn between wanting to get involved in their conversation and an even sharper desire to shut it out. Being a teenager had been stressful. Watching other people going through it felt a little like rubbernecking at a traffic accident.

She concentrated on inputting an out-of-print Beethoven CD of violin concertos that she’d had for a while. The Internet was actually the best place to sell something like this, since random customers browsing in a store wouldn’t know why a certain recording, and a used one at that, could cost twice as much as most other CDs. It took a specific buyer.

Lou came back in, an album tucked under his arm. “I thought I’d give you this one to sell.”

It was an old CBS edition of *Pictures at an Exhibition.* Very common. “You should hold on to that,” she said, continuing typing. “It’s not worth anything.”

Too late, she realized her words had lacked tact.

“It’s a great record!” he said, nearly shouting.

The two kids stopped their discussion of the spring dance to look up at them.

“It *is* a great recording, but it’s Leonard Bernstein, Dad. It’s been reissued a bijillion times. That’s why it’s not worth anything.”

Her words did little to smooth his ruffled feathers. "It's worth something to me."

"All the more reason you should keep it for yourself," she said.

He glowered at the piles of records and CDs and stalked away.

"That wasn't very nice," Lily said to Grace. "Why would you tell him his record was worthless?"

"Because it is. Just because something's good doesn't mean it's worth a lot."

Lily pursed her lips. "That's a mercenary viewpoint."

Crawford snorted.

"What?" Lily asked.

"She's running a business here. Money's the whole point, idiot."

Lily sprang to her feet. "I'm not an idiot! I just don't happen to believe scraping money together is the most important thing in the whole world!"

"Well, what is, then?" Crawford asked.

Her face was mottled red. "Learning—and being smart enough to know not to insult people. Especially people who . . ."

"Who what?" Crawford asked.

"Oh, never mind!" Lily wheeled on the balls of her feet and stormed out the door.

"Lily!" Crawford called after her. He glanced over to Grace and rolled his eyes. "Am I supposed to run after her and apologize?"

"Only if you want to make peace."

He released a long-suffering sigh. "What was she doing over here anyway?"

"Can't imagine," Grace replied.

"She's always over here and she never does anything."

"Maybe she enjoys our company."

His expression darkened and he turned back to his pile of CDs. "Is a prelude different than an impromptu?" He held up two Chopins for her to inspect.

"No, those can go in the same batch," she told him.

He nodded and seemed absorbed in the task, but a few minutes later he blew out a breath. "I guess I *should* go over and apologize, but it seems a little stupid, doesn't it? I mean, she's obviously not an idiot. She'd have to be a moron to think I really meant it."

"Before you apologize, you might want to consider your wording."

He stood up. "I've got the five piles here worked out, anyhow. That's two hours. Do you need me anymore today?"

"No, but if you have time tomorrow . . ."

"I'll be here after school," he promised.

He was turning to leave when he walked smack into Jordan. She was panting, and he reached out as if to hold her up by her arms. "What's the matter?"

She hopped backward to avoid his touching her. "Do you have a car?"

The question sent a tremor of frustration through him. "No!"

"Shit!" Jordan looked at Grace, her eyes pleading. "Can you help me? *Please?* My friend is having an emergency! She's really sick. I think she needs to go to the hospital."

"Shouldn't you call an ambulance?" Grace asked.

"She says she can't afford an ambulance!" Jordan snapped. "I'm really worried about her. If I had the money for a cab, I'd get one and pick her up, but I don't."

"I have money!" Crawford said.

Jordan's eyes lit up. "Really?"

Before Crawford could offer up all his hard-earned savings, the savings he had just been telling Lily he was loathe to part with for anything other than a car, Grace intervened. "I'll take you," she said, grabbing her purse off the desk. "It will be faster than a cab."

Jordan blinked at her. "Seriously?"

"Sure, come on."

Jordan turned, swinging her snaggle of recently dyed peach-and-black striped hair over her shoulder.

"Hey!" Crawford said. "You want me to go with you?"

"No, that's probably not necessary," Grace told

him. Then she remembered her dad. "But if you could stick around here for a little bit . . . ?"

"C'mon!" Jordan cried as she clattered down the stairs. "This is life and death!"

Crawford's disappointment was palpable, but he shrugged and answered, "Sure. I didn't have anything else to do." Then he called out, "I hope your friend's okay, Jordan!"

Jordan was already out the front door.

Poor Lily, Grace thought. *She'll never get that apology now.*

26

Even Hemorrhoids Have Their Uses

Jordan sat erect in the passenger seat, hands flat on the dashboard in front of her as if she could push the car forward from within. She was practically vibrating in panic.

"I'm really worried. She's not even answering her phone anymore."

"We'll get there soon," Grace told her in an even voice. "It's not that far."

Jordan wished she could have found anyone else to help her. Grace seemed to be making a big show of being calm. Or maybe she *was* calm, which was even more irritating. "I know what you're thinking," Jordan told her. "You're thinking that Heather's just some sort of freak. Not worth the trouble. Because of that other time."

"That's not what I was thinking. I'm anxious for her. That's why I'm doing this."

A stiff moment of silence followed.

"She's not tripping, either, if that's what you suspect," Jordan said. "Just because she stole a couple of egg rolls doesn't mean she's a junkie."

"I never said—"

"She might have something really wrong with her, like a disease, or food poisoning—people die of that, right?"

The light turned green and Grace accelerated again, but not as fast as Jordan would have liked. She sighed impatiently.

"She's not going to die," Grace said.

Jordan snapped her gaze toward that composed profile. "How do you know? I was talking to her. She sounded *really bad.* It's not like people never die!"

"Right, but—"

"People *I* know die," Jordan said. "Maybe you've heard—I'm a curse."

Grace frowned but didn't say anything for a second. "I hadn't heard that, and I wouldn't have believed it if I had. It's nonsense."

"Oh, sure. When you're cozying up to Dominic and Lily and Dad, they never mention me."

"Of course they mention you, but no one's said you were a curse. Not to me."

"Well, I am, okay?" Jordan swallowed past a lump of fear in her throat. "I might even be a murderer, which is what Lily calls me. If it hadn't been for me, my mom and Nina would still be alive. You knew *that,* didn't you?"

"I've never heard anyone say you were responsible."

"You know why Mom and Nina were driving down that road in the first place? To retrieve me, the family delinquent. Because I'd been arrested."

"Why?"

"It was all so stupid! My family was at this dumb Hill Country lake house my mom had rented for spring break. It was so boring there. But I'd met a few kids in town, and we were driving around one afternoon and there was this dairy farm in the middle of nowhere. On both sides of the gate to this farm there were these wood cutout cows—cutesy cows, like for an advertisement. So these guys I was with decided it would be hilarious if we moved the cows to make it look like they were humping. Which is what we did—and it wasn't easy.

"But then, just as we were finishing, the owner drove up and the guys jumped in their car and just left me there. And the farmer called the police, who came and picked me up. They caught the other guys, too, and eventually we all ended up waiting at the sheriff's office ten miles away. That's where I called Mom from . . ."

She drew in a ragged breath. "And I was still there later when they came and told me what had happened—that Mom and Nina had been killed. Just a mile or so away from the stupid humping cows. That's what they probably saw before they died. Maybe that's even what Nina was thinking about while she bled to death waiting for the ambulance to show up."

Grace didn't say anything.

"They told us she probably died right before the ambulance arrived." Jordan's voice cracked, and she stopped to swallow. "But it didn't get there for *twenty minutes.* She was in that car with our mom for twenty minutes, and Mom was—"

Grace interrupted. "You didn't murder anybody."

Jordan pushed back against her seat and squeezed her eyes shut. What was the matter with her? Why was she spilling her guts to Grace? She hadn't even told this much to the therapist.

"It wasn't your fault," Grace said. "You weren't even there."

Jordan scowled at her and began punching numbers on her cell phone again. "You so don't get it."

"It was an accident," Grace said. "You weren't driving the car that hit them."

"I might as well have been."

She angled away from Grace and watched the city speed by as they drove along I-35's access road. Heather still wasn't answering her phone, and Jordan almost missed the turnoff coming up.

"Turn here!" she yelled, pointing so late at the street that Grace almost had to do a U-turn to make it. "It's this little apartment complex up on the right."

As soon as Grace pulled her clunky old Subaru into the parking lot, Jordan jumped out of the car, ran to Heather's door, and knocked sharply. She tried the doorknob, but it didn't turn, so she pounded some more on the door itself. "Heather!"

After a minute of this, the muffled sounds of someone stirring inside came closer, and Heather finally unlocked and opened the door. Her skin was a pale green, and sweaty. It looked like her legs could barely hold her up.

"Oh, God," Jordan said, suddenly frozen. Now that she was here, she didn't know what to do.

Grace stepped past her. "Heather, I'm Grace. We're going to take you to a doctor."

"I'll be fine . . ." Heather coughed and wobbled and let out a groan of pain.

Grace surged forward and caught her as she started to fall. "We'll get you to the ER."

"I might as well die," Heather said, bursting into tears. "I'll die on my couch, next to Buns. Poor Buns!"

Grace shot Jordan a questioning glance over

Heather's drooping head. *Rabbit,* Jordan mouthed back.

Heather's moaning about Buns seemed especially delirious because for weeks she had been whining about how she couldn't afford to take care of the rabbit and needed to get rid of him.

"You need to get well to take care of Buns," Grace said in a kindergarten teacher voice. "We'll take you to the emergency room, but first we need to find your purse."

Heather lifted a limp arm to a chair where her huge canvas bag had been thrown, its contents spilling all over the seat cushion.

Grace scooped it up and directed them to turn back toward the door.

They reached the hospital faster than Jordan would have expected, and when they got to the ER with Heather—who, as if on cue, puked as they stumbled through the automatic doors—a nurse came to whisk her away. Grace and Jordan stayed back to try to give Reception all the information they could. Just as they were finishing up the paperwork, a doctor came out and addressed Grace. "Mrs. Levenger needs an emergency appendectomy."

Jordan and Grace moved to surgery's waiting room. Jordan tried to act as calm as Grace looked, but inside she was a quivering wreck. *Heather can't die.* That would be too awful. Heather was the only friend she had. She treated her like an adult—she'd even started asking Jordan to go out to nightclubs sometimes. Just last Saturday Jordan had snuck out after midnight to go with Heather to see a band. Heather had a crush on the lead singer of a group called Swingin' Love Carcass. It hadn't been much of a band, but it was fun to go out like a real person. She was seventeen now, after all.

And Heather was the one who had seen a notice for a summer art program for high school students, at a college in San Francisco. Jordan was going to apply, and Heather had promised to write her a letter of recommendation. Jordan didn't want to spend another dreary summer in Texas. This winter had been dreary enough. Christmas had been a joke. They'd gone out for Indian food and exchanged perfunctory gifts almost as if they were embarrassed to be acknowledging the holiday.

About the only thing grimmer than Christmas had been her birthday, an occasion her dad had been adamant about marking even though Jordan would have just as soon skipped it. He'd acted almost manically determined to be nice to her that day—almost as if someone had instructed him to. He'd even brought home a cake from a bakery and insisted on singing "Happy Birthday" to her. Everyone had gone along, a little dazed, but during the song Lily had burst into tears and ended up running from the room, and her father had sunk into his chair, looking defeated. Jordan hadn't been able to breathe, so she'd had to blow out each of her seventeen candles individually. The first time she'd ever blown out birthday candles all alone. Even Dominic, who usually could inhale several pieces of cake before any presents were opened, sat hunched over his plate as if the fluffy coconut cake were made of mud.

Jordan had gone to bed that night thinking of her mom, who used to make such a fuss over birthdays. What would she have thought about their sad attempt at a celebration? And of course, it was impossible to avoid thinking about Nina, her partner in birthdays for as long as she'd existed. How was she supposed to spend the rest of her life getting older, passing milestones, while Nina remained stalled at sixteen forever? Every birthday of her life would be a reminder of that other life that had been cut short. All that potential, snuffed out.

All her fault.

The surgery seemed to be taking forever. Jordan got sick of brooding, worrying, and pretending to read *People* magazine. She'd probably flicked past the same article on Angelina Jolie fifteen times already.

"It's really good that you panicked like you did," Grace said, looking over at her. "You were right to."

Jordan felt a moment of satisfaction—finally, she'd done something right!

Then her lips curled down and she turned to Grace. "She was dying. Any idiot could tell that."

Grace leaned back and folded her arms. "That apartment really smells. Maybe we should clean it."

"It's pointless. I've cleaned it before and within days it just goes back to the way it was. I should probably take care of Buns, though. Would you mind swinging by . . . once we figure out how the surgery goes?"

"No, of course not."

After another hour, the surgeon came out and told them that Heather's surgery had gone well, she was in recovery, and they could visit her that evening.

Back at Heather's apartment, Grace picked her way across the floor to the kitchen while Jordan went back to find Buns. The poor animal was hovering in the corner, thumping his back foot on the floor of his filthy cage, which was out of food and almost out of water. She unhooked the plastic water bottle from the bracket that held it to the cage bars and went to the kitchen.

"I'm taking the rabbit with me," Jordan announced as she leaned around the open cabinet door to reach the sink.

Grace gave no indication of having heard her. "Where are the garbage bags?"

"There are none. Heather doesn't believe in them."

She straightened. "How can you not believe in garbage bags?"

"They're not eco-friendly, because they're made from petroleum or something."

Grace's mouth twisted. "Does she have paper bags?"

"Nobody's had paper bags since, like, 1940."

"But—" Grace looked around, seeming almost more hysterical over the lack of garbage bags than she had when they'd been driving Heather to the hospital.

"You don't have to clean," Jordan told her again. "She wouldn't want you to."

"Everybody feels better in a clean apartment."

"Not Heather. If you'll just help me load up the rabbit cage, we can blow."

"Jordan—"

"What?" Jordan shouted back. "I didn't ask you here so you could start doing your Hazel routine. I just came *to get the rabbit.* I told you that, remember?"

Grace lifted her arms and then let them flop back at her sides, a gesture that struck Jordan as being *really* irritating.

"What is it with you?" Jordan asked.

Grace rounded on her in surprise. "With *me?*"

"It's not like I can't see what's going on, you know."

"Oh—I can't wait to hear this," Grace said. "Tell me. What's going on?"

"You're just trying to suck up, which is probably why you volunteered to help in the first place. Now you can go back and tell my dad that you really saved the day, and he'll be *so grateful*."

Grace just stood there with her hands in fists at her sides, her mouth working open and shut like a guppy's at feeding time. "*You* asked for my help—for the second time. Against my better judgment, I haven't said a word about the Chinese restaurant. I've barely spoken to your dad since your little Thanksgiving tantrum. So if you don't trust me now, that's *your* problem."

"Yeah, whatever," Jordan said, turning to go get Buns.

From behind her, Grace called out, "You do realize that you make it hard for anyone to like you, don't you?"

"Thank you, Miss Broken Record of 2011." Jordan turned. "You do realize I don't care whether anyone does or not, don't you?"

There went the guppy face again. But at last Grace stopped and shook her head, sighing. Surrendering. "Just grab the flippin' rabbit and let's get out of here."

27

An Invitation

Grace inspected a Deutsche Grammophon label on an album, trying not to get her hopes up. According to her research, the record was worth either two hundred dollars or twenty-five cents, depending on how the tulip design looked. The trick was deciphering whether she had a gold mine tulip or a dud tulip.

The slight acceleration of her heartbeat as she checked the details was saying gold mine.

Her father hadn't stopped pushing choice items from his record collection on her—even as he deplored her giving up her store and selling things on-line. Most days started out with his bemoaning the fact that she was in Austin at all. But she knew he wanted her here; anyway, it was a fait accompli now. They had informed Darla Swinton her services would not be needed. Grace was the live-in help.

The record she was inspecting was one of Lou's Telemann Viola Concertos. She wouldn't have thought of selling it, but he actually had two copies because Sam had bought him a duplicate one year for Christmas. And she was beginning to think that Sam was a genius, because this one seemed to be an original stereo pressing, which could be worth quite a bit.

Someone knocked at the door and she braced herself, preparing for it to be her dad bugging her about the album again. Once he'd handed it to her to sell, it was all he could think about. After all the albums he'd lugged in for her to look at—all of which she'd had to declare without value—he would be gleeful.

Without turning, she announced, "You're sitting on a gold mine."

Behind her, Steven said, "Glad to hear it."

"Oh—sorry. I thought you were Dad." She frowned. It was the middle of the day on a Thursday. "What are you doing here?"

He took a seat on a folding chair. From her desktop he grabbed a push puppet of a burro in a serape and sombrero and started fidgeting with it. "I drove Muriel home, so I decided to drop in."

"Muriel Blainey?" That name, and the formally casual tone of his voice, shot off a warning flare in her mind.

He nodded, pulsating his thumb so that the burro nodded too. "Turns out, we share a divorce lawyer."

The world's longest business trip was officially over, evidently.

"As Muriel pointed out, we're both in the same boat." Steven's expression was grave. "Of course, she's worse off than I am. I might have had to leave my old practice, but she's being forced out into the workplace, back to her old profession."

"You make it sound like she was selling her body."

He drew back. "She was a real estate agent."

"Oh, sorry, I was wrong. It was her soul she was selling." Grace laughed. "Real estate agent. It fits."

"I don't see anything funny," Steven said. "The poor woman's had her life turned upside down."

Poor woman? "Oh, Steven, be careful."

"Careful of what?"

"Can't you see? She's one of those bulldozer women you always end up with."

He sputtered. "That I—? *What?*"

"Sara . . . Denise . . ." She arched a brow. "Now Muriel Blainey."

He was not convinced. "It sounds to me like you're projecting. Ben jerked you around, so now you think the same thing's going to happen to me. But what's Muriel done to make you so suspicious?"

That was a good question. And the answer was . . . nothing. Maybe she *was* just projecting. But what was she supposed to do about that gnawing queasiness in her stomach at the idea of Steven in Muriel's clutches? Even though, God knows, Steven was not without faults. He wasn't exactly Valentino, and he had a complete lack of sentimentality.

For the first time, she noticed that he had

brought a bundle of letters in with him. "What's this?" she asked, picking it up off the desk.

"Your mail."

Out of the stack she picked out a cream-colored envelope that looked like an invitation.

"I got one of those, too," he said.

She eyed him questioningly, and when he didn't clue her in, she tore open the envelope. Inside was a wedding invitation. *You are cordially invited* . . .

To Truman and Peggy's wedding!

Steven shook his head. "I don't know why they just didn't go to city hall months ago."

There. No sentimentality.

"Because this is a big deal. Huge." Even though she had been irritated by their coupledom in the beginning, even she could see the momentousness of their marriage. "Uncle Truman giving up bachelorhood at eighty-two? Peggy throwing off her spinster schoolteacher mantle at seventy-four?"

"All the more reason for them to hurry up and tie the knot without any fuss. At their spot on the actuarial tables, time is of the essence."

"They want to make it an occasion," Grace told him. "I can understand that. I just worry about Dad."

"Why would Dad care? He knows Truman's asked her."

"But still. Peggy's his old friend. His companion."

"Dad never was her *companion,*" Steven argued. "They were just friends."

"Bull. That's just what Peggy's saying now."

"You romanticized them, but you weren't around that often."

It was so irritating. These first-wave Olivers could always trump her with the you-weren't-around argument. "But when I *was* around, so was Peggy."

"Well, of course—because she liked you. Naturally she'd want to come visit more often when you were here."

Grace had never considered that possibility before.

"The wedding's in three weeks," Steven told her. "Doesn't give you long to rustle up a date."

"You could be my date," she said.

He squirmed uncomfortably, and the burro began flopping over again.

"Oh, no," Grace breathed. "You didn't invite *her.*"

"Muriel had already received her invitation. So naturally when the subject came up . . ."

Grace groaned.

"What's the matter? It's just a small family wedding."

"Whose wedding?" Lou asked from the doorway.

Steven and Grace both jumped. They hadn't heard him come in. He frowned, looking from one to the other.

Grace took the invitation out of her lap and handed it over. “We were talking about this. Truman and Peggy’s wedding invitation.”

Lou took it and examined it. As he did, Grace studied his rough hands. His fingernails were dirty and jagged. Should she suggest a manicure? Nail care was one of the many things she’d never considered for her dad—little day-to-day things a person did that you took for granted until you realize that suddenly they weren’t doing them at all.

He tossed the invitation on the desk. “I knew about that. Truman told me.”

“You never mentioned it to me,” Grace said.

“I don’t have to tell you everything that happens, do I?”

“No, but—”

She was stopped by the expression on her dad’s face, which was mottled red with anger. He had done a double-take at something he’d seen on the desk. He picked up the Telemann record.

“What are you doing with this?”

“Oh!” She hadn’t told him yet. “Good news! I think it’s worth around two hundred dollars.”

“Over my dead body, it is!” he shouted at her. “Who gave you permission to go putting my things up for sale?”

The blood drained from her face. “You did.”

“Like hell, I did.”

She didn’t know what to say. Tears jumped to

her eyes, but she wasn't about to let them fall. This wasn't about her, she told herself.

This wasn't even really him.

She sent an imploring look to Steven, hoping he would intervene. He struggled for words. "Dad, Grace wouldn't—"

"Naturally you'd take her side," his father said, interrupting. He dismissed them both with a scowl and a warning for Grace. "Stay out of my things."

When he left, Grace and Steven lowered themselves into their chairs again and looked into each other's eyes. Neither of them could find words.

Crawford showed up to help her after school, and Lily filtered in and then back out when she failed to capture Crawford's attention. Dominic came in later to walk Iago before it got dark, while Grace fixed dinner. She and her father ate in silence, and then he sat down in the living room to watch an old DVD of *Columbo* that she'd found at the library. Since Christmas, he'd been watching DVDs more and reading less.

Grace felt cooped up in the house and went out to the backyard for air.

"Hey there," a male voice said over the fence.

She instinctively looked over toward Ray's house, even though she knew it was the wrong direction. Wrong voice, wrong fence, wrong guy.

Since Thanksgiving, things had been awkward

between them. Ray was keeping his distance from her—maybe he didn't want to upset his children, and she certainly didn't want to add to his family tension. Or maybe she'd only been imagining—or overestimating—the connection between them.

But she had also wanted to wall herself off a bit from him. In no way did she want him or anyone else to think her decision to stay with her dad had been influenced by the fact that Ray was next door. The idea was preposterous, really. A grieving widower with three kids and a communication problem? Not exactly the bachelorette's dream.

So they waved at each other occasionally from their respective driveways and heard news about each other from Lily and Dominic and left it at that. But she never quite managed to banish him from her mind.

Grace pushed off the porch and strolled toward Wyatt, who was grinning at her over the fence. "Care for a martini?" he asked, waggling his brows with mock seduction.

Or maybe that was actually his real seduction technique. With Wyatt there was no telling.

She laughed. "Sure."

What the hell. It had been a crappy day. A martini couldn't hurt.

By the time she made it around his gate, he was already busy shaking up a batch on his patio. "Outdoor living in the middle of February," he said, pouring her a glass. “This is why I love Texas.”

He handed her a drink and pointed her toward one of two chaise longues.

She flopped down and looked up at the sky through the limbs of a live oak. She’d expected Wyatt to take the other chair, but he perched at the foot of hers instead. He was wearing jeans and a tucked-in polo shirt, and smelled of cologne, cigar, and alcohol. It appeared that happy hour had started a while back.

She felt the first stirrings of alarm.

“Where’s Pippa?” she asked.

He laughed. “Pippa flew the coop.”

She hadn’t heard that—and it seemed like something Crawford would have told her. Not that she didn’t believe Wyatt. It couldn’t be easy for a man to admit his fiancée had dumped him.

She frowned. That afternoon, Crawford had mentioned that he was going to a friend’s house tonight. “So you’re all alone?” she asked.

He smiled. “Not anymore.”

She scooted up a little straighter.

“What’s the matter?” he asked.

“Nothing—I’m just not sure these chairs were meant for two.”

“Oh, sure. They can withstand a lot of action, if you know what I mean.” He chuckled and then sobered up again in the next second. “Sorry. That’s not what I meant to say. I meant to tell you

. . . well, that I know what you're going through."

"What I'm going through?" she repeated, mystified.

"With your dad. My grandmom had it."

"What?"

"Alzheimer's."

Her mouth dropped open. "How . . . ?"

"I've picked things up from Crawford," he explained, "and other clues. Like the time he set your house on fire. I put it together later. Mom was always having to watch my grandmom."

"I didn't know."

"It's heartbreaking. It almost killed my mother, taking care of her mom. She finally had to put her in a home."

Grace shuddered. "I couldn't do that."

"But it's hard staying with him all the time, right?" he asked. "You gave up your business back in Portland, Crawford said."

She shrugged. "I'm just transferring it on-line. The physical store was probably doomed anyway. This might not make as much money, but it won't be as much stress, either."

"Well, anyway," Wyatt said, "I just wanted you to know that there's somebody nearby who knows what you're going through. You're not alone."

For a moment, she found it hard to speak. She took a swig of her martini. "Thank you."

Wyatt frowned and touched her chin with his hand. "Hey."

Impulsively, she blurted out, "Are you busy March tenth?"

He drew back. "Why?"

"I was going to ask you on a date. I mean, I know the last time didn't work out so well . . ."

"I thought you didn't like me," he said.

"Actually, I thought you didn't like me, either."

"That's crazy." He chuckled. "Well . . . maybe not so crazy. But I can't deny I've been curious about something."

The look in his eye caused her to shiver, but whatever was in that martini had mellowed her nerves to the point that she didn't flee for her life. "What?"

"This."

He lowered his lips to hers, and she braced herself for the onslaught. Given her opinion of the man, she was expecting his kiss to be all slaver and tongue. But it was actually sort of . . . nice.

When he pulled back, she was left blinking in surprise. He smiled at her, and she blushed.

"So is that a yes?" she asked.

"Yes to what?"

"To March tenth. Peggy is getting married to my uncle Truman."

"I know. Got my invitation yesterday. Unfortunately, you're too late to claim my services as escort. I'm taking Pippa."

Had she heard him correctly? Pippa?

Fire surged into her cheeks, and she straightened

up as far as she could without kicking him out of the way. “You said Pippa had flown the coop!”

“Well, yeah, for the evening. She had a red-eye tonight.”

“Do you mean you’re still engaged?”

“Of course.” He grinned. “Do you mind?”

She gave him a hard thump on the arm. “You jackass! What were you kissing me for?”

“I told you—I was curious.”

“You’re not supposed to be curious. You’re engaged!”

“But not married. The fat lady hasn’t sung yet, baby.”

He leaned toward her and she put her hand against his chest and shoved. As he went sprawling onto the pavers, she scrambled off the low lounger as quickly and with as much dignity as she could. Which wasn’t much.

Am I losing my mind? She couldn’t imagine what lunacy had made her think that a quiet moment with Wyatt would be a good idea. She was obviously more screwed up by Ben dumping her than she had realized. All her thoughts about Ray . . . and now this. Pining after the impossible . . . hurling herself at the unspeakable.

“This day can’t end fast enough to suit me,” she muttered as she fled back over the property line. The only positive was that no one had been around to witness this humiliating scene.

28

ROAD TRIP

Even for Texas, winter had been puny that year, so after March arrived, Grace felt confident in declaring that spring was here. Time to get out more. What she and her dad needed was a barbecue road trip.

She mentioned it to Lou as she was driving him in his car to his six-month dental checkup, which Lou had forgotten six months ago, and she hadn't thought about, either. Or even known to think about.

"Why don't we take a road trip?" she asked him.

"Today? I'm going to the dentist."

"I know, but what about tomorrow? We could go to Belton."

"Why would we want to go there?" he asked.

"You know why. Schoepf's barbecue."

His eyes lit up. "If it's barbecue you want, we should go to Lockhart. To Kreuz's."

"The best barbecue in Lockhart is Smitty's," she said.

"Kreuz's."

"Smitty's," she argued back. "And that's why we should go to Belton. Because in Lockhart, we'll just have this argument all over again, and you'll never admit you're wrong."

He laughed. "All right. Have it your way."

She left him in the dentist's waiting room reading *National Geographic* and went back to the car. Steven's office wasn't far from the dentist, so this morning she had arranged to meet him for coffee. It was a gorgeous day. It had rained the night before, and the still-moist air carried the scent of spring.

At the office, whose walls now taunted her brother's mobility-challenged patients with pictures of tennis and basketball stars as well as ballerinas, Grace found Emily in a glum mood.

"Dr. Oliver told me to tell you that they would be waiting for you in the coffee shop," she said in a strained, clipped voice.

"They?" Grace repeated.

"Your brother and his friend. Muriel."

Ugh. "Feel free to call her Frau Blainey. Or even The Blainey," Grace said. "That's what I do."

For once, Emily cracked a smile. "Is it serious between them?"

"I'm hoping it's just temporary insanity."

At the sandwich shop in the building next door, Muriel waved Grace over. She was perched at a window table, waiting for Steven, who was at the counter picking up their order. On the table in front of her lay several glossy brochures. Grace looked at the title of the one on the top, *Live Oak Villa, an adventure in assisted living,* and immediately felt on her guard.

"What is *this?*" she asked as she sat down. Although it was perfectly obvious what it was.

When Steven brought their coffees and took a seat, she could tell by the anxiety in his eyes that he knew her blood pressure was already on the upswing.

Muriel got right down to brass tacks. "Steven thinks your father should be in a home. A residence center, I mean."

He turned on her. "No—I said that we could start *considering* it."

"But Dad loves his house!" Grace said.

"So would a lot of people." Muriel crossed her arms. "That's the point. Your father's house is worth a fortune. He would be able to afford to move into a really nice place."

"A nursing home?" Grace said.

Muriel rolled her eyes. "We're not talking about putting Lou in a skanky home that smells like urine and serves Vienna sausages for dinner. These are nice places."

"You don't understand," Grace told her. "He's lived in his house forever, practically. And now you propose to take him out of it at the exact moment when he most needs familiar surroundings and homey comforts? That would be the worst thing in the world for him right now!"

Why was Muriel here talking about this? She wasn't even part of the family.

"Here," Muriel said, pressing the brochures on Grace.

They felt like a pile of bricks in her lap. She leafed through one filled with pictures of tidy rooms done up in beige and mauve, and caring nurses hugging smiling old people. Her hand trembled as she turned the pages.

"You have to plan for these things." Steven eyed her with the same studied patience he probably used on patients who refused to believe surgery was necessary. "A lot of these places have waiting lists."

"Who does it hurt to have Dad staying where he is for as long as possible?" Grace argued.

"That's what I thought, too," Steven said. "But then, the other day . . . You probably don't see it, but Dad's going downhill, Grace. He's not going to be functional forever, and then it will be hard for you. And that would be unfair."

"Dad's not ready for a home," she repeated. "He's not."

Muriel leveled an impatient stare on her. "*He* might not be, but y'all have to think of the market. Character homes centrally located fetch a lot now, if you're willing to wait for the right buyer."

"Muriel . . ." Steven said.

"What?" She blinked at him, all innocence. "You said I should come here and talk to her about it."

"But not from such a bloodless, mercenary angle."

Muriel's eyes widened innocently. "Mercenary! Just because I'm being realistic? But of course *I'm* not emotionally hobbled by daddy issues."

Grace shot out of her chair. "I didn't come here to discuss Dad with neighbors, or to be insulted." She turned to Steven. "And I don't appreciate being ambushed this way."

She turned and headed out the door, tears in her eyes. She was determined not to fall apart. At least not until she was in the privacy of the car. When she started to dig in her purse for a tissue, she realized she had the brochures that she had been carrying in her lap.

Footsteps followed her, and she turned to see Steven approaching, a distraught look on his face. "I'm sorry, Grace."

"She's awful," Grace said.

"I know, but it's my fault. After that thing with Dad and the record a few weeks ago, I began to worry that you would be overwhelmed by taking care of him."

"Don't tell me this is for my own good," she said. "I shouldn't even be part of the equation. It's Dad who should decide, not us."

He nodded. "I guess you're right. I see that now. And please—don't think I care how much Dad's house is worth."

"I don't. I just don't understand how you can care about someone who does."

She stomped back to the car and was starting to

drive home when she remembered she had to go back to the dentist office. She needed to pull herself together. In the parking lot she looked at the worried face staring back at her in the rearview mirror and quickly worked to brighten herself up. She took a lipstick from her purse and swiped it across her lips, and then combed her hair out. Her father must have seen his car pull up, because he came out of the dentist's office door, saluted her with his cane, and started toward her. In a panic, Grace remembered the awful brochures for assisted living centers that she'd pitched into the passenger seat. She scooped them up, started to stuff them into the glove compartment, but thought better of it and slid them under the passenger seat.

A second or two later, Lou opened the door and got in.

"Everything go all right?" she asked.

He grinned. "Dr. Beckwith said I had the teeth of a sixty-year-old. How's that for a compliment?" He laughed. "What about you? Have you been up to anything interesting?"

She swallowed and kept her smile fixed. "No, not really."

The barbecue excursion was still on, but the next morning when Grace walked into the living room after getting herself ready, she found her dad drinking his second cup of coffee and staring at the old version of *The Forsyte Saga* he'd found at the library. He'd seen it when it was originally broadcast in the sixties and now he was on a full-throttle nostalgia trip. There were over twenty episodes in the series. If Grace didn't get to the library to pick up more DVDs, he'd rewatch the ones he had. Multiple times.

She waited for a break in the drama before she pressed pause. "Dad, we're going to Belton today, remember?"

As the word Belton sank in, his smile faded.

Her heart squeezed painfully. "You know—the road trip. Schoepf's barbecue."

He frowned in thought, then glanced down at the dog. "What about Iago?"

"He'll be fine. We'll only be a couple of hours."

He looked doubtful.

"We'd better get moving," she prompted. "You might want a jacket."

She held her breath, but he stood obediently and started for the stairs. Sometimes it was difficult to get him out if he was feeling stubborn. But when he came back down the stairs wearing his favorite hat—a greenish felt Tyrolean fedora with a rope band and festooned with one of those doohickies that reminded Grace of an old typewriter eraser—her heart lifted. He looked jauntier than she'd seen him in months.

Driving his car again, she got onto the

interstate and headed north. The traffic was light, and bluebonnets and a few early red paintbrushes dotted sections of the median and slopes running along the highway. Lou hummed along with Mozart, stopping every so often to shake his head at the way Austin kept sprawling. "Austin's going to spill right into Waco one of these days."

He had been saying that for twenty years and it always made her laugh. "I think we can trust Waco not to let that happen, Dad."

Grace had a homing instinct when it came to barbecue places. She hadn't been to Schoepf's in years, but she remembered exactly which exit to take.

As soon as they pulled off, however, her father grew agitated. He frowned through the windshield. "This isn't the way to Kreuz's."

Kreuz's? "Dad, this is Belton. We're going to Schoepf's. Remember? We decided not to go to Lockhart because you like Kreuz's and I like Smitty's . . ."

"Smitty's!" he exclaimed. "Why would you want to go there?"

"I don't, right now."

"Good. Let's go to Kreuz's."

She felt as if she'd fallen into an Abbott and Costello routine. "Dad, that's way on the other side of Austin. Schoepf's is right here. And you like it."

He looked as if he was going to argue some more, but he ended the discussion with a shrug. "I was only making a suggestion."

At the restaurant, his mood perked up again as soon as the door closed behind them and they were enveloped by the out-of-this-world scent of mesquite-grilled meat coming from a pit just feet away. It was like spa day for the taste buds.

They strolled over to where the pit master was waiting to take their orders.

"What do you want, Dad?" Grace asked.

"I want the turkey."

The man moved to oblige, but Grace stopped him with a raised finger. "Are you sure?" she asked her dad.

"Why not?"

"You never eat turkey here."

"Yes, I do." She looked at him doubtfully and he said, "You haven't been with me every time I've come here."

She couldn't argue with that. In any case, why did she want to? She needed to guard against this urge to tell him what to do.

At her nod, the man continued to pile up a plate with turkey, and then she ordered ribs.

She and her father made their way into the main part of the restaurant to order sides and iced teas and then sat down at the end of one of the long wood tables. Grace looked around contentedly at the walls covered in deer heads and crosses made from old license plates. It had been too long since she'd been here.

Lou interrupted her thoughts. He had taken a bite and was scowling at his plate. "This doesn't taste right."

"What's wrong with it?"

"It doesn't taste like it usually does."

That's because it's turkey. She held her tongue.

He took another bite, which he appeared barely able to gulp down. He chased it with a long swallow of tea. "Did they say that it would be like this?"

"Who? What?"

"The doctors? Did they warn you my taste buds would change? They didn't tell me. Nobody told me that."

"Dad, it has nothing to do with—" She stopped herself. Instead of arguing, she reached across the table, took his plate, and switched it with hers. "Here. Try the ribs."

He looked offended for a moment, but then tentatively picked up a rib and nibbled at it. His brows shot up. "This tastes okay." He looked at her with veiled accusation. "Why did you let me get that other stuff?"

A shriek rose in her throat, but she swallowed it. "All's well that ends well, Dad." She tucked into his plate.

"Do you like that?" he asked, nodding toward the food he'd given her, his nose wrinkling.

"Yes, it's good." *Not as good as those ribs. . . .*

They ate in silence for a few minutes. The lunch crowd was starting to pick up, and a few guys seated themselves at the other end of their table.

"Look at that! Men wearing baseball caps indoors!" Lou exclaimed, in a voice just slightly too loud. His green Tyrolean was neatly stowed on the unoccupied seat next to him. A bulky man with a Rangers cap on backward flicked an irritated glance their way. "Grown men with hats at the dinner table!" her father crowed. "Cary Grant loses, *Hee-Haw* wins."

"Dad!" she said.

He leaned forward, eyes round. "What?" he asked in a discreetly low voice that he unfortunately hadn't employed while he was insulting the diners surrounding them.

"Nothing." She didn't want to say anything that might lead to him loudly defending his belief that Neanderthals had won the style battle. That guy in the Rangers cap looked beefy enough to take Lou out with one slug.

After they had finished eating, they went back to the car. Grace put in a Percy Grainger CD and proceeded to make their customary loop through town, past the incredible white stone Bell County Courthouse. When she passed it, her father leaned against the window. "That's nice," he said.

She tightened her grip on the steering wheel and

kept driving. He couldn't have said anything that could have made her feel worse. *Nice?* While they had been restoring the courthouse, he had wanted to take her by every time she visited. Now he acted as though it was something he'd never seen before, a mildly interesting curio.

Gloom descended on her. This was how it worked, wasn't it? Things would slip away. What mattered one day wouldn't matter the next. Memory disappeared, leaving simple sensation. The writer Iris Murdoch had ended her days watching *Teletubbies*.

He's going downhill . . . That was what Steven had said.

But it wasn't true. He just had bad days sometimes.

Her father happily hummed along with "Country Gardens" as she accelerated onto the interstate, but nothing could dispel the tension she felt. The miles that had flown on the way up dragged now. She watched the exits—Salado, the Jerrell turnoff, Georgetown—wondering if they would ever get home.

Her father looked at her anxiously. "What's wrong?"

"Nothing."

"Was it something that happened back there?" he asked. "You didn't like your lunch?"

"Lunch was fine."

Stiff silence made the car feel claustrophobic.

"It was something I did," he guessed, depressed. "I missed something. I made a mistake."

The forlorn tone in his voice tore at her. "Don't angst, Dad. It's just that all that food I ate has made me sleepy."

At the Round Rock exit, she pulled off at a gas station.

"Aren't we almost home?" he asked, confused.

"I need a cup of coffee," she said, grabbing her purse. "Do you want anything?"

"No, I'll stay here."

She hesitated, worrying he would get out of the car while she was gone. She envisioned him somehow managing to toddle onto the interstate and walk along the shoulder with his cane. In her imagination, cars whipped past him, missing him by inches.

"I'll be *fine,*" he said. "I'm not a child."

She nodded, shut the door behind her, and went inside the service station, glancing back often through the plate-glass windows to make sure the car doors remained closed. The coffeepot on the counter looked as if it had been sitting on its hot plate since morning, cooking down the contents to a couple of inches of bitter caffeine sludge. Grace turned to the refrigerator cases, searching for something a little more appetizing. After passing over the million kinds of flavored waters and fruit juices, she scanned the sodas, Red Bull-type liquid jolts, and bottled coffee drinks. She finally grabbed a Coke, paid, and headed back out to the car.

At first she was relieved to see her dad sitting quietly, reading. All her worrying was for nothing; he hadn't wandered off. But when she lowered herself into the driver seat, an odd tension hung in the air. Lou was flipping through one of Muriel's brochures.

"Assisted living." When his gaze swung toward her, she could barely look him in the eye without flinching. "What are these doing here? You've had enough of living at home, so now you've decided that I should be stowed away somewhere?"

"No." She could feel her face turn red.

"I didn't even want *your* assistance."

"I know that," she said. "Someone gave those to me." She couldn't bring herself to say Steven's name. She didn't want her dad to think that his children had formed a cabal against him.

"Why would people think that I should be put away already?" he asked. "Was it the house fire? That was just a mistake—months ago! Since then, just little things."

She repeated, "I know."

He slammed the brochure shut and tossed the pile onto the mat at his feet.

She started the car and pulled out of the station's parking lot, heading toward the freeway ramp.

"Assisted living," he muttered, watching the scenery go by. It was the same beautiful day that had lifted their spirits on the way to Belton, but it didn't do the trick now. "They might as well call them death houses, because that's what happens in them. People go to those places as a last stop on the way to dying."

His eyes squinted at the glare of the sun through the windshield.

"You don't even need me, most of the time," she said, thinking aloud. At least, he didn't need her at home, all of the time. He hadn't done so well today, but today she'd taken him away from his world. But half the time he seemed his old sharp self. And he could still beat her at chess. That had to mean something.

She was relieved to get back to Austin and pull into the driveway of the old house. Apparently her father was too, because he got out even before she'd turned off the engine. Unlike his usual meticulously neat habits, he left the barbecue doggy bag container behind. Grace leaned over to pick it up and the brochures.

A door slammed from the direction of the West house and Grace looked up, hoping for a glimpse of Ray. Which was ridiculous, since it was the middle of the afternoon. He'd be at work.

It was Crawford who came crashing out of the West house. His head was down as he cut straight across Lou's yard.

"Hey there!" she called out. "Is something wrong?"

He stopped. His Adam's apple bobbed in his throat before he finally came out with, "*Everything* is wrong!"

He steamed across the lawn to his own house.

Frowning, Grace bumped the driver door shut with her hip and headed inside. Iago danced around her feet as she came in the door. Her father obviously hadn't taken the time to let him out. Upstairs, Wagner boomed. A few minutes later, as she was storing the leftovers in the fridge, a trumpet blast sounded next door from Crawford's house and for the next hour she was treated to an overpracticed UIL trumpet solo dirge coming from next door competing with Valkyries overhead.

Maybe she had Ray on the brain, but times like these, she longed for that sympathetic glance of his. Or even just a glimpse from those dark brown eyes that telegraphed the understanding that life didn't always turn out the way you wanted it to.

29

A Year Without Squeezies

From the moment Lily climbed out of bed that morning, something felt different. She couldn't put a name to the unsettled feeling, and if there was one thing that bugged her, it was not having a word for something.

She could only think it was nerves about the dance. The spring dance was in April, and lots of girls at school had already been asked to it. Crawford wasn't taking hints very well. She'd mentioned the dance several times, and from what she could fathom, he planned on going. At least, he never seemed completely bored by the topic, like a boy who had no intention of attending would have been. And she knew he had no girlfriend already because he never talked about one.

So he was probably going, and he knew she wanted to go, but he hadn't asked her yet. Maybe he never would. How was she going to handle that?

She shuffled to the bathroom, pulled her hair back off her shoulders, and looked in the mirror. Which she could only really do once she put on her glasses. *Ugh.* A blemish (she couldn't stand the word *pimple*) had cropped up overnight on her chin. Life was so unfair. She wouldn't have minded adolescence so much if she could have gotten breasts *and* pimples. But where was the justice in having cramps and oily skin when you were still encased in a body with the sex appeal of a twelve-year-old Romanian gymnast?

She sighed, scrubbed her face with cleanser, and slapped on a fresh coat of Clearasil. Maybe she should stay away from the professor's house today. If Crawford saw Mount Vesuvius on her chin, he would never invite her to the dance.

Occasionally she thought about just going ahead and asking him herself, but that would never work. If he said yes, she'd always wonder if he had just said yes so he wouldn't hurt her feelings. If he said no, she would want to curl up like a caterpillar being poked with a stick.

She dressed and went downstairs, where she was surprised to find not only Dominic but Jordan sitting at the breakfast table. Jordan hadn't gotten up early on a Saturday morning since her class ended back in the fall. Today she looked almost normal. Her hair was still a peach-and-black nightmare, but this morning she had it pulled back in an almost tidy fashion. Dominic was shoveling spoonfuls of cereal into his mouth, but he wore a clean, unwrinkled navy blue polo shirt. The sight of the two of them sitting there calmly, almost expectantly, made her nervous.

"What?" she asked when they looked up at her.

"Nothing," they said.

Uneasy now, Lily put a piece of bread in the toaster and poured herself a glass of orange juice. After she situated herself at the table and Jordan was sitting there staring blandly at her, arms folded across her chest, Lily asked, "What are you *doing?*"

"Sitting," she replied. "Is that a crime?"

Before they could start sniping, Dominic piped up, "We're waiting to see if Dad comes back."

"Dad?" Lily had just assumed he was in his study.

"He went out earlier," Dominic said. "In a suit."

Lily frowned. "Why?"

Jordan's expression straddled between astonishment and disgust. "You really don't remember, do you?"

"What?" Lily asked.

Dominic gulped a spoonful of sugar-drenched bran flakes. "It's been a year."

Lily froze. She had forgotten. A year ago, her mom and Nina had died.

How could she have forgotten? Maybe because the accident had happened during Spring Break. But Spring Break fell later this year. Or maybe she'd just become preoccupied.

She put her toast down, suddenly not hungry at all. How could she have woken up today of all days thinking about Crawford and the stupid dance?

"Are you okay?" Dominic asked.

"Of course she's not okay," Jordan said, surprising her by sounding almost sympathetic.

Dominic sighed and sat back. "Me neither. I wish we didn't have to remember."

"You don't want to forget Mom and Nina, do you?" Lily asked. She felt terrible for forgetting them this morning.

"I *won't* forget them," Dominic said. "But having this day to remember makes me feel awful for me, not for them. I keep thinking of all the things I miss about them, and I feel selfish."

"What do you miss?" Jordan asked.

Dominic blinked, as if it was impossible to know where to begin.

There were a million things, big and small. "Nina's brownies," Lily said. "She'd make them so that the centers were undercooked and gooey."

"Right," Jordan said, "and we'd start taking squares out from the center, so that in the end there was just a crusty brownie frame left in the pan."

"I miss hearing a stupid song Mom sang sometimes," Dominic said. "Do y'all remember? The one about Carmen the Chameleon?"

Jordan burst out laughing.

"What?" Dominic said.

"It's '*Karma* Chameleon.' "

Dominic frowned. "What's that?"

"That's the song." She sang a few bars. "It's from the eighties. You can YouTube it if you don't believe me."

Dominic looked down at his cereal bowl, disappointed. "Oh—I thought it was about a chameleon named Carmen. That's what it sounded like when Mom sang it."

"Mom was a really awful singer," Lily said.

Dominic sighed. "I miss that Mom and Nina weren't the only ones who gave squeezies."

Both Lily and Jordan stared at him, uncomprehending. "What's a squeezie?" Jordan asked.

"It's when someone hugs you so tight that you feel like you're going to have all the air squeezed out of you. Remember how they both used to do that?" he asked. "Nobody else does that."

Lily did remember. She hadn't ever thought about that till now. But Dominic was right. Their mom had possessed an internal radar that sensed when one of them was feeling down. Lily could recall trying to hide how bad she felt one time when she was being tormented in gym class by a group of girls who burst out laughing whenever she said anything, or even if she just looked at them. She'd thought she'd been doing a good job of carrying on as if nothing had happened until her mom came up to her before bedtime one night and gave her a hug that nearly shut out the awful memories, in addition to cutting off her circulation. Without words, her mom had known something was wrong.

Nina was like that, too. But Nina was so affectionate, she would also give you a hug or swing you around for no reason at all. And everyone always talked about Nina as if she was perfect, but she could be unpredictable, too. Lily remembered one time when she was little and she and Nina had been raking leaves. They had raked for two hours until they were achy and exhausted and all the leaves were in neat piles. And then Nina got a gleam in her eye and started tearing around the yard, plowing through the piles and kicking up leaves. For a moment Lily had stared at her, stunned, and then she had let out a banshee yell and followed suit. The two of them had gone crazy, but it was Nina, so it was fun crazy. Not crazy crazy, like Jordan.

"Sometimes I've felt like no one wants to touch me at all," Jordan said. "Or even look at me."

Lily took a bite of her toast and forced herself to chew. *She* hadn't wanted to look at Jordan sometimes. Most of the time. They were so different, it was hard to believe they were of the same species, never mind the same family. Especially now that Nina wasn't here. Nina had been their missing link.

"You see?" Dominic asked. "This is the problem. I'm just thinking about me. That's not what we're supposed to be doing, is it?"

"I'm not sure anyone knows what we're supposed to do," Jordan said. "There's no rule book, Nickel."

"Well, if there was, it wouldn't include feeling sorry for yourself," he said. "I'm pretty sure that's a sin or something, isn't it?"

Jordan bit her lip. "I'm not the person to ask about that."

They were interrupted by their dad, who came in abruptly. As Jordan and Dominic had said, he was dressed in a dark gray suit. "Do you all want to go with me?"

Nobody asked where. They just got up and filed

out to the car. They didn't argue over where to sit, either. Jordan got in the front, Lily and Dominic in the back. The drive out to the cemetery took about ten minutes in the light Saturday-morning traffic.

Their dad parked on the roadway not far from the graves. He and Dominic carried the big potted azaleas he must have bought while they were eating breakfast. They laid them down, first at their mother's grave, then at Nina's. Lily wondered if maybe Dominic was right. All year she'd felt grief—first painful, then slowly dulling to a persistent ache that flared up into occasional crying jags. But now . . . She was filled with the unbearable, wrenching misery she hadn't felt since the funeral last year. Especially when she looked at Nina's flat grave. She just couldn't believe Nina was there. Nina *wasn't* there. Not her Nina.

Her Nina had always been active, bursting with ideas for things to do. The rest of them complained about being bored all the time, but Nina, never. She'd played sports and always had some other weird project going on, like when she'd put on a puppet show for Dominic when he was five. Only, it wasn't just any old lame puppet show. Nina had tried to replicate the movie *The Little Mermaid* with sock puppets. If she'd had a fault, it was that she'd been impatient with people who didn't approach life with the same zeal she did. Her criticism could be more withering than Jordan's if you crossed her path.

A sharp guilt pierced Lily. She shouldn't think bad things about Nina. Not today. But she still refused to think Nina was here. If anything, Nina was up in heaven somewhere, shaking her head at them. *Just look at them all!* she was probably thinking. *Wasting this gorgeous day moping around a cemetery. . . .*

For a moment, Lily could feel her sister's presence so clearly that holding herself together was hard. She looked around to see if anyone else felt it, too. Jordan stood across from her, her face white. She appeared trembly but almost stoic next to Dominic, whose arms were rigid at his sides. He cried openly, tears streaming down his cheeks and dropping onto his shirt, creating damp streaks. Lily glanced around for their dad, and she found him still kneeling next to their mom's azalea. He'd never moved.

A wretched feeling swept over her, like a fever. All this time, she'd been thinking about how much she missed her mom and Nina, and about Dominic and his squeezies. She'd even spared a moment for Jordan and feeling guilty for disliking her so much. But she hadn't given a thought to how her father must ache, remembering their mom. About what a chore getting through every day must have seemed to him, too, this past year. Kneeling there, her father looked like the loneliest man in the world.

• • •

It was probably a dumb thing for them to be out in public, considering how gloomy they all felt. But on the way back from the cemetery, they stopped and ate. For most of the time nobody said anything beyond *pass the salt, how's your food?* and *fine* until dessert, which Dominic wanted but nobody else did. But nobody seemed to want to go home, either.

When Dominic was just starting on his cake, their dad made an announcement. "I'm thinking about putting the house on the market," he said.

"What?" Jordan asked.

He shifted. "Well, the house is . . . it's so big . . ."

"No!" Lily exclaimed, unexpectedly loudly. She couldn't help it. She thought about the few *good* things that had happened in the year—knowing Grace, and the professor, and Crawford. If her dad sold their house, she'd lose all that too. "We can't move!"

"You'd sell Mom's house?" Dominic gasped.

Their dad seemed shocked by their reactions. "I wasn't thinking of it that way."

"If we moved, how would I ever be able to see the professor and Grace?" Dominic asked. "Or walk Iago?"

His frown deepened. "It's just an idea I've been kicking around in my head."

"It's an idea that stinks," Jordan said.

Lily hoped it was an idea that he would soon discard.

Silence fell around the table.

Then, just as they were all calming down again, Jordan had to start talking. Naturally. "Have you given any thought to me going to California this summer?" she asked their dad.

"It's a long way to go and be all by yourself," he said.

"I'm seventeen now. I'm going to college next year, and you won't care if I go to the University of Timbuktu then. San Francisco now, Timbuktu U next year—what's the big diff?"

He shifted uncomfortably and worked his jaw side to side as he crunched an ice cube—anyone with half a brain could tell that he was fishing for the most diplomatic way to say no. "I work with people in California," he said. "I guess I could ask them if they've heard of the program."

"What would a bunch of software geeks know about an art program?"

Way to get what you want, Jordan, Lily thought. She didn't understand finesse at all.

In the spirit of the closeness she'd felt toward her sister that morning, Lily added helpfully, "The brochure says they're careful about supervision, Dad." Apparently, this program had to handle questions from lots of parents worried about sending their kids to San Francisco and having them freak out. "They have fifteen students per live-in supervisor, and besides, because of the rigorous program, students won't have much free time to explore the city aside from supervised outings."

Jordan blinked at her, astonished. "Did you go through my stuff?"

"No," Lily said. "Dad left the brochure on his desk. I just happened to see it when I brought the mail in."

"I must have skimmed over that part about the supervisors," he said.

Now he was at least starting to sound as if the idea was worth mulling over.

Lily and Jordan exchanged looks. *See?* Lily tried to convey with hers. *I could be your friend if you'd let me.*

Jordan's lips quirked into a half smile—the closest she could probably come to a thank-you—and she turned back to their dad. *"Please?"*

He looked down at his coffee, noncommittal but leaning favorably, Lily guessed. "I'll think about it," he said.

Dominic, his cheeks bulging like a squirrel's, only with Mississippi mud cake instead of nuts, looked at them all with equal parts apprehension and wonder. Lily could read his thoughts. *Dad sort of interacting, no one fighting, dessert freely offered . . .*

It had been forever since they'd gotten along this well.

The truce lasted all the quiet afternoon. The spring weather allowed them to keep the windows open, and they could hear violin music playing from Peggy's house down the street, where the wedding reception was being held. Occasionally the sound of laughter would float their way, too, and Lily would feel a pang of envy for those people in Peggy's backyard—guests at a wedding reception on a beautiful day instead of inmates in the house of perpetual mourning.

And then immediately she would feel awful for having such a terrible selfish thought. Even if it was true.

Anyway, weddings—even the weddings of senior citizens—made her think of romance, which made her think of her situation with Crawford. Granted, it wasn't much of a situation, since nothing had actually happened, but she still had hope.

Restless, she went down to the living room and sat on the opposite side of the couch from Dominic, who was playing a handheld video game.

He immediately launched into a defense. "I know—it's a complete waste of time."

"I didn't say anything," she said.

"But you were going to, weren't you?"

She shrugged. "Probably. You could have least given me the chance."

"Chance to what?" Jordan came in and flopped

sideways into a chair, dangling her legs over the chair arm.

"Nothing," Dominic said.

"He thinks I wouldn't be able to resist telling him that electronic games are a waste of time."

"I'll tell him." Jordan fixed her gaze on him. "Nickel, games are a waste of time."

He grunted and kept playing.

"Did my best," Jordan told Lily with a shrug. "Kids these days."

Lily hesitated to ask Jordan the question that had been burning in her mind lately. It seemed so stupid, but Crawford had mentioned it specifically, so she kept coming back to it.

"Jordan? Say you wanted to buy a formal . . ." she began in a casual tone. "What thrift store would you go to for that?"

Jordan's eyebrows darted up. "Big date?"

Lily confessed, "Not really. But I hope I'm going to the dance."

"Who with?"

"It doesn't matter," Lily said. "He hasn't asked me yet."

"Who?" Jordan insisted.

Some madness—some temporary amnesia regarding her sister's true personality—made her confess. "Crawford."

"Crawford!" Dominic yelled, appalled that a friend of his would be considered date material by his sister.

Jordan sputtered, almost laughing. "Whoa—that's a seriously hopeless case."

"Why?" Lily asked defensively.

"Because he asked me," Jordan said.

At first, Lily thought she must have heard wrong. But she knew she hadn't because the words kept echoing in her head.

She felt sick.

"When?"

"Yesterday," Jordan said. "I skipped last period and came home from school early. He must have been stalking me or something."

Lily's heart had stopped beating. She wasn't lying. Crawford hadn't been in band class the day before. "What did you say?" she asked, dreading the answer.

Jordan sneered at the question. "What do you think? I said no."

No?

Lily couldn't believe it. If Jordan had said yes, that would have been tragic. She wasn't even sure she could have stood it. But instead Jordan had said no, and she couldn't even feel relief. The nicest boy in the whole world! He probably felt awful. And now, so did she.

Jordan looked down at her black fingernails. "Dude's gonna run around asking girls who don't like him to the spring dance, he's gotta expect an epic fail."

"That's so mean! I hope he realizes how lucky

he is to not be going with you." She tilted her head. "Who *are* you going with?"

"*Nobody.* I wouldn't be caught dead at a moronic high school dance again."

The moronic high school dance that I've had my heart set on for months, Lily cringed at all the hours she'd spent daydreaming, the hints she'd dropped—when it had been hopeless all along. He liked Jordan.

Rage mounted inside her until she could barely stand it. She wanted to get up and stomp out, but she knew that would make Jordan laugh at her.

"You really are a bitch!" Lily was immediately angry at herself for having sunk to Jordan's level, but the word had just leapt out of her mouth.

Jordan's eyes bugged, as if she couldn't believe what she'd heard, and then she hooted with laughter. "And you're pathetic! Lusting after the neighbor boy—you probably dreamed he was Prince Charming or something. That would be about your speed."

Lily's throat felt so choked she wasn't sure she could speak.

To her shock, Dominic threw down his game. It glanced off her, and for a second Lily thought he'd thrown it at her on purpose, but apparently she was just collateral damage. He jumped up and faced Jordan. "Why do you have to be so mean?" he yelled. "Just when things were starting to seem a little better around here! You aren't ever nice to anybody!"

Jordan reached out to grab him. "Come on, Nickel—*we're* friends."

"No, we're not," he said, wrenching his arm away. "You never think about me. Not really. I'm just a house pet or something. You act all nice to me for about five minutes and then you ignore me! I hate it!"

When he was gone, Jordan looked as if she'd been smacked. "What's the matter with him?"

Lily shook her head. "You just don't listen, do you?"

"What? You think I treat you like a house pet, too?"

"No!"

"No, of course not. Because you were Nina's little pet. Nina and Mom's."

"I wasn't anybody's pet. Nina liked me because we had things in common, and because when you were in junior high you started behaving like an idiot. You even acted like you were too cool for Nina sometimes."

Jordan glared at her. "You don't know anything about Nina."

Lily released a bitter laugh that felt so good. "You thought because she was your twin you owned her or something, so you resented me when she hung out with me and invited me places. And you're still jealous!"

"Shut your yap!"

"Or maybe you're just feeling guilty."

Jordan's cheeks flamed. "Why?"

Lily crossed her arms. "You know why."

"Because I killed them, right? I'm a murderess—isn't that what you called me in that pathetic diary of yours?"

Lily froze. "What do you know about my diary?"

"You left it on the kitchen table one morning. I had to read something with my Shredded Wheat. So you see, I already knew all about your sad little crush on little Crawdad McHeartthrob."

She'd known? And she'd made her confess it anyway?

Lily tried to sound calm, but when she spoke her voice quavered. "You'll be sorry."

Jordan stood. "Oh—are you going to write me up in your diary again?" She walked away slowly, but once upstairs, she slammed her door. Seconds later, the thump of old punk music made the ceiling vibrate.

I'm not going to cry, Lily told herself. *Crying does no good.*

She rubbed moisture off her cheeks when her dad emerged from his study. "What's going on?" he demanded. "I heard all of you yelling—even Dominic—and then doors slamming, and now the whole house is vibrating to the Sex Pistols!" He glared up at the ceiling. "How does she even know about the Sex Pistols? They were before *my* time!"

"Heather, probably," Lily told him, pulling herself together.

"Who?" He shook his head. "I would think you all could try to get along—today of all days."

Today of all days. The reminder pushed her over the edge.

"Dad, can I talk to you about something?"

He looked wary. "What?"

"It's really important," she said. "But I need to talk to you in private. And I need to run upstairs and get something first."

"Okay," he agreed. "But while you're up there, could you please tell Jordan to ramp down the volume a little?"

"Sure," Lily said, although she had no intention to. It wouldn't matter to her if she never spoke to Jordan again for the rest of her life. She took the stairs two at a time and went straight to the second drawer of her desk, where she kept her journal.

Thinking of the journal, and Jordan looking in it, made her furious all over again.

No, she wasn't going to cry this time. This time, she was finally going to get even.

30

A Change in Constellations

The first person Grace ran into at the reception was Wyatt, who was joining the herd around the champagne table. Pippa, a petite, pretty blonde who looked way too nice for him, was on his arm.

"All alone today, Grace?" Wyatt asked, raising a brow at her. "*You* don't intend to wait till you're eighty to get married, do you?"

"I'm not alone," Grace said. "I came with the best man."

It was something she had to repeat over and over during the course of the afternoon. Today Lou had dressed in a dark blue suit and looked more like his dapper old self. He outshone the groom, although Uncle Truman had actually sprung for a new suit for the occasion. Truman was even taking Peggy on a honeymoon—they were driving to Natchez, Mississippi, to look at the old houses and spring flowers. Peggy's idea, surely, not Truman's.

Grace had been hoping to see Ray at the reception at Peggy's house. She'd spotted him earlier in the day wearing a suit, something he didn't usually even wear to work, and she had anticipated having at least one other unattached someone to stand next to. But Ray had not shown up. She wondered why—and why he'd been so dressed up. Another function to attend, evidently.

She hung around the fringes of the backyard reception and watched Peggy and Truman doing some pretty lively dancing on the patio to a string trio. The swing music had a reversing effect on the dance floor: the old people jitterbugged while the younger demographic shuffled awkwardly or lingered on the sidelines. But it didn't matter. The day was exactly right for a wedding—sunny and not too hot—and Peggy's spring garden was a berserk flower display. Everything seemed perfect.

Grace spotted Crawford, whose glum expression proclaimed the fact that he was not bursting with joy.

She went over to him. "Not dancing?"

"Dancing's not my favorite topic right now," he said.

She remembered seeing him storm out of Ray's house the day before. "Is something wrong?"

He held a glass of cola in his hands and kept his gaze focused on it, swirling the contents so that they made a noisy whirlpool of soda and clinking ice cubes. "Nothing's wrong, except that I never get what I really want."

"What happened?" she asked.

His face turned red. "Nothing."

"Did you have a fight with Dominic and Lily?" she asked.

He snorted dismissively. "Nah, *they're* all right." He obviously had no intention of opening up to her about whatever subject was really bugging him. "Do you think it would be bad if I left now?"

"Of course not. Just say good-bye to Peggy, to be polite and rack up brownie points. She might need someone to help with her yard this summer. It will get you that much closer to your car."

He smiled, obviously taking comfort in the reminder. Dreams were the best balm for disappointment.

She was chewing over what exactly might be going on to make Crawford so miserable, when Steven found her. He was alone. Even though Muriel was across the yard, wearing a low-cut fitted blue silk dress and pearls, Grace hadn't seen them dancing. Nor had Muriel been standing next to Steven with the family during the wedding ceremony.

"I keep thinking it's a shame Sam couldn't be here," she said as he approached her.

Steven eyed the cake. "I was thinking about Uncle Truman's diabetes."

At his typically unsentimental remark, Grace inhaled champagne and nearly choked. Her brother had to pat her on the back a few times, and she was so grateful to him in that moment for making her laugh that she forgot the resentment that had been seething inside her since her encounter with him and Muriel at the coffee shop.

Steven obviously didn't see anything the least bit funny in what he'd said. "I don't know what they needed a cake for," he grumbled. "This crowd's arteries are probably clogged enough already."

"You have to have cake at a wedding," she said. "Remember? You've had two of them."

His lips flattened into a grim line. "Not likely to have a third."

She glanced at Muriel, who was dancing with one of Uncle Truman's contemporaries, her head tossed back in laughter.

"I'm sorry about the other day, Grace," Steven said, his gaze following hers. "But in a way, I'm not sorry. I saw a side of her . . ."

A side that Muriel was probably hoping he wouldn't see—at least not for a while yet.

She let out a breath. That was one disaster averted, at least.

"Let's forget about it," she said.

"Agreed." He held out his hand. "Dance?"

The band was playing "The Tennessee Waltz." "Do you know how to waltz?" she asked him doubtfully.

"No clue," he said. "But how hard can it be?"

She laughed. "I guess my toes are about to find out."

• • •

She and her dad were both too full from snacking at the wedding to want to bother with dinner that evening. After he had beaten her at a game of chess, she set up the tea set on the back porch, but Lou had already resumed watching *The Forsyte Saga.* She went out alone, flipped on the porch light, and sat down with her dad's battered copy of *Modern Chess Strategy.* She was determined to learn enough chess maneuvers to win once or twice in her lifetime.

Her eyes were just beginning to glaze over halfway through a section called "The Equilibrium of the Position" when she became aware of someone nearby. She looked up and realized Ray was standing in his yard. From her vantage point on the porch, she could just see the top of his head over the fence. She closed her book and stood. He still wore the suit she'd seen him in that morning, only without the jacket. His hands were in his pockets and he was staring up at the new night sky.

"All dressed up and nowhere to go," she said, just loud enough to carry over the fence.

He didn't seem surprised to hear her voice. "Can you tell the Big Dipper from the Little Dipper?" he asked.

She glanced up. "I usually have a hard time just figuring out which one is Venus."

"Jen knew all the stars—all the ones you could

see with the naked eye. She was forever rattling on about Taurus and Cassiopeia—and I would just sort of look up and nod. I think she said something about how the dippers weren't actually constellations anymore . . ."

"Really? The way Pluto isn't a planet anymore? I know science is always advancing, but I wish they'd leave the third grade basics alone."

"Jen knew all that stuff, but I wasn't paying attention. Now I wish I had. I feel that way about a lot of things. It was as if she was telling me how to get along all those years, but I just wasn't listening. I took it for granted."

"You thought she would be around."

He kept his gaze focused overhead. "It's been one year."

For a moment she didn't follow, but in the next second, looking at the way he was standing there, so alone, she understood what *it* meant. She felt like an idiot for having made that crack about his being all dressed up with nowhere to go.

"Come over and have some tea," she said. "I made a cup for Dad, but he's staring at the television."

Ray came around through the gate and stepped up on the porch. When he sat down, the way his legs and elbows jutted out from the thin iron arms of the patio furniture emphasized how tall he was. In his everyday clothes he never looked so gangly. Or maybe it was the rawness of his hurt that made him seem so awkward and brittle. As if one more blow just might snap something.

Some of what she was feeling must have shown in her face.

"I didn't tell you about the—the anniversary to earn your pity," he said, apologizing. "It's just I haven't been able to think of anything else. I shouldn't have come over. I'll probably be a bore to talk to."

He was on the verge of popping out of the chair again, but she put a restraining hand on one shoulder and with her other hand lifted a cup of tea in front of him. "You won't bore me. It's been a long time since we've had a chance to talk. We've been ships passing in the night."

Which was a gentle spin for what they'd actually been doing—studiously avoiding each other after Jordan threw her hissy fit.

He took his tea and settled back again. "I know there was the wedding today. Peggy invited me. I couldn't go—not today. And I was too much of a coward to RSVP, because I thought I'd have to give a reason for not going, and I didn't want . . ."

"It didn't matter. No one missed you." Grace's words echoed for a split second before she added, "Bad word choice. Of course you were missed. *I* missed you—missed having someone sane there to talk to, I mean. I'm sure Peggy didn't mind."

They both sipped.

"Did you have a nice time?" he asked.

"It was fine, even though there's been some family weirdness lately."

A shadow passed over his face, and he sighed. "Yes, I've had my share of that, too."

"Today?" she asked.

"Everything seemed fine," he explained, "and then half an hour later all the kids were fighting. I couldn't understand where it all came from. Then, after the blowup, Lily marched into my office and informed me that Jordan had snuck out of the house one night after her curfew."

"Oh, no," Grace said. "Are you sure it's true?"

"Lily showed me dated journal entries, and she also had photographic evidence of Jordan getting into a car at night with some older woman. All the people she hangs out with seem to be too old now."

Grace assumed he was talking about crazy Heather. "What did Jordan say about all this?"

"She was livid, but she didn't deny a thing. I told her that she couldn't go to California this summer. There was a summer arts program she had her heart set on, but if I can't trust her here at home, how can I possibly let her loose in San Francisco?"

Grace nodded in sympathy. And yet she felt sympathy for Jordan, too. And a pang of guilt. After the second Heather incident, and seeing that awful apartment, maybe she should have warned Ray that Jordan's best friend was a serious oddball. Or at least told Jordan that she was heading down a path full of pitfalls.

Not that Jordan would have listened to her.

"Now all of a sudden it's as if war has broken out in the house," Ray continued. "I don't know how it's going to end. I don't know what to do for the kids. It's all I can do to hold *myself* together."

She thought for a moment of Crawford, and how upset he'd been. And how just the mention of his dream car had cheered him a little bit.

"People need something to hope for," she said. "To look forward to. Especially kids. I imagine Lily and Dominic and Jordan are dreaming of a time when they won't be so unhappy. A time when they won't wake up thinking about the worst thing that's happened. Jordan probably does, too."

"Something to look forward to," he said. "Like California."

Grace shrugged. "I don't know. You could start smaller. Maybe just interact with them a little more."

His eyes narrowed. "Family activities, you mean? Jen always took care of most of that—outings, vacations, birthday parties."

She felt a spike of frustration. "*You* have to step up, Ray. Don't say you can't and just hide away from them, working."

His brow tensed. "I know I've been distant. I've hardly been able to function myself. Oh, I realize you were probably thinking I was terrible last year—a workaholic dad. Or maybe you thought I was burying my grief in work, but the truth is, I had to work twice as much because it took me twice as long to do things. I was always dreaming about Jen, and wishing she were back with me. I've been going crazy, and the only way I knew how to hide it from the kids was just to avoid them. Obviously, that was a mistake."

"Yes, it was. But I understood. I think the kids understood, too. But you can't go on ignoring them, Ray."

He sighed. "We went out today and it was a disaster. My efforts to bring us all together just made things worse. What can I do for them?"

"You must have been good for something all those years."

"I don't know. I worked. I mowed the yard. I never even prepared the meals, except for grilling things every once in a while."

Her ears perked up. "See? That's something."

He straightened. "Is it?"

"Of course."

He thought about it for a moment. "We had backyard cookouts sometimes. Everyone enjoyed them."

"There you go."

"I could do that again." His eyes glistened with a growing enthusiasm. A crazed enthusiasm, actually. "I could have one next weekend, or the weekend after that. Or Easter, maybe. That would give me time to plan. I could invite the whole neighborhood."

Whoa. "You might want to start with something a little more intimate."

Oddly, though, he seemed truly taken with the idea. "No—the more the merrier. We've all been shut up for so long, and people have been so good to us. I need to repay everyone somehow. Why not a backyard party? Easter would give us time, right?"

She was wondering who he meant by *us*. Maybe he meant himself and his family. Or was he including her? "I guess."

"I need to start figuring this out." He got up and was already drifting away, lost in thought. In plans. Halfway to his own house, he stopped.

"You looked beautiful today, Grace," he said, as if it was both a matter of fact and a consolation.

And strangely enough, coming from him, it was.

31

Hell to Pay

Jordan jabbed paint on the canvas in front of her, distracted by the herd of emotions charging around her head. She didn't know why she bothered painting at all—sometimes the futility of it overwhelmed her. She wasn't going to San Francisco. She wished now she hadn't sent in her application to the program; it would be sickening if they rejected her, and even worse if she got accepted and couldn't go.

It had been a bad week. First had come Lily's treachery and their dad telling her that she couldn't go to California this summer. Then, after she'd bricked her last algebra test, she'd gone to talk to the teacher, Mr. Witt, ready to beg, plead, bribe—anything to encourage him to nudge her test grade from an F to a D. But after she'd blurted out her sob story—she was so busy, was still having problems adjusting to all the changes in her life, blah, blah, blah—Mr. Witt had frowned down at his desk for a moment, his mouth tensing into a flat line so that his lips disappeared.

"Part of my job as a teacher, especially as a teacher of mathematics, is to emphasize logic. And a large part of logic, unfortunately, is that actions have consequences."

"Yeah, but—"

"Actions have consequences."

As if she of all people didn't know that!

Mr. Witt wasn't going to change her grade. She was going to fail.

She looked at her painting, which wasn't coming out the way she wanted. She had found a silly little collapsible wooden toy on the kitchen counter and had intended to do a still life of it for an art project. But the little black-and-white cow with its flat features and segmented legs was proving to be a tougher subject than she'd expected.

There was a knock at the door and Dominic poked his head in. "What are you doing?" he yelled over her music.

She turned it down a hair.

He stepped in, nose wrinkling. "It stinks in here."

Jordan loved the smell of oils. If some company were to bottle it, she'd buy it. But there was Buns to consider, hunched in his cage in the corner. Buns was practically her best friend now. She didn't want the poor guy to asphyxiate. She walked over to pry open a window.

Dominic gawped at the canvas. "Grace's cow!"

She was taken aback. "Grace's? I found it in the kitchen."

He picked up the model. "Yeah . . . I sort of took it. Grace has a whole lot of these. She calls them push puppets."

"What does she do with them?"

He shrugged and put it back as it had been. "I dunno. They just sit on her desk, mostly."

What little enthusiasm she had for her painting waned now that she knew where her model had come from. But she had to keep going; she hated not finishing stuff.

Dominic crossed his arms. "Do you want to go do something?"

"I'm sort of busy here, Nickel," she said, distracted. "What's going on next door?"

"They're not home," he muttered, trudging back toward the door. "They went to Houston."

"Why?"

"So Professor Oliver can see a specialist."

"Is he sick?"

"Not really *sick.* He's got Alzheimer's."

Jordan straightened and looked over at him. "Seriously?"

He rattled the doorknob restlessly. "That's what Lily told me. Why?"

"Because that's *really awful,*" Jordan said.

Dominic frowned and kept on rattling the doorknob. "Really? He seems okay to me."

She turned back to look at her cow and shook her head. "Now, maybe. But people with Alzheimer's really lose it. Their brains turn to mush. Maggie Burton's grandmom had Alzheimer's and according to Maggie she basically just sat around drooling in a nursing home until she died."

"Yeah, but Professor Oliver's not that bad."

"Not that bad *yet,* maybe," Jordan said. "It's like one of the worst things that can happen to you." Poor old geezer.

"Oh," Dominic said.

"You didn't hear the phone ring, did you?" she asked him.

"No," he said.

She was hoping Heather would want to go out. But the truth was, the last couple of times Jordan had called Heather, she'd sort of blown her off.

She turned to ask Dominic where Lily was—it helped to keep track of her so she could avoid her altogether—but Dominic was already gone. She went back to painting, but the mere thought of Lily made her so hopping mad she couldn't concentrate. Lily, the life ruiner.

She should have wrung her scrawny neck when she'd told Jordan that she was jealous of her and Nina. Jealous, of Lily! What a pathetic delusion that was. Lily didn't know squat about Nina. Just because Nina talked to her about books, and because Lily was willing to let her whack tennis balls at her and talk her into doing goofy crafty stuff like making elaborate costumes for character day at school—all the junk Nina did that had seemed like a total waste of time to Jordan—Lily assumed they had been best buds. But that was nothing compared to the bond Jordan had had with Nina. Nina had meant everything to her, and then when Lily got older she started butting in, and . . .

Jordan's eyes started to water, and she wrenched her cell phone from its charger on the floor by the bed to check for messages. Nothing from Heather, or anybody. She felt all alone in the world.

She flopped onto her bed and thought about dyeing her hair pink.

But what did it matter? She had no future to need pink hair for. She was either going to spend her summer working at McDonald's or repeating Algebra II in summer school. And no one was ever going to call her again, evidently.

She heard something from down below and got up to look out the window. Her dad and Lily were dragging the lawn furniture around. Oh, yeah. She'd heard Lily telling their dad this morning that she'd *love* to help him spray paint the lawn furniture. Little Miss Suck-up. Their dad had turned manic recently. It was weird. He'd latched on to the idea of having a big party in the backyard, and now he was always trying to get them involved.

Jordan flipped off her music, grabbed her bike messenger bag, and left the house.

At first she didn't know where she was going, but she found herself on the bus headed for Heather's apartment. She dug through her bag for her cell phone, but then she remembered that she'd put it back in its charger. Damn. But it wasn't as if she hadn't dropped in on Heather before. As long as she brought a treat, Heather was always happy to see her.

She got off the bus a stop early so she could go to the 7-Eleven. In the store, she looked around for something Heather would like. Chips were always good, but this day cried out for super comfort food. She finally settled on a box of Little Debbie Star Crunches and a giant bottle of Dr Pepper.

Humidity hung thick in the air, and by the time she made it to Heather's she was hot, sticky, and tired. She was just stepping into the complex's driveway when the door to Heather's apartment opened and Heather walked out, followed by some guy.

They both stopped in midstep when they saw Jordan. Neither of them looked thrilled to see her.

"Oh, hey," Heather said, smiling but without much enthusiasm. "Clint, this is Jordan. You know . . . the kid I told you about."

Kid?

The unspoken desire between them to get rid of her was palpable. Clint's hair, she noticed now, was sleeked down and wet. Like he'd just taken a shower. Now that she thought about it, Heather's cornrows seemed sort of damp, too. Her hair was usually so oily and skanky that water tended to roll right off her head, so it was hard to tell. But clearly something of an intimate nature had occurred.

Hoping she was hiding the flush in her cheeks, Jordan said, "So y'all are going somewhere?"

"Yeah," Clint said. "There's a thing."

"I love things," Jordan said.

Heather rushed in. "It's kind of an adult thing."

Jordan let out a humorless laugh. "What—a porn party?"

Heather rolled her eyes. "No, but you know. There'll be lots of alcohol. And adults."

"Oh, and I've never been around those before," Jordan said sarcastically.

Clint let out a nervous chuckle. "It's just . . ."

"Yeah, I get it." It was just that they didn't want her there. She lifted her head. "Never mind. I just came by to hang out."

Heather looked down at the bag. "Oh—and you brought stuff. Sweet! You can leave it here if you want."

"No, I think I'll take it home. I need a sugar rush now. I had a sort of crappy week."

She hadn't even seen Heather since learning she wasn't going to get to go to San Francisco. She had left her a message, but Heather hadn't called back. Hadn't even texted. Which was perfect—her life had been ruined because she'd gone to some stupid club with Heather, and now Heather was making her feel like a pariah.

"Aw, suck-ass," Clint said sympathetically.

"But that's what being in high school is all about, isn't it, kiddo?" Heather asked. "Learning to deal with crap."

Kiddo?

Heather glanced at her watch. "You need us to drop you at the bus?"

She didn't even rate a ride home anymore, apparently.

"No, thanks." Face blazing with embarrassment, Jordan walked back to the corner and didn't even acknowledge them when they cruised by in Clint's truck. While she was on the bus she realized she was dying of thirst. She opened up the two-liter plastic jug of Dr Pepper and started swigging it. The woman sitting next to her changed seats.

Screw Heather, Jordan fumed. She didn't care if she never saw her again. Only, she wasn't going to give her Buns back. Heather had been talking about giving Buns to the Humane Society anyway.

Forsake your rabbit, forsake your friends. Why hadn't she seen it coming?

After she'd made her way back to the house, she realized that barely an hour had passed. Sixty minutes that had resulted in her life getting even worse. Lily and their dad were still in the backyard, and Dominic was in the living room, laid out on the couch like something half dead.

"What's the matter?" she asked him.

He groaned. "I ate five bowls of cereal. One right after the other."

"Why did you do that?"

"I was worried about what you'd said about Professor Oliver."

"That's no reason!"

But she felt a stab of guilt as she wedged herself between his feet and the edge of the couch. She'd said that about Maggie's grandmom without thinking.

He looked at the plastic carrier bag in her hand. "What did you get?"

She remembered that she was wagging around a dose of sugar solace too. “Little Debbies.”

He sat up. “Can I have one?”

“No! You’ll hurl, Nickel.”

“Star Crunches are my favorite.”

She remembered what he and Lily had said about her—that she treated Dominic like a puppy. It would be easy to give him a treat and walk away, to go upstairs and wallow some more in her own woe. But she couldn’t. She was so depressed, but when she looked into Dominic’s round eyes, she felt a weird jolt. Like maybe she wasn’t *totally* alone after all. And hadn’t been, ever.

“Let’s go a movie,” she said.

He tilted his head. “You can’t drive.”

“So?”

“Nina used to say that when she learned to drive, she’d take me to the movies.”

Yeah, Jordan remembered that. It was Nina’s leverage with their mom for taking driver’s ed and getting her learner’s permit as soon as she legally could. She’d promised she would help hauling the kids around. She probably would have, too.

Now for a whole year, no one had hauled Dominic and Lily anywhere.

“Well, we’ll take a bus,” she said. “There are a couple of theaters we can get to that way, easy. I’ll go check the Internet.”

Dominic hopped up, then stopped. “Shouldn’t we ask Dad first?”

“Huh? Oh, yeah—I guess so. Except maybe you should do it. And tell him it’s Pixar.”

“What is?”

“The movie we’re going to see.”

“What *are* we going to see?”

“I don’t know. Just tell him it’s a cartoon thing. That way he won’t think I’m going to drag you off to watch *Deep Throat.*”

His eyes widened. “Is that a slasher movie?”

“Just say Pixar,” Jordan repeated.

Dominic ran out the back and Jordan was heading upstairs when she glimpsed something out of the corner of her eye. Lily’s journal was sitting on the sideboard in the dining room, next to a filthy pair of gardening gloves.

She hesitated, then hurried over to it. Without allowing herself to ponder the pros and cons of what she was doing, she grabbed the book and shoved it into her plastic bag next to the Star Crunches.

Lily thought she’d already won the war, but she was so wrong. Jordan hadn’t even begun to fight.

32

I Wouldn't Do That If I Were You

In Houston, Lou underwent one more brain scan and met with yet another neurologist, whose patiently earnest stonewalling and nondivulgence of useful information made Grace realize with textbook clarity that he was a man with no good news to tell.

During the tense moments, the waiting, she found herself daydreaming about Ray and wondering how the spray painting of the patio furniture was coming along. At one point she was on the verge of calling him to remind him to buy protective goggles. It would have been just like him to be so wrapped up in what he was doing that he would forget and end up spattering a pair of glasses beyond all repair.

And then she gave herself a stiff mental slap. *Enough with the mother hen already, Grace.*

Enough with thinking about trivialities so she didn't have to focus on her dad's painstakingly dignified gait and sad expression as they navigated the unfamiliar medical complex.

She couldn't imagine what was going through her father's head. Beyond mentioning the scenery,

Lou didn't speak much on the way home. She didn't even know what hopes he'd had when they went to Houston, or if he'd harbored any hopes at all. Steven had recommended he go, and now he'd gone, and he didn't seem inclined to confide in Grace about his disappointment over the medical evidence that his condition had deteriorated since last summer—something that Grace—and probably Lou, too—had already known.

The only real conversation they had on the way home had been about the party, and Ray's family.

"I don't know how this party is going to come off," she said as they approached the fringes of Austin. "Planning it seems to have popped Ray back to life a little, though."

Her dad had grunted at that. "A man doesn't get over a tragedy like his in a year, or two, or even a decade. I didn't, when I lost Joyce. And I guess I made my big mistakes during that time."

She gritted her teeth. Her mom was the mistake he was talking about.

He drummed his hands on his knees as he looked out at a patch of Indian paintbrush and observed, "We don't see as much of Lily anymore."

"She's been busy helping Ray—and I think she's trying to avoid Crawford."

"Why should she do that?"

"Why do you think, Dad?"

He frowned. "Is she breaking his heart?"

"Other way around. According to Dominic, he likes someone else. Lily's sister, actually."

Lou pivoted, shocked. "I should give that boy a thump on the head. Lily's got twice as many smarts as that crazy-haired hoyden."

"Don't mention it, Dad. Crawford knows nothing about how Lily feels. Anyway, he's brokenhearted, too. According to Dominic, he asked Jordan to a dance and she turned him down flat."

"So it's good times all around." He drummed his fingers on his knees. "Well, maybe this thing of Ray's will liven up everyone. Is it this weekend?"

"The next."

"Yes, that's right."

Grace couldn't decide if watching Ray pop back to life that April was gratifying or frightening. For the past several weekends, he had been a whirlwind of action. Whenever she gazed across the fence now, there were always ladders out, or tarps spread, or gutters being cleaned. He would return from Saturday morning shopping outings laden with plants, hanging baskets, and even Chinese lanterns. Dominic would come over to walk Iago, looking tired or exasperated, and tell them what his dad and Lily were up to.

One of the biggest mysteries coming from the West house now was the question of what had happened to Lily's diary. At some point, the journal had disappeared, and Lily wasn't at all reticent about placing the blame squarely on Jordan's shoulders. The war between the West sisters continued to escalate.

On the day of the delivery of a long cedar table—the table Ray had bought when he decided the old patio furniture alone just wouldn't suffice, even after he and Lily had gone to the trouble of painting it—Grace went over to inspect the new purchase. Jordan made a rare appearance in the backyard to look at it too.

"This is going to be a two-table affair then?" Grace asked.

"Oh, yes," Ray said. "We're still going to be squeezed as it is."

Jordan folded her arms. "If there's a kid's table, I'm not sitting at it."

"What about if there's a thief's table?" Lily asked.

Jordan turned on her, laughing. "Give it a rest. I didn't take your stupid diary."

"Why don't I believe you?" Lily wondered aloud.

"Because you're a paranoid 'rhoid," Jordan said. "What the hell would I do with it?"

Ray busied himself inspecting the connecting braces of his table. If he had heard the exchange between Lily and Jordan while he was hovered underneath that wooden tabletop, he pretended not to. When he came back up to standing, he announced, "This thing is actually pretty well constructed. I bet we'll still be using it a decade or two from now."

Grace felt an ache in her chest as she looked at his pep rally smile. He was trying so hard but still missing the connection. *Say something to them,* she wanted to tell him.

"If *I'm* still sitting in this backyard two decades from now," Jordan muttered as she stalked away, "someone please put arsenic in my Geritol."

Ray watched her go, mystified, as if he'd never heard a discouraging word and the skies were not cloudy all day. "What's the matter with her?"

When Lily went inside to get something, Grace brought up a subject that had been bothering her. "It's awful to have your heart set on something and then have it pulled out from under you."

He frowned. "What are you talking about?"

"Jordan. She's so alone. I haven't even seen her hanging out with that weird woman anymore."

"Good."

"But she doesn't seem to have anyone she relates to. At the art program, she might find a bunch of people just like herself."

"Oh, Lord."

"Or people who would be sympathetic to her."

Ray's brow crinkled, and he stood with his hands on his hips, staring at the grass. He released a long sigh. "Maybe you're right. I've been worried about her, the way she wanders around by herself with that rabbit, or else shuts herself away.

The only one in the family she seems to talk to is Dominic. I asked her if she wanted to go back to the therapist and she just laughed at me. Maybe she does need something else."

Grace felt as though she had made a little headway. Though as the cookout approached, when she was helping Ray more and started catching more glares from his older daughter, she sometimes wondered why she had bothered.

She didn't understand those glares. It wasn't as if she was actually a threat. She might have had a bit of a thing for Ray, but she had never acted on it. She had no idea what Ray was thinking about her. Only occasionally would she feel his gaze following her. But they were never alone, and usually they were arguing good-naturedly with one another about things such as whether the Chinese lanterns were a decorative touch too far.

Ray liked the lanterns.

She shouldn't have cared one way or another about him. He was at a difficult spot in his life, he had a daughter who despised her, and he appeared to have kept his emotions sealed off even in the best of times. And however hard he was trying to hide it, he was still grieving.

She didn't want to become someone's biggest mistake, like her mother.

Not to mention, she had her own problems. First and foremost, she had her dad to worry about and take care of. And rigolettosmusic.com to oversee. Beside which, *she* was on the rebound, after Ben. Although she wondered how long a person could remain on the rebound without actually hitting anything. At some point didn't you become just a loose ball, a dud?

But then Ray knocked on the door one evening to ask if they had a former neighbor's e-mail address.

"Bob Cassidy," he told Lou.

"I do have it!" Lou said with a certainty that lifted Grace's spirits. "Bob sends me those end-of-the-year update e-mails. Like a family advertisement. I've never understood how those caught on."

Grace and Ray exchanged amused glances. "I can send the e-mail to you," she said.

"Why?" her dad asked. "I've got it. I'll just go and write it down for Ray right now."

"Or just e-mail it to Ray, Dad."

Lou raised a brow. "Why e-mail it to him when I can run upstairs and write it down? He's right here."

She opened her mouth to answer but her dad was already stumping up the stairs as if he'd won the argument.

She turned back to Ray with a gesture of amiable surrender.

Ray obviously hadn't been inside Lou's house often, because he scanned the room, inspecting the bookshelves and furniture as if he were a traveler taking a house tour. It occurred to her that they usually talked outdoors, where they mostly crossed paths by chance. Indoors, he seemed to take up more room, and she could actually smell the soapy scent of his skin—after his day's work he'd apparently taken the time to get Zestfully clean.

"Thank you for helping me think of all this, Grace. You were right. It's made all the difference to be focusing on something. I feel as if I'm about to be relaunched into the world. Sounds stupid, I know."

She shook her head. "No. I sometimes feel I need to be relaunched, too."

His brows arched in surprise. "You?"

"You don't think?"

"No—that would be terrible. My launch is sort of a leap over a mental hurdle. If you launched, I worry you'd leave."

She lifted a brow. "That would be bad?"

"Awful."

She couldn't help smiling.

"Dominic would be heartbroken," he added.

She tried to keep the smile in place, but she wasn't sure how successful she was. *Dominic* would be heartbroken, the man said.

Her father came down, leading with his outstretched hand holding a sheet of paper. "Here's the address."

Ray gave the impression of snapping to attention. He took the paper without looking at it. "Thanks."

"Care to sit a while?" her father asked Ray.

"No, I should get back."

"Game of chess?" Lou pressed.

He shook his head. "I've never been that great at chess."

"You could still beat Grace."

Ray smiled awkwardly, as if he didn't know whether he should actually be smiling or not. "Thank you anyway."

After he was gone, Grace suddenly went saggy with disappointment. *Dominic* would miss her.

Her father sat down and leaned back. "That poor man. Such a tragedy. He'll never get over it."

Gritting her teeth, Grace went to the kitchen and swept, even though it didn't even need sweeping. Iago was trying to take his prebedtime nap under the kitchen table and made growly sounds whenever the broom came too close to his snout for comfort.

When she heard another knock, she grumbled all the way back to the door. Her father must have gone upstairs to get ready for bed, because the living room was empty. She swung the door open and was surprised to see Ray again.

He held up the strip of paper. "Your father gave me a phone number, not an e-mail."

"Oh. Well, can't you just call Bob? That sounds simpler anyway."

"This is not Bob's number. It doesn't even have an Austin area code."

She squinted at it. "That was my number when I lived in Oregon."

He smiled. "So I got your number without even having to ask for it."

"It's defunct. I can give you my real one." His gaze froze, and she immediately wanted to kick herself. "Kidding," she assured him. "I mean, not kidding—but you know. There's no reason you'd want my number."

"Yes, there is."

She blinked.

He hesitated but then blurted out, "What I said before, about Dominic missing you? That was only half the story. I'd miss you, too. That is, I think I would." He grabbed her hand. "I'm so . . . I don't know how to say it."

"Don't then."

He looked into her eyes. "You're right." He tugged her hand and she seemed to slide right toward him. It helped that he was still standing on the porch, which put them on equal footing. Their lips met and she was amazed by the hunger she sensed in him in just a brief kiss. He held her tight, almost like a man hugging a life buoy, until she pushed away.

"I'm not sorry," he said.

She laughed. “I’m glad to hear it.”

He wasn’t laughing, though. Instead, he was studying her face as if he’d never really noticed it before. “I half suspect I could fall in love with you, Grace.”

She’d been feeling a glow under his intense gaze, but now she froze. *Half?* Half *suspected?*

He wasn’t even willing to lay odds?

Her Romeo backed away. “Well. Good night.”

She watched him turn and imagined herself not going to his stupid party. For a brief moment she thought she could send her regrets and stay indoors until she was an old lady.

But before he’d cleared the last porch step, she poked her head out the door.

“555-4692,” she called after him.

He turned.

“You said you wanted it,” she explained. “Should I write it down?”

He shook his head. “No need. Numbers, I remember. They’re the one thing in life I’m good with.”

“I’ll send you Bob’s e-mail,” she promised.

“I don’t know what I’d do without you, Grace.”

They said good night again and she sank against the door as she flipped the bolt. Her legs wobbled beneath her, and her body felt half weightless, half hopelessly earthbound.

It was probably very dangerous to lose your head over a man who thought of you in terms of not being able to do without you—like a garlic press or a good can opener.

It was even more dangerous when your heart felt it was lost already.

33

Things Fall Apart

The day of Ray's party, bulbous cumulous clouds crowded overhead, gray and menacing. Grace kept peeking out the window to see if they had dispersed. But by noon it hadn't rained, and she began to suspect it was going to be one of those spring days where clouds hovered overhead and nothing at all happened.

Ray was upbeat. "I think it's great. Whatever blew in last night has cooled it down a little. It's only supposed to be seventy-eight today. Perfect!"

The kids all seemed in a good mood too—even Jordan, who was carrying Buns around with her and a large Easter basket that no one, not even Dominic, was allowed to look into.

At one point, Ray tugged Grace into his office. For a breathless moment she thought he was going to kiss her again, but as soon as he'd shut the door behind them he let go of her arm and hurried toward his desk. "I have something to show you."

He unfolded a piece of paper and handed it to Grace.

It was a "pleased to welcome you" letter telling Jordan she'd been accepted into the art program.

"Jordan left it on my desk last night," he said. "Probably a last-ditch effort to make me change my mind."

Or to make you feel guilty.

"I've thought it over," he continued, "and I've decided you're right. I'm going to slip the news into the conversation during the meal. You know . . . if someone brings up summer plans. I can say 'Well, Jordan's going to be spending her summer in California.' Very offhand. She'll be excited, don't you think?"

Even though she harbored doubts about making the news a public announcement, Grace couldn't help smiling. What would a happy Jordan look like? It was difficult to imagine.

The guests began to arrive just after noon. Wyatt brought beer, and he and Ray popped them open and headed for the grill to make sure the coals were firing up properly. Lily appointed herself official greeter and posted herself at the gate to the backyard.

Grace saw Muriel arrive, followed by Truman and Peggy. The two had dropped by the house after they'd returned from Natchez—a visit that felt stiff and formal, like the post-nuptial calls couples were supposed to make in nineteenth-century novels. But it had been a kind gesture, and a few days later while Grace had been out, Peggy had brought over some strawberries that Lou had pronounced the best strawberries he'd eaten in the past twenty years.

Dominic asked Ray and Lou if he could bring Iago over to join them, and soon there was a black-and-white floppy-eared food Hoover winding between guests, picking up dropped potato chips or anything else that touched ground. The smell of charcoal and meat was so strong that when they all finally sat down at the tables, Grace was almost as frantic for food as the dog was.

That was when everyone noticed the origami birds set in front of each place.

"Oh—fun!" Pippa exclaimed, picking up one and holding it in her palm. "A little birdy!"

Grace was seated at the end of the table where Ray was going to be. Lou, Truman, and Peggy installed themselves on the other end. Jordan, who had stowed Buns away for the meal, placed herself in the middle of the long table, facing everyone. She seemed serene. Disturbingly so.

"Who made these?" Muriel asked.

Ray brought more plates with hamburgers. Everyone was about to dig in as he was finally able to sit down too. "I don't know. Did you do these, Lily?"

Lily, who looked put out to be sitting at the metal patio satellite table—the children's ghetto, Jordan had dubbed it—stared at her origami bird with suspicion. "No."

If ill-at-ease could have had a face at that moment, it would have been Lily West's. The boys sitting next to her—Dominic, Crawford, and a cousin of Crawford's who was visiting for the Easter holidays—were making honking and quacking noises with their birds. This was obviously an uncomfortable setup for Lily on many levels.

"I can't imagine who else could have made these." Ray sent Grace a barely perceptible wink.

She held her breath, waiting—hoping—for him to make the announcement about Jordan.

"Lends the whole affair a little extra touch of class," Wyatt observed before flicking his bird to the side of the beer bottle.

Peggy was exclaiming over how beautiful they were when a gust of wind blew up. As one, all the people at the table reached forward to keep the birds from flying away.

"Oh, look!" Pippa said excitedly. "My birdy has writing on it. "Should I unfold it?" Everyone started inspecting their birds again as Pippa unfolded hers and read aloud. " 'Having my dad for a father is like having no father at all.' " She pulled a perplexed face. "Is that a riddle?"

"I don't get it," Muriel said.

"Maybe it's a game," Peggy said, prodding Truman to open his.

" 'I'm so in love with Crawford I could die,' " Truman intoned.

"What?" Crawford screeched.

Wyatt joined in. "'My little brother is a whiny fatso.' It's got a date on it, too."

A sickening, sinking feeling took hold of Grace, especially when she glanced at Lily. The girl's face was tomato red, and her jaw hung open in shock. At the other table, Jordan was smiling placidly with her arms crossed, peering over at the piece of paper in Peggy's hand with satisfaction.

The mystery of what had happened to Lily's journal had just been solved. Lily had been as accurate as Sherlock Holmes. She just hadn't guessed her sister's diabolical plan for it.

Grace longed to snatch up the birds before any more damage could be done—before more feelings were hurt, before Jordan's big summer plans were irrevocably lost.

But it might have already been too late for that. Judging from Ray's face, he also knew what had happened.

The boys erupted in fits. "No, she didn't!" Dominic yelled angrily.

Crawford's cousin yanked the paper out of his hand. "'Tonight I saw Mr. Carter making out with Grace right in his yard. It was disgusting! January fourteenth.'"

"What?" Pippa squeaked. She jerked toward Wyatt. "We were already engaged in January!"

Wyatt looked over at Grace, as did practically everyone else.

Grace sank deeper into her chair. If it had been at all possible, she would have crawled under the table. Maybe crawled back to her own house, too.

"It seems odd that none of them are about me," Muriel said, opening hers impatiently. She frowned, almost disappointed. "No, this is just about Grace's nasty granola."

Grace was almost glad when Crawford's cousin reached over and read Lily's aloud, if only because it might take the attention off of her for a moment. " 'Professor Oliver is the nicest man imaginable, but I worry Grace might be psychotic.' "

Grace choked on her tea and looked at Lily, who had tears standing in her eyes.

Lou erupted in a burst of laughter. "You're not coming out of this too well, are you, Grace?"

She chuckled back, more from tension than anything else.

"Well, is it true?" Pippa demanded, glaring from Wyatt to Grace.

" 'Course it's true!" Truman barked. "I've been saying for months now that Grace is nuttier than a squirrel!"

"I meant about the other thing!" Pippa huffed.

Wyatt shrugged sheepishly.

Pippa threw her bird at him. It bounced off his head and whirled away on a fresh gust of wind. The same wind seemed to lift Pippa, who tossed her napkin on the table as she stood. "I don't know who wrote these nasty little notes, but thank you! I for one am grateful!" She stomped off just as the first heavy drops of rain splattered the table.

"We'd better get out of this before it starts to pour," Truman announced. "I knew this would turn out badly."

People jumped up, grabbing plates and glasses and dashing back inside as old leaves and origami birds were whisked through the air. Ray and Grace stayed seated. So did Lily, even as Jordan approached her and bent toward her, close to her ear.

"Oh—forgot to tell you, Lils," she taunted. "I found your journal."

Lily's chest heaved in tortured breaths as the downpour began. She kept her gaze focused on the uneaten, increasingly soggy hamburger in front of her.

"How does it feel to have your secrets out in the open?" Jordan shouted in her ear.

Lily finally turned toward her. "I hate you."

Jordan grinned maliciously. "I don't care."

Grace watched the exchange in horror. Besides herself and Ray, everyone else, even Iago, had already scrambled for the house. She expected Lily to turn and run, too. Instead, Lily launched herself at Jordan, springing on her like something feral. Grace gasped and stood up, but not before Jordan, taken by surprise, had been wrestled to the ground and had her face pushed into the wet spring grass.

Ray jumped up and pulled them apart. "For heaven's sake—stop it! We have guests!"

Those guests, especially the boys, were watching the whole thing from the other side of the sliding patio doors. Avidly.

Lily looked ready to launch herself at her sister again. Her expression was ferocious. "I hate her! She never has to pay for what she does!"

"You don't know anything!" Jordan yelled.

"No, *you* don't," Ray said, glaring at his older daughter.

Foreseeing his next words, Grace stepped forward to stop him. Too much had been said in anger already. "Ray, she doesn't deserve—"

He cut her off. "Don't say anything, Grace."

Jordan, still wiping dirt and grass clippings off her face, practically snarled, "Oh, she's probably *dying* to say something—if she hasn't already. *'Jordan doesn't deserve anything. Jordan has screwed-up friends. Jordan's a thief.'* Right, Grace?"

Grace shuddered mournfully as Ray turned toward her in confusion. "A *thief?*" he asked.

She shook her head, remaining silent.

He pivoted back to his daughter. "For your information, before you pulled this stunt I was about to tell you that you could go to San Francisco. Obviously, you won't be going now."

Jordan's face fell. "What? That's not true!" But as she looked from Grace to Ray, realization dawned. She'd just blown it. "Oh, shit," she said, collapsing onto a bench. She repeated the curse again, knowing there was nothing left to lose.

Lily, still wound up, stood over Jordan and yelled at her back. "I wish you *would* send her away! I don't want to be in the same house with her," she told her father. "I'm going to live with Granny Kate!"

She spun on her heel and then ran for the house.

Grace stayed long enough to get the outside tables cleared and the dishwasher loaded. When that was done, she looked up and noticed that Ray had disappeared. She found him in his study, standing next to the window and looking out on the backyard tables. "Well, you were right about one thing," he said. "The Chinese lanterns were a waste of money."

"I'm so sorry."

He released a sigh. Even though he'd made the little jest about the Chinese lanterns, he seemed as depressed and discouraged as she'd ever seen him. It didn't help that he was still wearing his wet clothes and that his hair was plastered to his head at odd angles.

"Lily was right about me," he said. "They'd be better off having no father at all."

"No. Ray, forget that. You don't even know why

she wrote those words, or when. A teenager's moods are all over the place. When I was fifteen, I probably hated my parents every other day."

"The difference is, Lily's right. I've been useless since Jen died. They would have been so much better off if it had just been me in that car. Without me, they would have stayed a family. There wouldn't be this gang war atmosphere."

"It's awful what happened," she said, "but they're just working through this. . . ."

He laughed bitterly. "Grace, that wasn't friendly mud wrestling out there. If we hadn't intervened, I'm pretty sure the afternoon would have involved an ambulance."

She didn't know what to say.

He shook his head. "I never should have taken your advice about today and throwing this stupid party."

"*My* advice?" she repeated, stunned. "I didn't tell you to do this."

"Of course you did. I talked to you that night on your back porch, and to me it seemed like you had all the answers."

"But—"

"And then there's the matter of you and me. That night when I kissed you—that never should have happened, either."

She was taken aback. And miffed. "I'm sorry, are you referring to that time when you said you *maybe could possibly* bring yourself to like me?"

Being dumped by Ben after two years had been bad enough. But this felt like being dumped from a hypothetical relationship in someone's head. All the pain without even a nice dinner and a movie. "You'll be relieved to know that as far as I'm concerned, Ray, there never was a you and me. There was just a kiss. You've obviously got your hands full with family matters, and so do I."

He didn't deny it, or backpedal, or apologize. In the long silence that followed, Grace wondered if he intended to speak to her again at all, but finally he cleared his throat. "I never knew that a year could be so long," he said wearily. "I never realized that the world could feel so dark and cold for months on end. In all that time, it seemed that there was just one glimmer of light—you. You listened to me and helped me talk out some of my grief. And most of all, you helped my kids."

The words should have warmed her, but they didn't. She could hear the *but* coming down Fifth Avenue.

"But now . . ." He shook his head. "Now I suspect you had your own needy agenda. It appears you weren't above encouraging them to be sneaky and underhanded."

Her eyes flew open wide. "What?"

"Thieving?" he asked. "My daughter was caught stealing, and you knew about that?"

She opened her mouth, but it took a moment to form words. "It was just a minor incident at a Chinese restaurant. Jordan didn't even do anything—her friend got caught stealing egg rolls. I talked to the owner."

"*You* did?" he asked. "Who gave you the right to act as her parent?"

Her face was hot. She didn't know what to say.

"What else has there been?" he asked.

"Nothing!" she said. "Well . . . just an incident when we took her friend to the hospital." In response to his alarmed look, she added, "With appendicitis."

"What friend? The older one I saw in the picture?" he asked. "Was that the screwed-up friend Jordan mentioned?"

"Yes, as a matter of fact."

"And did you know she was screwed up?"

Grace shut her eyes, resenting the inquisition but unable to lie. In hindsight, her actions really did seem worse than they had in real time. "Yes, I knew."

"But you still didn't say a word to me about it." His lips twisted in a sour, disgusted frown that she found infuriating.

"Look," she said, "I'm sorry. I probably should have mentioned what happened to you, but I didn't, and you know why? Because Jordan was concerned about you. She said she didn't want to upset you, and I didn't either. You seem to have already forgotten, Ray. For the past year the kids were pretty much in loco parentis for themselves, because you had checked out."

Twin splotches of red crept into his cheeks. "I was grieving, but I wasn't so out of it that I would have ignored my daughter's problems if I had known about them."

"But how could you have known?" Grace fired back. "You hid yourself away, and walked past your own children without really seeing them. They even had a word for it—'Dad's zombie days.' "

"I could have known if *you* had told me. You lured my kids to your house like some pied piper. Of course they loved it there—they could tell you everything and know you would do nothing, because ultimately you weren't really responsible for them."

"What should I have done?" she asked angrily. "Turned them away from my door? Left them to your benign neglect?"

"You could have been open with me," he said. "Truthful. I thought we were friends. I thought we were . . . Now I don't see how I can trust you at all. So I'm afraid I'm going to have to ask you to stay out of my family's business. We can deal with our own problems."

She felt winded, as if someone had punched her. "I assume you don't want me to show your children the door if they choose to visit—but I won't encourage them to come over, if that's what you want."

"That's what I think would be best for all of us."

"Fine." She turned to go, but after a few steps she pivoted back around. "I know it's none of my business," she said bitterly, "and that I should probably just shut up now, but there's just one more thing I need to say."

"What?"

She didn't know why she was sticking her neck out, but she felt compelled to. *Last time.* "I think you should let Jordan go away this summer. Punish her some other way that doesn't crush her dreams. Keeping her here will just demoralize her."

He shook his head. "I just don't know. I'm overwhelmed. All I can think is that I'm not up to handling this. I need Jen."

There was no answer for that.

She backed toward the door. When she spoke, she tried to sound businesslike and not wounded. And not like she wanted to strangle him, which she did. "I tidied up a little," she told him, referring to the kitchen. "There's still a lot to do, though."

He nodded.

"Good-bye," she said.

"To you, too. And good luck."

It was as if she were moving across country instead of walking right next door. As she was turning to go, he shook his head as if remembering something.

She paused midstep. "What?"

His eyes held such emotion, she wondered if it might be longing, or regret. She thought he might be on the verge of an apology.

She thought wrong.

"Did you actually kiss Wyatt?" he asked.

She sighed. Not longing—disgust. She couldn't read him at all.

But she didn't see the point of explaining herself at this point. She let the silence speak for her and stalked out. *Thanks, Lily,* she thought.

But what was going on with Ray wasn't Lily's fault. It was the grief. And the places they both found themselves in.

As she left the office, shutting the door behind her, she almost tripped over Dominic. His eyes were worried.

"Are you leaving?" he asked.

She forced a smile. "Yes—traveling all the way to the other side of the fence."

"But I can still come over, right?" he asked, seeming unconcerned that he was giving away the fact that he'd been eavesdropping. "And see the professor, and Iago?"

She couldn't help giving him a quick bracing hug. "Anytime. Remember, no matter what happens, my door will always be opened to two men—Daniel Craig and you."

34

Wherever Apologies Are Accepted

Two days after the debacle, Lily knocked on the kitchen door. She held out a bouquet of flowers for Grace. "I've come to apologize. For the things that I wrote about you."

"You shouldn't have to apologize to me," Grace told her, taking the flowers. They were roses. "You were writing in your diary. You didn't know your thoughts were going to be broadcast."

"I know. It was all Jordan's fault. But who's going to remember that? They'll just remember that I wrote it."

"Most probably won't remember at all."

Lily looked gloomy. "Dominic told me that Mr. Carter and Pippa have broken off their engagement. *She'll* remember." She sighed. "I don't know where she lives, so I can't take her roses. But I doubt she'd want them anyway, do you? Not from me, anyway."

She leaned against the counter as Grace retrieved a vase and arranged the flowers. They were beautiful—and fragrant. They did take a little of the sting out of having the entire neighborhood know that she and Wyatt had experienced a moment of madness.

Lily tilted her head. "How many brothers and sisters do you have?"

"Four."

Lily's eyes widened. *"Four?"*

"My two half brothers here," Grace explained, "and my younger half brother and sister in Portland."

Lily looked astonished. "You never talk about the Portland people."

"They're a lot younger than me. I was eleven when my half brother Jake was born, and I was already a teenager by the time Natalie came along. She's just finishing up high school."

Lily took a moment to absorb this information. "Do you hate any of them?"

The question caught Grace off guard. "No. Of course not."

"I'm pretty sure I hate Jordan. And it's not just what happened at the party—Jordan ruins everything. I blame her for what happened to Nina and Mom."

"That was an accident."

"But they wouldn't have been driving if it hadn't been for Jordan! I'll never forgive her for that," Lily said. "Never."

Grace thought about letting the subject drop, and staying out of it. *Not my problem.* Ray had warned her not to interfere, and though his words had stung, and she'd thought he was being an illogical ass, maybe his instinct was right. She couldn't help remembering how angry she'd been when Muriel had told her that her father should be in a home. Outsiders shouldn't butt into family business.

On the other hand, here was Lily, wounded and distressed. She couldn't just wave her out the door. *Thanks for the roses, sorry you hate your sister. Have a nice day.*

"What if it had been you who your mom and sister were picking up?" Grace asked her.

Lily's eyes bugged. "*I* wouldn't have been arrested!"

"Okay. But what if you had called from band practice and asked your mother to come get you, and then she and your sister had had an accident picking you up?"

"But that didn't happen. This was totally unexpected, because Jordan was at a *police station.*"

"Did the police station have anything to do with the car crashing? Shouldn't your anger be for the person who actually hit them? Or was it the condition of the road, or the time of day? Maybe the sun created a glare and the other driver didn't see their car. None of that was in Jordan's power—or anyone else's—to control."

She didn't know what she had expected. A teary Hallmark moment of understanding and forgiveness, maybe.

Instead, by the time she'd finished, Lily's face had turned a darker hue of red. "Why are you taking *her* side? She doesn't even like you!"

"Yeah, I sensed that."

"It wouldn't matter if you had twenty brothers and sisters," Lily railed at her, "you don't know what it's like to live with Jordan. Even if she wasn't *directly* responsible for Mom and Nina, she's made my life a misery. And she'll never change!"

"That's probably true."

Lily looked as if she was about to continue her rant, but at the last minute she doubled back. "What's true?"

"She won't change—or if she does, the change probably won't be what you would have expected, or wanted."

"Great!" Lily said. "Thanks. That's really comforting."

"You can change yourself, but other people are out of your control, unfortunately."

"There's nothing the matter with me," Lily argued. "*I'm* not the problem."

"You're the problem if you're unhappy," Grace told her, amazed how easy it was to channel Deepak Chopra when faced with an unhappy teenager.

"You're not *listening,*" Lily said. "I'm telling you, if it weren't for Jordan, I *would* be happy."

"Look, I'm not saying you have to like Jordan,

or even get along with her. But the fact is, she's going to be your sister forever. Even if you become the kind of siblings that live on opposite sides of the continent and don't even send each other Christmas cards, she's going to be out there, and you're going to think about her. So for your own peace of mind, you should figure out something about her that *doesn't* make you crazy—just one little thing. That way when you're giving lectures at Princeton and she's serving her life sentence in the women's correctional facility in Chowchilla, California, you won't have this awful gunk festering away inside you. Instead, you can think to yourself, *'Gosh it must be difficult for a free spirit like Jordan to be spending her life making license plates.'* "

Lily bit her lip to stop her face from crooking into a smile. "But there's *nothing* to like about her. You couldn't find anything either, even if you tried."

"Yes, I could. I know she's a talented artist. I have a painting she did of a demented smiley face."

Lily's mouth dropped. "You have Egbert?"

"It's up in my room. And sometimes on the worst days I can look at that crazy picture—and I don't know why—but it makes me feel better. It really does."

"I thought Egbert was gone for good," Lily said. "I thought everything of Nina's was gone."

"No, it's just dispersed," Grace assured her. "Egbert found a good home."

Lily folded her arms. "I still don't think Jordan's all that great."

"I was just trying to give you a coping mechanism," Grace said.

The girl narrowed her eyes and focused on a spot on the linoleum. "I'm going to cope by leaving. I'm going to go live with Granny Kate."

Unexpected sadness welled up in Grace at the news. "Your dad would miss you. So will Dominic. We will here, too."

Lily pursed her lips. "I don't believe it. Sometimes I think I'm one of those invisible people that no one remembers after they leave a room."

Grace couldn't help laughing. "If you think that, you don't know yourself at all. I remember the moment you opened the door when I went to your house to find Iago. And the moment you came over to return the cheap plastic cookie plate—looking for Crawford but not saying so."

Lily's hue turned a shade redder. "How pointless was that? I was crazy, thinking any cute boy would look twice at me."

Grace held back for a moment, wondering if she should not interfere in this, either. *In for a penny . . .* "Look—don't take this wrong." Lily stared up with wide eyes, and Grace continued. "You have a very distinctive appearance. But teenage boys aren't really known for favoring distinctive."

"What about Jordan? She has peach and black hair and the personality of a viper—but Crawford fell in love with her anyway."

"I'm not sure I'd call it love. And Jordan also wears make-up and clothes that make her stand out."

"Make her look like a skank, you mean."

Grace wasn't going there. "But the thing is, dating and stuff—it takes a *little* effort."

Lily glanced at her sharply. "You mean I ought to make myself look just like everybody else. But how can I do that? Everybody knows who I am already. How stupid would I seem if I suddenly showed up at school attempting to look like the cover of *Seventeen*?"

"You wouldn't look stupid. You might feel awkward for a day or so. And then . . ."

Lily shook her head. "I shouldn't have said anything. You don't know what it's like. Anyway, *you* look sort of normal, and Ben still dumped you, and I haven't noticed men flocking around here. Except Mr. Carter, and he's not exactly particular."

Sort of normal? What part of her wasn't normal? She was interested to know, but she probably shouldn't be asking a fifteen-year-old.

Grace lifted her shoulders in a shrug. "Well, do as I say, not as I do."

She had the sinking feeling that nothing she'd said had made the least bit of difference. "The only thing I want to do is flee," Lily said.

35

The Toast of Little Salty

Fleeting thoughts of home scratched at the back of Lily's mind during her summer in Little Salty, along with a vague discomfort that she was in the wrong place. But then she'd hear Granny Kate singing "Copacabana" and all her misgivings would melt away.

Every day in Little Salty offered some kind of fun. She and Granny Kate buzzed around town shopping in the mornings—sometimes they even went to Midland—and in the afternoons there was bridge club or Jazzercise. She learned to play bridge, and by mid-June she could actually participate in Granny Kate's club if they needed another person and if she didn't have anything else to do.

But that wasn't often, because other activities crowded in. She went to Granny Kate and Pop Pop's church and had been recruited by the choir, despite the fact she really couldn't sing all that well. Plus there was the church's youth group. She joined the community band, too, which was going to have a big concert in the town park on the Fourth of July.

She felt like a wallflower who, as if by magic, had discovered her dance card was full. Granny

Kate and Pop Pop's friends fussed over her, and the kids she met were curious about her because she was new and from Austin—exotic, almost. The older teens kept telling her that she must be bored in Little Salty, without all the wild and fun stuff there was to do in Austin. To them Austin was Sixth Street, South by Southwest, the ultimate party town, the Live Music Capital of the World. Lily couldn't bring herself to confess that if she'd been home in Austin she would be baby-sitting her brother and hanging out with a seventy-seven-year-old chess fanatic.

Here, everybody said she was so supertalented, so smart, and so not like her weird sister. Jordan evidently had *not* been the toast of Little Salty.

If Little Salty was paradise, Granny Kate was her fairy godmother. She noticed that Lily had—in her delicate expression—"filled out some" and bought her some new bras and summer clothes that fit better. Remembering what Grace had told her, Lily asked if she could get contacts, an idea Granny Kate leapt on—"to show off those beautiful eyes." She took her to the mall for a makeover and ended up buying her a ton of make-up. Lily got her hair cut shorter, in a layered cut that looked great at the salon but wasn't so easy to replicate at home. Nevertheless, everyone told her she'd bloomed.

Grace had been right. Transforming herself hadn't been the awkward ordeal she had feared.

But maybe it was easier because the people here didn't have a picture of her old geekier self burned into their brains for all time.

Over the summer, Lily tried hard not to think about Jordan, but it wasn't easy. Granny Kate sometimes dished the dirt about the hellish time she and Pop Pop had had with her. (Granny Kate didn't say hellish, but that's how it must have been.) Jordan had slept late, she hadn't picked up after herself or offered to help—not like Lily did—and she'd always sulked, even when they were doing fun things, like trips to Midland and lunches at Applebee's. Jordan had to be browbeaten into Jazzercising and then would sit around all afternoon eating up all Pop Pop's ice cream (they didn't say anything to her about it, but they'd noticed) and watching some hippie painter on public television.

And then there was the business with the room. The final straw. According to Granny Kate, it had taken *three coats* of paint to completely de-Jordan the walls. Now the guest room was beige, with floral pink curtains and a matching bedspread.

Hearing Granny Kate crab about Jordan should have been a balm. But thinking about Jordan tended to set off flashes of them wrestling in the grass, and of the volcanic anger that had erupted out of her after hearing snatches of her journal read aloud, in front of everybody. She wasn't proud of herself.

In the end, her father had let Jordan go to California. Naturally. Jordan always got what she wanted when push came to shove—people gave in to her just to get her out of their hair. But even if they were in different states, something felt unfinished between them, and Lily began to wonder if it would always be like that. Maybe this niggling feeling was what Grace had been warning her about.

In July, Granny Kate started bringing up the subject of Lily's transfering to Little Salty High for junior year. Some of the kids in youth group were encouraging when Lily mentioned this. They promised she'd have fun and be superpopular. Not to mention, she'd be the smartest kid in the class, maybe the whole school. Without warning, Granny Kate spoke to Lily's father about it on the phone one night. After the call, she announced that Ray had agreed to talk to her about it, if Lily thought she would be happier there.

When Lily heard this, her throat tightened. He was willing to let her go just like that? She couldn't imagine leaving her father and Dominic forever, but the lure of Little Salty was strong. She was happy. She sort of fit in. And wouldn't she have to leave Austin to go to college in two years anyway?

She received e-mail from Dominic sometimes, and as the summer stretched into the end of July and all the fun new things became more routine, she became more impatient for news of home. Because both she and Jordan were gone, their dad had hired a college girl, Jeanine, to come in during the day during the summer and look after Dominic. She wondered what Jeanine was like, and what else had changed in the neighborhood since she'd left.

Unfortunately, Dominic was one of the worst e-mail writers on the planet. Most of the time Lily just skimmed his messages with a sagging feeling of letdown.

But sometime in late July, she received an e-mail that made her stop and read it twice.

Hi lily
The bad news tday is that prof. o fell and now his arms hurt bad. I went over there and grace looked really worried, even though her brother the doctor said that it could be worse. Especially if he brk a hip. But he didn't so thats good.

Poor professor Oliver! He had to be really demoralized, having another accident just a year after he got hit by the car.

She e-mailed Grace to tell her that she was worried about the professor and hoped he would get better soon.

Grace replied before Lily had logged off the computer.

Lily! It's soooo great to hear from you! Dad and I talk about you all the time, wondering what you're getting up to in Little Salty. In fact, Dad was just asking me to hunt down your address. He wants to send you his copy of *The Small House at Allington.* It has a character named Lily in it, who, according to him, "is just as resolute as our Lily."

Dad is doing fine, all things considered. He had a pin put in his wrist after his accident, and the operation seems to have affected his memory a little, which he was already having problems with, as you know. It's been another challenge for him. He's a little slower in moving those chess pieces than he used to be. I don't think he likes the game as much anymore, to tell you the truth, but he still beats me whenever we play.

I can't give you much more news of home, I'm afraid. I haven't seen much of your dad. He seems to be back to working long hours. Jeanine, Dominic's minder, is twenty-one and—according to Dominic and Crawford—incredibly hot. She seems to spend most of her time sunbathing on your back deck.

I have a Clarinet Concerto CD that I think you'd like. If you send me your address, I'll

include the CD along with the Trollope book.
I'm so glad you're having a fun summer! Maybe you've found your geographical niche!
Love,
Grace

Grace's e-mail made her want to cry. And it wasn't just because of Professor Oliver's accident, or the idea of her dad backsliding into his post-accident routine, or that teenage boys were pathetic and shallow. It was because there were people who thought of her, who tried to understand her. It was because the world she'd left, her world, was going on without her, and for the first time in two months, she really missed it. So much that she understood what the word *heartsore* meant. She thought wistfully of the tag end of last summer—which had been an awful time in so many ways—hanging out at the professor's house with her feet up on the uncomfortable velvet sofa in the front room, listening to classical music, and pretending to read a book while she daydreamed.

How could she be happy in one place, but still long for another place?

At the beginning of August, life ground to a halt in Little Salty. Everyone seemed to be taking a vacation except for Granny Kate and Pop Pop. Pop Pop didn't like to leave his pharmacy when he was so close to retiring anyway, and Granny Kate said every day of her life was a vacation, so she didn't need one. The youth group went on a retreat, but it had all been planned before Lily had moved to Little Salty, so she couldn't go.

For the first time all summer, she started to feel lonely. Restless.

One day while Granny Kate was at bridge club, Lily did a little snooping. Along the top shelf of her grandparents' closet, she found several photo albums. She pulled them down and sat on the floor among the clothes that smelled of mothballs to look at them. She flipped through her grandmother's whole life, starting from the black-and-white baby pictures to the strikingly bright Polaroids from the fifties and sixties. Later Granny Kate almost disappeared, photographically overpowered by her own daughter. And then the grandkids.

When she came to the photos of her and her siblings, Lily slowed down. She couldn't help it. She'd seen them all a hundred times—the awkward Sears portraits and school pictures, the crooked or blurry candid shots. Most were copies her mom had sent to Granny Kate. One, though, stopped her cold.

The photo was of her and Nina—they looked to be about eight and ten years old. It must have been snapped in the summer, because Nina was wearing shorts and a tank top and Lily, barefoot, was riding piggyback on her and wielding what must have been a plastic sword of Dominic's. Standing to the side, half cut out of the picture, she could make out Jordan wearing her soccer uniform. Lily had the sword raised and her mouth was stretched open in what was obviously a full-throated cry—she and Nina were on the verge of charging at something—and Nina was laughing so hard it looked as if she was about to buckle over.

Tears brimmed in her eyes. The picture captured exactly how it had felt being with Nina—that happiness that obliterated everything else. Every worry, every bad thing, every hurt. She wanted so fiercely to crawl back inside that picture, back to that time, it was like an ache. If she'd had to live every moment of her life again, even the most awful, even seventh grade, she would have, just to be back in that moment, laughing with Nina.

A tear splattered the clear film covering the photos, which she pulled back. It took her a moment to pry the picture off the page's sticky backing, and when she had it, she shut the book and put all the albums back on the shelf in the proper order. Maybe taking the picture of her and Nina was theft, but she didn't care.

She wandered to the kitchen and found a bottle of diet cream soda. Usually they bought cans, but this stuff had been on sale. The trouble was, she couldn't open the darn bottle. In one of the kitchen drawers, where Granny Kate kept less-used utensils and the emergency flashlight, she found an opener.

Something else caught her eye—a cheap MP3 player, the kind that was just a little bigger than the data sticks that plugged into a USB port. It seemed an odd thing for Granny Kate or Pop Pop to have. She couldn't imagine them downloading anything; they barely had e-mail nailed down. She frowned at the gadget and then stuck it in her pocket. She had headphones on her iPod upstairs. She could listen to it sometime.

She retreated to the living room and sat on the sofa while she channel surfed and gulped diet cream soda. On her journey through the channels, she hit upon a middle-aged white man with an Afro painting a mountain. She watched for ten minutes before finally turning off the television. She would never understand Jordan, not in a million years.

The next day she decided to go to the pool. As she walked through Little Salty, it seemed emptied out, eerily so, like a Wild West town before the villains are due to ride in.

At the pool, she found a secluded spot far from the lifeguard. She lay on a towel, soaking up the sun and wondering if, should she actually go to Little Salty high school, she would finally get a boyfriend. One of the girls in youth group had told her a boy named Brandon liked her, but the trouble was, Lily didn't like Brandon. He wasn't as cute or as nice as Crawford. She dozed off thinking how great it would be if she could merge the things she liked about Austin with all the good things about Little Salty to create her own perfect Lilyland.

The next thing she knew, she was waking up, and it was obvious she was in trouble. For one thing, it hurt to open her eyes. She looked down at herself and to her horror saw that her skin, which used to be white and pasty, now was a dull pinky red. She staggered up, dazed from sun, and winced as she slipped her T-shirt over her head.

When she walked into the kitchen, Granny Kate cried out. She led Lily upstairs, told her to lie flat on the bed, and brought in a fan to blow on her full blast.

For the next two days Lily lay on her back and was all alone except for when Granny Kate came in to give her food or slather her down with aloe vera gel. Lily cycled through all the music on her iPod until she was tired of hearing it. Finally, she remembered Granny Kate's MP3 player that she'd swiped from downstairs. She crawled out of bed and retrieved it from her shorts in the laundry basket. When she was reclined and re-gelled, she inserted her headphone jack into the new player, turned it on, and closed her eyes.

The first notes startled her. They sounded like the Indian instrument called a sitar. Expecting easy listening, she'd set the volume too high. But this was not Barry Manilow.

A pause followed, and then a bashing drum jolted her for a few bars. Her eyes opened as Mick Jagger's voice started singing "Paint It, Black." She knew that's what it was as soon as she heard his voice—the song that had led to all the problems. Granny Kate must have confiscated the player last summer.

The odd thing was, she liked the song, with that raw voice singing the strange angry-sad lyrics to a persistent, melancholy, thumping beat.

When it ended, she played it again three times in a row.

Had Jordan lain in this same twin bed last summer, staring at the ceiling and hearing those words? She must have. She would have done all the things Lily had—walked the same streets, gone to the pool, felt restless. It had just been a few months after their mom and Nina had died. Lily listened to the song once more, imagining for once how it must have been to be Jordan last summer. Feeling not only sad, but guilty. Feeling as if no one wanted to look at her.

She decided she wouldn't have wanted to be Jordan. Not for anything.

That afternoon, Granny Kate brought a box up to her. "UPS just delivered this," she said, depositing the box on the bed. The return address was Grace's. Lily ripped into it eagerly and extracted the contents—the CD and two books. One was the Trollope novel, but the other was a red cloth-bound blank book, its cover faded. Grace had included a note.

Dear Lily,

Here is the book Dad wanted you to have. And the CD I told you about. I'm also including an extra—a blank book. It's one that Dad gave me years and years ago, when I was uprooted. You'll notice that it's as blank as the day I received it. I've never been much of a writer, but I think you are. Don't let anyone stop you.

Love,
Grace

How could anyone have had a blank book all these years and not have written in it? Lily flipped through the thick, yellowed pages until she caught a flash of spidery script. Grace was wrong. Something had been written in it—on the inside cover.

Where we love is home.
Home that our feet may leave, but not our hearts.
Oliver Wendell Holmes

"Do you want to come down and watch television?"

Lily jumped. She had forgotten Granny Kate standing in the doorway. "No, thanks." She was eager to start reading. Or writing. Or to listen to that song again.

"I talked to your father today," her grandmother said. "I felt I should tell him about your sunburn calamity. Just to keep him posted."

Lily pushed herself up straighter. "What did he say?"

"Nothing much, except that your sister's back. Apparently her hair is orange now."

Lily frowned. "Orange? Like Bozo?"

"I have no idea," Granny Kate said. "It wouldn't surprise me. I think your father should have left her in San Francisco. That's probably the kind of place where a girl like her is going to end up anyway."

"Did he say anything else?"

"No—oh, yes. Dominic had to have a cavity filled."

"I mean about Jordan."

"I didn't ask for details about Jordan."

Lily considered her grandmother's perspective for a moment. "I guess it's hard to forgive Jordan for all the trouble she put you through. And the money it took to repaint." Those three coats.

"Well, I'll give your sister her due. She sent us the money for that. God only knows where she got it—I didn't ask."

Lily frowned, and then wished she hadn't. Her forehead felt like parched earth—a stretch of dried riverbed on her head. "She sold her furniture," she said, understanding now. "She sold almost everything she owned. Her stuff and Nina's."

Granny Kate let out a humorless chuckle. "That sounds typical. She never cared about possessions. She never wanted to belong to anything, either. She never seemed to care about being part of her family, or being on a team, or school spirit. It was always Jordan for Jordan."

"She really loved Nina." Lily heard the words come out of her mouth and wondered if she was possessed. *Why am I defending her?* But somewhere in the back of her mind, she could hear Grace's voice telling her to find that one good thing about Jordan. Maybe this was it. "She loves Dominic, too."

"Well. That may be," Granny Kate replied. "I don't mean to say anything against her. She's a character, I'll grant you that."

She left Lily alone again. What had seemed natural and right to Lily before—people complaining about Jordan—now made her uncomfortable. Weren't grandparents supposed to like their grandkids just a little? Unconditional love was sort of the point of grandparents, wasn't it?

She fell asleep and woke up about a half hour later, roused by an uncomfortable feeling that had nothing to do with her sunburn. It was that niggling itch at the back of her mind again. She'd missed a connection somewhere. She leaned over to the drawer of the bedside table and pulled out the picture she'd stolen from Granny Kate's closet. The one of her and Nina.

She studied the girl standing off to the side—the half a person in a soccer uniform. *"She never seemed to care about being part of her family, or being on a team,"* Granny Kate had said. It was true. Their mother was always signing Jordan up for arts camp, or theater programs. Never sports. Nina was the one who had played soccer.

"Oh, no," she whispered, staring at the picture in a whole new way.

Here came that tug again, that unsettled feeling deep inside her. Only this time, instead of a tug, it was a painful wrench. Days ago she thought she would have given anything to be with the sister in that picture again. But now . . .

Now all she had to do was leave the place where she fit in and go back to the place she'd felt like a natural-born outcast. Put aside her swan plumes and go back to ugly-ducklingville. The place her feet had left, but not her heart. It was so unfair! It was unfair that there was actually a voice in her head telling her to do it. In fact, it was telling her that she might regret it forever if she didn't.

36

What You Don't Know Can Hurt You

Jordan intended to float through the year, serving out the last of her childhood sentence in Austin by dreaming of the future and talking to all her new friends on Skype. Then, in just one short year—so soon she could almost taste it—she was going to art school.

There was just one hitch. The schools she and her friends from San Francisco talked about applying to wanted you to have decent grades; some even required three years of math. What math had to do with being an artist was a puzzle. But the upshot was, she had about four months to show college admissions offices that she wasn't a complete academic write-off. She was going to have to study very hard . . . and take Algebra II all over again. The worst part was, because she had screwed up last year, now her algebra class had Lily in it.

As she trudged home from school, she came to the painful conclusion that Lily might be her last best hope. It hurt, but she was going to have to suck it up and ask for help. Throw herself on her little sister's mercy.

"Hi!"

Jordan looked up and immediately wished she'd had her iPod so she could have pretended not to hear. Grace was waving at her, although God only knew why. The woman was juggling about twenty little bubble-wrapped mailers, carrying them to her car.

"Oh. Hey." Jordan inflected her voice with as little enthusiasm as humanly possible.

Grace dumped the mailers on the hood of her car. One dropped to the ground and she rolled her eyes before stooping to pick it up. "I should really have stuck these in a bag."

"Yeah." Duh.

"I think I have one in my car," Grace continued, as if she thought Jordan might actually want to have a conversation. "That's the worst part about what I do—I live at the post office."

Jordan frowned. "What do you do?"

Grace looked surprised that she didn't know. "I sell CDs online. Rigolettosmusic.com."

"Oh." Maybe Dominic had mentioned that before. She hadn't really paid attention.

"Classical mostly."

It figured.

Except . . .

One of her teachers from the summer had told them about *Einstein on the Beach.* "I've been listening to Philip Glass," Jordan said. It wasn't a total lie. She'd been thinking about listening to him, at least. "He's very intense."

Grace laughed. "Intensely headache inducing."

Every molecule in Jordan's body seized up. What a 'rhoid. "Yeah, well, I just happen to think Philip Glass is a genius, but then, I'm not an expert or anything," she said in disgust. "I don't run an *online music store*."

"I didn't mean to—" Grace shook her head as if it wasn't even worth her time to argue with Jordan. "How was your summer?"

She had a lot of crust asking. The last words Jordan remembered Grace saying were *She doesn't deserve* . . . As in, *Jordan doesn't deserve to go to California this summer.* "It was great. No thanks to you."

She turned sharply and walked away, enjoying her last glimpse of the woman's stupefied expression.

When she opened the door to the house, she heard the unmistakable rattle and clatter of dice being thrown against cardboard and peeked into the dining room to investigate. Lily and Dominic were playing Yahtzee.

"Afterschool family fun time?" Jordan asked, wandering over.

Lily glanced up. Sometimes Jordan couldn't believe she was looking at her little sister. She'd never imagined summer in Little Salty could be a transformative experience for the better, but here was living proof. Lily had ditched the glasses and the ponytails and now looked less like Poindexter girl.

She'd expected her sister to say something snarky to her, but instead Lily turned her attention back to the board and advised Dominic, "I'd take my twos if I were you."

Elbows on the table and his chin propped on his fists, Dominic muttered, "I *really* need a full house," before relenting.

During the next play, Jordan drifted closer to the table and finally slipped into a seat. "Who's winning?"

"Guess," Dominic grumbled.

"You can still catch up," Lily said. "It's just luck." She rolled. "Oh, excellent! Four of a kind—with sixes!"

Dominic moaned.

"Hey Lils . . . are you going to do your homework tonight?" Jordan asked.

"I always do my homework."

Jordan watched them play another turn and then cleared her throat. "I was wondering if I could study with you."

"Tonight?" Lily asked.

"Every night, actually."

Lily's eyes widened. "You must be *really* desperate to get a good grade!"

"I am," Jordan said. "That is . . . well, you know. I have to get into a decent college. It might already be too late, but if I at least show I'm trying . . . and write a really good essay . . . maybe . . ."

Lily deliberated for a moment. "Okay."

A few seconds passed before Jordan would allow herself to believe her ears. Lily had agreed? Just like that? No arguing, no negotiating?

Apparently so.

She exhaled in relief. "Good. With you helping, I at least have a prayer."

"You'd have a prayer anyway, if you would just concentrate."

"But that's it—it's hard to concentrate on numbers and symbols. They don't seem real."

"Not *real?*" Lily looked almost offended. "What's more real than numbers?"

"Speaking of real numbers," Dominic said, butting in, "will you roll already?"

Lily picked up the dice and rolled, but she was still shaking her head.

"Why does everybody get all snarky whenever I express an opinion?" Jordan asked.

"I didn't *get all snarky,*" Lily said.

"Who else got all snarky?" Dominic asked at the same time.

"That woman next door."

"Her name is *Grace,*" Lily said irritably.

Jordan rolled her eyes. "She's such a know-it-all. She had to make a snide remark about Philip Glass."

Dominic's brow puckered. "Who?"

"He's a composer," Lily explained to him.

It irked Jordan that her sister knew that. How did Lily manage to absorb everything?

"He's really cool," Jordan said. "But of course that woman Grace doesn't like him. She's so bourgeois and judgmental."

"You don't even know her," Lily said.

"Oh, please. I know her enough to see she's always had it in for me."

Dominic stood up suddenly. "You're crazy! You owe Grace *everything.*"

Jordan laughed. "Oh, right. Sure."

"You do," Dominic insisted. "*She* was the one who talked Dad into letting you go this summer."

"What?" Lily looked as stunned as Jordan felt.

"I don't believe it," Jordan said.

Dominic nodded. "After the party last spring, Dad was ready to—I don't know—lock you up in your room all summer or something. He was *really mad.* It was Grace who talked him out of it."

"How do you know this?" Jordan demanded.

"They were in Dad's study." He shrugged sheepishly. "I happened to overhear. And there was other stuff, too."

"Like what?" Lily asked.

Dominic looked reluctant to divulge any more, but Lily kept at him. "Okay," he said. "Dad said something like 'It was a mistake for me to kiss you.' "

"What?" Lily and Jordan said the word in unison. Yelled it, practically.

"I'm only telling you what I heard. I felt sort of

bad for her. He made it sound like he blamed Grace for the whole thing."

Jordan frowned. She was still trying to wrap her mind around the fact that Grace had told her father to let her go to California. "What whole thing?"

"The party—you know." Dominic lifted his shoulders. "The way it all turned out—even some incident about a Chinese restaurant Grace hadn't told him about."

Heat crept into Jordan's cheeks, especially when Lily shot her a sharp look.

"I didn't know," Jordan said.

Her brother and sister just stared at her until she slank away. Her feet felt like lead weights as she climbed the stairs. *Grace.* She'd always disliked her so much just on superficial grounds, and because Lily and Dominic thought she was so great. She'd never guessed she'd had a secret advocate living right next door.

37

Assisted Living

On a Saturday morning, Truman and Peggy took Lou out—"to give you a little time," Peggy explained to Grace. They were going to have brunch and maybe do a little shopping. They were gone four hours. Grace started to get antsy after three.

When they all returned, she offered Peggy and Truman something to drink while Lou hurried to his room. "He's probably tired, I guess," Grace said.

Truman jumped in. "Him? Why should he be tired? *I'm* the one who's eight-two!"

Peggy laughed. "We should probably go. Methuselah here needs a nap."

They called good-bye up the stairs and then traipsed out, arm in arm, looking like newlyweds.

Her father came down a little bit later and wanted to watch *Animal Planet.*

"I think I'll see if any orders have come in," Grace said.

She made a pass by her computer and checked the Rigoletto's Web site, but there were no new orders to process. She sighed restlessly. Now what? *When all else fails, do laundry.* She went into her bedroom and scooped the laundry hamper out of her closet. Then she went to her dad's room.

She had dumped the contents of his hamper into hers and was heading downstairs with it when a flash of something on his bureau caught her eye. A brochure.

The glossy booklet for Live Oak Villa on Town Lake was familiar to her because it was a replica of the brochure she'd thrown into the recycling bin months before. This version was so brand-new it still let off a fresh ink smell. She felt her chest rising and falling as she forced herself to draw in deep breaths.

Her father had *sneaked out* to look at Live Oak Villa? Last spring he'd been outraged at the idea of being packed off to live at an assisted living facility.

She picked up the brochure and hurried downstairs. In the living room, she picked up the remote and zapped the television screen. It flickered to black, causing her father to turn in alarm.

"What is this?" She held up the brochure.

A surge of anger crossed his face. "You got that from my room!"

"Yes, I did," she said, unrepentant. "Where did *you* get it? Is this what you and Peggy and Uncle Truman were doing today?"

"Don't blame Peggy. It was my idea. I asked her and Truman to take me."

No wonder they'd fled so quickly after dropping him off.

"But *you* were against this last spring!" she exclaimed. "Why would you even want to go looking at a place like that?"

"Because I can't stay here forever. I have to make plans."

"Why?"

The look he leveled on her broke her heart. It was a look that told her that all the fears she harbored were his fears too. All her dread was amplified in his eyes by a power of ten.

Because he had been so quiet about his illness

these past months, especially since the accident with his hand, she had hoped that he was just adjusting to living with slightly diminishing capacities and uncertainty of what the future would bring. Or that Alzheimer's had already relieved him of long-term worries. But that look told her he could still remember what he was losing.

"Don't be mad, Grace. Do you really think I'm going to let you be my nursemaid? It was wrong of me to even let you come here to live—to give up your business, leave your friends."

Her throat felt tight. "You didn't *let* me. I did it, and now I'm here. Are you going to abandon me?"

"It would be for the best."

"For who?"

He forced a smile. "Whom."

She wanted to scream. "I won't let you do it. If you're worried about me—"

"I'm worried about *me.* And you, too. I can't abide the thought of you taking care of me as if I were an infant." He smiled at her. "You've become bossy enough already."

Tears stood in her eyes and she had to look away. She tossed the brochure on the coffee table. "This is a mistake. Living among strangers? How will that help you?"

"How will it help me to live here with you and see you fritter away your life?"

"I'm not frittering away anything! I *want* to be here. With you."

"It's not your decision to make. It's mine, and I don't want to put off making it until it's too late."

She looked down at him for a moment longer. He was so tranquil about it all, while she felt as if there was a tornado of rage being whipped up inside her.

She barely croaked out, "I don't accept this," before she had to run back upstairs to her room. She threw herself facedown on the bed and blamed her brother for planting this seed in their father's mind last year. And Uncle Truman and Peggy for abetting her father. She remained indignant even against the onslaught of Heathcliff and Earnshaw's soothing purrs.

Maybe *eventually* he would have to think about moving out—maybe—but right now he was nowhere near that stage. It was outrageous.

She remained upstairs, entering a couple of CDs she had found at a garage sale this morning.

Later, when the more mellow light of evening was coming through the windows, she heard a knock at her bedroom door. Her father ducked his head in.

"Why don't we go out to dinner?"

"A public setting is no guarantee that I'll be any calmer than I am at home," she warned him. "Just ask Uncle Truman."

"I want Mexican food," he said, as if he didn't know what she was talking about. Maybe he didn't remember.

She relented. Twenty minutes later they were seated in the first wave of Saturday night diners at Fonda San Miguel. During the drive over she had worried about how they were going to handle the subject of Live Oak Villa when it came up, but she could have saved herself the anxiety. The whole dinner, Lou chattered about Forsytes, even though he'd spent most of the afternoon watching shows about pelicans and Komodo dragons. Even discussion of the perfect mole sauce, which usually would have merited at least a mention, was bypassed in favor of Forsytes.

But the dinner did cool her off somewhat. When they got home and Lou suggested a game of chess, she slipped obediently into her old spot. She hadn't played in weeks.

The game started as their games always did. She always felt a little sorry for that first doomed pawn she pushed forward. As the black and tan pieces marched toward each other, she braced herself for the onslaught. When a gap opened up, leaving a castle in plain view of a bishop, her father held back, which made her suspicious. What did he see that she couldn't? In the next few moves he started munching her pawns, tearing down her meager defenses.

After he'd caught both her knights, she decided to make a mad move with her queen and brought her out as a sort of last-ditch, flags-flying, hopeless-cause charge toward his king, which was still flanked by pawns. She took out a bishop and a castle, putting herself in position to grab the pawn standing between her queen and his king, which was boxed in.

“Check?” Her voiced wavered a little in amazement. She’d said the word so rarely.

“Hmm.” He looked down and studied the board. What seemed like an interminable amount of time passed, and then he castled her knight at the other end.

“Dad . . .” she said.

“What?” He glanced up at her with his eyes wide open. “Go ahead.”

She couldn’t believe it. Suspecting a trick, she slowly moved her piece forward and bumped off the pawn.

Her father stared at the board in surprise. “Is that checkmate?”

“I said check earlier,” she reminded him.

“I heard you.” He looked up at her. “Well, go ahead.”

“What?”

“Take the king. You won.”

“Yeah, but . . .”

He sat back and sighed contentedly. “Do you want to watch an episode of the Forsytes with me?”

She was still in shock. She’d dreamed of victory for so long, she’d expected that when it finally came she would be jumping up and down, pumping her fist and whooping madly. She'd thought—on the off chance that she ever did win—her father would have some scathing things to say about her scattershot strategizing, or maybe just the law of averages. Instead, he was already strolling back to the television, as if what had just happened was of no moment at all.

She studied the board, devastated, trying to figure out where she'd gone right. It had to have been a mistake on her part. The urge to drag her father back to the board and play the whole game over was almost unbearable.

"Grace?" he asked, so sweetly that she couldn't help walking over to the television and turning it on for him. She was fairly certain her father had already watched the particular episode he clicked on—watched it five times, probably—but she didn't say anything. She couldn't say anything. Nor could she focus on the story.

A few minutes in, when her father's face registered his absorption into this familiar fictional world, she slipped out quietly and went to the back porch for air. She was surprised to find Dominic sitting there, petting Iago. She'd forgotten she'd let Iago out when she and her dad had come in from Fonda San Miguel.

She sank down on the porch on the other side of Iago.

"Is something wrong?" Dominic asked.

She shook her head, but she felt a tear rolling

down her cheek and had to shrug her shoulder to wipe it off with the arm of her short-sleeved shirt. "I beat Dad at chess tonight."

"Wow," he said.

"I know. I can't believe it."

"No—I mean, *wow,* he was actually winning all that time?"

She sent him a sharp look. "What's so strange about that? He always beats you too."

"Yeah, but . . ." He shifted uncomfortably.

She froze. "Dominic, are you saying you've been *letting* him win?"

He gaped at her. "Well, *yeah.* I just assumed everybody was."

"For how long?"

He puffed his cheeks and then exhaled. "Since . . . I don't know . . . May?"

"That's four months!" she exclaimed.

Four months. All this time, she had been telling herself that—from the chess angle, at least—Lou was tack sharp. That he had to be doing okay because he could still beat the pants off her at his favorite game. It was the thing she'd been clinging to—her benchmark for proving to herself that he wasn't getting any worse.

Dominic fidgeted uncomfortably. At first she thought he must feel embarrassed to see her so upset. But when he spoke, she realized his reaction stemmed from something else entirely. Pity.

"You must really suck at chess," he said.

• • •

The woman, Diane, was perfect for her job as tour guide at Live Oak Villa. She was outgoing without being overbearing, sensitive when she needed to be but not creepily so, and most of all, upbeat.

Grace trailed after the woman through forest-green carpeted hallways, peeking into the dining room, the all-day snack bar, the conference room, the rec room, and the library that boasted two thousand volumes and a grand piano. Then they toured a couple of the apartments, which were standard one-bedroom units with kitchenettes. The whole place seemed great—almost like being in a college dorm again, only with nicer digs.

"Of course, these are the supportive housing units for our more independent residents," Diane told her. "I'm showing you these because when I spoke to Mr. Oliver, I sensed he still values independence and privacy."

Grace latched on to the flip side of this tidbit—the sinister hint of a hidden place where they intended to exile him to later, where there was no privacy or concern for him as an individual. "So when he gets to a later stage, you'll move him over to a group ward?"

Diane smiled patiently. "We call it a Special Care Unit. All rooms are private, but our SCU building is based more on a communal model, to keep residents with more rigorous supportive needs in a social, secure environment."

“I’d like to see this SCU,” Grace said.

Diane smiled at her. “Of course. But first, why don’t I show you the garden?”

A stalling tactic, obviously.

Grace was expecting an institutional courtyard with benches, but instead there was a large plot of land with waist-high raised beds where flowers grew, and tomatoes. And beyond it were shaded walking paths. “A feature we’re very proud of,” said Diane. For a moment Grace forgot the dreaded Special Care Unit.

“Dad could walk Iago back here,” she said.

“Who?”

“His dog.”

The woman’s forehead creased with lines. Grace felt a clamping sensation in her stomach. “Dad has a dog. Didn’t he tell you that? Iago’s very important to him.”

“No, he didn’t say anything about . . . Is it a small dog?”

“He’s a basset hound. Maybe sixty pounds?”

“We only allow small pets, and only in the apartments,” Diane told her. “Cats and small dogs. And of course fish and birds are fine.”

As far as Grace was concerned, this was the deal breaker. Her father might want to move, but he would never abandon Iago. “Well, that’s it, then,” she said.

Diane looked alarmed. “Don’t get me wrong. We love animals here, and we all understand the therapeutic effect they can have on people. Every few weeks we sponsor a Pets for Wellness visit."

"Like a petting zoo?" Grace couldn't help asking with a little sneer.

"It's a therapy dog group."

"Iago isn't a therapy dog. He's a member of the family."

She went through the motions of the rest of the tour, which was quick anyway.

When she returned home, her father, who had been out to lunch with Steven, asked her how she'd liked Live Oak Villa.

"I can't see you being happy there, Dad. They won't let you keep Iago."

"I know."

She gaped at him. "*You know?* And you're still considering it?"

"I can find Iago a good home," he said. "A better home, where he'll be taken care of."

"But you're his person!"

"I am, but I'm seventy-seven, and he's eight. Iago could live another ten years, and as he gets older, he'll need more care. I was going to ask Dominic if he would take him."

He had already thought this through? "When did you plan on moving?"

"This fall, I hope. As soon as I can get everything settled. I'll have to sell the house, of course. Steven says our neighbor Muriel is a real estate agent."

Swallowing took effort. Of course he would sell the house, and most of the things in it, too. He couldn't take it all with him.

He couldn't even take his dog with him.

"I'm going to need your help, Grace," he said. "I won't be able to manage it all, Steven says."

So she would be coerced into doing the very thing she found most odious. Being a party to his carting himself away to a home. It made her sick.

"You really intend to do this," she said. "You've probably been thinking about it for a while, too."

"I just didn't have the courage to tell you," he said. "I was afraid you'd be angry with me. You're not angry, are you?"

He sounded so frightened, her anger melted away in her need to reassure him. "No, Dad. I'm not angry."

For the next few days, Grace tried to be stoic. For the most part, she avoided thinking about Live Oak Villa. Even when Muriel came through the house in real estate agent mode, critiquing their paint colors and their old kitchen Formica countertops, she held her tongue. Occasionally she would catch herself clinging to the hope that her father would forget all about this and they would just continue to muddle along as they were.

It became harder to keep her head in the sand when the For Sale sign was planted at the end of the walkway.

The afternoon it appeared, she was up in her room when the front door opened and a brouhaha exploded downstairs. Her father and Dominic's raised voices penetrated her closed door, punctuated by a few barks from Iago. Then, to her surprise, heavy footsteps clomped quickly up the stairs and Dominic burst in.

"You didn't tell me you were moving!" he shouted. "Professor Oliver says he's going to live in a place way over on the other side of town! Why?"

"Because it's a place for . . . seniors."

"But that's *crazy!* Why would you let him do it? Why would you let him give up Iago?"

"He told you about that?" she asked.

"He wants me to take him," Dominic said. "But Iago's not my dog, and he's going to feel totally abandoned. Professor Oliver said I could bring Iago out to visit him, but I don't even have a car or anything, so how am I ever going to visit him way out there?"

She gulped. For some reason, she hadn't anticipated Dominic being this upset. Now she wondered why. "I don't know. But you'll see him again."

"But it won't be the same, will it? We won't be neighbors. He'll be gone, and you'll be gone too, won't you?"

"I'm not sure where I'll be."

"And what about Heathcliff and Earnshaw?"

The sad fact was, Earnshaw was looking shakier

every day. Grace was trying not to think about that, either. "I'm sorry, Dominic. I know it's awful to lose a friend like this . . ."

"No, you don't! I always lose everybody. I hate it!"

Tears ran down his face. She got up to give him a hug or even just a touch on the shoulder, but he ducked away from her just in time to maintain his adolescent dignity. "I'm not even sure my dad'll let me have Iago," he said.

"Do you want me to talk to him?" she asked.

His face registered surprise. "I doubt he'll listen to *you*."

She might have laughed, but his words smarted. Apparently, her stock was still not high at the West house.

"I'll talk to my dad," Dominic said. "Maybe if I sound pathetic enough, he'll give in."

She trailed after him downstairs, but Dominic left without another word. She went out and checked the mail. Nothing had arrived except an electric bill, junk mail, and down at the bottom of the box, a small package addressed to her.

The small box seemed odd. She shook it, but it didn't make any noise. She took it inside to the kitchen, where she could cut through the packing tape with a knife. When she lifted the lid she saw a little toy, a push puppet, lying on a bed of cotton.

At first, Grace couldn't believe what she was staring at. Instead of a cow or a pig or a figure in kitsch folk-wear, this toy represented a little old man with gray hair. He had a cane attached to one of his carved hands, and one of his legs was covered in a large white cast. But it was the face that shocked her, because it was so little yet so finely carved. The long nose, the set of his eyes, even the clothes that had been painted on him . . . it couldn't have been anyone else. It was her dad.

Carefully, she depressed the plunger inside his little pedestal, and the little old man with the cast collapsed. Then, when she let up again, he sprang back. She smiled.

Who had done this? She looked on the packaging for a return address, but there wasn't one. The package bore an Austin postmark.

"Who sent you?" she asked, before it occurred to her that she was talking to a puppet.

Clearly, it had been a long day.

38

Making a Mountain Out of Muriel

A car pulled up alongside Lily one day as she was walking home from school. She flicked a sidewise glance toward the street as Crawford was lowering the red Honda Fit's passenger side window. "Want a ride?"

Her pulse jumped, and it was only with

enormous effort that she forced herself to shake her head. Coming back to Austin, she'd made two resolutions: One, she wouldn't fight with Jordan. Two, she was not going to pine after Crawford. The second had proved a little easier than the first because she hadn't really spoken to Crawford since school had started. Now that he had his car, he was a lot more popular.

"No, thanks." She forced a pleasant smile and kept going. "I don't mind walking."

"C'mon, Lily," he said. "You've never even ridden in my new car."

"I know."

He puttered alongside her. "I'm going home too, and it would be pretty stupid for me to keep inching along this way for fifteen blocks. . . ."

She stopped. How could she say no again without sounding like a pill? Besides, pining was an emotional thing, while riding in a car was just a physical act. She could handle it. Without an actual verbal assent, she turned, pulled open the car door, and slid into the passenger seat.

The car, only a month old, still smelled new. "People must be paying you a lot to mow their yards," she said.

Crawford ducked his head and accelerated. She'd almost forgotten how his shorn-off curls looked this close up, and how green his eyes were. "My dad paid for most of it," he admitted, glancing at her. "Think I'm spoiled?"

She shrugged.

"I'm getting a weekend job to pay for gas and insurance and stuff, though."

"It's none of my business," she said.

"I know—but for some reason I can't stand the idea that you would think I didn't deserve something that I got."

"Why?" she asked.

He shrugged. "I don't know. I always get this feeling you're judging me."

"Well, I'm not. Why would I? I hardly have had time to think about you at all, I've been so busy. In fact, you can just drop me off here. I'm going to take a bus to the library downtown."

"I could drive you there," he suggested.

She lifted her chin. "Thanks anyway. I'd rather walk."

He looked almost hurt as he stopped. "Well, okay. See you around."

After she got out, he faced forward and sped off without another word. Lily felt a knot in her chest as he turned at the intersection and disappeared. Riding in cars might just be physical, but it could jump-start pining faster than anything.

"Where's Dad?" Lily asked Dominic later that evening, at home.

"I think he's next door."

"At the professor's house?" Lily asked, surprised. He never went over there.

"No, I think he's over at Muriel Blainey's."

She dropped into a chair in exasperation. "I need him to sign my permission slip for our band trip."

"I've got to talk to him, too," Dominic said.

"About what?"

"Professor Oliver wants to know if I can take Iago. For good."

"What?"

"He's going to move to an old folks' home. He's selling the house and everything. Didn't you see the sign in their yard?"

No, she hadn't. That's what came of being distracted by love. "Why would he move? He's got Grace."

"I don't get it, either. But he's going, and he can't take Iago with him, so he wants to know if I'll adopt him."

"Dad'll let you—don't worry."

"But doesn't it seem weird, taking Professor Oliver's dog away from him?"

"He's giving him to you."

"I still feel weird."

Jordan banged through the front door. "There's a For Sale sign in the yard next door!"

Lily, still stinging from not having noticed that sign herself, brought Jordan up to speed.

"This is screwed up," Jordan said. "Grace moved all the way down here to take care of her dad, didn't she? What's she supposed to do now?"

Lily crossed her arms. "Since when have you ever cared about the professor or Grace?"

Jordan dropped into a chair and dangled her boot-clad legs over the arm. "Since never. It just seems screwed up, that's all." She looked toward their dad's study door, which was open. "Where's Dad?"

"He went next door," Lily said.

"Oh—then he'll probably be able to give us all the poop on what's going on."

"The *other* next door," Dominic clarified. "Muriel Blainey's. I'm waiting to talk to him about adopting the professor's dog."

"And I'm waiting for him to come back so he'll sign a permission slip," Lily added.

Jordan gaped at Lily as if she were nuts. "Why don't you just forge his signature?"

"It's for a band trip to San Antonio. He's got to sign it. Otherwise he'll wonder what happened to me when I disappear one day."

"You think?" Jordan asked.

Dominic laughed. "What if we all disappeared? Do you think he'd notice that?"

"What's he *doing* over there?" Lily wondered.

"Muriel came over and said she was having computer problems," Dominic explained. "She wanted him to come take a look."

"Poor Dad."

"She really needs to get a new computer," Dominic said. "She was always having trouble with it this summer too."

Lily found her gaze seeking Jordan's, which reflected the same jolt of foreboding that she felt.

"And did Dad go over and help her?" Jordan asked casually.

"Sometimes."

Dominic noticed Lily and Jordan exchanging glances again. "What?"

"Nothing," Jordan said quickly. "Mountains out of molehills, probably."

This made their brother all the more worried. "You could at least tell me what the molehill is."

"Muriel Blainey," Lily told him. "And Dad."

Dominic rolled his eyes. "She just needs Dad's help with her computer because he knows all about that stuff and Muriel's husband's not around anymore. I think they're divorced now."

Jordan groaned just as the front door opened and their dad came in, humming. "Oh—here you all are!" He balanced a cellophane-wrapped plate in his hand, waiter-style, which he then put down in the center of the coffee table. "Muriel sent these over for you all. Wasn't that nice of her?"

The three of them stared at the cookies as if they were radioactive.

"They're chocolate chip," he said, his smile fading at their reaction. "She made them especially for you guys. She was thinking we could all get together sometime, for dinner or . . ." As he noticed their decided lack of interest, his voice petered out. ". . . or a movie?"

"It's a really busy time right now," Jordan said.

"What movie?" Dominic asked, before Lily kicked him. He let out a sharp *ow* in surprise, then piped up, "Not that I have time to watch movies. There's *so* much homework in seventh grade."

Ray frowned, puzzled. "Even on weekends?"

"Seventh grade is that make-or-break year, Dad," Lily said.

His eyes widened. "Well . . . it was just a suggestion. Muriel's all alone now, you know."

Jordan sent him a flat gaze. "Yeah, we know."

"I feel sort of sorry for her." Their father continued into his office and shut the door.

Lily forgot all about getting him to sign her permission slip, and Jordan looked lost in thought, too. Although not so lost that she didn't spot Dominic's hand reaching for the cookie plate.

"Nickel, if you eat even a bite of those cookies, we'll never speak to you again."

It took a moment for Lily to absorb the idea that she was the other part of Jordan's *we.* It took another moment of shock for her to agree.

"They're chocolate chip," Dominic argued.

"They're poison," Lily told him.

"Y'all are crazy!"

"Are we?" Lily asked him. "When was the last time you heard Dad hum?"

Dominic thought for a moment, moaning as the truth finally sank in. He collapsed against his chair back. "Muriel Blainey? This can't be happening."

Jordan drummed her fingers on the armrest. "It might not be. Yet."

"If he had to like a neighbor," Dominic said, "why couldn't he like *Grace?*"

Gloom settled over the room.

Jordan swung her feet back to the floor and sat up straight. "We have to do something, guys."

"What can we do?" Lily asked. "They're all adults. We can't tell them not to . . ." Lily couldn't even bring herself to think the words *fall in love,* much less say them. Not when she was thinking of Muriel Blainey.

What a disaster.

"This is the deal, guys," Jordan said. "Muriel Blainey as a stepmom? We have to think positive. We *will* find a way to stop this from happening."

Lily scrunched her lips. She never thought she'd see the day when she'd be accepting words of wisdom from Jordan.

Frighteningly, that day had come.

39

Impostor Parents

But we might not receive an offer on the house for months." Judging by her expression, Muriel was not impressed with Grace's logic. She had come to light a fire under Grace, to get the ball rolling. Grace was not showing can-do spirit. "We won't get *any* offers while this place is crammed with junk," Muriel declared, marching through the house, opening cabinets and tut-tutting over their contents.

Grace grew hot. "The possessions of a man's lifetime are not junk."

"Maybe not to the person who collected them, but to the rest of the world they're junk."

"S-so what are we supposed to do?" Grace sputtered. "Empty the place out?"

"You're going to have to do it sometime." Apparently there was no *we* when it came to accomplishing this. Muriel's eagle eye fixed on an object on the counter—a push puppet of a little boy. She held it up as Exhibit A. "I mean—stuff like this. Honestly, Grace! People going through a house don't want to think some creepy old pack rat lived here."

Grace stepped forward and snatched the toy from her. It had been delivered the day before, along with a companion figurine of a black-and-white dog. The boy had round eyes and painted-on chestnut hair like Dominic's. She still wasn't quite sure who was sending these little gifts, but it chafed her to have Muriel calling them junk.

"You need to decide what's actually worth something and find a way to dispose of all this stuff. The rest of it needs to be hauled away." Muriel stood in the middle of the kitchen and turned, trying to imagine it. “Empty, this place might look like something.”

“It looks like something now. It looks like a home.”

“You can’t just bury your head in the sand, Grace. The sign is in the yard. For Sale. It’s going to happen.”

“I know,” Grace said, growing agitated. “But what am I supposed to do? How can I get rid of everything?”

“Craigslist.”

At the sound of an unexpected voice, the two women whirled toward the doorway where Jordan stood. Somehow she had managed to sneak up on them, which seemed remarkable considering the amount of leather and metal she was wearing, and her orange hair.

“I got rid of a lot of things on Craigslist last year.” Jordan smiled at Grace. “If you want, I could help you.”

“There!” Muriel looked thrilled to have someone on her side, even if that someone was a teenager with hair the color of a traffic cone. “You’ve already got a helper, Grace!”

“Kitchen stuff, clothes, and knickknacks you could probably get rid of at a garage sale,” Jordan said. She pointed at the little toys on the counter. “Like those goofy things. Those would probably be snapped right up.”

Grace snapped them up now. “They’re not for sale.”

Jordan shrugged. "The bigger stuff you should probably list individually. Last year I advertised a partial estate sale and sold everything all at once. But I think I could have done better if I'd planned ahead better."

Muriel was still grinning, totally entranced by this punk fairy godmother providence had sent to bolster her argument. "Isn't this incredible, Grace? Who would have guessed there was a Craigslist genie right in our midst! This will be perfect." She beamed her Pepsodent smile at Jordan. "I'm going to tell your dad about this next time I see him! He'll be so proud!"

When Muriel finally left, Jordan glowered after her. "*That woman* is a walking billboard for Preparation-H."

Grace would have laughed if she hadn't been so confused. "What are you doing here?"

"Oh! I brought you cookies." She dug through her leather bike messenger bag and produced a cellophane-wrapped plate of cookies. She placed it in the middle of the chrome dinette, pulling off the cellophane and making a little ta-da gesture.

"Why?" Grace couldn't help asking.

Were they poisoned? What was Jordan doing here?

" 'Cause we had some and I thought you might like them." She shrugged. "Dominic's really upset that you guys are leaving." She tilted her head.

"He said the professor's going to an old folks' home."

"It's an assisted living facility."

Jordan's lips compressed at the distinction. "Yeah, right. Okay. But where are *you* going to live?"

The question had been in the back of Grace's mind for weeks now. She hadn't allowed it full volume because she didn't want to be swamped by panic and despair. *Back to Portland?* That was the most obvious answer. Her mother would be happy to have Grace out of the Olivers' clutches again. But she couldn't leave the city where her dad was. *Rent an apartment, find a new job, start over?*

"I'll figure something out," she said finally.

"Seems to me this really sucks from your point of view," Jordan said. "That's why I thought you might like some chocolate chip therapy."

Grace was still looking askance at those cookies.

"Also," Jordan said in a rush, "I wanted to apologize for being such an asshat. Last spring. And a couple of weeks ago. And, well, basically 24/7 my entire life. I'm sorry. Seriously."

Grace shifted.

"And I really will help you with getting rid of your stuff," she added. "If you want me to."

"That's okay," Grace said. "That is, I still don't know what I'm doing. But thank you."

Jordan shrugged. "Up to you. You know where to find me."

She slunk out just as quickly as she'd come in, leaving Grace in a semidaze. She couldn't look at those cookies without feeling a shiver of paranoia. What was going on?

When her father came through, he looked at the cookies and reached for one. "Who brought these?"

"Jordan."

"Who?"

"Dominic's sister."

His hand froze. "The hoyden?"

After a perfunctory knock, the side door opened and Dominic came in. He headed straight for the cookies and sat down. "Can I have one? Jordan wouldn't let me eat them over at our house."

Grace frowned. "Why not?" Maybe they really were laced with cyanide or something.

But he gulped one down with no visible harm and reached for another. Iago came trotting in, and Dominic petted his head and grinned as the dog snuffled around the floor, anticipating crumbs. "Can y'all come to my school on the night of the twenty-second?"

That was two weeks away. "What for? Are you doing some sort of presentation?"

"Not really. It's St. Xavier's Parent Night."

"We'd love to go!" Lou exclaimed, before Grace could signal caution. "Thank you for inviting us."

"Wait," Grace said. "Shouldn't I talk to Ray?"

Dominic looked at her as if she were crazy. "Dad? Why?"

Grace shifted awkwardly. "Maybe he would think we were being . . . intrusive."

"Lots of kids have other people besides their parents come," Dominic said. "Grandparents or aunts, stepparents. Last year Jonah Renfrew brought his nanny . . . but that *was* sort of weird, actually."

"Yes, but—"

"Dad's probably not even going to make it, so if y'all don't come, I won't have anybody."

It was settled, then, that they would go. Lou seemed to look forward to it, and despite her own misgivings about overstepping into Ray's territory again, Grace couldn't bring herself to rain on her dad's parade, or Dominic's. What did it matter? They would just pop in, smile at a teacher or two, and pop out before too many people absorbed the fact that they were impostors. No biggie.

"Do you need us to drive you to school on Parent Night?" Grace asked him.

He shook his head. "No, I have a ride."

During the intervening days, she barely had time to think of Parent Night. She had to keep the house spotless in case people came to look at it, and then vacate when prospective buyers wanted to tromp through. She was also busy with the usual business of selling her CDs, and now she wondered if she should start trying to sell some of her father's books online too. Feeling as if she was taking her life into her own hands, she broached the subject with him.

Though braced for a blast of indignation, all she received was a shrug.

"I enjoy looking at them," he said, "but not enough to carry them all with me."

His nonchalance upset her more than a full-scale opposition would have.

By the time Dominic's Parent Night rolled around, she had almost forgotten all about it. Lily reminded her the night beforehand.

"Saint Xavier's is sort of snobby," she informed Grace.

"I'm sure I can handle it," Grace said.

Lily didn't look convinced. "Do you own a dress? You're supposed to look nice."

Grace laughed. "I won't embarrass Dominic, I promise. Besides, Dad always looks dapper when he goes out. He'll provide the wow for the both of us."

"You should be wow too," Lily argued. "Do you want me to pick something out for you?"

Grace practically had to bar her from the staircase to keep her from marching up to her room and ransacking her closet. Up to that moment, she hadn't realized how much she must have let herself go in the past year, but if even a fifteen-year-old self-professed former geek wanted to give her fashion tips . . .

The next day she went for a haircut, dragging her father off with her to the salon. She dug a dress out of her closet that she hadn't worn since leaving Portland. It felt like an outfit from another life. When she was checking on her dad, he was putting on a suit that was fresh out of a dry cleaner's bag.

"How do I look?" he asked.

"Very Savile Row," she replied, although he'd made a complete shambles of his tie. She reknotted it for him and combed his hair. "I don't think Dominic will be embarrassed by us."

As they were ready to leave for the school, Dominic knocked on the door. "Are y'all ready?"

Grace stepped back, confused. "Do you need us to drive you after all?"

"No—I told Dad y'all are coming with us, so he'll drive."

Dominic turned and gestured toward Ray, dressed in a suit, standing on the porch. Ray swept his gaze up and down Grace's person, taking in her fancied-up appearance.

"C'mon, Professor Oliver," Dominic said, practically vibrating with nervous energy. "We're going to go in my dad's Prius!"

He pulled Lou out of the house and led him to the car.

"I *did not* do this on purpose," Grace declared, before Ray could say anything. "Dominic invited us. I had no idea—"

"It's all right, Grace. I understand what happened."

"But Dad and I don't have to go. If you'd rather—"

"It's fine," he said. "I'm glad you're coming along."

She couldn't believe that. "Really?"

A horn honked from the driveway. "Dad, *let's go!*"

Ray's lips twitched into a smile at Grace. "Okay!" he called back.

At St. Xavier's, they started out in Dominic's homeroom, where there was a contest to guess how many gumballs were in a jar. In secret, the parents had to write down an estimate of what half the total number would be, and then the following day the students would put down their own guess for half. The two numbers would then be added up and the parent-student team that came closest to the actual tally would win something.

Grace and her father held back, looking at photos the students had taken, but Dominic grabbed Grace's arm and dragged her over to the gumball jar, which Ray was staring at intently. "C'mon," Dominic said. "Y'all have got to make a guess. There's a really good prize—it's a vacation!"

"Seriously?" Grace asked. She'd never gone to the kind of schools that gave away real loot.

Dominic pointed to the flyer taped to the

blackboard behind the gumballs. The vacation was a two-night stay at something called the Winecup Lodge and Spa in the Hill Country.

"How many do you think?" Ray asked her.

"I can't know your guess," Dominic said, backing away from them. "I'll go introduce the professor to my English teacher."

He disappeared.

Grace leaned in toward Ray. "I really am sorry. If I'd known you were coming . . ."

"You wouldn't have come?" he asked.

Actually, she supposed that *was* what she had meant, but she hadn't wanted it to sound so blunt. "I just assumed that you would be . . ."

"Too busy for my kids?" he asked. "I'm not entirely negligent."

"That's not what I meant. I only wanted—"

He cut her wittering short. "Grace, one way to get over the awkwardness here might be to focus on the gumballs. Do you have a guess?"

His open strategizing to defuse the tension made her laugh. "One hundred and sixty?"

"I was going to say a hundred and fifty."

"Make it a hundred and fifty-five and you'll have a bargain."

He smiled and wrote it down on one of the slips of paper provided.

Another couple, obviously parents, sidled up to the gumball jar. The woman smiled at Grace and introduced herself as Julie Otley-Richardson.

"And this is my husband, Todd. We're Alissa's parents. She's going to be playing harp at the recital in just a little bit."

"I'm Grace," she replied, only realizing the pitfall in the situation once she'd already begun. "I'm here with Dominic West. But I'm not really a parent. This is Dominic's father, Ray."

Julie Otley-Richardson's bright smile remained firmly in place. "Significant other, then?"

"I'm not really significant," Grace said quickly. "That is, not a significant other. Just a friend. Of Dominic."

"And me," Ray told her.

"Well . . ." Grace felt her brow pinch as she looked up at him. "Friend, yes. I mean, we're neighbors. But not *significant* . . . that's what I meant."

"Oh." His eyes registered that he suddenly understood the distinction she was trying to establish. He turned to confirm her assessment for the Otley-Richardsons. "No, not really significant."

Julie and Todd's faces had frozen into expressions of shared bemusement.

"Maybe we should go find Dominic," Grace suggested to Ray, dragging him away.

As they moved through the hallway, passing well-heeled couples with their sheepish children in tow, Grace murmured, "I'm glad Lily told me I needed to dress up."

Ray stopped to give her another once-over.

"You look great. You did something to your hair. It's pretty." He added quickly, "I mean the color. I've always been intrigued by it. Is it red, is it brown . . . ?"

"Auburn."

"Exactly—one of those sixty-four box Crayola colors."

She laughed. "Like raw umber. I never knew what that meant."

"Blizzard blue was always my favorite," he said. "It only made sense if you didn't think about it. But I guess they didn't need more names for white."

She laughed.

Impulsively, he reached for her hand. Even though their end of the hall was emptying out—everyone seemed to be herding in the opposite direction—Grace felt awkward. She tugged at her hand, but he held it fast.

"I'm glad you're here, Grace. Probably a hundred times I've wanted to knock on your door, to apologize."

"There's nothing—"

"Yes, there is."

"Hey!" Dominic skidded toward them, and Ray dropped her hand. "There's a music recital. Everyone's supposed to be there, so you have to go even if it's boring, which it probably will be."

Ray laughed. "That's great salesmanship, Dominic."

They entered the small auditorium as people milling about were starting to be seated. At first, Grace took the seat on the aisle next to her father, but then Dominic asked her to switch with him, so she moved in. She had only just sat down next to Ray when her father poked her on the shoulder. "Dominic has something he wants to show me. We'll be right back."

Grace cast an uneasy glance at a man wheeling a harp onto the stage. "Why don't we all go?"

"No," Dominic said quickly, stopping them from getting up. "I mean—we won't be long."

After they had left, she turned and smiled at Ray. "I think Dad's having a good time."

One of his eyebrows darted up. "Are you?"

A couple sidled past them to get to seats in the center of the row. In an effort to get out of their way, she and Ray half stood and shifted, colliding with each other. They collapsed back in their seats, facing forward. Grace absently rubbed her upper arm where he'd bumped it.

After a moment, Ray leaned toward her. "I wanted to tell you that I'm sorry for . . . well, for practically everything I said last April. Later, when I'd had a chance to think, I wanted to kick myself."

She shrugged, carefully nonchalant. "It's been a bad year for both of us."

"Dominic would talk about you, and about your father's troubles, and I would want to say something to you, but I held back. At one point last summer Lily said she wanted to stay with her grandparents permanently, which devastated me. I wanted to talk it over with you, too, because I knew you would understand how I felt . . . but after all the things I'd said to you—and with so much anger—I expected you would slam the door in my face."

"That, I would never do," she said. "And I wasn't exactly calm that day, either."

"Everything's been better lately—because of you. You were right, straight down the line. I let Jordan go, and she's come back relatively sane. And Lily's doing well too."

She had forgotten how his voice, rich and deep, affected her. She turned to him, bracing herself to look into his dark eyes, and smiled.

"It was you, Grace," he said. "I'm glad—"

Impatience spiked within her when his words broke off. "You're glad . . . ?"

"That you came along," he said.

A rush of emotion knotted in her throat. Until just this moment she hadn't realized how much she'd missed him—how many times she'd wished he was there to talk to.

As the lights dimmed and the spotlight came up on Alissa Otley-Richardson, who was a quarter of the size of her harp, Ray leaned toward Grace and added in a whisper, "I almost asked Muriel."

She stiffened. "Muriel?"

"We've been hanging out a little," he confessed.

Grace was grateful for the dimmed lights, because she was pretty sure the flush in her cheeks would have been visible otherwise. He hadn't meant that he was glad she'd come along into his life, which was the conclusion she had jumped to. He'd meant that he was glad she was there *tonight.*

She faced forward, arms crossed. She was even glad to hear the opening plucked strains of "Ave Maria," so she wouldn't have to render an opinion on Ray *hanging out* with Muriel Blainey.

40

More Invitations

Lily waited until she knew Grace was alone before knocking, but even so, she had to rap twice on the door and stand waiting for a while. Grace finally answered, her face puffy and her eyes red. The words Lily had rehearsed flew out of her mind. "What's the matter?"

"Oh, nothing." Grace shook her head. "Dad just left on a walk with Dominic. Would you like to come in?"

Lily stepped into the house. "I brought you this."

Grace took the small old glass bottle from her and studied the label with a furrowed brow. "Cinnamon sticks?"

"I read on the Internet that you should boil them in water before people come over to look at the house. It's a psychological thing. It will make the house smell homey and then people will want to buy it."

At her words, Grace went from looking slightly depressed to openly weeping. She barely squeezed out a trembly "Thank you!"

"Is something wrong?" Lily asked.

Grace gulped a few times before attempting to speak. "Earnshaw died," she squeaked.

"Dominic told me. I'm really sorry."

She waved her hand in front of her face as if to cool off her tears. "It's okay. It's stupid for me to be so upset—she was really sick. I mean, I knew it was going to happen."

Lily nodded, but didn't want to say anything more. The only times she'd glimpsed Earnshaw, she hadn't been very impressed. The cat had spent months squatting under furniture, looking hunted. "Is Heathcliff okay?"

"*He's* never been better," Grace said with a trace of bitterness. "All these years, I thought the two of them were devoted to each other—that they couldn't live without each other. But Heathcliff is gamboling about like a kitten. He's never been so frisky!"

"Maybe he's glad to have you all to himself. Maybe *you're* the one he's devoted to."

Grace considered this. "I still feel disillusioned."

She held up the tiny jar. "Anyway, thanks for the cinnamon sticks. I suppose I should try to use them—although I'm secretly tempted to sabotage any possibility of a sale."

"I wouldn't want to leave this house, either. It's so much cooler than ours."

"Your house is bigger."

"Yeah, but it's never felt right since . . ." She didn't finish, but she didn't need to. Grace was nodding in understanding.

A small object on the bookshelf caught Lily's gaze. An object that looked strangely like herself. "Hey!" She picked the piece up and examined it. It was one of the little push puppets that Grace collected, but this one was painted with her face, and was even carrying a tiny plastic clarinet. Just to test it, she pushed the plunger and watched herself collapse and pop back up again.

"Where did you get this?" she asked Grace.

"It's a mystery. They keep appearing in my mailbox. So far I've got Dad, Iago, and Dominic. And now you."

"Where do they come from?"

"I don't know. They arrive in little boxes with Austin postmarks."

"But you must have some idea," Lily insisted.

"I have a suspicion."

Lily narrowed her eyes. *Who would do this?* They were so cute, it would have to be someone with a sense of humor. Also, someone who knew

Grace pretty well. And who was good at woodworking.

“I think I know who it is,” Lily announced.

“Who?”

“I’m not going to tell,” she said. “I want to find out for sure, first.”

Grace smiled. “So I guess we share a suspicion.”

Lily suspected Crawford. Crawford had carved a box out of the wood from the old elm tree and given it to Grace last Christmas.

If it was Crawford, she was doubly glad the figurine of her looked like the new her and not the old her. There were no glasses painted on her face, and her hair was loose, not in a ponytail. Aside from that, it was hard to know if her likeness was flattering or not. She was certainly flat-chested, but that wasn’t necessarily the artist’s fault. A cylindrical segmented body didn’t exactly give an artist much to work with.

The important thing was that Crawford—if it was Crawford—had been thinking about her.

She was so wrapped up in the puppet that she almost forgot the reason she had come over. The cinnamon sticks had just been cooked up as an excuse. “You and the professor are invited to our house for Thanksgiving,” she told Grace. “We kids want to make dinner. Do you think you’ll be able to come?”

Grace frowned. “Well, thank you, but—”

“Please? Say you’ll come. Last year was so

awful—and this year Granny Kate and Pop Pop are taking a trip to Florida to visit Great-Aunt Jeannie."

"It's nice of you to invite us, but Dad has it in his head to have Thanksgiving here."

"Again?" Lily hadn't foreseen this. "But last year was a disaster!"

Grace laughed. "I know, but since this will be our last Thanksgiving here . . ."

Lily left the house soon after. *Mission not accomplished.* Jordan would be annoyed that she hadn't been able to persuade Grace to come for Thanksgiving. Now what were they supposed to do?

Crawford pulled into his driveway. He got out and smiled at her over the roof of his car. "Hey! Seems like I haven't seen you in two hours."

He was referring to their last-period band class. "I was talking to Grace," she said. "She received a new one of those puppet thingies in the mail." She watched him closely for his reaction.

His face twisted in puzzlement.

Oh, he was good.

"Didn't you offer to drive me somewhere in your car?" she asked, crossing the yard toward him. Risks were worth taking when there was a mystery to be solved.

Now he looked really confused . . . but not displeased. "Okay—hop in."

She did and he reversed out of the drive and

sped off down the street. When they were stopped at a light, he turned to her. "You want to go grab something to eat?"

"Sure," she said.

Crawford drove to Taco Cabana. Lily just ordered a Coke; her stomach was too jittery to actually eat. They hadn't been alone together since last spring, and back then it had only been when someone else had happened to leave the room. It had never been on purpose—at least not on Crawford's part.

After they sat down, Crawford took a bite of a burrito—he wasn't too nervous to eat, apparently—and gulped it down with a swig from his drink. "You seem different this year," he said.

"Well?" she asked. "That's a good thing, isn't it?" She sounded so defensive, she immediately wished she'd kept her mouth shut.

He tilted his head. "Why did you leave this summer? I never understood."

"Just to get away," she replied.

"From your sister?"

"Mostly," she admitted.

His brows scrunched together. "But Jordan went away too."

Did he still like Jordan? From his expression, she couldn't tell. She sucked on her straw, fighting against all the old feelings that threatened to come roiling back.

"Did you have fun while you were with your grandparents?" he asked.

"Yeah, I did, but somehow it didn't seem real. It was like I wanted to belong there more than I actually did."

"But Dominic said that you were actually thinking of living in that place."

"I was."

"So why did you change your mind?"

"Because of something Grace said. Although I suppose it was really something Oliver Wendell Holmes said about your feet leaving a place but not your heart."

He laughed. "Well . . . you still talk in the same whacked way. *That* hasn't changed."

She smiled.

"All this time since you got back, I've wanted to talk to you," he said. "But it seemed sort of weird because of . . ."

"Last spring," she said.

"Yeah."

She hoped he couldn't see her shudder. After that episode, Crawford had probably thought she was a little psycho stalker. It was so embarrassing. "I'm sorry."

"Hey—don't apologize to me. As far as I'm concerned it all worked out great. Dad and Pippa broke up."

She sat up straighter. "You used to like Pippa."

"She was okay, but she and Dad would never

have lasted. So there would have been a lot of arguing and stuff, like there was with my mom, and then they would have gotten a divorce. So what was the point?" He leaned forward. "Besides, without having a steady girlfriend, Dad got sort of into looking for cars with me. That's how I ended up getting a new one. He hated all the used cars I looked at that I could have afforded on my own. So, if you think about it, I have you to thank for my wheels."

He really was reaching. "That's nice of you to say—but I was so embarrassed. I still am. I basically insulted everyone in the neighborhood."

"You didn't insult me," he said.

She felt a blush creep up her face and she hunched over her drink, sucking Coke through a straw so she wouldn't have to say anything. She'd spent her whole life reading books, but when she really needed words, her brain blinked out on her.

And yet Crawford, who usually didn't talk that much at all, was able to keep the conversation afloat.

"So I guess you're bummed about Grace and the professor moving," he said. "I know I am."

Here was her opening. She crossed her arms, preparing to watch his answer *very* closely. "Have you thought of doing anything . . . for Grace, I mean?"

He blinked. "Like what?"

"Oh, you know . . . any special farewell gift or something?"

"Not really." Frowning, he asked, "Why? Do you think she expects me to?"

"Not if you don't want to. I mean, I was just thinking, because you're so good at making stuff, you might have had something in mind."

He shrugged. "I haven't had time."

Lily frowned. He didn't seem to be hiding anything. So apparently there was *some other* woodworker out there making her into a puppet. Weird.

As they were driving home, he asked her, "Would you ever be interested in going to a movie or something?"

For a moment, she couldn't believe she'd heard him right. He was asking her to a movie. As in, *on a date.* No one had ever asked her on a date before. It had always seemed such a remote possibility that even in her imagination she'd never gotten to the part about how she was supposed to react. Her tongue felt frozen.

He darted a nervous glance toward her. "No? Yes? Think about it?"

"Yes," she blurted out. "Of course yes. I mean, it sounds fun."

When she got home, the moment she shut the door she wanted to whoop with joy. Or toe dance through the foyer. Or bound up the stairs three at a time.

But Jordan was waiting at the door for her, practically tapping her watch like an impatient parent. "Where have you been? You went over to Grace's hours ago!"

"Crawford offered me a ride in his car." She was still floating, so she didn't feel compelled to add that he'd only offered once she'd asked him first. "We went to Taco Cabana."

"Congratulations," Jordan said. "Did you talk to Grace?"

"Yeah . . . but it's not good. She said no."

"*What?* And then you just went out joyriding?"

"What else could I do? Grace said that the professor wants to have Thanksgiving at their house."

"Did you try to talk her out of it?"

"How could I do that? It's obviously the professor's decision. Grace is really depressed about its being the last year at their house."

"Crap!" Jordan plopped down on the stairs. "Now what do we do?"

Lily lifted her shoulders. "Give up, I guess."

Jordan's head snapped up. "Give up? With Muriel Blainey on the prowl? There's no telling what that woman has planned for Dad over in her lair."

Lily twisted her lips, thinking. "Maybe Dominic will be able to convince Grace to take the spa trip."

Too late she realized bringing up *that* topic was

akin to poking her sister with a pin. Jordan roared in frustration. "What is the matter with her? We go to all the trouble to win that stupid trip, and then she won't even go!"

Lily still experienced a pang of guilt whenever she thought about those gumballs. "We shouldn't have done that. It was cheating."

Jordan, on the other hand, entertained no guilt about having sneaked into Dominic's classroom during the Parent Night recital and counting gumballs when no one was looking. "It was *necessary* cheating, for a worthy cause. Or it would have been," she grumbled, "if the cause would cooperate."

Lily thought for a moment. Apart from missing an opportunity to have her father and Grace together in a social setting, she dreaded Thanksgiving alone, with just the family. Things might be better than they were last year, but another holiday alone with just the four of them would be grim. Almost as grim as last Christmas, when their father had given them all watches and taken them out for Indian food.

"We'll just have to try a different tactic," she told Jordan.

"What do you have in mind?"

"Being pathetic."

41

Grateful but Unwilling

Dominic's eyes were Grace's undoing. Those big brown eyes melted her resistance and persuaded her where mere pleas had failed. It was all the eyes—and maybe the bit about Ray taking them out for Indian food.

At first, Grace tried to laugh it off. "Maybe they'll have tandoori turkey on the menu."

That was when Dominic had turned those big brown eyes on her. "No pie, though." His voice contained such sadness, he might as well have said *no love.* "Just mango custard."

His four kinds of pie lament from last year came to mind. It was as if there were a cinch around her heart, squeezing.

"Or a little soupy rice pudding," he droned on.

Grace couldn't take any more. "Why don't you all come over here?"

"That would be a lot more work for you," Lily pointed out.

"It's no more work to buy a bigger turkey," Grace told her.

The two kids raised up for a moment, their faces hopeful. Then their gazes met and they both deflated. "Dad would say we were imposing," Lily explained.

"He'll send one of us over here to tell you no."

"What if *I* talk to him?" she suggested.

They brightened up again. "Would you?"

"Of course."

Lily warned, "Dad'll probably try to convince you that he had big plans mapped out."

"Yeah—he'll make out like he was going to make a turkey on his own," Dominic said. "But that's just because he's too proud to ask for help."

"He is?"

Dominic nodded. "He'll act like he's got it all under control."

"Well, I'll be diplomatic," she promised.

As it turned out, Lily and Dominic's predictions were spot on.

"Thanks for the invite," Ray said, "but I think I've got Thanksgiving under control."

"You have plans?" She very nearly asked him which Indian place they were going to this time.

"We're having dinner here. Gonna attempt a turkey myself, I think."

Poor guy. His kids really had him pegged.

She swung into manipulative mode. "I guess you've heard, Dad is moving in December."

He nodded. "I'm sorry. What will you do?"

"I'll spend the month of December selling off the rest of Dad's stuff, and I guess in January I'll move to an apartment or something."

"I'm sorry," he repeated.

"I've known it was coming. It's . . . well, you

know. It's not just Dad. I'll miss the house, too. All those years I was in Portland, it was the home I dreamed about. I guess I just assumed it would always be there."

"Because you assumed *he* would always be there," he said, understanding.

"The thing is," she continued, getting back to the point, "Dad probably won't have much more opportunity to see Lily and Dominic after Thanksgiving."

Ray weighed her words for a moment. "I could send them over after dinner."

Was he really that desperate to avoid her company? She started to feel irritated—and challenged. "Ray, the fact is, I've already invited the kids over. All of you, actually. I think they have their hearts set on it."

His brows arched. "Jordan too?"

"Jordan too. We've declared a truce."

He seemed impressed.

"I'm sorry if I stepped out of line," she said. "I didn't know you would kick up an objection. But I can't rescind the invitation. It's against my policy."

He smiled. "Mine too. That's why there's a problem . . ."

Lily didn't find out about the extra guest until Thanksgiving day, when she was counting places in Grace's dining room. As Grace explained about the extra chair, Lily's composure snapped. "You invited *Muriel Blainey?*" She was almost yelling. "Why?"

"What could I do? Your dad said they'd already talked about spending the holiday together. If I hadn't invited her, she would have been by herself all day. Ray might have sent you all over here and spent the day at her house. Alone with her."

She exchanged a significant glance with Lily.

"Oh."

In truth, when Grace had heard that Ray intended to spend the day with Muriel, she was tempted to wash her hands of the whole business. First her brother, now her neighbor. Was she going to spend her whole life dealing with the Blainey threat?

On the other hand, she had promised the kids.

At least including five new people would add another layer of interest to what was shaping up to be a bittersweet holiday. Thanksgiving was the prelude to her father's exodus from the house. The first weekend of December—the weekend of her birthday—he was going to be moving to his new place, and she would spend the next month boxing things up, selling, and shipping, and trying to figure out where she was going to go herself.

When Sam, who had flown in to spend a couple of weeks, heard about the situation with Ray's family, he cornered Grace in the kitchen to crow in amusement. "So are you on a one-woman mission to save the world from Blainey-kind?"

She smiled. "Not a mission. Just helping out."

"Exactly," he said. "Just helping out so that she doesn't snag your guy."

"Oh, please! Have you been upstairs dipping into my old *Sweet Valley High* books again?" Sam had found several in a Goodwill box and had been pestering her with dramatic readings from them all day. "Ray's not *my guy*—not by any stretch."

He arched a brow. "Not even in your imagination?"

"Not even there," she said. "I like him. Last year I felt a sort of . . . I don't know . . . camaraderie building there. But then things went south."

"Every romance has its ups and downs."

"It's not a romance," she said. "Never was."

"The kiss was just accidental?"

She whirled on her heel. "Who told you about that?"

"I might be a gossipy bigmouth," he said, folding his arms across his chest as he leaned against the counter, "but I'm also a journalist. I never reveal a source."

Who could have told him? Only Ray knew—and Ray was the very opposite of a gossipy bigmouth.

"The kiss was a mistake."

"Uh-huh," Sam said.

She handed him a bowl of olives. "Put this on the table."

"Why? So you can have a moment to think of a rationalization?"

"Yes."

"Well, forget about it, because when I come back I intend to pester you for info about this new girlfriend of Steven's."

"That's not a girlfriend. That's Emily."

"I hate to contradict, but I saw them standing together next to Truman and Peggy, and Steven had his hand at the small of Emily's back."

Grace's jaw dropped. She had given up her dream of anyone ever getting past Emily's tough shell. Especially Emily herself.

Sam left, almost bumping into the woman herself on her way in. She did look a little different. She had cut her hair and given it a light perm, softening up the sharp edges and angles of her face.

"Is there another gravy boat, Grace? Frau Blainey is warning that the dining table is going to have a condiment dead zone."

Grace laughed. "Don't worry about it. I'll dig up something."

"Give me something to do," Emily begged. "I hate to stand around feeling useless, and Steven's deep in a conversation with your uncle about his knee."

Steven? Not Dr. Oliver?

Sam was even more perceptive than she'd ever given him credit for.

Grace picked up the water pitcher and handed it to Emily. "The water glasses need filling. Be my guest."

"I thought we already were your guests." Jordan slouched in and with her sharp-nailed fingers pincered a carrot stick off a tray. "I didn't know we had to work, too." She crossed to the stove and started lifting lids off pots. "Isn't this stuff ready yet? I'm starving."

"Almost."

"What's the deal with Sam?" Jordan asked. "He's cuter than you and your other brother. Doesn't he have anybody?"

"He does, but he doesn't really admit it. The guy's in Africa."

"Cool—what's he doing there?"

"Planting trees."

Jordan chewed this over. "Interesting. So . . . it's really just you who's not paired off."

"Thanks. I hadn't dwelled on that fact in the past ten minutes."

"You want to know why you're alone and your brothers aren't?" Before Grace could say no, Jordan continued, "Because men don't do lonely. Women do, since they're pickier. But men will just take whatever comes down the pike."

"I'm not so sure about that."

"Look at my dad and Muriel. That's all the proof you need."

"But they're not together . . . not really." When

Jordan didn't say anything, she asked, "Are they?"

"Only a matter of time, I'd say." Jordan edged closer as Grace was sticking rolls into the oven. "Dominic says you're not going to the spa. Why not?"

That spa again! Dominic had been whining to her about it for weeks. Lily too. "I don't have time. Besides, your dad should go and take you guys."

"Or Muriel," Jordan said.

The idea rankled, but Grace forced herself to say calmly, "If that's what he wants."

"But you won it!"

"We did it together."

"Then you should go together."

Grace shook her head. "I really don't have time. We're moving Dad next weekend, and then it's going to be busy right up through Christmas. And then . . . who knows?"

She thought that would be the end of this particular discussion. Wishful thinking, evidently. Even during dinner, the subject of the damn spa popped up.

This time it was Steven who mentioned it. "So when's the big spa trip?"

Grace put down her forkful of mashed potatoes. It was hard not to send a glance in Ray's direction. He'd already been looking awkward enough, wedged between Muriel and Grace. "It's not happening. I don't have time."

"It wouldn't be a long trip," Lily said quickly. "It's just two nights. Anyone can manage two nights."

Muriel looked around at everyone, eyes wide and alert. "What trip is this?"

"Grace and Dad won a trip to this place in the Hill Country when they went to my school's Parent Night," Dominic told her. "But now Grace won't go."

"Well," Muriel said dismissively, "I never thought spas sounded like too much fun anyway."

Even Emily put her oar in. "I sure wouldn't pass up a getaway like that. It's free." Her laser gaze buttonholed Grace. "Are you accustomed to throwing money away?"

Grace shrank a little at her tone. Maybe the woman had a little bulldozer in her after all.

"You should go, Grace," Sam said, smiling.

"Yes, you should," Peggy put in, her round face encouraging. "It would do you good."

What was this? A conspiracy?

Grace searched everyone's faces; her fears were confirmed. It *was* a conspiracy. "I have no time," she said. "We're moving Dad next weekend, remember?"

"We can manage that," Sam said quickly. "Can't we, Steven?"

"I don't know. I'll be on call." As silence fell, Steven's gaze traveled nervously around the table. "Oh—but of course, we don't need Grace just to make sure Dad's stuff gets loaded and moved."

"There!" Jordan said. "Next weekend. Mark it on your calendar. Right, Dad?"

Ray looked shell-shocked. "I'm not sure. They might be full up. And what about you all?" he asked, looking at his three children.

"We're coming too," Jordan said. "And it's off-season—they have rooms. I checked."

"Oh, but—" Ray didn't seem up to an argument with his kids in front of Grace's family.

"Why not?" Dominic asked. "We aren't doing anything else, are we?"

"That's several more rooms," Ray pointed out. "A lot more money."

"Jordan and I can share a room," Lily piped up.

"Yeah," Jordan said.

Cutlery clanked against plates, and a stunned hush fell over the room. If Lily and Jordan were willing to share a room, the Muriel threat had to be more deadly serious than Grace had suspected.

Muriel jumped in. "Of course you couldn't leave the kids behind, Ray." Her eyes narrowed. "What is this place called?"

"The Winecup Lodge and Spa," he said.

She tilted her head. "I think I've heard of it. I've always been curious about places like that. I might look into it myself!"

When Grace heard a groan, she worried it had come from herself. But she pinpointed the source—Dominic, who had sunk a foot lower in his chair. Over his head, Lily and Jordan exchanged a quick look, but that one glance spoke volumes. The war between the sisters was over.

The battle against Muriel Blainey had just begun.

The day Grace was to leave for the spa, on the eve of her father's move, Sam was running between rooms to help both of them. Lou required the most assistance; he grew more agitated as his possessions disappeared. As soon as one box or suitcase was filled, he would fretfully start taking things out again, looking for a favorite shirt.

Grace could hear them down the hallway, both growing increasingly frustrated. In the old days, they had argued over politics and aesthetics; now they got their dander up over what went where.

"Dad, *all* your clothes are going. You don't need to worry."

"But I especially want that one. The red one."

Moments later, Sam appeared at Grace's door, as he had twice before, and didn't seem any more pleased with her progress than he had been with Lou's. Perhaps because there had been none since the last time he'd come to badger her. His voice rose in frustration when he saw her perched on the edge of the bed, petting Heathcliff. "Why aren't you packed? You're supposed to be leaving. You've got a two-hour drive."

"I'm not going," she said.

He rolled his eyes. "Yes, you are."

"I need to stay here. With Dad. Now of all times."

"No, now of all times you need to leave. We'll manage fine. Steven's coming over later tonight. We'll probably spend the evening repacking all the stuff that Dad's going to pull out of the suitcases."

"Put *The Forsyte Saga* on," she instructed him. "As long as it's playing, Dad will be distracted and you can finish doing everything. And as soon as you're done packing something, take it to the car, or stack it on the back porch so he won't see it." Steven and Sam were hiring a rental van for the big move the next day.

Sam absorbed her words, nodding. "Clever girl."

"See? You need me here."

"No—you'll just be in the way. And you'll start weeping."

"No, I won't!"

"Grace, you're crying now."

She lifted her hand and felt her damp face with a little surprise. She hadn't noticed. "This doesn't count. I'm only really crying if I'm sprawled across a piece of furniture, wailing and bashing my fists into cushions."

Sam sat down next to her. "It's okay, Grace. He'll just be on the other side of town."

"But we won't be together. Not here, in this house. At home."

"You might be the only thirty-one-year-old feeling empty-nest syndrome for her father."

"It's easy for you to laugh—you were always a true blue Oliver. But for the first time this past year, I was actually starting to feel like part of the family. Like I really belonged. And now it's all disintegrating."

He looked into her eyes. "Did you think we were living some kind of *Leave It to Beaver* life while you weren't around? We were always an odd bunch, lost in our own activities. To my mind, you *were* part of the family. The best part."

She tilted against his shoulder, leaning against him as she absorbed those wonderful words. It was so great to have a brother here to talk to. Even though she and Sam had been separated by extreme distances most of their lives, nothing could break that bond of his being the closest sibling to her in age.

"Anyway, it's totally understandable that you'd feel like crying today." Sam paused before adding, with just a slight twitch of his lips, "There's so much stuff moving."

She straightened, stone faced, and when she had gathered up all the indignation she possibly could, she gave him a firm shove.

He fell against the bed, hooting with laughter as she stood and left the room.

"Grace!" he called after her. "Grace—don't be so sensitive!"

She marched down the hall. Her father had gotten into the bathroom box. Towels and washcloths covered a wing chair in the corner. "Hey, Dad, do you want to watch the Forsytes?"

He looked up, his eyes eager. "Do you?"

"I can probably squeeze in an episode before I have to leave."

They went down and she put a disc in—the one he pointed to—and they settled themselves down on the couch. The flat-screen television had been a birthday gift a few years ago from Steven, and at the time Lou had scoffed about it to her over the phone. "When I was young," he'd said, "companies attempted to design their televisions to seem like they belonged in a home. They were pieces of furniture—almost works of art, some of them. But this thing! It's as if a hideous Cineplex screen were sprouting in my parlor."

She never would have guessed that the last moments she and her father would be spending together in this house would be in front of that hideous screen, and that he would be glued to it almost to the exclusion of everything else.

He turned to her, smiling happily. "Are you comfortable there, Gracie?"

She bit her lip, nodding. "Just fine, Dad. Press play."

42

Treasure Hunt

She drove for two hours—twenty minutes of which was spent lost on a lonely back road—and when she arrived at the spa, it was already dark. Ray, the kids, and Muriel had gotten there hours before. Grace had called ahead to tell them not to wait for her to eat dinner. As she checked in at the lodge-style old lobby, the separation from her father and everything that was happening in Austin was making her feel torn in two. She barely spared a glance for the immense stone tiles on the floor, or the vaulted ceiling overhead.

A bellboy of sorts, a rangy-looking teenager in a cowboy hat, led her to her room. She followed him past a low-lit dining room with vast picture windows on two sides, and then back outside down a covered walkway to another building—one of three of similar modest gray stone appearance—and was shown into her room. Her surprisingly sumptuous room. There was a queen-size bed with a down coverlet festooned with a ridiculous number of fluffy pillows. Across the room, double doors opened onto a patio, which she decided to wait until morning to investigate. She crossed to the bathroom, which was like something out of a magazine. Just the sink itself, an elegant bowl fashioned from pink marble, seemed almost museum worthy. Plush white bathrobes hung on brass hooks next to plump towels. And light-colored tiles led to a sunken tub big enough for three people.

What was she doing here? All the pampering and lavish excess seemed so crazy, given her present mood. It was wasted on her. How was she going to survive till Sunday?

The kids came by to inspect her room, which Jordan, with true disappointment, declared not as cool as hers and Lily's. Dominic was more interested in showing her how to use the television, which had satellite and a Wii player connected.

Finally Ray came by and rescued her, after Muriel had retired for the night. Grace felt a strange sort of flush, a loss of equilibrium when she met his gaze, which she chalked up to the strangeness of seeing him there, on foreign soil. They were both unwillingly out of their element.

"I was worried you would decide not to come," Ray said. "You must have had a hard day."

Grace nodded. "Hard, long, sad."

Ray wasted no time herding everyone out of the room. Yet Grace was glad when he lingered a moment after the others had gone. "I'm happy you're here," he said.

"I'll be more in the spirit of things tomorrow," she promised, even though she had her doubts.

But when she woke up the next day and looked

outside through the glass doors, a rush of excitement took her by surprise. Because she'd driven in after dark the night before, she had not realized that the scenery would be so spectacular. The spa was situated in an area where light gray granite bluffs rose above the Guadalupe River. Through the millennia the rock had been worn down in places, so that the granite formed a lip over the low-water river, and at various higher elevations the stone jutted precariously out into space like jagged granite balconies. Live oaks dotted the landscape and smaller bushes, some also evergreen, clung to the thin topsoil on the shelflike protrusions.

She slipped into the fluffy terry-cloth robe provided in her bathroom—a robe so soft it was a little like stepping into a plush cocoon. Then, she threw open her doors and went out onto her patio. Moisture hung in the air and she had to hug her arms around herself to ward off the bracing morning chill. Even so, the clean air brought a blissful smile to her lips.

She didn't realize she wasn't alone until she caught a flash of orange out of the corner of her eye. When she turned, Jordan was peering at her critically from the next patio over.

"You do wear make-up, then," Jordan said. "I wondered, but it's pretty obvious when you're *not* wearing it."

"It's eight A.M.

"Yeah, but shouldn't you . . . I dunno . . . make yourself look decent?"

Grace laughed. She couldn't believe she was getting a fashion critique from the girl with Ringling Brothers hair. "I'm hoping to get a facial this morning."

"That's good," Jordan said. "Just so long as you're finished by one o'clock. At one we're going on a geo-caching treasure hunt."

"I have no idea what that is," Grace admitted.

"It's like a treasure hunt, only you use GPS devices."

Grace frowned and looked out toward the river. "Actually, I was hoping to hang out around here and relax. Maybe read a book."

"Well, you can't," Jordan said. "We already signed you up."

Lily rushed out in her bathrobe. "What's going on?"

"She's saying she won't go geo-caching this afternoon," Jordan said, clearly miffed.

Lily gasped. "But you have to!"

"She says she wanted to read."

"You can read anywhere," Lily said. "Wouldn't you rather explore with us?"

It was a topsy-turvy world when Lily told people they *shouldn't* read and a chummy Jordan and Lily invited her out for rambles in nature. But rambling with Jordan West didn't strike Grace as a dream vacation.

Looking into Lily's pleading eyes, however, she felt powerless to resist.

"Okay," she said, caving. "Count me in."

She spent the rest of the morning getting massaged and facialed, buffed, manicured and trimmed. By the time she presented herself at the treasure hunt meeting place, the kids were waiting, although neither Ray nor Muriel had arrived at the designated spot yet. Dominic scrutinized Grace closely as she approached, his face taking on a relieved expression when she stopped next to him. He turned to his sisters. "She looks okay to me."

Lily tactfully ignored him. "We're waiting for Dad and Muriel," she explained. "Muriel wanted to play golf, so they went out to a driving range. I hope she hasn't tired him out."

Grace laughed. "I think your ancient dad still has a two-activity day left in him."

He certainly seemed perky when he and Muriel ambled up. Ray was wearing jeans and a long-sleeved polo shirt, but Muriel was decked out in her Dinah Shore golf clothes—white golfing shoes, a baby blue skirt, and a matching knit top. Grace wished Sam was there to see it.

"Okay," Jordan announced, barely giving the late arrivals time to catch their breaths or say hello to Grace. "Here's your tracking device, Dad." She handed him a small plastic doodad about the size of an iPod. "And here's a list of the stuff you're supposed to bring back. You and Grace are on one team, and Muriel, Lily, and I are on the other team. We'll all be going for the same treasure, but our team will start by trying to find position A and work down to G, while you guys start at G and work the other way. The coordinates for each letter are programmed into the device. Oh—and you can only grab one item at each location. And no cheating. Got it?"

Lily and Jordan were already starting to head out when they noticed the adults weren't following. The two girls were forced to turn around.

"Is there a problem?" Jordan asked, hands on her hips.

"How did these teams get picked?" Muriel asked.

"*When* did they get picked?" Ray followed up.

Grace added, "And what about Dominic?"

In a disturbingly Jordan-like gesture, Lily rolled her eyes. "Since y'all were late, we went ahead and picked. We only have until dinner, so there's not a lot of daylight to waste. And Dominic isn't playing. He signed up for pool chess."

Grace glanced over at Dominic, not quite believing this could be voluntary. "Really?"

He nodded mutely.

"We could do three teams of two," Grace suggested. "Dominic and I could be a team."

"No, you can't," Jordan said quickly. "Because

Dominic wants to play pool chess in the luxurious heated indoor pool. Don't you, Dominic?"

Dominic nodded again.

"But shouldn't the rest of us draw straws or something?" Muriel asked.

"We drew for you," Jordan said. "Congratulations—you won. You're coming with us."

"Unless you don't want to be on our team," Lily said, challenging her. "I mean, if you just don't like us or something."

Jordan and Lily stared at Muriel so pointedly that Grace almost felt sorry for the woman. To respond she would either have to lie or be offensive.

Sensing her dilemma, Muriel capitulated with a huff. "Well, at least let me carry the cockadoodie list!" she grumbled, snatching the list out of Jordan's hand as she stomped past.

After they were gone, Grace turned to Dominic. "You can still join us, you know," she said. "Even out the numbers."

Dominic shook his head. "I signed up for pool chess. I figure I have a pretty good chance of winning after all my practice with Professor Oliver."

Grace also figured he had a pretty good chance of getting clobbered by his sisters if he dared joined Ray and Grace's team.

Ray turned to Grace with an amused smile. "I guess that leaves you and me chasing G to A."

They set off down a well-worn path, Ray walking slightly ahead. Now that they were alone, Grace felt awkward, and a little miffed. She wasn't so desperate that she needed two teenagers to fix her up with their dad—especially since it was clear they were doing so only because she was less loathsome than the alternative.

Especially when their dad seemed just as happy with the loathsome alternative.

Ray flicked a glance back at her. "Is something wrong?"

"Why?"

"You're walking a few steps behind me, as if I were a king."

"Sorry—I had the impression that you were walking ahead of me, as if I were a leper."

He slowed down.

"Although you have seemed a little kinglike lately," she pointed out. "You seem to have your would-be consort orbiting around you." The minute she said it, she wanted to slap her hand over her mouth. Where had *that* come from?

He stayed focused on the screen of the GPS device. "I have no idea what you're talking about." He pointed to a smaller path. "This doohickey is telling us to go this way."

She nodded, grateful for once for his studied obliviousness.

G turned out to be a plastic bag hanging from a tree. They hauled it down and examined the contents, then compared it to the list. Two of the things they needed were in the bag—a kazoo and a red plastic heart.

Ray frowned. “We can only take one thing from each site.”

“So we’re gambling that the thing we don’t choose will be in another cache?”

“Right. So which do we choose?”

They both thought for a moment.

“Heart,” she decided.

“Kazoo,” he said at the same moment.

They laughed. “We’ll go with the heart,” he said.

She shook her head. “No—the kazoo. That way if we get hopelessly lost, we’ll at least have music.”

“That decides it. We’re definitely taking the heart.”

After that, the ice, if not broken, was at least chipped a little. She and Ray rambled down pathways and picked up a tiny mirror at F.

“So where next?” she asked.

He arched a brow. “I think that would be E.”

Wiseacre. “I know the letter, but what direction?”

He punched in F and then gave the letter E as their destination, and the words *north 100 yards* flashed up on the screen. “That way.”

“Wouldn’t north be over there?” she asked, pointing to their right. “The river bends sharply here, doesn’t it?”

He frowned. "How do you know that?"

"They had a drawing on the place mat at breakfast. Didn't you notice?"

Judging from his expression, her argument wasn't very convincing. "We're supposed to use your foggy memory of a place mat as a road map?"

"It's a very clear memory of a place mat," she argued.

"Okay—but don't say I didn't warn you."

Her memory might have been right, but after ten minutes it seemed as if the place mat wasn't. They had to double back in the direction of the river.

"This will probably cost us," Grace said, wryly apologetic. "We'll probably be out here forever now."

He sent her a strange look—whether hurt or exasperated, she couldn't tell. Pained, probably, at the idea of being stuck out here with her much longer.

"I'm sure Muriel would never have gotten you lost."

He didn't say anything.

She wanted to slap herself upside the head for the sting of jealousy she felt. Why was it that the minute you started to play a game, no matter how old you were, the desire to beat the pants off the other team kicked in?

In her case, the person whose pants she wanted to kick was Muriel.

Maybe he *did* like Muriel. More power to him. It was certainly no skin off her nose if the two of them wanted to live happily ever after. She was foolish even to have come on this expedition.

She walked ahead.

From behind her, he called out. “Grace, what’s wrong? What did I say?”

She stopped—not that she had much choice. She’d reached the edge of the bluff overlooking the river. “Nothing,” she said, turning. “You didn’t say a thing. I just suspect you wish we weren’t out here doing this.”

A laugh sputtered out of him. “Oh, and you’re thrilled to be here, I can tell.”

“It’s beautiful!” she said. “And yes—I thought we were having a reasonably good time. In spite of being forced together.”

He caught up with her. “I got the impression that you’d rather be out here with anyone else.”

“Me?” She laughed. “I wasn’t the one who questioned the method of team picking as soon as they were announced.”

He frowned down at her. “No—you were the one who wanted to drag Dominic along the moment you thought you would have to be out here alone with me. Not that I blame you. After last spring.”

“Forget last spring! I wanted to drag him along because he so clearly wanted to come,” she argued.

"Then why did he sign up for pool chess?"

"Can you possibly be this thickheaded?" Grace asked aloud. When he recoiled in surprise, she attempted to enlighten him. "His sisters put him up to it because they didn't want you out here with Muriel Blainey. In fact, I'm certain this whole setup, if not this entire weekend, was just a way to make sure you spent as little time as possible with Muriel. Surely you can see that."

He looked genuinely perplexed. "Why would they care?"

"Because they're so desperate to have you not involved with Muriel that they're willing to spend the afternoon with her themselves. That's sacrifice, Ray. They've jumped into the volcano, for you."

"But why? I have no intention of getting involved with Muriel. We're just neighbors."

"No—*we're* just neighbors, Ray. You and Muriel are something else."

He took a step forward. "You're as misguided as they are, then. You've got it completely backward. Muriel means nothing to me. While *we're* . . ."

He stopped. Their gazes locked.

She swallowed. "What?"

He reached out and took her arm, tugging him gently toward him. She stumbled a step and found herself against his chest, enveloped in a kiss. It was a surprise, but there was none of the rush of the time before, the furtive kiss stolen on her dad's porch. This time, his lips explored hers more casually, more forcefully. And she didn't step away. She couldn't—not with a forty-foot drop behind her.

He pulled away and pushed a lock of hair behind her ears, then hugged her and kissed the top of her head. "Raw umber."

"It's auburn," she said, burrowing against the soft cotton of his shirt. It felt so good just to stand here, alone, away from their problems. Away from everyone.

"I should never have come along on this trip," she said, sighing. "I'll always feel we were set up by Jordan."

"I would have been miserable if you hadn't come," he confessed. "Every time I've looked at that damned FOR SALE sign, I've felt sick, as though I was losing you, even though you weren't mine to lose. It only felt like you were, because without you I don't know how I would have survived last year."

"Oh, Ray."

"When I see that sign, I want to rip it out of the ground, sabotage the sale . . . anything to keep you from going."

She smiled. "I've wanted to do the same thing myself."

"But not for the same reason. You're heartbroken about your father, while I was worried you would leave before I could—"

Something dropped to the rocks. She felt the muscles in his arms tense.

"Ray?"

He groaned.

"What was that?" she asked.

"That was our GPS tracking device."

She twisted to glimpse over her own shoulder at the drop below. "What do we do now?"

He looked down at her, eyebrows arching above the frames of his glasses. "Forfeit the game and find some other activity to keep us occupied?"

She smiled and settled her arms around him again. "Good plan."

43

Lost

Things really went downhill when they got to D. They'd been squabbling since they'd left the spa—and this time Jordan swore it was not her fault. Come to find out, put a list and a GPS device in Lily's hands and the girl morphed into Indiana Jones. She knew exactly where the treasure was, and she wasn't going to let anyone—especially Muriel Blainey—contradict her.

Until C, Lily's sense of direction had been right on. After that, they'd ended up circling some stupid pond that smelled very strongly of animal dung and something dead. Then, when they arrived at D, it started to look as if they had chosen the wrong treasure token when they were at B. Against Muriel's advice, they'd picked the pencil and passed on the kazoo. Now they were halfway through the game and they hadn't seen another kazoo.

"I told you that's what we should have picked up at B," Muriel complained. They were supposed to be moving on to E now, but she apparently wasn't about to let the kazoo thing drop. "What are the chances that we're going to run into another kazoo?"

"Why shouldn't we?" Lily argued. "We've run into three shoelaces already, and they aren't even on our list."

"Exactly," Muriel said. "That's why we keep seeing them. Now we're going to be out here all the livelong day, and we're going to lose, to boot. We might as well just go back to the spa."

Nevertheless, they kept going. Five minutes later, they were back at the stinky pond.

"Give me that!" Muriel said, grabbing the GPS device out of Lily's hand. "Are you sure you're reading this correctly?"

"Of course!" Lily turned in a circle, trying to figure out where they had gone wrong.

Muriel inspected the device and then whacked it against her palm. "Crappy little thing!" she muttered. "You'd think for the money we're paying at this place, they could give us OnStar."

"What would be the fun of that?" Lily asked.

Muriel laughed dryly. "What's the fun of *this?*"

"Uh, guys?" Jordan had to lift her T-shirt collar over her nose in order to breathe without passing out. "Can we go somewhere else to argue about this? Something is seriously putrefying in this pond."

"Probably the remains of lost guests," Muriel muttered.

Jordan shuddered. "I think there's a bug crawling on me."

"Squash it, then," Lily said.

"I can't. It's on my back." She twisted uncomfortably. "I can feel its little appendages digging into my flesh."

"Yes, well, we've all got problems," Muriel grumbled, staring at the screen. "A blood-sucking insect on your back is the least of them, frankly."

Jordan groaned. "Why did we ever come out here? I'm going to be eaten alive."

"You're so whiny!" Lily said. "You spend most of your time trying to prove how tough you are, but you can't even stand up to two hours of hiking."

"Because I'm not made for Outward Bound idiocy like this."

"It was your idea!" Lily said, exasperated.

"Only for Dad's sake! Not because I wanted to go wandering around some stinky bug-infested hellhole."

"Would you both just shut up!" Muriel yelled at them.

Jordan and Lily turned toward her. The woman's face was completely red. Jordan started to wonder if she was going to have a stroke or something.

"What did you mean, you came out here for Ray's sake?" Muriel asked.

"Just . . ." Lily's words faltered and her mouth clamped shut.

Muriel looked from one to the other. "This was all to get those two alone together, wasn't it?"

"Not entirely," Jordan said.

"Oh, right. You also wanted to keep me away from him. Is that it?"

Neither Jordan or Lily responded.

"Well, fine! Ray is with the sallow neighbor woman," Muriel said. "Mission accomplished, girls. Well done. But believe me, you don't need to worry that I'm going to try to get my claws into Daddy. I don't know where you could have come up with such a ludicrous idea. I don't need a man—I'm a real estate agent! So you see, there's no reason for me to be out here with you two squabbling brats!"

She turned and stomped away.

When she was out of sight, the two sisters exchanged a joyous high five.

Jordan let out a long sigh of relief. "Now that Her 'Rhoidness is gone, can we clear out?"

Lily knit her brow. "Would you call Grace sallow?"

"Who cares?" Jordan replied. "Can we just go back before I catch malaria or something?"

Lily bit her lip. "We've sort of got a problem."

"What's that?"

"Muriel took the tracking device with her."

The news swept through Jordan like a shiver. "I thought *you* had it."

"I did—but then she took it. Which you would have realized if you had been paying attention instead of whining about bugs."

"Why did you let her wander off with it?"

"I was just so glad she was gone. I forgot." Lily let out a long breath. "I screwed up."

"How are we going to find our way back?"

"It's not that big a deal," Lily assured her. "It'll be a lot easier than finding these stupid caches."

"You think?"

"Sure. The lodge is on the river. We just need to find the river and walk along it."

"When was the last time we saw the river?" Jordan asked. "Which way is it?"

Lily pointed to her right. "I think it's that way."

"But we could wander that way and get even more lost."

"Do you have a better suggestion? We can't just stand here."

Jordan followed her. If she hadn't been starting to get hungry, she would almost have hoped they *wouldn't* find the river. Just to prove Lily wrong.

But of course Lily was right. They came upon the bluff over the river in five minutes.

"How did you know that?" Jordan asked, impressed.

Lily lifted her hands. "It just seemed right."

"Now we just have to figure out how far we are from the spa."

"Probably not far. I bet you can look down the canyon and see the buildings from here," Lily said.

"You do that. I'm not getting close to that edge." She turned. "I'd rather climb a tree and look out that way, or better yet, just start walking."

Behind her, Jordan heard a yelp and then a heavy thud farther away. She whirled on her heel to see what had happened and saw—nothing.

"Lily?" She stared at the spot where her sister had just been standing. Nothing but air there now. As the horrible yet probable explanation sank in, tension looped her voice up an octave. *"Lily?"*

Jordan sidled up to the edge of the bank and looked over. Approximately fifteen feet below, on a shelf of granite jutting out from the canyon, Lily was sprawled on her back. Her arm was sticking out from her collarbone in a way that made Jordan wince. "Lils? Say something!"

She bent down, straining to hear. She could have sworn she heard a moan, but it might have been the river, or wishful thinking. She yelled her sister's name again as a feverish heat started to creep into her cheeks. *What am I going to do? Run for help?*

But she couldn't leave Lily lying there. What if she woke up and rolled over? Just a foot and a half and she would topple off the ledge and fall another twenty feet or more.

Jordan groaned. Damn! She hadn't brought her cell phone, and she was sure Lily hadn't, either. Who would have thought they'd need one? As cautiously as she could, mindful that her limbs were quivering with nerves, she got down on all fours and edged as far out as she could to peer over again. The rocks were uneven and jagged all the way down to the place where Lily lay. There was a possibility she could get down there to make sure Lily was still alive—and to see if she could help. On the other hand, there was also the possibility that she too would get trapped on the ledge. Or fall.

At some point, her dad and Grace should be coming along this way. But waiting for them would be risky. Maybe they had already passed them while she, Muriel, and Lily were wandering around the stink pond, lost. Or maybe they had given up the game altogether. She couldn't know. How long would it take them to figure out they were missing and send a search party? Lily needed a doctor as soon as possible.

That is, if she wasn't . . .

Jordan turned away, ready to run for help. But her feet wouldn't move. She couldn't leave Lily on the ledge. She just couldn't. Not without checking on her first.

Looking down, she visually mapped out a path with foot and handholds, and then, starting on her hands and knees, began to lower herself down. It would have helped if her hands weren't so sweaty. And if her stupid legs would stop shaking. And if her head would stop saying, *I've killed Lily. I told her to look over the ledge, and she fell.*

Her foot slipped off its perch and for a moment, a moment that felt like a century, she hung suspended over the cliff, her hands clinging to rock and the root of some plant. Her stomach jumped into her throat until she managed to get her feet back into place. *Calm down, Jordan. Or you'll both be lost.*

She finally made it down to the ledge, although she couldn't forget that what felt solid beneath her legs was just a few feet of rock jutting out into space. Could it hold the weight of both of them? She edged along the cliff face and then knelt next to Lily. Her face was chalky white. "Lily?" she asked. "Lils—say something!"

Receiving no response, she held her sister's hand and lowered her ear to Lily's chest.

"What are you *doing?*" Lily moaned, her eyes fluttering open momentarily.

Jordan could have wept. "Lils! You're okay."

"No, I'm not." She shut her eyes again. But maybe that was just as well.

"I'm afraid to move you, Lils. I'm going to have to get help." She didn't have the heart to tell her that she couldn't have moved her if she'd wanted to. "But you're going to have to remain perfectly still. Get it? Don't move!"

"I can't. My arm! I think it's gonna fall off."

That wasn't possible, was it? Jordan drew back and looked at that arm again, jutting out from her collarbone at a freakish angle. "I think it's your shoulder."

"And my head."

"Yeah, well, you thumped down pretty hard. I'll be back in a snap. Are you cold?" Jordan took off her jacket and draped it over her sister's torso. "Here—you can wear my favorite black leather jacket. Now you know I'll be back."

Lily's lips quirked into a smile and she opened her eyes. "I know you'd come back anyway."

"Yeah, probably," Jordan agreed. She looked down at her little sister's head lying back against the dirt and rocks. That couldn't be comfortable. She pulled her long-sleeved shirt off and wadded it up. "I'm going to lift your head and give you a pillow."

She raised Lily up a bit and her sister let out a piercing scream.

"It hurts that much?" Jordan asked.

Lily nodded. "But the pillow feels good. Only, you're half-naked now. Aren't you cold?"

Jordan looked down at her bra—glad at least that it wasn't one of her more ratty ones. "I'll be fine."

How were they ever going to get Lily out of there?

For that matter, how was she ever going to get back up the cliff face? She leaned into the rocks, sent up a silent prayer to whoever was listening, and started a quick ascent. She tried not to think of the sheer drop below her, or the fact that one loose rock or unstable branch could send her falling to her doom.

When she finally heaved herself back onto level ground, she knew what it was to want to kiss the earth. But there wasn't time to waste even for that. She got up, dusted herself off, and ran.

Although the hotel was closer than she and Lily had supposed, by the time Jordan had run all the way she'd still managed to work up a sweat. She streaked through the spa's lobby, glancing quickly around on the off chance that her father was there, but saw only employees and guests gawping at her as if they'd never seen a frantic girl in a bra before. She hurried on, out the back door, down the covered walkway and into the building where their rooms were. She rapped on her dad's door, and when Dominic opened it she burst in. Her dad and Grace were sitting around a table drinking beers.

"Thank God you're here!" Jordan panted.

"What's happened?" her father asked, hurrying to her. "Muriel came by—she was very upset."

She shook her head, gasping for air. "No time. Call—"

"Why aren't you wearing a shirt?" Grace asked.

"Call 911, Dad!"

"Where's Lily?" Dominic asked.

"She fell! She's stuck on a ledge!" She sucked in a breath and tried to string together some coherent sentences. "I think she broke her collarbone. Something weird. She can't move without screaming. I don't know how they're going to get her out of there. I didn't want to leave her, but I didn't have any way to call for help."

Her father was already on the phone, speaking to someone in a low urgent voice, while Grace flipped open his suitcase and pulled out a long-sleeved T-shirt that looked exactly like the one that her father was wearing at the moment, only it was burgundy instead of navy.

Grace signaled for her to put the shirt on. "We'll need to hurry."

"I want to go!" Dominic said.

"No," Ray told him. "You stay here."

"But I want to go!" Dominic yelled.

"I need you to stay here," Ray said. "We'll be back as soon as possible."

Traveling along the river path in her father's car, they made it back to the spot. All the while, Grace was on the phone, giving directions to EMS. The sun was lowering in the sky as they all peered down at Lily, who lay with her eyes closed.

"Lily," her father breathed.

Lily's weak voice traveled up to them. "Hi Dad."

Jordan got down on all fours and started lowering herself over the edge. "What are you doing?" her father barked at her, panicked.

"I'm climbing down to see if she's all right."

"Do you want to get yourself killed?"

"I did it before. It's not that hard. And you all need to wait for whoever they're sending."

"You are *not* climbing down there," her father said.

They were the last words he spoke to her as she lowered herself step by step down the cliff face. It wasn't quite so terrifying this time, now that she knew the footholds better. When she was back on the ledge, she squatted next to her sister.

"Help's coming," she assured Lily. "They're sending an ambulance."

"How will I get up?" While alone, Lily had obviously had time to consider her predicament. "I can't even sit up."

"Let them worry about that. It's their job."

"What if I can't move? What if they can't get me out of here?"

"Don't be stupid," Jordan told her. "They get climbers off of Everest, don't they?" *Did they?* Jordan wasn't even sure, but it sounded good.

"Getting you off this rinky-dink ledge will be a snap."

A siren blared in the distance, and Lily closed her eyes in relief. "You saved my life," she said as the sound neared.

"Yeah, right. I almost killed you. I told you to look over the ledge and got you in this mess."

Lily smiled. "It wasn't your fault. A chunk of rock where I was standing must have chipped off. I slipped."

From above, their father called out, "The ambulance is almost here!"

As if they couldn't hear that for themselves, Jordan thought, rolling her eyes.

"That's another good thing about you," Lily said. "I'm up to three now."

Jordan had no idea what she was talking about. The pain was probably making her delirious. "A good thing is that I almost got you killed?"

"No—that you saved my life." Lily smiled.

Above them, red lights flashed and a vehicle door slammed. Jordan was torn between trying to listen to what the paramedics were saying and paying attention to Lily.

"It's for when we're living on opposite sides of the country," Lily explained. "Grace said I needed to have good things to focus on when I think about you."

Jordan bit her lip. "I don't think I could think of three myself."

"One—Nina and Mom loved you. Two, you love Dominic."

Jordan leaned back and crossed her arms over her chest. After all the running around and worrying she'd done, it would be stupid to fall apart now that it was almost over. "Dominic's not the only person in the world I love," she said, her voice a rasp.

Lily looked at her. "There's something I was going to show you. It's in my suitcase in our room. In my diary."

Jordan released a dry laugh. "Not going there."

"I give you permission."

A paramedic had rappelled down the cliff face and now was yanking Jordan out of the way. "You need to go back up," the man instructed her brusquely. "Let me attach this harness . . ."

"I can climb," Jordan said, instinctively flinching away.

"We're not going to save one sister only to watch the other one topple into the river." He started wrapping the harness around her and clipping it securely.

"You should be doing something for Lily," she complained. "She's the one in pain."

"I'll tend to her just as soon as you're off this rock."

Jordan sighed and the man signaled to the people above them that they could start hoisting her up. As she began her ascent, Lily called out to her. "Jordan, wait!"

Jordan looked over at her. "What?"

Lily couldn't lift her head up, but she tilted it so that their gazes met. "You shouldn't blame yourself. It could have happened at any time. It was just an accident."

Their dad went with the ambulance, while Jordan and Grace returned to the hotel to pick up Dominic and clothes for Lily. The paramedics had had to cut the shirt she'd had off of her—but by that time Lily had been so zonked on morphine she hadn't freaked out like she normally would have.

Jordan headed directly to her and Lily's room. Dominic was on the lookout for her and emerged from his room as soon as she was at her door.

"What's going on? Is Lily in the hospital?"

"She's on her way."

"Is she going to be okay?"

"Yeah, I think so."

He followed her into the room. "What happened?"

Jordan made a beeline for Lily's suitcase. First she grabbed some clothes, and then she found the diary and started flipping through it.

"Is Grace going to drive us to the hospital now?" Dominic asked.

"In a sec. She's waiting for us."

"Then why . . . ?" He looked at what she was doing and groaned. "Oh, no! That's Lily's diary!"

"Don't worry," she assured him. She held the book by its spine and shook it. "She told me to look in it. It's supposed to have . . ."

A photograph dropped out of the book. Jordan tossed the book back in the suitcase and scooped the photo off the floor before Dominic could grab it.

The picture was of Lily—little Lily, maybe seven or eight years old—riding piggyback, her mouth wide open and wielding some kind of toy sword.

Dominic crowded in to look. "Where's that from?"

Jordan shook her head in wonder. She didn't remember the photo being taken, but she did remember the silly games they used to play when they were younger. Lily was so cute. And she . . .

"Look at Nina laughing!" Dominic said. "She looks like she's about to fall and take Lily down with her."

Jordan lifted her free hand to her lips. She almost hadn't recognized that other girl, either. Not because she confused herself with Nina—Jordan was always surprised that people couldn't tell them apart—but because of where she was in that picture. The center of everything. The anchor. And how happy she seemed.

She *did* remember it. Not the day, exactly. But she could remember the laughter, and the certainty that if her legs gave out beneath her they would all catch their breaths and then get back up again.

"What's the matter?" Dominic asked. Then he looked down again. "Sorry—dumb question. Does looking at her make you sad?"

"Yeah, it does, but not because it's Nina," Jordan said. "That's me."

Dominic's forehead crinkled. Even her own brother couldn't tell.

"That's really me," she repeated.

44

Everything Must Go

While waiting for the doctors to tend to Lily, Grace and Ray decided that Grace would drive Dominic and Jordan back to Austin the next morning, Sunday, so he could stay with Lily until the hospital released her.

Initially, Dominic and Jordan protested that they couldn't abandon their sister. But a night spent hanging out on the uncomfortable orange bench seats of the hospital waiting room convinced them that being cut out of the loop wasn't such a bad thing. Sibling devotion couldn't overcome boredom, or hunger.

"Can we stop for breakfast on the way back?" Dominic asked as they were leaving. "Someplace with pancakes?"

"Dominic wants to celebrate the fact that Lily's okay," Jordan said, shooting Grace a wry look.

"Yeah," he said.

Declaring Lily okay was a bit of a stretch. She had fractured an arm, dislocated her shoulder, and suffered a concussion. Bad as it was, though, Grace couldn't get the picture of that ledge out of her mind. If Lily had been standing a few feet to the right when she'd fallen, the outcome would have been another tragedy for the West family.

"Pancakes it is," she agreed.

During the drive back, they stopped at a roadside diner full of Sunday brunchers. After they ordered, Grace's cellphone started vibrating across the laminated tabletop.

"Is it Dad?" Dominic asked.

She checked. "It's my brother Sam."

"You can talk to him here," Jordan said when Grace started to get up. "We'll pretend not to listen."

Sam shouted into her ear as soon as she picked up. "Happy birthday!"

She was stunned. "Oh my God—I completely forgot. So much has happened—but I can tell you about it when I get home. I'm on my way now."

"You should tell me now, then. Rainbow and I are on the way to Houston. I ran into her at Whole Foods. We decided to make like the old days and road trip to see a show at the Alley."

"Oh, great."

"I figured you had better things to do on your big day than hang out with your brother."

She tried hard to swallow her disappointment that he wouldn't be there when she got home. That no one would. Instead, she gave an abbreviated recap of Lily's accident.

"Sounds like the weekend was eventful." He paused, then asked, "Anything else happen?"

His tone made his meaning perfectly clear. She turned slightly away from her breakfast companions. "Not what you're obviously thinking."

He sighed. "I wash my hands of you then. You're hopeless."

"What about Dad?" she asked. "How did it go? How is he?"

"He's all settled, and he seemed fine. Although it took me forever to get his furniture positioned the right way."

"I'll go see him as soon as I get back," she said.

"Actually . . ." He hesitated, then explained, "The director of the place requested that Dad not have visitors for a week. Or phone calls."

"What?"

"I know, it sounded weird to me too. But she said Dad should have some time to adjust and get to know people around him—and not just shut himself up and wait for his family to visit."

"But that's crazy! Dad will wonder where I am. Who's going to look after him?"

"They are. That's why he's there."

Her heart was racing. "But without visiting or

calling, how do we know that they're treating him well, or that he has what he needs?"

"Grace—"

"What if he's lonely, and miserable, and at loose ends?"

The silence that crackled over the line was filled with pity. For her. "I think you need the week to adjust, too," he said.

She bristled. "That's ridiculous. I'm fine. I just don't trust them."

"You're going to have to. Just give it a week."

A week! A week seemed like an eternity to her all of a sudden.

"Oh, and Grace?"

"Hm . . ." she said, distracted.

"Have a happy birthday. We'll do it up big when I get to Austin!"

When she hung up, she took a gulp of coffee. Her hand was shaking over what Sam had told her about her dad. She didn't care what Sam said—the one-week policy stank. What if her dad thought she had abandoned him? Sure, he would have been informed of the policy, but sometimes he forgot things right after he heard them.

"When we get home, should I come over and get Iago?" Dominic asked.

She nodded. She had forgotten about Iago. Now he would be gone, too. A tear slipped down her cheek.

Dominic and Jordan focused their eyes on their plates but darted wary surreptitious glances in her direction. “Is everything okay?” Dominic asked.

“Today’s my birthday,” she explained.

Their heads lifted. “Happy birthday!” they said in unison.

For some reason, their rote exclamations made her feel even more depressed.

“How old are you?” Dominic asked.

“Thirty-one.”

“God,” Jordan said. “No wonder you’re crying.”

After she parked the car in the drive in Austin, Grace expected the kids to unload their stuff and troop back over to their house, but Dominic followed her to her door.

“Is it okay if I go ahead and take Iago home with me now?” he asked.

“Sure,” Grace said, trying to be cheerful about giving up her father’s dog.

When she opened the door to her father’s house, Iago was right there. He certainly looked ready to go. He was doing the front-paw hop he performed whenever he saw Dominic. She petted him, trying not to mind the hole in the living room where Lou’s television had been. Or the absence of his favorite armchair. Now there was only the martyr’s chair, but with no chess set on the table next to it. For some reason, the absence of that game got to her more than anything. The quiet house felt drained of life, as if its heart had been torn from it.

Or maybe that was just how she felt herself.

As Dominic hurried to the kitchen to collect Iago's bowls, food, leash, and flea meds, she couldn't help remembering the other dogs that had lived in the house. Her father had never been without a canine friend for long. When she was growing up, there had been Desdemona, and at the end of Des's life, a Chihuahua mix named Cassio had come on board. And then Iago.

She had asked her father once why there had never been an Othello. "I would never give a dog the lead," he'd explained. "There would be no living with him."

Dominic looked reluctant to leave. "You're not going to start crying after I take him, are you?"

She smiled. "No."

" 'Cause I could leave him here a few days, I guess . . ."

She shook her head. "Look at him—he's raring to go." She smiled. "Besides, I still have Heathcliff."

His expression was doubtful, but he led Iago out anyway.

Speaking of Heathcliff . . . She went upstairs to check on him. She didn't worry that he had been traumatized by the move, because he generally confined himself to her bedroom and the Rigoletto's office, and those rooms hadn't been touched by relocation madness yet. In the next few weeks, though, they would have to be boxed up and emptied out, too. *Everything must go.* This was her job now: to make sure that nothing was left.

In her bedroom, Heathcliff was lounging on the bed in a patch of sun. He winked one eye open, saw her, and then shut it again. Then he arched, stretched, and flipped over to face a large box that was lying in the center of the bed.

It was just a big white clothes box, with an envelope taped to the top. She opened the envelope and took out a card with a picture of George Eliot on it. She remembered it from a set of famous author note cards she'd sent her father once on *his* birthday.

Gracie,

It's your birthday, and I can think of nothing more precious to leave as a gift to mark your thirty-one years. I know I am right in thinking that it is best left in your safekeeping.

Love,
Dad

She pulled the lid off the box. Inside, surrounded by tissue paper, was the old chess set. She picked up one of the pieces and fell back on the mattress, laughing. His treasure, her torment. But he was right—she would keep it with her until the last breath left her body.

But that didn't mean she couldn't loan it out on occasion.

She hopped up and picked up the box. Rules be damned. She didn't care what anyone said, it was her birthday and she wanted to see her father, just to spend a little time with him and make sure he had everything he needed.

On the way out to Live Oak Villa, she stopped at a barbecue stand that had never been on her father's A-list, but which was still probably better than the institutional food he was getting. Having the to-go bag sitting on the passenger side seat lifted her spirits; barbecue was the most effective aromatherapy in the world. She imagined her father's face lighting up when he saw it.

When she appeared at his door bearing all her goodies, though, she discovered that he wasn't in his rooms. It was the right apartment, she was sure of it. The number was the one they had written down as his address, and his furniture was there. But no Lou.

As she prowled the carpeted corridors in search of him, she half expected to be collared by the assisted living police. The last place she looked was where she should have started, given that it was going on six o'clock. The dining room.

He was seated at a round table with two ladies, both with perfectly set gray hair. A walker stood sentry next to one of the ladies' chairs. The other woman seemed to be telling a story, and Lou was watching her intently, a smile on his face. When Grace approached the table, he turned the same smile on her. For a moment, there was no flash of recognition, no connection. The gaze was impersonal, as if she were a nurse, or someone coming to take his plate.

As if he didn't really know her.

She froze, pierced by a pain so sharp she wanted to double over. Did he really not know her? Her own father?

She took a deep breath, remembering a time before, when he'd been in the hospital. It was just the unexpected that caused the delayed recognition. She took the empty chair next to him and gave him a kiss on the cheek.

"Hi, Dad."

He took her hand. "It's so good to see you!" He turned to his two companions. "This is my daughter, Grace." He introduced her to the two women, Frances and Brenda, who made a fuss over her. Brenda encouraged Grace to take her tapioca cup. Grace declined politely.

It was as if she had issued a challenge.

"Go ahead and take it," Brenda said. "I can always get another one."

"Me, too." Frances was already twisting toward her walker, ready to hit the dessert buffet on Grace's behalf.

"No, really," Grace said, trying to stop her. "I'm

not hungry." She was holding out for barbecue, hoping that she and her father could go back to his room and talk. Maybe play a game of chess.

"Would you like a roll?" Frances asked her.

"The asparagus casserole was good. I have a little of that left." Brenda pushed her plate toward Grace, who laughed in frustration.

"No, thank you."

"I know what she really wants," Lou said. "Birthday cake. It's her birthday!"

The two ladies beamed in delight. "They didn't have cake tonight."

"But we could sing," Brenda said, brightening even more.

"Oh, no," Grace said, cringing. "That's not necess—"

But stopping those two ladies from launching into "Happy Birthday" at that moment would have been like trying to hold back the dawn. And once they started, the surrounding tables got in on the act, and by the end, the whole cafeteria was singing. Grace hunkered stiffly in her chair, grinning, praying for it to be over. Unfortunately, when the song ended and the room burst into applause, someone in the back started the song all over again.

She should have just accepted the tapioca. When round two was over, Grace was introduced to thirty people whose names she knew she would never be able to remember after tonight. Finally, they began to filter away and she turned to her dad. “Do you want to go up to your apartment?”

“Why?” he asked.

“I’d like to get the tour.”

“It’s nothing special,” he said.

Brenda turned to her. “It’s Sunday night! We’re having a movie tonight. You should stay for it.”

“Oh—I don’t think I can.” She was still half expecting the powers that be to come collar her for premature visitation.

“Why not?” her father asked.

“It’s *Top Hat*, with Fred Astaire,” Frances said.

Lou lifted his brows. “There are people here who could stand to take some style pointers from Fred Astaire.” The ladies laughed.

“We’re going to go to the rec room and get good seats,” Frances said, getting up. “Should we save you one, Lou?”

“Oh, yes, please. I’ll be right there,” Lou said.

Grace shook her head in frustration.

“Well, let’s go upstairs,” he told her. “Not much to see, I’m warning you. Just the same old furniture. I might have you help me move the couch, though. Sam swore I wanted it in the wrong place, but I don’t like it where he put it. There’s a glare from the morning sun.”

They took the elevator up. “I brought you something,” she said when they got there. She showed him the barbecue she’d left on the table, and the chess set.

He sniffed at the food. “But I just ate.”

“I forgot that you’d probably be at dinner.”

“You should take this home with you. The chess game, too. I don’t know anyone here who plays.”

“*We* could play.”

“Tonight?” he asked, looking panicky. “What about *Top Hat*?”

She took a breath. “Don’t worry, Dad. You won’t miss the movie. I’m just going to put this food in your fridge.”

“All right.”

He brought up the couch again. She helped him shift some pieces around, during which time she wondered if they should splurge and buy him a replacement for the uncomfortable velvet couch.

Moving the furniture took all of five minutes. Then he was heading for the door.

“Where are you going?”

“*Top Hat*,” he reminded her.

“Dad . . .”

His eyes widened. “What’s wrong?”

She shook her head. “Nothing.” She gathered her purse, in a hurry to leave before she started to cry. This was shaping up to be the weepiest birthday ever.

He looked at her anxiously. “There is, I can tell. Did I do something wrong? Do you want me to eat dinner again? I will, if it will make you happy.”

“No, Dad. Save it for tomorrow . . . or whenever.

It's just . . ." Her throat closed up, making it hard to gulp in a breath.

"What's wrong?" he asked again.

"It's just so hard to have to leave you here."

His face pinched into a frown and he came toward her, taking her hand. "Christopher Columbus."

She flicked a tear off her cheek. "What?"

"Remember?" he asked her.

She remembered, but how did he?

He gave her hand a squeeze. "Always new places to go, separations," he said. "But we've always managed to find ways to be together sometimes, haven't we, Gracie?"

She nodded, not trusting herself to speak.

Then she escorted her father down to watch Fred Astaire with his new friends.

45

Memorizing the Future

When Grace got home, her first stop was at the remnants of the small woodpile Crawford had given them after chopping up the elm tree branch. The previous winter hadn't been very cold, so they hadn't used much firewood. It wasn't cold this night, either. She just craved the coziness of a fire.

Inside, she stacked the wood in the grate and

tucked a few twisted newspapers left over from packing around the logs as kindling. She intended to go to the kitchen and fix something to eat, but the flames mesmerized her. Her mind wandered randomly through memories: of the hospital waiting room where she had spent the night before, and of riding her tricycle to Peggy's, and of a giant Styrofoam boulder collapsing at a prom she'd never attended. She might have sat there hypnotized all night if someone hadn't knocked.

When she opened the front door, she found herself face-to-face with a massive red poinsettia. Her spirits lifted on the assumption that this was Ray, so that when another man's face poked over the top of the plant, disappointment crept into her voice. "Oh. Wyatt. It's you."

Her lackluster greeting did nothing to dim his smile. "Yes, it's me, Wyatt—coming to wish my favorite neighbor happy birthday."

"If a pretty coed moved into the student house next to you, I'm guessing my most favored neighbor status would be rescinded instantly." Nevertheless, she let him in, closing the door behind him to keep the chill out. "How did you know it was my birthday?"

"I woke up this morning and the birds singing outside my window told me."

She crossed her arms. "How did you really find out?"

"I ran into Muriel Blainey today." He laughed.

"Hell hath no fury, Grace. You're the talk of the town today. Or at least the talk of the street."

"Muriel didn't know it was my birthday."

"Actually, Crawford went over to Dominic's house and came back with the news." One of his eyebrows shot up. "But then I saw you poking around your woodpile, puttering around all alone on your birthday, and I decided to run out and remedy the situation."

It was a thoughtful gesture. There was even a card buried among the leaves. "Did you write me a poem, too?" She pulled the card off its plastic stick to see.

He frowned in confusion. "Oh—wait!"

He reached out to grab the card, but she feinted to the side and read aloud, *" 'Mary Jo—Forgiveness is divine. Yours, Wyatt.' "* She laughed. "I'm touched! You shouldn't have gone to the trouble."

"Okay, Mary Jo flew to Denver before I could give this to her." He looked shamefaced. "Still, it's a perfectly good plant. You wouldn't want it to go to waste."

"No, it's not the poinsettia's fault."

Behind them, there was a knock, and, still laughing, she turned and pulled the door open. Ray, holding a slightly lopsided cake with a single blue candle in it, looked surprised—then dismayed—to see Wyatt standing behind her.

For a moment, the two men gazed from

poinsettia to cake, measuring up their respective gifts.

Wyatt greeted him with a terse "West."

"Hello, Wyatt." Ray turned to Grace. "Happy birthday, Grace."

"Should we sing?" Wyatt asked.

"I would be unbelievably happy if you didn't," Grace told them. "When did you get back, Ray?"

"This evening. They released Lily this afternoon."

"Is she doing okay?"

He nodded. "She's still exhausted and zonked from the painkillers they've given her—especially from the morphine shot last night."

"Poor thing." Wyatt shook his head and addressed Ray. "Crawford told me what happened. You probably want to get right back to Lily's bedside."

"I think she's actually fairly content now that it's all over," Ray said. "She's over there now, propped on the couch and giving people orders. Crawford was going over to visit her as I was leaving." He turned back to Grace. "Anyway, Dominic and Jordan made this cake for you this afternoon. It's white with chocolate icing, I think."

She looked into Ray's eyes, and the memory of kissing him by the river came back to her. The desire to kiss him again surged in her. So did the desire to get rid of Wyatt.

She and Ray both looked at him, and in his eyes

they could see realization dawning. In the battle of plant vs. cake, cake had won.

"Well!" Wyatt said, handing the poinsettia over to Grace. "I should be running along. Got phone calls to make tonight, evidently."

She opened the door for him. "Good luck."

When she turned back to Ray, he asked, "I hope I wasn't interrupting . . ."

"Only from Wyatt's perspective, and I don't think he really minded. When it comes to romance, his skin is as thick as rhinoceros hide."

"I'm sorry I didn't buy flowers for you."

"Don't worry—Wyatt didn't, either." She led him toward the kitchen. "And the cake is even better. I was just about to resort to making dinner."

"You haven't eaten?" He started searching through all his pockets.

"What are you looking for?"

"Matches."

She laughed. "That's okay. Honestly."

"No, I promised the kids that I would do this right. Even if you won't let me sing . . ."

It seemed strange suddenly that Jordan and Dominic, or at least Dominic, hadn't come over to present the cake in person. "Dominic didn't want to come over and have a piece?" she asked. "Or Jordan either?"

Ray finally found an old matchbook that he'd obviously dropped into the breast pocket of his shirt for this purpose. "They said they wanted to watch a movie." He struck the match and lit the candle. "There. Make a wish."

For the first time in her life, Grace didn't know what to wish for. All the things she wanted—for her father to be well, to not lose the house—were out of her grasp.

She wished for them anyway and blew.

She cut off two hunks of cake and put them on plates from the set of everyday china that would soon be boxed up like everything else. "Why don't we eat in the living room?" she suggested. "Next to the fire."

From the leftover furniture, Grace dragged an old end table to set up next to the martyr's chair. Another chair—an unmatched replacement chair that had been in the dining room before the dining room table had been hauled away by an antique dealer Muriel knew—she brought in for herself.

"Oh!" Ray dug into a jacket pocket and pulled out a small wrapped cylinder. "From Jordan."

She took it from him. It weighed very little.

"I'm sort of curious to find out what it is," Ray said, encouraging her to open it. "Jordan wouldn't say."

Grace unwrapped the package—although *unwound* it would have been a better term. The paper was rolled around the small object, and when she pulled it away, she found herself holding a push puppet of a tall man with brown hair and wire-rimmed glasses.

Laughter bubbled out of her. Mystery solved.

Ray frowned. "What is *that?*"

She pushed the plunger, demonstrating. "Actually, I think it's you."

She handed it over to him and smiled as he inspected it with a sort of wonder growing in his eyes. "Where did she get this?"

"She made it." Grace pointed to the mantel, where the parallel push puppet neighborhood Jordan had been fashioning resided at the moment. "She made all of those, too."

Ray inspected them. "*Jordan* did these?" he asked. "How?"

"She's an artist."

He smiled. "I think she must be." He pushed Iago's plunger and laughed. "I've wondered what she's been up to, locked up in that crazy room of hers. I never would have guessed this." He looked at Grace. "Did you know?"

She shook her head. "I only suspected."

"You think you understand people," Ray said, "even your own kids, and it turns out you've barely nicked the surface." He sat down in the armchair. "I'm sorry I don't have a real present for you, Grace."

She smiled at him. "Don't let it go to your head, but just your being here is a sort of gift. I'd resigned myself to the fact that I was going to have a lonely birthday night at home with my cat. How pathetic does that sound?"

His gaze held hers. "You miss your dad already, don't you?"

"More than anything," she said, choked by a jolt of sadness.

Ray leaned toward her in sympathy. "I'm sorry. I wish there was something . . ."

She shook her head and lifted a forkful of cake. "Eat cake. It's good for what ails you."

As they ate, they talked about what had happened at the hospital after she left, and about chauffeuring Lily home with her in the backseat requesting he change the satellite radio every five seconds until they came upon the Sirius audiobook channel. They had hit the middle of *Wuthering Heights* and Lily had made him listen to it all the way to Austin, even though they had missed the beginning and Ray really didn't have much idea of what was going on. And then he'd missed the end.

"It couldn't have turned out well," he guessed.

"It didn't," she confirmed. "Unless you think being ghosts, wandering the moors and creeping people out generally is romantic fulfillment."

"No, I don't. Lily said you do, though."

She laughed.

"After that, we finally arrived home and discovered the dog had moved in and Dominic had made a cake. I didn't remember it was your birthday."

"Did I ever tell you?"

“Well, no.” He shrugged. “It just seems like one of those things I should know about you. One of many things. Sometimes I feel there’s the relationship I think we have, and the relationship we actually have. Does that sound odd?”

She laughed again. “I’ve felt the same way too. Maybe it’s just proximity that does that to people. The neighbor thing.”

“That’s not what I meant.” His expression was serious. “I always felt that there was a connection between us.”

“The first couple of times we met, you barely seemed to remember who I was,” she felt compelled to remind him.

“Really?”

She nodded.

“But later,” he continued quickly, “once we started talking—I can’t tell you what that meant to me. I probably bored the stuffing out of you, but sometimes it felt as if you were the only person in the world who I could talk to. And you seemed to understand me *and* what the kids were going through. You were like a magnet for all of us.”

“A grief sponge.”

“No.” His hand covered hers. “Maybe I should stop talking about the past.” He stood up and coaxed her to her feet, too. “Could we take up where we left off yesterday?”

“Isn’t yesterday the past?” she joked.

“Grace . . .”

She looked around the room. "I'm sorry. I'm in a funny mood. I haven't felt so unbalanced since I was a kid." She pulled away from him, remembering. "When I was seven and my mother was moving us to Oregon, I remember I came and stood in this room and tried to memorize everything. I put my hands up like this—like a camera lens—and tried to stare at everything, every nook and cranny, so I could memorize it. I worried I would never come back." She dropped her hands to her sides. "But now I'm here, and the house I knew is slipping away from me anyway."

"Try this." Ray moved behind her and, reaching with his longer arms, lifted her hands again, keeping them locked in viewfinder position. "Look at the shelves and see your CD collection there, and your books, and your puppet collection on the mantel." He turned her slowly. "And the furniture—well, it would probably be a mishmash of old and new, but everything comfortable, just how you want it. Definitely keep the chair. And over there, at the dining room table, there are a couple of kids playing Yahtzee, and a black-and-white dog underneath waiting to catch any crumbs that fall off the table."

Her heartbeat quickened. "You want to buy my dad's house?"

He lowered his hands and wrapped them around her waist. "I want you, Grace. In this house, or any house, mansion or hut."

She exhaled a nervous laugh and turned in his arms so she could look into his eyes. "Are you out of your mind? Just yesterday I was wondering if you had a thing for Muriel!"

He shook his head. "That would be an indication to me that you were out of your mind, actually."

She laughed again, amazed to find herself so tempted by the ideas he was spinning. "We hardly know each other."

"We've known each other for a year and a half. Maybe house hunting would be premature. But surely a year and a half is long enough to start thinking about kicking a relationship up to the next level?"

He smiled and brought her to him for a kiss. She floated into him, letting herself sink into his arms. The kiss tasted of chocolate icing and optimism, a tantalizing combination.

He pulled back, looking worried. "But of course, I realize I'm not exactly a dream guy. My kids . . ."

"I love Lily and Dominic," she said. "Of course, there's also . . ."

"Jordan."

The anxiety in his eyes made her laugh—as if he thought his other daughter might be a deal killer. "She brought us together, didn't she?"

His worried expression turned to astonishment. "I hadn't thought about it. I guess she did."

"Jordan and I have made our peace. In fact, I

think she's starting to make her peace with the world."

He shook his head and encircled her in his arms again, squeezing her in a supportive, tender embrace. "You work miracles, Grace."

"Not me," she said. "Time works miracles. Time, and love, and belonging."

46

A Billion Times Happier

"There are just a couple of lights on downstairs," Jordan said, peering through her sister's binoculars. Unfortunately, the curtains at the side of the Olivers' house were closed.

"You shouldn't spy on them." Lily was sitting next to Crawford on the couch. In spite of her bandages and her arm's being in a sling, she had color in her cheeks, and her eyes were bright.

Jordan sank back on her heels in her chair. "They've been over there a while, though."

Dominic had been stretched out on the floor with Iago, ignoring everyone, but now he sat up. "A while? It's been an hour! They've probably eaten the entire cake by now."

Jordan and Lily and Crawford exchanged looks.

Dominic searched their faces. "What?"

"They're probably not just eating cake," Jordan said.

"Well what else *could* they be doing?" Dominic asked. "Professor Oliver took the television."

For a moment, Jordan tried not to laugh, but after Lily let out a snort she couldn't help herself. Even Crawford was laughing.

Dominic growled in frustration. *"What?"*

"We're hoping they're having a romantic moment," Lily said.

"Like, kissing?" Dominic asked.

"Yes!" Jordan said.

"The cake was just a pretext," Lily said.

"Oh." Dominic frowned. "A what?"

"An excuse," Jordan translated.

Lily looked at her, impressed. "Very good."

"You're rubbing off on me," Jordan said. "Terrifying, but true."

Dominic stood up, took the binoculars from Jordan, and peered through the window with them. "So . . . do y'all think Dad and Grace are going to get married?"

"I hope so," Lily said.

"Me, too," Jordan agreed.

Crawford looked surprised by that. Everybody did. "You do?"

"Of course." Jordan shrugged. "If that's what Dad wants."

"But last year you said you didn't want a stepmother," Lily reminded her. "Especially not Grace."

"So? I feel different than I did last year about a

lot of things. I'm about a million times happier than I was then."

"Me, too," Lily said. Jordan could tell she was trying not to look at Crawford, but her blush said it all.

Jordan wondered if this was the beginning of one of those high-school-romances-becoming-forever-love things, or if poor Lily would end up getting her heart smooshed.

"I can't see a thing," Dominic said, giving up on espionage and turning away from the window. He looked at Jordan thoughtfully. "So . . . maybe if you're a million times happier this year, next year you'll be a billion times happier than last year. And then the next year, you'll be a trillion times happier, and after that, you'd be like a balloon with too much air, and you'd pop."

"That could get messy," Crawford said.

Lily let out a sound of disgust and whacked Crawford playfully with her free hand. Crawford seized the opportunity to grab it. He didn't let it go, either.

Jordan stood up. "Hey, Nickel, let's go walk the pup."

She hustled her brother and the dog out the front door.

Dominic still held the binoculars and walked several paces in front of Jordan as she pulled Iago from tree to tree down the sidewalk. Every once in a while, he would peer through the binoculars again, up at the sky. The night was clear, and the half moon hung low and bright. Jordan thought of how her mom used to name the stars she saw, and babble about celestial navigation, which always seemed so goofy. Now Jordan wondered if there wasn't something to it. She'd like to think that her mom was up in the heavens, exploring all the places she'd stared up at for so long when she was earthbound.

Dominic fell into step beside Jordan again. "You're thinking of Mom, aren't you?"

She nodded.

"Me, too," he said. "It's weird, but when I feel depressed, I really miss Mom and Nina. But when I'm happy, like right now, it's almost like they're here with us."

A cool breeze blew around them, shivering the trees and sending maverick leaves tumbling in their path. Along the street, a few early-bird Christmas decorators had strung lights on porches and in trees, which now illuminated the sidewalk like bonus stars. They reminded her of Nina. Nina had always loved looking at the holiday lights.

Jordan darted her arm around Dominic's shoulder and gave him a fierce squeeze. "I think they are here, Nickel. I really think they are."

Center Point Publishing
600 Brooks Road • PO Box 1
Thorndike ME 04986-0001 USA

(207) 568-3717

US & Canada:
1 800 929-9108
www.centerpointlargeprint.com